Charles Rice

Proceedings at the Celebration of the Two Hundredth Anniversary of the First Parish at Salem Village

Charles Rice

Proceedings at the Celebration of the Two Hundredth Anniversary of the First Parish at Salem Village

Reprint of the original, first published in 1874.

1st Edition 2024 | ISBN: 978-3-36884-877-4

Verlag (Publisher): Outlook Verlag GmbH, Zeilweg 44, 60439 Frankfurt, Deutschland
Vertretungsberechtigt (Authorized to represent): E. Roepke, Zeilweg 44, 60439 Frankfurt, Deutschland
Druck (Print): Books on Demand GmbH, In de Tarpen 42, 22848 Norderstedt, Deutschland

Chas B Rice

PROCEEDINGS

AT

THE CELEBRATION OF THE TWO HUNDREDTH ANNIVERSARY

OF THE

First Parish at Salem Village,

NOW DANVERS,

OCTOBER 8, 1872;

WITH AN HISTORICAL ADDRESS

BY

CHARLES B. RICE,

MINISTER OF THE PARISH.

BOSTON:

CONGREGATIONAL PUBLISHING SOCIETY.

CONGREGATIONAL HOUSE,

BEACON STREET.

1874.

C. J. PETERS & SON,

ELECTROTYPERS AND STEREOTYPERS,

73 FEDERAL STREET, BOSTON.

1281063
PREFACE.

THERE has been an unavoidable delay in the preparation of these materials for the press. Since the day of the celebration, the Historical Address has been much enlarged; and it has been revised repeatedly with very great care. The work having been once reluctantly undertaken, I was unwilling to leave it until it had been done, if not in fulness, yet with somewhat of thoroughness, so far as it might reach. How much of time is required for such a purpose, and with results so little to be noticed by an ordinary reader, they only who have been engaged in a like employment can understand. There have been with me, also, frequent calls to other work, besides the ample occupations of the pastoral office.

While I have read whatever might be found in print, touching upon our local history, I have very seldom depended upon any such authority, having found it altogether unsafe to do so. The "History of the Town of Danvers," prepared and published in 1848, by Rev. J. W. Hanson, while containing much interesting matter, is not reliable wherever exactness and certainty are required.

The work of Mr. Upham is a different affair. And from him almost alone, having had frequent occasion to test his accuracy, I have in some instances adopted statements of fact, without making original examination.

That the narration, as now printed, should be wholly free from errors, would be too much to expect. It has also many deficiencies in the way of omission, which it has not been possible to supply, with the time at my command.

I have received valuable assistance from Hon. Charles W. Upham and Wm. P. Upham, Esq., of Salem; from Dr. Henry Wheatland, President of the Essex Institute; from Deacon Samuel P. Fowler, and Andrew Nichols, Esq.; and also from very many members of this society. Acknowledgment for materials furnished by some of these persons will be found in due place. Special mention ought to be made of Mr. Moses Prince of this village, to whose most remarkable memory concerning all things local and personal I have had resort continually. That portion of the history covering the last one hundred years has also been read to a considerable number of elderly persons in the parish, with others having particular interest in the matters treated, who have met together several times for this purpose, and who have thus given to the record the benefit of their suggestions.

I have not entered upon the details of the period intervening between the first settlement of the town and the organization of the parish. Mr. Upham has enlarged upon it with fulness, in his " History of Witchcraft, and Salem Village," already referred to; and it would have been a waste of labor to have reviewed it. A similar remark may be made respecting the witchcraft delusion itself. I have done no more than was necessary to carry the history of the parish fairly past that point. In the references made to that topic, I have by no means followed Mr. Upham blindly. I have become acquainted with nearly every thing that has been written upon it with any originality or authority, and have of course observed the points that are held in dispute. It is proper to say that my judgment is in agreement, generally, with the views advanced by Mr. Upham ; and that his narrative appears to me to be, in the main, eminently fair and trustworthy.

This is not a history of the town, but of the parish ; and it has been held with some steadiness and unity to that aim. At the same time, the relations of town and parish, though peculiar in this instance, were exceedingly close ; and their history for a long period is almost identical. The parish territory corresponded, also, nearly to that of the town as now constituted. It was therefore natural, and it seemed suitable, in dealing with the more modern periods, to give some account of the general progress and condition of the town, and also of the other religious societies that have sprung up upon the same territory. For this reason, and as a record in large part of that period during which the whole population of Danvers was united in one parish, this publication may have an interest for all our citizens.

The statistics of other societies have been furnished, in most cases, by persons having official connection with them ; and in every matter of doubt they have been subjected to careful revision.

The form of the original address has been preserved in many parts, with the changes and additions that have since been made; and references appropriate to the day of the commemoration have been retained.

The book is to be stereotyped. The additional expense involved has been generously provided for by Deacon Samuel Preston, whose name is thus fittingly connected with a publication in which he has taken, from the first, a lively interest. The plates, by his direction, will become the property of the church. They will be left in the keeping of the Congregational Publishing Society at Boston. New copies may thus be readily produced, if they shall be needed; or, in distant future times, the history may be reprinted, with the added record of other centuries.

That the sketch now published, by the instruction and the encouragements it brings from the past, may be of service to this church, in promoting its peace and stability and strength, and may help to make more fair that record of the coming times, and that it may thus also contribute in its measure to the enlargement and beauty of the kingdom of God in the world, is the earnest wish of its author, as it has been his chief motive and hope in the labor of its preparation.

C. B. R.

BI-CENTENNIAL ANNIVERSARY OF THE FIRST PARISH IN DANVERS.

———◆———

PURSUANT to public notice given on the preceding sabbath, the first meeting of persons interested in observing the two hundredth anniversary of the commencement of preaching in this place was held in the vestry on Wednesday evening, Feb. 14, 1872.

George Tapley was chosen chairman, and Edward Hutchinson secretary.

The object of the meeting was stated by Augustus Mudge, who also read some extracts from the early records of the society. After some discussion, and interchange of opinion, it was determined to appoint a general committee, to have charge of the proposed commemoration; and the following persons were constituted this committee : —

SAMUEL PRESTON,	DEAN KIMBALL,	JASPER POPE,
GILBERT TAPLEY,	GEO. TAPLEY,	E. G. HYDE,
W. R. PUTNAM,	CHAS. P. PRESTON,	W. B. WOODMAN,
ELIJAH HUTCHINSON,	REUBEN WILKINS,	G. B. MARTIN,
CHAS. B. RICE,	EDWARD HUTCHINSON,	FRANCIS DODGE,
AUGUSTUS MUDGE,	ELIAS NEEDHAM,	NATH'L POPE.
MOSES PRINCE,	S. B. SWAN,	

Other meetings were afterwards held, at which the order of proceeding was fully considered; and sub-committees were appointed as follows : —

On the Memorial Address, Speaking, and Order of Exercises.

SAMUEL PRESTON,	AUGUSTUS MUDGE,
WM. R. PUTNAM, ·	CHAS. P. PRESTON,
EDWARD HUTCHINSON.	

On Invitations.

CHAS. B. RICE,	AMOS PRATT,
EDWIN MUDGE,	GILBERT TAPLEY,
S. B. SWAN,	CHAS. LAWRENCE,
GEORGE TAPLEY.	

On Collecting Information.

MOSES PRINCE,	WM. R. PUTNAM,
ELIJAH HUTCHINSON,	REUBEN WILKINS,
NATHANAEL POPE.	

On Music.

E. P. DAVIS, ·	JOSHUA PRENTISS,
GEORGE TAPLEY,	FRANK K. DAVIS,
GEORGE WOOD,	JOHN SWINERTON,
EDWARD HUTCHINSON.	

On Entertainment.

EDWIN MUDGE,	S. A. TUCKER,
ALFRED HUTCHINSON,	RUFUS HART,
E. G. HYDE,	S. B. SWAN,
W. B. WOODMAN,	AMOS PRATT.

On Decorations.

D. HERBERT COLCORD,	WALTER NOURSE,
CHAS. TAPLEY,	GEORGE PRATT,
W. W. EATON,	ALBERT H. MUDGE,
GEO. W. FRENCH, JUN.,	JASPER POPE, JUN.,
MOSES P. KIMBALL,	E. A. H. GROVER.

On Finance.

Geo. B. Martin,	Geo. W. French,
G. A. Tapley,	Jasper Pope,
Edwin Mudge,	Adrian Putnam,
Francis Dodge,	Chas. P. Preston,
Dean Kimball,	S. B. Swan,

Geo. H. Peabody.

On Printing.

Augustus Mudge,   Wm. R. Putnam,
George Tapley.

An effort was made, but without success, to engage Rev. Dr. Braman, late pastor of the church, to prepare the memorial address.

The work of preparation was carried on with great vigor and thoroughness by these various committees, who were also assisted by the ladies of the parish at all points where their help could be needed.

The appearance of the meeting-house within, upon the day of the observance, is thus described in " The Boston Journal " of the next morning.

" The church was most beautifully decorated with bouquets of flowers, delicate trailing vines, and festoons of evergreen and forest leaves. The pulpit was fringed with smilax, which drooped in graceful cables in front. On either side there was a profusion of choice plants, and bright clusters of flowers. On the table in front a beautifully arranged bouquet of flowers rose from a bed of smilax ; and beside it stood on either side a white cross covered with trailing evergreen. The gallery was trimmed with evergreen cables gracefully looped beneath the names of pastors of the church, which were encircled with evergreen, and separated by forest leaves tastefully arranged. The following mottoes were also displayed in evergreen letters on the balcony fronts : ' Thy law is love ; ' ' God is our Refuge ; ' and opposite the pulpit, ' 1672 — Praise ye the Lord — 1872.' The windows were ornamented by baskets of choice flowers suspended by evergreen cables and loops of evergreen, fastened with rosettes of forest leaves.   As a significant portion of the ornamentation of the room, two century plants, one on either side of the pulpit, reminded the audience of the commemoration."

The day without was stormy and unpropitious.   The severe rain of the morning did not, however, prevent the gathering of an audience respectable in its number, and notable in its character.   Many persons were present from abroad, former residents of Danvers, and once belonging to the parish, or their descendants, with prominent citizens from various parts of the county and with members also of the other religious societies of our own town.

The services were opened by music from the organ, with an anthem by the choir, under the direction of Mr. E. P. Davis.   Very appropriate selections of scripture were read, and prayer was offered, by Rev. James Brand, pastor of the Maple-street Church ; and an original hymn, written by Miss Mary S. Patterson, was sung by the choir.   Next followed the historical address by the pastor of the church, as it is given below, with enlargements since made.

HISTORY OF THE FIRST PARISH,

BY CHARLES B. RICE.

MEMORIAL ADDRESS.

I COULD have wished that the preparation of this sketch might have fallen into other hands. There are those, the natives of this or the neighboring soil, and long residents upon it, whose tastes or occupations have caused them to be well acquainted with the history of this village from the first. The little of such local knowledge which I have gained has been bought with a great sum of labor, while they were wise-born. If to any of these persons the narration which I have to make may seem to be barren and imperfect, I shall not profess to be, on their account alone, very much grieved; since the endurance of it to-day is an infliction to which they, not having themselves undertaken the work, may appear to be justly subjected. It should, however, be observed that the earlier portion of this history has already been treated in a thorough and satisfactory manner by Mr. Upham in his "History of Witchcraft, and Salem Village;" so that there is less occasion now to dwell upon it. And for nearly the whole of the two hundred years from the commencement of preaching in this place, there are in existence the ample records of the parish and the church. These I have read throughout with care; and as very few others, if any, have ever done this, or are likely to do it, I have thought it might not be a thing wholly without interest to bring out the main facts from this mass of material into a form for more easy and popular use. But information has also been diligently sought from all other available sources.

I have been able to do less in the way of giving detailed accounts of individuals and families prominently connected

with this religious society in former times, than might have
been wished. It is in this matter especially, of personal and
family history, that I have missed the knowledge which comes
with residence among a people from early life. The materials,
withal, for much of this history are now difficult, if not impossible, to be had ; and, in any case, to gather them up would be
a work requiring far more than the limited time that has been
at my disposal. The lack, therefore, of such details in this
recital is unavoidable, however it is to be regretted.

The territory of Danvers was originally a part of Salem.
There were settlers upon it as early as 1632 or 1633 ; though
that portion of it included within the limits of the "village,"
to be shortly defined, was not probably entered upon until
two or three years later. At that time, or about 1635, there
began to appear a purpose to plant a settlement in a somewhat formal manner in this neighborhood. It was to be
styled a village ; although that term, according to present
usage, would have been more appropriately applied to the
central establishment at Salem itself.

The houses were widely scattered ; and there was not for
a long time, nor indeed scarcely until within the memory of
those now living, any considerable collection of them anywhere upon this territory. The district was also more popu-
larly and fittingly known in early times as "The Farms ;" and
the inhabitants were called distinctively "The Farmers."
They used this title also with respect to themselves ; and in
the records of their first assemblies the form is : "At a meeting of the Farmers."

As population increased, the inconvenience of the connection with Salem began to be seriously felt. They were far
from the place of meeting, both for the transaction of business
and for public worship. They accordingly began to move for
a separate parochial organization. A petition to this end was
presented in 1670. The town of Salem gave a conditional
assent in March, 1672 ; and the General Court granted the

requisite authority, Oct. 8 of the same year. This is the event we to-day commemorate. As this date is given in the old style, the time was really OCT. 18; and, if it had occurred to us seasonably, that might have been the better day for our observance. Exact people can have liberty to mark the occasion on Friday of next week, and well toward the morning of Saturday. (See Appendix A, p. 231),

The following is a copy of the order of the legislature, which was really an act of incorporation, as it appears in the records of the parish : —

" At a generall court held at Boston 8th of October 1672. — In answer to the Petition of the farmers of Salem Richard Hutchinson Thomas Fuller &c the Court judgeth it meet that all persons living within the tract of land mentioned in the town's grant of land to the Petitioners together with all lands and Estates lying within the said bounds shall Contribute to all Charges referring to the maintainance of a minister and erecting a meeting house there and that they shall have liberty to nominate and appoint persons among themselves or town of Salem not exceeding the Number of Five who are hereby impowered from time to time for the making and gathering of all rates and levies For the ends above expressed — and that in case of refusall or non-payment of the same by any person or persons amongst them that then the Constables of Salem shall and hereby are empowered to make distress upon the goods of any that shall so neglect or refuse to afford their help in that use. And the same to deliver to the persons aforesaid to be improved accordingly and that when a minister shall be settled amongst them they shall be freed from Contributing to the minister's of Salem — That this is a true Coppy taken out of the Court records attests Edward Rawson Secretary."

For the boundaries of the tract thus set off, a starting-point was taken at " the Wooden Bridge " over " Cow-House River," known afterward as Endicott, and now as Water's River. This bridge was undoubtedly where the present road crosses the small stream near the brick school-house by Felton's Corner, Peabody. Thence the line ran west, a few degrees south, passing through the middle of the pond near the present village of Brookdale, to the Lynnfield border. Setting out again from the " Wooden Bridge " toward the north, the boundary followed what has been known as the " old Ipswich road," crossing Crane River below the cemetery, and entering along Ash Street upon the ground of the modern village at the Plain, and continuing across Frost-fish Brook, on the line of the road, to the " Horse Bridge," so called, at Bass River, in North Beverly, just beyond Cherry Hill and the residence of Richard P. Waters. From this point the boundary bore to the north-west until it reached the Wenham line ; then turned westerly on that line to the present boundary between Danvers and Wenham, which it followed to the Topsfield border ; and thence, turning to the south-west, it kept near by the present line to the Ipswich River, holding the same general direction over the river and across a considerable bend of the stream until it passed it again at a point not far from the north-western corner of Peabody, and thence following the Peabody line on the border of Lynnfield until it met the line first laid down, reaching westward from the place of beginning.

Besides this, there was added on the north-western margin a large, four-sided tract, now included in Middleton, and embracing about half of that town. This enlargement covered what was known as " Bellingham's Grant," and was added at the petition of its owners, and notably of Bray Wilkins, who wished for many public reasons, and especially for his love to the Salem church, to be within the limits of Salem.

It will thus be seen, that, besides this part of Middleton, the village embraced in the south-west a large section of Peabody, and on the north-east a considerable portion of Beverly ; * while it did not include in the south-east and south the Endicott farm, or any part of the territory now known as Danvers Port, formerly " New Mills," and still earlier " Skelton's Neck." These still remained with Salem. And they had for a long

* That is, so much of Beverly as lies upon the north of the above-described "old Ipswich road." For a long period the town of Beverly embraced a much larger portion of this original village ; since the border between the town and Danvers was farther to the westward, upon " Frost-fish Brook." The present boundary — by which what is now known as " East Danvers " was detached from Beverly, and annexed to Danvers — was established in 1857.

period no parochial relation with us ; saving, indeed, that the people living upon these lands might often, and did, enter into some voluntary and informal connection with " the Farmers."

There was also a disputed territory on the border of Topsfield, which, no doubt, fairly belonged to our fathers of this village, but which they were never able finally to get, though they fought stoutly for it.

This territory was thus set off from Salem for parish purposes only, being still in all other respects a part of the original town. But parish purposes in those days were broad, and somewhat ill-defined. Besides, therefore, what pertained to the support of preaching, the villagers had a care, at times, for schools, and to some extent for roads ; and later for the raising of men and money in time of war ; and, in fact, for nearly every local interest that might arise : so that the organization was, in part, municipal as well as parochial ; and the parish went near to be a town, and was sometimes called by that name.*

It was understood that no church was to be formed at first in the new district.

The church at Salem appears to have been unwilling to part at once with such a considerable number of its members ; and it had, perhaps, some distrust of what they might do if allowed to set up wholly for themselves. There being thus no church, it occurred, almost of necessity, that the distinction generally made at that time between church-members and others, as to voting, was not followed in this instance ; and all householders were allowed a share in the management of parish affairs. The arrangement in this particular, as the matter then

---

* By the general usage of that time throughout the State, the town and parish were territorially the same : parochial business was done in town-meeting, the parish being a kind of adjunct or incident to the town. These conditions in this case, by the territorial separation of the village as a parish, were in a manner reversed : so that there was here a parish with certain incidental functions as a town.

2

stood, was liberal and just; but the practical working of it was nevertheless, in this case, not most advantageous: though the misfortune should be attributed not to the enlargement of the franchise, but to the want of a church itself, which should have been planted at first with its appropriate organization and appointments. The ecclesiastical system of those times, withal, though full of the seeds of our present liberty, was only half Congregational, and abounded in inconsistencies and imperfections. The State, or the associated body of churches and ministers, held too great a control within it.

The first meeting of the Farmers was held on the 11th of November.* Lieut. Thomas Putnam, Thomas Fuller, Sen., Joseph Porter, Thomas Flint, and Joshua Rea were chosen a committee "to carry along the affairs according to the court order." They instructed the committee to lay taxes on this basis: "All vacant land at one halfpenny per acre; all improved land at one penny per acre; all heads and other estate at country price." This "country price" was probably a rate established in the Colony. It was also voted to make a rate of forty pounds that year for Mr. Bayley.

Mr. Bayley had been in the village perhaps some few months at the date of the organization. By this vote he became not the settled pastor of the people, but what we might now call a "stated supply."

At a meeting held on the "26th of the 10th month," that is, in December, 1672, it was voted to build a meeting-house "of 34 foot in length, 28 foot broad, and 16 foot between joints;" and Nathanael Putnam, Henry Kenny, Joseph Hutchinson, and Joseph Putnam were joined with the gen-

---

* The dates will be given in old style, as upon the records. To bring them to the present reckoning, add, as usual, ten days for the seventeenth century, and eleven days for the eighteenth, until 1752.

For the convenience of the reader, however, the number of the *year*, in the months from January to March, will be given according to the present custom, by which the year begins with Jan. 1.

eral committee before chosen, for a building committee. It was agreed that a rate or tax should be made, to pay for the work. And a little later in March, the record runs that "at a meeting of the farmers it was voted that the fifth part of the rate for building the meeting-house and finishing the same shall be paid in money, or butter at five-pence a pound or wheat at money price, and the rest of the pay in such pay as shall carry it along. This money and butter and wheat is to provide nails and" [glass probably: the word is partly gone from the page] "for the meeting-house." "Money and butter and wheat" were things choice; and with these they could buy the two articles of building material which alone in the plainness of those times they were not able to furnish themselves.

This meeting-house was built according to vote; though it was not altogether completed for a considerable time. Thus in 1684 it was voted that the meeting-house "shall be filled and daubed at where it wants below the beams and plates. And that six casements shall be Hanged in the meeting-house, and that there be a canope set over the pulpit." And a little later galleries were added.

THE FIRST MEETING-HOUSE.

The wood-cut herewith given affords, it is believed, a good representation of this first meeting-house.* These "casements" were probably glass windows, made to swing outwards in opening. No glass therefore, it is likely, had been bought before ; but though such votes with the Farmers were not always effective, there is reason to think that these six casements did then in fact " be Hanged." Aside from these, the openings at the windows were closed, if at all, by swinging or sliding shutters of wood.

The house stood upon the flat, north-east of the present site, upon the north side of Hobart Street, — which is the old meeting-house road, — and between the houses now occupied by John Hook, sen., and Hiram Hook. Joseph Hutchinson, who lived near and owned all that meadow, gave an acre of ground about the meeting-house, to the " Inhabitants of the Farms," " for the Meeting-House and ministry amongst them."

Liberty was given to any that pleased to put up " a house for their horses," . . . " on that side of the meeting-house next the swamp," that is, at the rear towards the north-east. Provision was made in these houses, or sheds, for the horse only, with no respect to carriages, of which there were none.

For his second year's salary Mr. Bayley had forty-seven pounds. He was to find his own fire-wood ; or he might, if he preferred, give up the extra seven pounds, and have his wood furnished by the parish committee. It appears from his receipts that he chose to do sometimes one, sometimes the other. The records further show that from thirty to thirty-six cords of wood was reckoned a supply for the minister's yearly use. If the value of butter at five-pence to the pound may be taken as a basis for comparison, it will appear that Mr.

* The engraving for this meeting-house, and for the three next in order, was done chiefly from drawings made under the direction of Moses Prince. Some changes in the details have since been made. Pictures of other churches of the same age, which certain of these are known to have resembled, have also been made use of. Great care has been taken, both by Mr. Prince and by me, to secure the truthfulness of these representations.

Bayley's salary of forty pounds was equal in purchasing power to about $675 at the present time. Or, if the comparison were made with wood, then sold at five cords for a pound, the salary would equal $2,000.

In this second year of the organization of the parish, 1673, it was voted to build "an house for the minister:" the dimensions to be " 28 foot in length, 13 foot between joynts and 20 foot in breadth, and a leentoo of 11 foot at the end of the house." But this does not appear to have been carried into effect; for seven years later, in February, 1680 (1681 N. S.), we find the vote renewed: " the Dementions of the House are as followeth: 42 foot long, twenty foot Broad: thirteen foot stude, fouer chimleis, no gable ends." This time "a Ratte" was made to meet the expense, to the amount of two hundred and twenty-one pounds, nine shillings, and sixpence. Accordingly on " the 26th of Genewary" in the following year, the work appears to have been well under way; and in February of 1683 (1684) the house was so far done as to stand in need of being " Repaired."

This house stood some fifty rods to the north-west of the present parsonage, and a little less than twenty rods from the course of what is now Centre Street, on the north-eastern side, to the rear of the houses of John Roberts and Henry Prentiss, upon land now owned by E. & A. Mudge & Co. A lane just above the house of John Roberts leads in towards the site.

It was upon the south-western border of a lot of land containing about five acres, which Joseph Houlton had given, in 1681, to the inhabitants of Salem Village, " for the use of the ministry."

The record for these years is fragmentary and very imperfect; partly because four pages are missing from the book, and partly because some votes were purposely expunged. That which we now have is not, in fact, the original record at all, until about the year 1687. It is a new book transcribed from an older one, and with certain omissions, made by direct order of the parish, and for reasons which are soon to be considered. Among the votes thus omitted were some that were passed during the ministry of Mr. Bayley, with respect to the building of a parsonage.

The delay in this matter of a parsonage was an occasion of annoyance and expense to Mr. Bayley; and of disputes between him and the parish, to which further reference will be made.

Of Mr. Bayley, and, indeed, of either of these village ministers for the first twenty-five years, I can add little of importance beyond what Mr. Upham has gathered up. Mr. Bayley was a native of Newbury, a graduate of Harvard, and twenty-two years of age at the formation of the parish. His ministry was not a peaceful one. The people do not appear to have been united upon him from the first. Something, too, in the manner of his engagement gave offence. There were family jealousies and dissensions of such a sort as would have been likely to have stood in the way of any very cordial agreement upon a minister. And he himself was young, without experience, and without any special fitness for a position requiring judgment and tact. Troubles continued or sprang up year by year. They came to such a height as to need to be brought before the parent church at Salem, and at last before the General Court of the Colony. But this was to little purpose; and, no prospect of harmony appearing, Mr. Bayley's ministry was closed, probably near the end of the year 1679. It is not certain whether he could have remained any longer if he had chosen. It is pretty clear that it would have been better if he had left before. The people, indeed, may have deserved the most of blame for the difficulties that arose; and they were certainly in a temper to enter too readily into a quarrel. But, however that may have been, and in every such case where the minister is involved, the remedy, by removal at least, rests with him; since he can, at all events, go from the parish, while the parish cannot readily move away from itself. This remedy, moreover, is commonly the better the sooner it is applied. In this instance the dissensions had grown too deep and bitter for any such curing.

Mr. Bayley did not, in fact, make a complete removal. In the year 1680, certain of his late parishioners — Thomas, Nathanael, and John Putnam, Joseph Hutchinson, and Thomas Fuller, sen. — made him a gift of about forty acres of land, lying in part upon the hill and meadow east of the meeting-house. Here he had a house, which was his home, apparently, for several years, and which, Mr. Upham says, he continued to occupy occasionally "for some years after the witchcraft transactions."

This gift of land, however, had been promised, if not, as it would seem, actually made, several years before, and soon after his engagement to preach. Among the papers that went up to the General Court in 1679, bearing on these ministerial difficulties, and which are now preserved at the State House, is one which purports to be a copy, probably from the original Village Book, of a record of a gift of upland and meadow-land, amounting to about forty acres, to Mr. Bayley, and from the same men above named, save that Jonathan Ray occupies the place of Thomas Fuller. The land was in several lots; but the most of it was situated upon "Hadlock's Hill" and "Cromwell's Meadow." The hill was that upon which the houses of Mr. Benjamin Hutchinson and Mr. Geo. H. Wood now stand; and the meadow was on the Ipswich River. This instrument bears date "21 — 12mo — 1672" (that is, March 3, 1673, N. S.).

It is likely that this gift had not been carried out in full, or the title, at any rate, had not been made complete; and hence the recorded deed of 1680. But it is probable that some portions of the land had been all along in Mr. Bayley's possession. The site of Mr. Bayley's house is known to have been near the present residence of Mr. Hutchinson, and a little to the westward from it. We may conclude, I think, that he had built this house during the period of his ministry, with his own means, after waiting in vain for some time to see if the parish would take any steps in that line. There is confirmation for this opinion in the fact that in a letter addressed by Mr. Bayley to the parish in 1679, and preserved at the State

House, he speaks of his being obliged, "in order to a settlement, to expend considerable estate" amongst them.*

Under the peculiar circumstances of the case it was not wise
for Mr. Bayley to remain in the village. His staying kept the
old troubles alive in memory, and excited also continually the ·
wishes of his friends that he might be again employed as their
minister. The matter was made worse by the connection
which had been formed with one of the principal families of
the place, through the marriage of the sister of his wife with
Thomas Putnam, jun. There is no evidence, so far as I can
discover, that Mr. Bayley was ever himself a mover in any of
these projects of his friends; nor does he appear to have been
at all involved in the fiercer strifes of the witchcraft delusion.
His faults may probably have been, for the most part, of a
negative sort. That he went no further in the ministry, leaving
it thus early in life, for no strong bent toward any other pur-
suit; and that he entered another profession only, as it
would seem, doubtfully and late, — may show that he was
lacking in steadiness of purpose, and force of character. There
are other indications to the same effect.

After leaving the ministry, Mr. Bayley became, in time, a
physician, practised in this profession at Roxbury, and died in
1707.

There is still standing upon the place he once owned a pear-
tree, dating from Mr. Bayley's time, and bearing both native
and grafted fruit. I have tasted this year of the product of
the tree. The native pear is neither pleasant to the eyes, nor
"to be desired to make one wise;" and, if the village pastor
was accustomed to eat freely of this fruit, any peculiar crooked-
ness of temper he may ever have shown might, perhaps, be
naturally accounted for.

The papers already referred to, on file at the State House,
relating to the affairs of Salem Village in Mr. Bayley's time,

* Since writing the above I have observed that one of Mr. Bayley's letters at
the State House, written in August, 1679, is dated "from my house." This
makes it certain, that, as I had been led to suppose, he had a house of his own
before the close of his ministry.

are interesting in many particulars. The handwriting in several instances is, in the judgment of the author of this sketch, at least peculiar. The matters set forth are certainly not less so.

Mr. Bayley addressed a letter to the inhabitants, complaining of the uncertainties of his situation, and mentioning the expense to which he had been subjected. Fifteen of his parishioners, under the lead of Nathanael Putnam and Bray Wilkins, answered that he was not fairly settled among them; that they "doubted if he could prove his call;" that as to his estate, they "were sorry he had not been better advised;" and that they were not edified with his preaching. To this a much larger number made rejoinder, that the engagement was in due order ; that he was virtually "settled" among them by his "promise not to leave without consent of the people." And they add a remark, referring to certain names among the fifteen, that must have been meant to be impressive, and the like of which it would hardly occur to any one in our times to make: to the effect that it was a strange thing that they, "who think themselves the only persons capacitated to act about a minister, should so contradict themselves as to admit of Thomas Wilkins, Henry Wilkins, John Kenny, &c., as competent judges of a minister's abilities"!

These persons, some of whom, if not all, were afterward in good repute in the parish, and holders in some instances of public office, may then have been young men, and perhaps below the standard, in those times, for sobriety of manners.

From these papers we learn that the number of church-members in the village — members, that is, of the church in Salem — was "about 11 or 12," and that of the householders "about fifty."

The General Court, in its endeavors to settle the village troubles, had directed, that, although there was no church, two men should be chosen each year "to supply the place of deacons," and specially to receive the money collected by the parish committee, and settle with the minister. The first officers bearing this name were Lieut. John Putnam and Nathanael Ingersoll, who were chosen in December, 1679. The next year a change was made ; and the deacons were Lieut. Thomas Putnam and Sergeant Jonathan Walcott. After three years, in 1683, Nathanael Ingersoll was put again into the place with Lieut. Putnam. In 1686 Jonathan was put instead of Thomas Putnam.

From this time unto the organization of the church there is no mention upon the records of any election of deacons. The same persons may have continued in the office.*

Mr. George Burroughs, another Harvard man, came to the village to preach in November, 1680. For his support the Farmers voted as follows : "That Mr. Burroughs for his mentenance amongst us Is to Have for the year enseuing sixty pounds In and as money one third part in mony cartain the two thirds in provision at money price as followeth : Ry and barly and malt at three shillings per bushel : indian corn at two shillings a bushel beaf at three half-pence a pound and pork at 2 pence a pound Butter at 6 pence a pound and this to be paid at each half year's end : it is to be understood that It shall be at the Inhabitants Liberty to discharge the wholl Sixty pounds in all mony if they se cause and his firewood."

But the friends of Mr. Bayley were not at ease ; and troubles continued. Mr. Burroughs gave up his engagement, and left the place early in 1683 ; his ministry covering two years, and probably one-quarter of the third.

Little is known of Mr. Burroughs beyond what appears in connection with the history of this village. His experiences here were stormy and sad, both during his brief stay as

---

* The keeping of the records passed, in 1687, for a time out of the hands of the excellent clerk, Thomas Putnam, jun., and was but imperfectly done. Mr. Upham speaks of Edward Putnam as having been deacon for some time previous to the organization of the church. He may possibly have been in the year 1687 or 1688 ; but, as to evidence that he was, Mr. Upham, whose care for details is a matter of admiration, was misled by an inaccurate reprint of documents in the Salem Court House, respecting the difficulties between Mr. Parris and his parishioners, and having a reference to the deacons.

preacher, and afterward to the tragic end. He was neglected
as to his salary, and saw but little of " mony cartain." His
wife died ; and he had not of his own wherewith to pay for her
burial. He was insulted in public, and publicly arrested for
no cause, he only being wronged. And he was not safe when
he had departed. Years afterward, in a time when all evil
passions were let loose, the animosities of the people he had
left went after him to the wilds of Maine, and brought him
back to a trial in the mockery of justice, and to a death from
the barbarity and shame of which he alone, of all concerned,
was clear.

At a meeting held Dec. 27, 1681, it was " agreed upon and
voted for the futer by the Inhabitants of Salem Village : that
the Ratte made for the Defraiing of all our charges for the
year 1681 : both for Houses and Lands with all other Consarnes belonging to thee Ministry amongst us shall Be entered
In our Book of Records with the names and perticular
summes : And that it shall not Bee Lawful for the Inhabit-
tants of this Village to convey the Houses or Lands or any
other consarnes Belonging to the Ministry to any perticular
person or persons not for any cause by voat or other ways :
But this estate to stand good to the Inhabitants of this place
and to their successors for ever (for them)."

Both of these votes are significant with respect to the nature
of the troubles existing among the Farmers, which had to do
largely with pecuniary affairs. Of this fact there are many
other clear indications. The attempt to prohibit in this
manner the transfer of the real estate belonging to the parish
was of course impracticable ; since what was once fixed by
vote only could be at any time by vote unsettled. Whether
the original conveyance of these ministerial lands to the parish
should not have secured them against alienation ; and whether,
indeed, it did not in some cases do this by just force of law, — is
another question of some importance in this history, and, perhaps, not wholly without some present interest. However
that may be, there can be no doubt but that the aim in this
action was a wise one.

It is evident, too, that some movement had already been made or threatened, looking toward the gift of these properties to the minister, — a business that afterward caused more of trouble. Whether this effort was made in behalf of Mr. Bayley or Mr. Burroughs I find no means of determining with certainty; though all the probabilities indicate that it was for Mr. Bayley. To whomsoever it had reference, the reflections which it suggests concerning him are not pleasant.

The direction for the full recording of rates and of all money transactions indicates what we know also from other sources, that there were uncertainties, and consequent disputings, as to how much had been paid by individuals, and what might be still due from them or to them.

If the wholesome rule expressed in this vote had never before or afterwards been disregarded, I am persuaded that a great proportion of these strifes among the Farmers might never have arisen. Such mischief comes of breaking the divine command to "provide things honest in the sight of all men."

The "rate" for 1681 follows immediately upon the record; but similar entries were not made with uniformity and fullness until fifteen years later, and with the coming of better times.

I transcribe here this first record of assessment, since it gives the names of the men who then lived within the village, and shows something of their rank as to property; although some of these persons were undoubtedly taxed also for parish purposes in Salem, upon property lying in that town, outside the village.

RATE OF 1681.

	£	s.	d.		£	s.	d.
Lieut. Thos. Putnam	10	6	3	Jonathan Walcott	3	6	0
Richard Hutchinson	2	9	6	Israel Porter	1	10	0
Nathanael Putnam	9	10	0	John Buxton	3	15	0
Lt. John Putnam	8	0	0	Lot Kellom	1	4	0
Joseph Porter	6	3	0	Joseph Holton, senr.	3	6	0
Henry Kenny	2	5	0	Isaac Goodall's widdow	0	10	0

	£.	S.	D.		£.	S.	D.
Thomas Flint	5	2	0	John Darling	0	10	0
Gilles Gory (Cory)	0	4	0	Joseph Holton, jun	1	12	0
Joseph Pope	3	0	0	Jonathan Putnam	1	16	0
Elisha Cuby	0	3	3	Edward Putnam	1	17	0
Wm. Nichols	0	10	0	Thomas Haile	0	7	6
Isaac Cooke	0	4	3	Daniel Andrew	5	19	3
William Sibley	4	16	0	Sam. Brabrook	0	16	0
Joseph Roots	0	4	9	Zacca. Herrick	0	12	0
John Giles	0	6	3	Nath. Felton, jun	0	5	0
Andrew Eliot	0	5	0	Thos. Fuller, sen.	8	6	0
Wm. Dodge	0	6	6	Henry Renols	0	2	3
Joseph Boys.	0	3	3	Jerimy Watts	1	5	0
Samuel Sibley	1	18	0	Joseph Hutchinson	6	12	3
Job Swinerton, sen	3	0	0	Nath. Ingersoll	3	12	0
Job Swinerton, jun	4	10	0	Joshua Rea	7	7	0
Peter Prescott	1	4	6	John Brown	3	1	6
James Smith	1	4	6	James Hadlock, sen	1	9	3
John Burroughs	1	5	6	James Hadlock, jun	1	4	0
Thomas Keny	1	10	0	Francis Gefords's farm (?)	1	7	6
William Way	1	10	0	Thomas Haines	2	2	6
Thomas Putnam, jun	2	14	0	Jonathan Knight	1	10	0
John Putnam, jun	2	14	0	John Kenny	1	10	0
George Flint	1	7	0	Aron Way	1	19	0
John Flint	1	7	0	William Jerland	2	5	0
William Osburne	0	3	0	Thomas Fuller, jun	2	8	0
Nath. Aires	1	4	0	John Sheepard	1	10	0
Thos. Bayly	0	13	0	Zaccary Goodell	2	14	0
Daniel Rea	3	0	0	John Gingill	3	10	6
Thomas Cane	0	3	0	Bray Wilknes	2	12	6
Peter Cloys	1	8	6	Samuel Wilknes	1	16	0
Abraham Walcott	0	9	0	Thomas Wilknes	2	16	9
Peter Woodbery	0	2	6	Henry Wilknes	1	10	0
Francis Nurs	0	18	0	Benj. Wilknes	1	16	0
Samuel Nurs	1	4	0	Edward Bishop	2	8	0
John Tarbill	1	4	0	Joseph Herrick	3	0	0
Thomas Preston	1	10	0	Thomas Rament	2	14	0
William Buckley	1	4	0	Ezekill Cheever	0	13	0
Benjamin Holton	1	1	0	Joseph Mazary	2	0	0
Joseph Woodrow	0	15	0	Alexander Osborn	2	2	0
Thomas Clark	0	13	0	John Adams	1	2	6
John Nickols	0	10	0	William Rament	0	9	9

The whole tax amounted to a fraction above two hundred pounds; indicating the collection of a considerable sum in payment for the minister's house, then in process of building. The number of names is ninety-four, representing a population of not far from five hundred.

Next came Mr. Deodat Lawson. His first name belied him. He could not have been divinely given to this people, save in the way of bare allowance. He was long in coming. The people began to move to get him in May of 1683. He may, probably, have preached occasionally in the summer or autumn, but not with any regularity. They tried in vain "to treat with him." They sent to Boston to see him (for he was a Boston man); but he kept them in suspense. It is possible something in the terms they offered may have justified this, but not probable. For he appears to have come at last upon the same salary with Mr. Burroughs; and this, it is likely, they were ready to have given at first. Perhaps he was waiting to see if Providence might not call him to some larger place. In December they were nearly ready to give him up. Mr. Daniel Epps, meanwhile, had supplied the pulpit for many weeks.* But in January they tried him again, offering "Mr. Burroughs his salary of sixty pounds only corn at 2s. 6d. per bushel." Corn had risen; and these Farmers were not the men to lose that advance of a quarter. This proposal Mr. Lawson seems at last to have accepted; and he came soon after, probably in February, 1684, to make his residence in the village. Neither Mr. Epps nor Mr. Burroughs had at this time been paid in full, — notwithstanding the people looked so sharply after their corn; and, if Mr. Lawson had made a stand to have these accounts settled before he closed his bargain, nobody could have blamed him. It is not most pleasant paying for one's food long after it has been eaten; and the same thing would seem to have been true of this preaching.

As to Mr. Lawson's ministerial work in this parish, little, really, is known. This only, is certain, — that there continued to be dissensions among the people, both old and new, and with increasing bitterness.

The condition of the Book of Records attracted attention. It was judged that it contained votes improperly recorded,

* This was the famous Salem schoolmaster of that name.

and that some votes were omitted ; and concerning yet others, though the entry was not questioned, it was thought that the action itself recorded was ill-advised, and injurious to the interests of the inhabitants. After much difficulty, the matter was finally arranged by the procuring a new book, — that which we now have, — into which was transcribed the substance of the old, leaving out such parts as were objected to. The proceeding was, perhaps, injudicious. It certainly has become the occasion, when viewed in the light of later occurrences, of much suspicion cast upon these Farmers ; and it has helped, no doubt, to make their conduct appear worse than it was. It would have been better if they had contented themselves with repealing the obnoxious votes. I am convinced, however, that in this particular they have suffered in reputation somewhat beyond their deserts. And in this matter almost alone, I think Mr. Upham has done them, without meaning it, some slight injustice. I do not believe that any dark doings of much account were so attempted to be covered up ; nor that there was any special thought at all in what was done, of the scrutiny or judgment of future times upon the record of their parish action. They had, rather, in mind, we may think, certain business matters in which they were or might be then engaged, and the record of which had become in some cases confused and entangled. They were money matters undoubtedly ; and of no great consequence, the most of them, beyond the time then present. And it must not be forgotten that the original and apparently the chief ground of complaint, with regard to the book, was in its alleged inaccuracy and incompleteness. The main grievance was, not that it told too truly what had been done, but that it failed to tell it truly. This might be abundantly established by the most copious quotations from the record. There is indirect evidence too, of the most decisive kind, bearing on this point ; as in the votes that were passed, one of which has been already cited, directing that greater care should be had in setting down all particulars of money transactions. Another instance of the same sort appears in an order adopted in March, 1685 ; that " the Com-

mittee in Being shall keep the original papers that the voats
are written on : and at the ,year's end they shall be compared
with the Book: when the committee shall give an account of the voats that have passed." Conformably to this
we find, that, when the various disputes of the people were
referred for advisement to a committee of five gentlemen from
Salem', they recommend in their report that "for the future
no votes be recorded but in the presence of the assembly that
votes them : or at least at the next lawful meeting being again
publickly read which if it be done and the vote read publickly
after it is recorded will undoubtedly prevent any reflection for
the future upon the Book or Book keeper." This shows plainly
that doubts existed with regard to the value of the record itself,
and that precautions were thought to be needed to make sure
its accuracy. It is to be admitted, indeed, that some votes were
finally expunged that had been once properly recorded. But
even as to these, there was in some cases an underlying dispute
as to the legality of the action itself thus recorded. And this, too,
appears in the repeated directions given, as to the mode of
warning the meetings ; and in the order of June 5, 1683, that
no matter should be acted on at any meeting that had not
been mentioned in the warrant.

Altogether it was not, perhaps, so strange that the Farmers
should have thought it best to begin again with a new and
clear book. They are not open, either, to so severe a censure
as a legislative body would be in the like proceeding : since
the doings of a legislature are more thoroughly public, and
enter into the history of the State ; while this matter was
thought to have to do chiefly with their own internal and
temporary business affairs.

It is important, also, to notice that the final adjustment was
one that met with unanimous approval, distinctly and formally
given ; and it must thus, it would appear, have been reached
without serious wrong done to any individual.*

---

* Special mention is made upon the record (February, 1687), of Joseph Hutchinson, Job Swinerton, Joseph Porter, and Daniel Andrew, as having "aggriev-
ances relating to the publique affairs of this place." A month later a committee

There were friends, too, of Mr. Bayley, and doubtless, also, we may think, of Mr. Burroughs, who would have objected if any gross injustice had been done them in this revision.† Furthermore, it was voted that the original book should be preserved ; and, though this has not in fact been done, yet there is no evidence of any general desire, or any desire at all, to have it finally put from sight ; nor does it appear that, the new record being settled to their minds, the old one was cared for, or that it perished otherwise than by neglect. It is not quite unnecessary to add, since there have been some popular misapprehensions on the subject, that all this took place several years before the breaking-out of the witchcraft troubles, and that the revision therefore was not made with any purpose at all of covering up that dark chapter of history.

The state of the record for these first years having been thus referred to, it is proper to add that, for the period covered by this history, the records of the church and parish, as now existing, are full and exact, taken as a whole, much beyond what is common.

of six was chosen, having upon it three of these men, with Joseph Hutchinson for chairman, with instructions to them to " view our Books of Records [the new one was then in process of making] and to coppie out any enteries that are therein which they conceive to have been grievous to any of us in time past, or that may be unprofitable to us in time to come," and to bring them before the people. And this committee are afterward mentioned again, by name, as approving, for the main part, of the form in which the record was finally left.

† The designation of this matter, so far as relates to these two ministers, in the vote by which it was finally adjusted, is as follows : " Tho there are summe voates left out that past in Mr. Bayley's Days and summe voates left out that passed in Mr. Burrough's Days that are not transcribed : which we conceive will be of noe great use to us for the time to come which we leave to Ly in ye old Book of Records as they are."

One of these omitted votes of Mr. Bayley's time has happened to be preserved, being among the documents sent to the General Court at Boston for its consideration. It is of date July 3, 1673, and is a promise to "give Mr. Bayley 40 pounds in Boardes and Brick and Clay and Stones for Suller and Well and they to be digged and ground to be fenced and broken up for the seteling of Mr. Bayley amongst us in the work of the ministry." It is to be admitted that Mr. Bayley, on his part, found this vote of the Farmers "of noe great use" in the matter of house-building ; and I do not mean to deny that the old record may have had upon it other matters discreditable to the people, but only to state my belief that the getting of any such votes out of sight was not the main motive in what was done.

We need not, however, undertake to clear the people of this village from great blame for the spirit they manifested in general through these years of contention and bitterness. They had become habitually quarrelsome, beyond a doubt, and violent and rancorous in their quarrels. These early occupants of the parish were clearly of a vigorous stock, energetic, and strong-willed. Many of them were men of decided character and marked individuality. When contentions arose in such a community, it was natural that they should be stoutly pressed. Some of these disputes were such as they were not altogether, if at all, responsible for, as to the origin of them, — as those that had to do with the bounds of their lands, in which respect we must believe they were most unfairly dealt by. And they were not fortunate on the whole, it must be safe at least to say, with respect to the ministers that came among them. These were men that did little towards bringing to bear upon the distracted people the powers of the gospel of peace.* But, whoever was most to be blamed, it must be admitted that this village in those years was but an undesirable place to live in.

John W. Proctor, Esq., in his interesting and very characteristic historical address, † has said of the descendants of these men in a later generation, meaning it in commendation, "They were none of your milk-and-water heroes : salt pork and bean porridge constituted the basis of their diet." If this were also true of the village men at the period of which we are treating, and if it had any thing to do with their habits and temper, we might wish that their diet had contained some slight mixture of water and of milk.

---

* I have been slow to frame so severe a sentence concerning these men, my predecessors in the Christian ministry in this place ; but I am not able to change it. It is not possible, in this sketch, to give all the grounds on which such a judgment must rest. Something further will appear as we proceed. The main judgment, I fear, can never be shaken. It is confirmed, among other things, by turns of expressions in letters or other writings, and by the *absence* also of expressions which the letters of a Christian minister should have contained.— This with regard to some. For all the *appearance of the record* is condemnatory. It is the record of the parish, to be sure ; but a minister in such times, earnestly working for peace, might have stamped upon it some sign of his desires.

† At the centennial celebration of the town of Danvers, 1852.

As it was, the good offices of their friends at Salem, which they were obliged to call in, hardly sufficed to keep within bounds the animosities of the people.

For the connection which all these quarrels had with the parish and the ministry, and soon with the church, we may remember that those strifes are always worst that arise in what ought to be the best associations of life. We do not break up our homes, and set aside wholly the family relation, because the most uncomfortable and scandalous of all contentions may sometimes break out in these domestic circles. No more are the troubles of which we are speaking to be set down as of any evil in the Christian Church itself, or in the institutions of religion. They sprang up, not because of the existence and use of Christian institutions, but by their abuse, — by the failure, really, to use them; and because these appliances had made as yet no sufficiently thorough and deep impression upon the community.

Efforts had been repeatedly made by a portion of the people to secure Mr. Lawson's permanent settlement among them. But the resistance was too strong; and, matters growing no better, Mr. Lawson left the parish during the summer or early autumn of 1688. He visited the neighborhood again in 1692, in an evil hour, and bringing evil with him. The little which is to be known further of his clouded life — darkening at length into the utter night — may be read in the history of Mr. Upham.

Next came Mr. Samuel Parris; and it was no change for the better.

Mr. Parris was born in London; and was thirty-five years old at his first appearance in Salem Village, in the autumn of 1688. He had been a member for a time of Harvard College, but without graduating; and he had been also a merchant in the West Indies and in Boston. Negotiations were soon afoot for his settlement in the vacant office. But he too was

slow in coming.   His wits had been sharpened in trade ; and
he was equal to the making a bargain with these villagers.
And he meant to do it.   The business was not concluded for
nearly or quite a year.   The record for this period is imperfect.
What were the exact terms of his settlement, became a matter
of dispute between the minister and his parishioners, and
was a question which they were never able to settle.   It
is not possible now, either from the record or from the depositions afterward made in court by Mr. Parris and by various
persons prominently connected with the affairs of the parish,
to determine precisely what was done.   Under date of June
18, 1689, there is an entry of a vote offering to Mr. Parris a
salary of sixty-six pounds, one-third in money and two-thirds in
provisions at specified rates ; he being required to find his own
firewood, and to keep the ministry house in good repair.   But
Mr. Parris never admitted that he made his engagement upon
the basis of this vote.   So vehement were his feelings on this
point, that when, some time after his ordination, the entry
was read in a parish meeting at which he was present, he
declared, according to the sworn testimony of three of his
parishioners, that he knew nothing of any such vote, and
would have nothing to do with it, and that " they were knaves
and cheaters that entered it," — a saying, we may observe, upon
such an occasion, not showing much wisdom on the part of
the pastor that could make it.

Upon the 10th of October, after mention of the repeal of
the vote of 1681, forbidding the conveyance by sale or gift of
the real estate belonging to the parish, it is said to have been
" voted and agreed by a General Concurrence that we will give
to Mr. Parice our menestrye house and barne and two akers of
Land next aioyneing to the house : and that Mr. Parice take
office amongst us and Live and dye in the worke of the
menestrye amongst us."   But here again many of the people,
on their part, had no better opinion of the means by which this
entry came on the book.

Nevertheless, Mr. Parris, supposing he had gotten the property, was now ready to take the office.   Accordingly, on the
19th of November (29th, N. S.), 1689, he became the minister

of the parish, and pastor of the church, that same day organized.*

The following is the covenant "agreed upon and consented unto by the Church of Christ at Salem Village, at their first Embodying, on ye 19 Nov. 1689." It is entered upon the church book of records in the handwriting of Mr. Parris. The missing words in the first paragraph, indicated by bracketed spaces below, are lost from the worn margin of the leaf. The covenant was probably drawn up by Mr. Parris ; and I have been able to find no other from which it could appear to have been modelled. Its last three paragraphs, with the names of the twenty-seven signers, are given in their place, reproduced with absolute exactness by the new process of "heliotyping."†

"We whose names (tho unworthy of a name in this (church ?) are) hereunto subscribed, Lamenting our own great unfitness (for such) an Awful and solemn approach unto the Holy God and (deploring ?) all the miscarriages committed by us, either in the Days (of) our unregeneracy or since we have been brought into acquaintance with God, in the communion of his churches (which we) have heretofore been related unto: And yet apprehending ourselves called by the Most High to Embody (ourselves) into a different society, with a sacred covenant to (serve) the Lord Jesus Christ and Edifie one another according (to the) Rules of his holy word, Being persuaded in matters (of Faith ?) according to the Confession of Faith owned and (consented) unto by the Elders and Messingers of the churches (assembled) at Boston in New-England.

---

* It should, however, be observed that Mr. Parris considered his engagement with the parish as beginning in some sort with the 1st of July preceding. His receipts for his salary are reckoned from that date. He was counted, we may suppose, after the manner of those before him, as "stated supply" until this time of his becoming the settled pastor.

The account of the organization of the church and parish in Mr. Nason's "Gazetteer of Massachusetts," just published, contains within its first seven lines nine material errors ; and, if this very remarkable instance of condensation had to be paralleled, I do not know where one might more hopefully look for another like it than in that same book.

† Printing in ink from a photographic impression.

May — 12 — 1680 (which) for the substance of it, we now own and profess

"We do, in some measure of sinceritie, this day give up our selves unto God in Christ, to be for him and not for an-other,* at the same renouncing all the vanities and Idols of this present evil world.

"We give up ourselves, and offspring, unto the Lord Jehovah, the one true and living God, in three Persons, Father, Son, and Holy Ghost. To God the Father of our Lord Jesus Christ, as to our Reconciled God and Father in Christ Jesus: and unto Christ Jesus, as our King, Priest and Prophet, and only Mediator: And unto the Holy Ghost as our only Sanctifyer and Comforter: As to our Best good and Last End: promising, (with divine help) to live unto, and upon, this one God in three Persons: hoping at length to live forever with him.

"We do likewise give up ourselves one unto another in the Lord, engaging, (with divine aid) as a church of God to Sub-mit to the order, Discipline and Government of Christ in this his church, and to the Ministerial teaching, guidance, and over-sight of the Elder (or Elders) thereof, as to such as watch for our Souls; And also to a mutuall brotherly watchfulness according to Gosple Rules, so long as by such Rules we shall continue in this Relation to each other: And promise also to walk with all regular and due communion with other churches of our Lord Jesus, and in all cheerful endeavor to support and observe the pure Gospel institutions of our Lord Redeemer so far as He shall graciously reveal unto us his will concern-ing them.

"In order hereunto:

[Continued by *fac-simile* on opposite page.]

---

* There will be noticed the occurrence, at several points, of phrases which have kept their place to the present time in the Covenant and Confession of Faith of the church.

We resolve uprightly to study what is our duty, & to make it our greif, & reckon it our shame, whereinsoever we find our selves to come short in the discharge of it, & for pardon thereof ~~to betake~~ humbly to betake our selves to the Blood of the Everlasting Covenant.

And that we may keep this covenant, & all the branches of it inviolable for ever, being sensible that we can do nothing of our selves,

We humbly implore: the help & grace of our Mediator may be sufficient for us: Beseeching That whilst we are working out our own salvation, with fear & trembling, He would gratiously work in us both to will, & to do. And that he being the Great Shepherd of our souls would lead us into the paths of Righteousness, for his own Names sake. And at length receive us all into the Inheritance of the Saints in Light.

Samuel Parris · Pastor.

Nathaneel Putnam

John Putnam

Henry Wilkins · 79.

Joshua Rea:

Nathaniel Ingersoll

peter Cloyes

Thomos putnam

John Putnam jun.

Edward Putnam

Jonathan putnam

Benjamin putnam

Ezekiel Cheevor

Henry Wilkins

Benja. Wilkins

william way

× Peter Prescott

The Women which embodyed with us are by their severall Names as followeth Viz.

1. Eliz: (wife to Sam:) Parris
2. Rebek: (wife to John) Putman.
3. Anna (wife to Bray) Wilkins.
4. Sarah (wife to Joshuah) Rea.
4. Hannah (wife to Jno (jun?.) Putman.
6. Sarah (wife to Benja.) Putman
7. Sarah Putman.
8. Deliverance Walcott Perris
9. Peiry (wife to william) Way.
10. mary (wife to Sam:) Abbie.

Illi quorū nominibus hoc signum præfigitur
+ è vivis cesserunt.

The signatures of all the men are in their own writing, excepting Henry and Benj. Wilkins. These two, with the names of all the women, were recorded by Mr. Parris. He seems to have omitted, at first, his wife Elizabeth ; and afterward, in order to place her name at the head of the list of the women, he changed the numbers which he had before placed against each one in the column below. The figures against the name of Bray Wilkins indicate his age at that time.

The sign of mortality the pastor did not have occasion, during his stay, to prefix to the names of any of these original members.

The printed Manual of the Church, now in use, is in error in omitting four of these names ; and also in many other points respecting the membership of the church and the pastoral succession.

The covenant itself gave promise of better things than shortly followed.

We all know of the delusion which, a little more than two years later, overspread the village ; and of the fearful scenes of violence and wrong that were here enacted. The witchcraft demonstrations began to be made near the end of February, 1692, and continued, with fierce excitement, through the spring and summer to near the middle of the autumn of the same year ; by which time there was a return of reason. All the neighboring towns were more or less involved. Twenty persons suffered death at the hands of the law ; and imprisonment, loss of property, exile, and innumerable other evils, befell a much greater number. The mischief began in the house of the pastor of the church ; and he, more than any one else, urged on to the deeds of public wrong that were wrought.

Of Mr. Parris himself, it is not easy to know how one should speak. He was by profession a Christian man and a minister. He fell, it may be granted, upon evil times. He had occasion to carry out to its full practical results the prevalent belief of his age ; and, in so doing, he incurred an odium which, for this particular matter only, and regarding him in comparison with

others of his contemporaries, is no doubt beyond his deserving.
It is not for us to decide that his motives in what he did could
have been only evil, — which, indeed, we have no reason to think;
nor may we judge that he possessed nothing of the Christian
character. But it is not unjust nor uncharitable to say that he
failed to do among this people the work of a Christian minister
or man. And, whether or not it is unjust or uncharitable, it is
not untrue that the writer of this account has often wished,
as he has been reviewing of late the story of those wretched
days, that his predecessor, this first pastor of the church, were
personally present, that he might lay hands upon him other
than in an apostolic fashion. And, indeed, it may be the
most favorable judgment that can be formed of him, that
would place him with that class of men — conceited, punc-
tilious, officious, perpetually wrapt up and encumbered with
their fancied dignities — to whom a thorough shaking might
sometimes be a means of grace. But, though I thus speak,
the record is one to be read in sadness more than wrath.

The book of the parish contains no mention whatever of the
witchcraft troubles. And it never contained any; for there
are no erasions or missing leaves. The record of the church,
kept by Mr. Parris, has but little, so far as concerns the proceedings connected with the immediate outbreak; but it is
full with regard to the strifes which followed it and grew out
of it. And it is with respect to these later difficulties only,
that I feel disposed to speak positively of the temper exhibited by Mr. Parris.

The question has, it will be seen, distinct and broad divisions. As to witchcraft itself, Mr. Parris is not to be specially
blamed for having no more light than belonged to his age. And,
for the great zeal he showed in pressing on the prosecutions,
it might be thought, and is thought by some, that he did
no more than to fulfil vigorously, as his habit was, the
duties which he held to be providentially imposed upon him
in the position he occupied; though, on this point, it will
still seem, that, as *pastor of this people*, he should have chosen
that some other person than he might be most prominent in
bringing upon any of them the last severities of the law.

Leaving this in part, but keeping upon the same branch of the subject, there is the further charge, heaviest of all if it were true, that Mr. Parris was moved in what he did, not only in a general way, by a hard and wilful temper, but directly by personal enmity toward those that were accused ; and that he thus maliciously took advantage of the outbreak and the excitement connected with it to bring ruin upon his enemies, and to break down all opposition to himself within the parish. Mr. Upham has pointed out numerous facts which look in this direction. But, after a most careful consideration of whatever has come to light bearing upon the case, I do not feel that we are quite compelled to come to such a conclusion. When we remember the intimacies between some of the accusing children and the family of Mr. Parris, it will not appear strange that they should have cried out against certain of those known to be opposed to him in parish affairs, even without any direct suggestion from him. And so long, at least, as the matter lies open to any doubt, Mr. Parris should have the benefit of the uncertainty. I prefer therefore to think, that, however he may have shown a bad spirit in these prosecutions, he did not push them forward, and stir up also the passions by which they were sustained, with the purpose, known distinctly to himself, of gratifying private animosities or compassing personal ends.

But what ought we, then, to have looked for from Mr. Parris, when the fury of the outbreak was over ; when it had come to be generally understood that the persons put to death had been condemned unjustly, or, at the very least, upon wholly insufficient evidence ; and when there was time for reflection upon all that had occurred ? When he considered the desolation that had been brought into those homes of his people, what must this Christian pastor have done ? If he were conscious of no malice, or of no distinct evil motive in the part he had taken, and even if he were not yet quite sure that the judicial course pursued had in fact been wholly wrong, — yet, when he thought of these most heavy sorrows, in the causing of which, for whatever intent, he had assumed so large a share, must he not have felt that the utmost tenderness should at least be shown towards those that had been thus bereaved ? Should

he not have thought that even their unjust reflections upon himself should be patiently and considerately borne ? And would
he not have conducted himself with carefulness and gentle-
ness, if not with the manner of penitence, in all that might
relate to the sad events through which they had passed ? There
were those involved in the same transactions, that ever afterwards reviewed them in this spirit. For Mr. Parris, we are
unhappily too sure he did not. This is, to me, the most
unpleasant memory connected with his ministry.

The part which he took in all the subsequent controversies,
as set forth by himself, no one can now look upon except as
most unwise and unbecoming. On the 14th of August, 1692,
that is, in the very worst stage of the excitement, and while the
executions were still going on, Mr. Parris caused the church
to remain after service, it being the sabbath day, and brought
before them for discipline the case of sundry persons who had
been absent from the communion for a time, and some of them
also from public worship. These persons — Peter Cloyes,
Samuel Nurse and his wife, and John Tarbell and wife, — were
all near relatives of Rebecca Nurse, who had just been put to
death, Mr. Parris assisting ; and one of them, Peter Cloyes,
had at the same time a wife in jail who narrowly escaped the
like fate. Under these circumstances, the proposal of the
pastor of the church to inquire after them, and to institute
proceedings against them, indicates an insensibility to the
most ordinary sympathies of humanity, that is shocking to
think of. These proceedings, thus indecently begun, were
carried on in some form for years ; though the persons com-
plained of became shortly, in their turn, complainants, and
formed the nucleus of that party in the church and parish by
which the removal of the minister was finally secured.

This whole affair Mr. Parris managed to the last in the
same spirit in which he began it. He took no pains to con-
ciliate those whom he had offended, or to make such amends
as he might for the wrongs they had some of them suffered.
He remained hard and unyielding. He was sharp in all his
dealing with them, standing for trifles, tenacious of all the
ground he held. This appears, for one instance, in the nego-

tiations with respect to the calling of a council to consider their difficulties. He opposed it as long as he might. He delayed it in every possible manner, and upon the most shallow pretences, when direct opposition had become too hazardous. And he did not finally consent to its coming together until it had become evident that the whole moral effect of a council would be had, whether one were called or not; and that it would go more strongly against him if he did not agree to its assembling.

His confession, too, which he finally made of his error in the witchcraft prosecutions, is of such a sort, that it might nearly or quite as well have been omitted.* His strongest expressions of humiliation are on account of the breaking-out of the delusion in his own family; and these, though suitable enough, are entirely consistent with the maintenance of the ground that the treatment of the evil was what it should have been. On this last, which was the main point, he does, indeed, go on to admit that some mistakes may have been made by him, with others. But he gives no intimation of any wrong intent or spirit on his part that needed to be acknowledged; but, on the contrary, appears to deny that there was any such; concerning which, we can only observe that if, by any stretch of belief, this might be allowed to be true, then, indeed, he was justified in maintaining it. The only passage in which he refers distinctly to those upon whom alone the direct and most terrible evils involved in the outbreak had been brought, is the following: "As to all that have unduly suffered in these matters (either in their persons or relations), through the clouds of human weakness, and Satan's wiles and sophistry, I do truly sympathize with them; taking it for granted that such as know themselves clear of this great transgression, or that have sufficient grounds so to look upon their dear friends, have hereby been under those sore trials and temptations, that not an ordinary measure of true grace would be sufficient to prevent a bewraying of remaining corruption." This must be

* Mr. Parris does not himself call this document, which is found at length in the records of the church, a confession; but entitles it, "My Meditations for Peace."

looked upon as a very remarkable paragraph in such a connection ; the only reference which the whole paper contains to "corruption" or real sin being thus, in this apologetic and back-handed manner, cast upon his opponents! It is not strange that the "dissatisfied brethren," after duly weighing this variety of confession, should have made answer, that "they remained dissatisfied."

We need not follow minutely the history of these years. The council which met on the 3d of April, 1695, was constituted unfairly with respect to the opponents of Mr. Parris. But it made a not very unjust distribution of censure and advice on either side ; and did, perhaps, all that could have been expected of it in the interest of peace, upon the condition that Mr. Parris was to remain in the pastorate. But the large and increasing minority of the people were not at rest ; and they made such further demonstrations as brought within a month, from several prominent members of the council, including both the Mathers, a letter to the pastor and church, advising that Mr. Parris should resign his office. But neither he nor the larger part of the church was yet ready for such a step.

A year later, however, Mr. Parris had determined to give up the contest. Whether, at that time, he could still have rallied a majority of both the church and the parish to sustain him further, there are no means of knowing with certainty. But, as to the parish, it is probable he could not ; and there are many indications that his withdrawal, though voluntary in form, was seen by him to be of necessity, and by the force of a hostile sentiment against which there was no longer any hope of continued successful resistance. But it is in fairness to be added, that the adherence to Mr. Parris for these four years of so many of his people, including the most of the leading men among them, should be regarded as somewhat to his credit ; for this support is not to be wholly explained by the fact that several of these men had been themselves actively concerned, along with their minister, in the witchcraft proceedings.

The ministry of Mr. Parris ended with the last sabbath of June, 1696. But the troubles with him did not cease with his resignation. Pecuniary difficulties remained. The questions touching the original terms of settlement were unadjusted. Then there was the ministry house, and two acres of adjoining land, which Mr. Parris had held by the vote of the inhabitants, after some sort, and which he now refused to give up. However it stood in law, he may have thought there was some moral right in his possession, since, in whatever way the vote was passed, the land had been with him a consideration in his settlement. Into this quarrel with their late pastor the people, on their part, seem to have gone with almost· entire unanimity, and, if we may so speak, with a hearty good-will. The business had to them, no doubt, a certain pleasing flavor of familiarity and of ancient and established usage. Not even Thomas Putnam the clerk now stood by Mr. Parris ; though he, with his family, had been intimately involved in all the most violent doings of the spring and summer of 1692. The depositions preserved in the court-house show that he entered into the popular movement to regain the parish property.

The matter went to court, and thence to a board of arbitration, consisting of "the Hon. Wait Winthrop, Elisha Cook, and Samuel Sewall, Esqrs." They awarded to Mr. Parris, from the inhabitants, besides the arrearages of his salary, the sum of £79. 9s. 6d. ; and required him to give a quit-claim to the ministry house and land. .

The affair was not concluded until September of 1697. For the larger part of this time Mr. Parris remained in the village, occupying the parsonage. Nor, indeed, was his legal connection with the parish completely sundered previous to this judgment of the arbitrators. (See Appendix B, p. 234).

Now at length he was gone. There is little among us to join his name with the common and kindly memories of humanity, saving that his wife died just after his resignation, and that he set a monument by her grave. The stone may still be seen in the Wadsworth Cemetery, bearing the inscription : —

"Elizabeth Parris, aged about 48 years, Dec. July y° 14 — 1676.
   Sleep precious Dust, no stranger now to Rest.
   Thou hast thy longed wish in Abraham's Brest
   Farewell Best Wife, Choice Mother, Neighbur, Friend.
   We'el wail thee less for hopes of thee i' th' end.   S. ·P."

Of this Christian woman, upon whom, besides the ordinary weariness of mortality, there had been cast the peculiar burden of these painful years, we may well imagine that she should have longed for that rest of which her earthly life, for its outward conditions, would seem to have afforded but so small a foretaste. It may be noticed here, as somewhat remarkable, that each of these first four ministers buried a wife during his residence in the village. Mr. Bayley lost also three children, and Mr. Lawson one, during the same period. The place of their burial is not marked nor certainly known; but it may probably have been in the Wadsworth Yard.

Mr. Parris, after his removal from our town, was employed in the same year to preach in Stow, and afterwards at Dunstable and at Sudbury. At this last-named place he died, Feb. 27, 1720. His later years were darkened with poverty and with manifold troubles; of which I make mention only as a matter of personal history, and not as if they should be taken as any proof of the disfavor of God upon him.

Into the history itself of the great witchcraft delusion I do not purpose to enter at all. It has been fully explored by Mr. Upham. I shall make only, in passing, some notes of reflection upon it, and specially upon the connection it may seem to have with Christian doctrine and the Christian ministry. These reflections will of necessity be short and summary.

Belief in witchcraft, with its allied superstitions, has not been peculiar to Christian countries. The evil has existed, and does exist, and in more obstinate forms, among heathen nations. The disease, indeed, as it broke out in this village, was in part a heathen importation, — coming in with Mr. Parris's Indian man John, and Tituba his wife.

There is no reference at all in the Bible to any witchcraft of the kind supposed to have been practised here ; and of course there is no authority for any such mode of dealing with it as was followed in this case. The witches mentioned in the Bible were persons *professing of themselves* to have in their keeping power or knowledge of a preternatural order ; as by sorcery, magic, necromancy, or divination. This profession on their own part is essential and characteristic. They did not need to have the thing charged upon them. They avowed it and claimed it. They had their living by it. Their successors in modern times, so far as they have any, are to be found with the impostors whose advertisements are to be seen in the newspapers of the lower sort ; and who, to the disgrace of our communities, are still able to live by the pretence of fortune-telling, and of the practice of occult arts. The Salem witchcraft was altogether a different thing, both in theory and fact. No one professed to practise it. The persons charged with it denied it. If either party involved in these proceedings bore any likeness to the ancient witches, it was *not the accused, but the accusers.* They — these young persons by whom the charges of witchcraft were brought forward — did themselves make profession of mysterious and extra-natural knowledge. They, if any one, might have been proceeded against and silenced by some scriptural and reasonable warrant.

That many Christian men of those days thought differently, may be of small concern to us. We are interested in showing that Christianity itself is not involved in their errors ; and, beyond that, our chief business with the mistakes of our fathers is to see that we do not fall into them ourselves.

Going beyond the particular theories and methods held and followed in this case, it may, however, be thought that the biblical teaching with respect to the existence and power of evil spirits gives at least some general support to what were then the popular beliefs. The Bible does, indeed, warn us concerning the Devil, that he may do us harm. It exhorts us to resist him ; and we shall do well to give heed to the counsel. It tells us, too, what armor and weapons are to be taken, — the girdle of truth, the breastplate of righteousness, the preparation of the gospel of peace, faith, and prayer. But the weapons used here were all unlike these, — bitterness, wrath, anger, clamor, evil surmisings and speakings, false witness, every shape of hatefulness and malice. These are of the Devil's own forging; and they can never be turned to much purpose in fighting against him.

The Devil's aim, too, according to the Bible, is to bring evil on the *souls* rather than the bodies of men, however the latter might please him. It was no doubt true, as Mr. Parris said, that this great "enemy of all Christian peace had been most tremendously let loose" upon this village; but he did his worst work when he stirred up these enmities and evil passions in the hearts of its inhabitants. And it may be that he wrought nowhere a greater mischief than in the bosom of this very Christian minister who thus deplored his coming.

Furthermore, it may be allowed to be true that in some cases, and perhaps in this with which we are dealing, the power of degrading and dangerous superstitions, and of the excitements to which they give rise, is temporarily augmented by influences arising from the Christian religion. The original endowments of man, and those of the highest with which he is furnished, render him susceptible to the force of impressions from unseen things. These endowments are liable to perversion; and they have been often and too far perverted. Once thrown from their appropriate balance, the pressure upon them of added motives from the invisible world, though these motives are in themselves of solid and wholesome truthfulness, may increase, for a time, their disordered action. The Christian revelation has not sought to withhold the play upon us of these powers from the unseen world, as the manner of some now would be, — a thing impossible, in truth, to be wholly done, and weakening and deadly, if it were possible, to all that is noblest in the estate of man. It has followed the style of all manly culture, and made it its aim not to lessen the force of these agencies, of whatever rational order, that may bear upon the soul, but to raise up and strengthen the spirit itself, that it may control and command and use them. Possibilities of evil are thus involved in these possibilities of the highest good. And it may sometimes be, both with individuals and communities, that the powers of religion to agitate and alarm may *precede* somewhat, in their working, its powers to elevate and calm and fortify. Nevertheless, all its own proper tendency is toward this last result, and not another. They in whom its highest efficiency is realized are not the men most open to debasing fears or uncontrollable agitation. They are calm, rather, and confident in the presence of dangers, which yet they may allow to exist, whether from the visible or the invisible world. The great words resonant along all the line of Christian revelation are, "faith," "hope," and "love,"— faith, not fear; for "God hath not given us the spirit of fear, but of power and love, and of a sound mind." And this line, comprehensive of the scope of our religion, should have been written betimes over the doors of that ancient and dishonored house of worship, which witnessed so much of the shame and misery of these proceedings.

As to the connection of this delusion with the ministry, it might be added that a physician first pronounced the manifestations to be those of witchcraft; that lawyers and judges had their full share in the prosecutions; and that the official responsibility for what was done in the name of the law rests primarily on them. And they, it should be noticed, were not residents of Salem Village at all, — upon which place, therefore, that odium must not rest. They were from abroad, and were among the foremost men of the Colony. Nor is there any thing in the whole history more humiliating, or more nearly incredible in its folly, than the reception in those courts, as conclusive testimony, of a mass of matter in the whole of which there was nothing whatever, saving only the confessions extorted by fear, that bore the slightest resemblance to rational evidence. And for the ministers, besides, Mr. Upham has said with truth, that, with certain grievous exceptions, they were of the first, if not as a class foremost, in discovering and checking the course of crime that had been commenced.

With respect to the "afflicted children," as they were called, who were the chief immediate agents, and by whose testimony the persons accused were pointed out and convicted, *they* alone, if any one, and not the victims of their false accusation,

4

were in conspiracy with invisible powers of evil. They should have been stopped at first by a quiet family discipline ; with resort even if necessary, as has been often before remarked, to the use of that remedy long ago pointed out by the wisdom of Solomon. The preparatory dealing they had for many weeks, though only in pretence or imagination, with spirits, real or imagined, was a meddling with beings, imaginary or real, that never brought a ray of light or any thing of good to our world, and whom it is most wise and safe to leave undisturbed within their own shadows.

I will not profess to decide whether, in the frenzied state into which they were finally wrought, their experiences were in part real, or wholly in pretence and fraud. But it may be observed that they belonged clearly with an unhealthy physical condition, of whatever origin.

They were nearly all young women. The student of social history will not fail to remember how prominent a part persons of this class have had in other times in similar wild excitements. The follower of medical science may add the observation, that with this same class, in such unhealthy conditions, there often appears a mixture of disease and deceitfulness which no one can separate. That delicacy of structure in woman, which is so closely associated with her superior grace and refinement, causes her to be exposed to. such peculiar dangers. The more carefully should she be guarded in her youth from all influences of that unwholesome order to which these unfortunate persons were so fatally subjected.

Finally, we may consider that there was perhaps some issue of good in the overruling providence of God, even from the fierceness of the outbreak in this village. The people here and in the neighboring region were of a kind to take the matter in hand stoutly, if at all. They carried out to the full the mistaken beliefs of the times, and caused their folly and atrocity to be clearly seen. The world was beginning to be ready to learn the lesson far enough so that it could be made out when set forth so plainly. It may be, therefore, that fewer persons in number have perished the world over since that time, through the power of that delusion, and that thus less mischief has been wrought by it than would have been if this dark scene in the history of our village had never been enacted, — (See Appendix F, p. 247.)*

But better times were at hand. After Mr. Parris had left, it was not easy, as may well be imagined, to find ministers who were willing to settle here, or to preach with that in view. And there appears even to have been considerable difficulty in procuring a supply for the pulpit in any manner. Overtures, more or less formal, were made to several in rapid succession, and, among others, to Mr. Bayley their first minister; but all to no effect. Reflections suited to their situation were being awakened in the minds of the people. At a meeting of the inhabitants it was voted "by a unanimous consent that we will keep Tuesday the 12th of this instant October (1697) as a day of fasting and prayer to seek direction of the Wonderful Counsellor about providing us a minister." On the 19th of November following, — though another had in the mean time been in vain applied to, — they agreed "by a unanimous consent," as the record runs, in the choice of a committee "to treate with the Rev. Mr. Joseph Green; to see if they can prevaile with him to come and preach with us a while in order to a further settlement."

The committee consisted of Capt. Thomas Flint, Dea. Edward Putnam, John Tarbill, Samuel Nurse, John Buxton, Benj. Putnam, James Putnam, Alexander Osborne, Benj. Wilkins, Jonathan Putnam, Benj. Hutchinson, John Putnam, jun., and Daniel Rea. The business was evidently thought a weighty if not an arduous one. And it may be noticed that the committee embraced a fair representation of what had been the minority party in the old troubles, — a practical sign of good, appropriate to come after a day of prayer.

The next week the church had also a special appointment for fasting and prayer ; and a meeting was held at the house of Dea. Edward Putnam. They prayed "that God would provide a paster for this his church, according to his promise made to

his people that he would give them pasters after his own heart
who should feed his people with knowledge and understanding
that his church may not be as sheep without a shepherd."
And the account proceeds : "After prayer being ended, the
church having before this day had some experience of the ministerial preaching and teaching of Mr. Joseph Green amongst
us, it was then consented to and voted by the church that we
desire him to continue in the same work still amongst us, and
that in order to take office upon him : if it shall please the
grate Shepherd of the Sheep to besto such a blessing upon us."

On the 20th of December in the same year, the parish took
corresponding action, "by a universal consent." This same
term appears with the vote fixing the salary ; the record seeming, in these pages, to exhibit a satisfaction that began to be
felt in this new and unaccustomed harmony. They offered
him a salary which was ultimately fixed at seventy pounds,
with the use of the ministry house and land, and his firewood,
which last was after some years commuted for eight pounds.
Mr. Green came, and remained with them many months, his
settlement being wisely deferred, that it might be seen if they
would hold in the same mind concerning him, and be at peace
among themselves. In the June following, the church renewed the call, as the parish also did in substance. And in
response to this we find an entry in the church-book, the first
in the handwriting of Mr. Green, in these terms : "I gave an
answer to the church and congregation to the effect that
if their love to me continued, and was duly manifested, and if
they did all study to be quiet, I then was willing to continue
with you, and to engage in the work of the ministry," &c.

The new pastor was ordained on Thursday, Nov. 10, 1698 :
a good-omened day for this church and parish. Mr. Green
was a graduate of Harvard College, and lacked two weeks of
being twenty-three years old. He married in the following
spring Elizabeth Gerrish, a daughter of the minister in the adjoining parish at Wenham. If his acquaintance with this
young lady had begun some time before, it is, I suppose, conceivable that some agreeableness of neighborhood may have
had a place among the reasons that made him "willing to continue" in this village.

The parish presently appropriated forty pounds for repairs on the parsonage. Probably the amount was thought too large by some ; and objections appear to have been raised. Very soon after another meeting was called, at which a statement was made in behalf of Mr. Green : "that he was willing the vote of forty pounds should be lett fall : and that if the house be so repaired that it be decent and comfortable to live in it shall please him." It is an entry refreshing to come upon after the dreary pages that have gone before it on the parish-book ; and, so far as concerns the spirit in which affairs of this kind were managed, it is almost the first sign the history of this village shows of the existence of the Christian religion.

I may add in a confidential manner, for the benefit of any ministers present, that I believe the course taken by Mr. Green is the best one commonly *for the matter of getting a parsonage kept in good repair.*

This business was arranged in February. It may add to our interest in it to remember that Mr. Green was to be married on the 16th of the next month, and would thus naturally have some wish that the house should be put in good order ; or it may be that he supposed the parsonage would be pleasant as it stood, after the young lady from Wenham had once gone into it ; or, as they must have talked of the matter together, we may believe that the lady herself is entitled to some share of credit for the moderation and good sense that was shown ; or it may be that both of them thought it was not best, by asking too much, to run the risk of having the wedding put off till fall.

Mr. Green directed all his efforts towards the prosecution of the appropriate work of the Christian ministry. He had special care for the restoring and maintaining of peace among the people, who had been so long distracted, and who had also in so many of their homes the most mournful occasion for remembering the strifes through which they had passed. The church voted to drop the action that had been pending for years against the offending — or aggrieved — brethren ; declaring that they "looked upon it as nothing," and that it "should be buried for ever." And there is a minute by Mr. Green in the church-book for Feb. 5, 1699, of "a matter of thankfulness" in the presence of these persons at the communion with the church on that sabbath, for the first time since the dark spring of 1692.

A new era was upon them. In 1701 the brethren of the church desired that a day of thanksgiving should be had, on account of the peace and prosperity which God had given them; and in answer, as they believed, to the prayers offered on the day of fasting three years and a half before. The thanksgiving was kept on Wednesday, the 18th of June. "God smiled on the season," says Mr. Green; "and the work of the day was carried on by Mr. Noyes, who prayed, and Mr. Pierpont preached and concluded.* The Lord help us to live his praises."

It is pleasant and instructive to observe that this beginning of better things could thus be traced to the time before the settlement of Mr. Green. It was not all due to him, and to the blessing of God upon his labors. His coming itself, and all his work, were in answer rather to the prayers of the people, that had been offered before he came, and while they were without a pastor. The church had not been without godly and faithful members. Besides the deacons Nathanael Inger-soll and Edward Putnam, there were many others, we may not doubt, both of men and women, who grieved over the desolations of Zion, and whose hearts, in that time of darkness, were moved in penitence and trust to seek the Lord. And the Lord, according to his promise, had regard to the prayer of these his people, and did not despise their prayer. And this is here to be written in gratitude and counsel and hope, "for the generations to come."

The occasions, then, for thankfulness were indeed abundant. The change in all respects was great; and it has also been in

---

* Mr. Noyes, of the Old Church in Salem, had been present with Mr. Hale of Beverly, at the day of fasting in 1697; and the brethren of this church had a pleasant recollection of his services on that occasion. The connection of Mr. Noyes with the witchcraft proceedings had been unfortunate; and I refer to this as bringing to light some better views of his character.

a good measure permanent. Nothing, scarcely, of importance, before the settlement of Mr. Green, had been done by a united people. Nothing of importance, scarcely, since, in the space of a century and three-quarters, has been done in any other manner. No minister has been settled except with practical unanimity; and in each case but one, as I think, there has been no dissenting vote in church or parish. Nor has there been, in all that long period, a single serious and obstinate contention among the members of this church and society.

To one who follows the narrative along the records there is a sense of relief and of exhilaration not easy to express. It may not be extravagant, considering what scenes had gone before, if we recur in comparison to the emotions with which the most sublime of poets has described his ascent in imagination, from the gloom of hell and the storms and wastes of chaos, to the settled and ordered beauty of the world of creation and to the light of heaven. May the days of peace lengthen and grow bright; and may no shadow of the former darkness return, forever!

During these thirty years nearly, from the building of the meeting-house, it had gotten much out of repair with time, and probably also by ill-usage. It was too small for the growing congregation; and, more than all, many unpleasant associations were fixed upon it. In 1700 it was determined to build a new house. It was set on the "Watch-house Hill," upon the spot where we are now assembled; * but fronting toward the north upon the other, or "Old Meeting-house Road." † This spot is described as being "before Dea. Ingersoll's door." The house of Dea. Ingersoll stood nearly

* The watch-house was designed for observation and defence against the Indians, and was probably a strong building of logs. It stood upon the northern point of the hill, about twenty-five rods from the meeting-house, and within what is now the parsonage pasture. The "hill" itself is a slight diluvial and glacial ridge of bowlders and gravel, which has been much lowered in parts, and almost obliterated, by the removal of materials for roads, and by levelling for building-purposes.

† That which is now the main road, leading southward by the western end of the church, was then but a private way and a cart-path.

where the parsonage now does, but probably a little farther to the rear, or toward the north-west. Dea. Ingersoll gave the land ; but the condition was added that " Deacon Putnam, and John Buxton and John Putnam and Benj. Putnam becom bound in a bond of a hundred pounds apeece to defend the title of the said land to the peple as long as they make use of it to that end." This provision was made on account of some question, afterwards adjusted, with respect to the validity of the title by which Dea. Ingersoll held his real estate.

The building was not actually under way until the next year, although preparations had been made. The house was raised in the spring of 1701 ; and the work occupied something over a year ; so that the people first met in the new meeting-house on the 26th of July, 1702.

The dimensions were forty-eight feet by forty-two ; and twenty feet between the joints. It had a tower, or " turret," and a hip-roof, or " gable ends." There were galleries within ; and the walls were plastered up to the plates, but left unfinished above. The proposed cost was three hundred and thirty pounds, which fell short of the sum required. About thirty-six pounds were raised by subscription among the " neighburs ; " that is, persons attending meeting at the village, but living beyond the parish bounds. Mr. Green, however, as being a person not regularly taxed, set his name first to this subscription for the sum of ten pounds. Only one or two persons in the parish paid more. Some help was also received from Salem.

The building committee were Capt. Thomas Flint,* Mr. Joseph Pope, Lieut. Jonathan Putnam, Mr. Joseph Herrick, and Benj. Putnam. It was voted that those that had their road shortened to the meeting-house by the change of location should do the work of levelling the new ground. And, moreover, though the people were done with quarrelling, yet, since they had not been through so much litigation without having their wits sharpened, they took care to direct that the new

* Capt. Thomas Flint was a carpenter; and in the Genealogy of the Flint Family, p. 9, he is said to have built "the first meeting-house in Salem Village." But it does not appear to be certain whether it may not have been this second house, the first upon the spot now occupied, of which he was the builder.

MEETING-HOUSE OF 1701.

house should not be raised until this work of levelling was
fairly done.

A good representation of this house is given on the opposite
page. It stood through most of the century, to 1785.

The seats in these houses, as is well known, and until recent
times, were assigned to each person by a committee appointed
for the purpose. The seating committee were instructed to
have respect, first to age, next to office, and lastly to rates or
taxation. The men and the women were seated ordinarily
apart, and with little regard to the keeping of families together.
The old men thus sat near the pulpit on one side, and the aged
women on the other. The details of these seatings are still
preserved. The main body of the house was set with benches,
answering roughly to modern "settees." But permission was
given from time to time for persons mentioned by name, to
build other pews or seats, with explicit directions as to their
construction, and the individuals by whom they were to be
occupied. It is recorded that at one time "several young
women" had leave granted them to put up a seat, but with the
provision that they should "raise it no higher" than those adjoining. For what reason it should have been thought that
these young women might be inclined to make their seat
higher than the rest, I am wholly unable to imagine

During these years the attention of the people was directed
to the making some provision for the education of their
children. Before this time, though there had been schools in
Salem, yet there had probably been none, within the limits of
the present town of Danvers, publicly and permanently established. The first reference to the subject which I have
noticed in the parish records is for the year 1701, when it was
voted "that Mr. Joseph Herrick and Mr. Joseph Putnam and
John Putnam jun. are chosen and empowered to agree with
some suitable person to be a school-master among us, in some
convenient time ; and make return therefor to the people."
These men were the first school-committee in our town. It is
doubtful, however, if, with this committee, the "convenient

time" for hiring a teacher ever, in fact, came. The passage of such a vote in one of these meetings, it must be said, does not of necessity signify accomplishment. Money was of right to be expected, and was afterward received, from the town of Salem, where their taxes were paid. And the next mention of the matter is eleven years later, at which time a committee was appointed to receive whatever might be furnished by the selectmen of Salem. And they were directed with this money to make payment to "ye widow dealand" of "five pounds which is her due for keeping school in ye village formerly;" and also "to invite her to come and keep school in ye village again, and to engage her five pounds a year for two years, of that money that is granted to us by the Town for a school." Nearly a year later there is a receipt signed by "Katharin Daland" for this five pounds, due "for Keeping School at Salem Villig at ye School House near Mr. Green's."

The diary of Mr. Green, which has been fortunately preserved, gives us some further information. This diary has been printed, or the most of it, in the Historical Collections of the Essex Institute, with a preface and notes by Dea. Samuel P. Fowler. It covers the larger part of the period of his ministry, though the entries are often far apart. It is a memorial of great interest ; and it is the more interesting for its having been intended, evidently, only for his own use.

In the year 1708 he has this record : —

March 11. My lectures ; full assembly, few strangers. I spoke to several about building a schoolhouse, and determined to do it, &c.

18. I rode to ye neighbors about a schoolhouse, and found them generally willing to help. I went to Wenham P.M. Bad riding as ever was.

22. Meeting of the Inhabitants. I spoke with several about building a schoolhouse. I went into ye Town Meeting * and said to this effect : Neighburs, I am about building a schoolhouse for the good education of our children, and have spoken to several of the neighbors who are willing to help it forward, so that I hope we shall quickly finish it ; and I speak of it here that so every one that can have any benefit, may have opportunity for so good a service. Some replyed that it was a new thing to them, and they desired to know where it should stand, and what the design of it

---

* That is, a meeting of the inhabitants of the village.

was. To them I answered that Deacon Ingersoll would give land for it to stand on, at the upper end of the Training field, and that I designed to have a good schoolmaster to teach their children to read and write and cypher and every thing that is good. Many commended the design, and none objected against it.

25. Began to get timber for schoolhouse.

There are accounts following of the raising and underpinning of the building, of his preparing the work and getting the " mantle tree; " and on the 20th of September, he was still " hurrying about ye schoolhouse."

It appears thus that this first schoolhouse in Danvers was built by the village minister himself; he directing the work, and assuming the responsibility for it, and collecting among his neighbors what he could to assist in meeting the expense. The usual liberality of Dea. Ingersoll is seen also in this business. The place where this building stood may not be known now more definitely than by this description, that it was at the upper end of the "training-field," or common.* It is a matter of doubt how much this house was used for the purpose for which it was built. Within a few years it became common to direct that the school should be kept a few weeks in a place in several parts of the parish, rooms being had in private houses. The matter was frequently acted upon at annual or at special meetings.

But Mr. Green had not been willing to put off the school till the house was done. On the 7th of April he engaged " Mrs. Deland " for a teacher; and the next day he hired a room of James Holten; and within a week " Joseph and John went to school." These were Mr. Green's boys, and he had thus a special interest in the matter; but his public spirit is not the less to be observed. And the whole account gives a good illustration of the part that was commonly taken by the early ministers of New England in promoting the cause of popular

* This common was itself a gift of Dea. Ingersoll "to the Inhabitants of Salem Village, for a training field forever." There is a tradition that a schoolhouse stood at a later date, somewhat farther to the west than the present line of the common, a little beyond the house now occupied by Dea. Elijah Hutchinson; but whether this had any connection with Mr. Green's schoolhouse, I am not able to determine.

education. It might have been well if in this place his predecessors had entered upon it, and had turned somewhat both
their own spare energy and that of the people into this
channel.

It was not this first school of Mr. Green's for which there
was a debt due in 1712; for he makes mention of paying "ye
school dame" himself as late as the last month of 1709. The
five pounds was doubtless due to Mrs. Deland, — however the
name is to be spelled, — for teaching during the next year;
and then there was probably an interruption of the school for
some short space of time. Whether Mrs. Deland was engaged
again does not appear. In 1714 there was a movement to
secure a master for the school. It was voted that "Capt. Putnam and Lieut. Putnam wher choasen to look after Won, and
to get him as Cheap as they can for the benefit of the pepell."
This direction our school-committees have always followed.

The master thus employed was Samuel Andrew.* His re-
ceipt for his first payment of wages is in these terms:
"Saillem vileg November the 3 in the year 1714. These may
Certific hom it may Consarn thatt I have Reseived of Capt.
Putnam and Leutt. Putnam the sum of seaven pounds, and
forty shillings of Sevarall persons for teaching ther Chil-
dren, the wich nine pounds I have Reseived in full for keeping
scholl in Saillem villeg I say Reseived By me, Saml^l Andrew."
The master is not responsible for the spelling, which is that of
David Judd the clerk, by whom the receipt was copied.

From the days of Katharin Deland and Samuel Andrew,
there have not failed from this village school mistresses and
masters in goodly succession, and faithful in their work. But
to this present time, in spite of all their labors, the "w-i-c-h,"
like the grass of a similar name, has proved impossible to be
wholly extirpated.

The whole business of the school continued in the hands of

---

* I think Dea. Fowler must be in error in giving the name of *Daniel* Andrew.
See Essex Institute Historical Collections, vol. x., p. 78, note.

Daniel Andrew, living near the Wenham line, had sometimes had a class at
his house; and others may have done the like.

the parish until the incorporation of the town. The first notice of the thanksgiving collection for charitable distribution occurs in Mr. Green's diary in 1707. Whether the custom existed before that time is not known.

The use of the "Half-way Covenant" was introduced by Mr. Green. This was an arrangement extensively adopted at that time, by which persons who had been themselves baptized in infancy, but who did not feel prepared to unite with the church, were yet brought so far into connection with it as to be allowed the privilege of having their children baptized. I think, contrary to the opinion of some, that political considerations had little or nothing to do with it. These persons must be of a manner of life not in any wise scandalous; and they were required to make a certain form of Christian profession. This profession or covenant, in the form made use of in our church, was one suitable in reality to a genuine and thorough Christian life; and it is not easy to see how any person who was not a true Christian could have subscribed to it. It was not so understood, however, then. And from that time forward there were many that thus "owned the covenant," who did not thereby become members of the church, and who did not regard themselves as having become experimentally Christians.

This plan was entered upon with good intent, and to meet a serious evil. But it was found in the end to involve greater evils of its own; and it has been abandoned in all our churches. With us it was not set aside for more than a hundred years, and until after the settlement of Dr. Braman. The question itself of the relation of baptized children to the church is one which may be looked upon as still open to further and more satisfactory adjustment.

Mr. Green, though not a man of unusual ability, was an acceptable preacher. He was sometimes called upon to preach on public occasions in neighboring towns. After diligent inquiry, I am unable to find that any of his sermons have been preserved.*

---

* Dr. Samuel A. Green of Boston is a descendant of Joseph Green. He has no knowledge of the existence of any thing written by him, saving the diary.

His diary shows us much of his manner of life, and of the man himself. He had rural tastes, as was suitable. He was fond of his garden, his orchard, his farm, and his sheep and cattle. His business in this line was considerable. He owned lands beyond what he occupied as belonging to the parsonage.* He liked hunting, and killed eighteen pigeons once at a single shot. Now and then he took his boys to Middleton to try their hands at fishing. And he could catch men; for his mind was not all on these outside employments and diversions.

There is a delightful ease and naturalness about the journal. In the fall of 1700 they had been to Portsmouth; and he says : —

"Oct. 2. Came home with my wife, and got in all our winter apples.

17. Training and trooping at ye Village. I dined with Capt. Flint.

28. I killed a wild cat.

Nov. 3. I exhorted ye church to attend ye church meetings more carefully."

The wild-cats happily have disappeared; but I do not know but the exhortation might still be given with propriety.

There are many evidences that Mr. Green was sufficiently pointed in his preaching. He was a person of some spirit too, and not a merely inoffensive man who kept the peace himself because he did not know or care whether he was well treated. He understood his rights; and when he yielded them up, as he did not seldom, he did it of a purpose.

Dr. Green is connected with various public institutions in Boston. He has greatly distinguished himself during the last years by his vigorous action, as city physician, in arresting the spread of small-pox, which threatened the most serious ravages. I find him also pleasantly remembered by numbers of our soldiers, as an assistant surgeon in the late war; and am led thus to question whether a certain spirit of his ancestor may not have descended upon him.

* The inventory of Mr. Green's estate gives the landed property as follows : —

About 110 acres of land near ye ministry house — 400 Pounds Five acres of orchard lot westward of ye house — 120 Pounds Twenty four acres of meadow and upland at Will's Hill — 80 Pounds. Three hundred acres on ye north side of ye Merrimack — 150 Pounds.

Adding the personal property, the entire estate was, in round numbers, 1,050 pounds, from which debts of 200 pounds were to be deducted.

The farm north of the Merrimack was near Haverhill, and was bought by Mr. Green the spring before his death.

One fall Benjamin Hutchinson's horses had a grievous habit of getting into his orchard. He went to him, and prayed him to keep them out. Their owner told him, that, "if his feed was not eaten quickly, the snow would cover it;" an answer partaking, it would seem, of the coolness of the approaching winter. The horses were in the field every night that week. He sent for Mr. Hutchinson again, and prayed him to mend his fence, which he did; and the beasts were kept out for a single night. Then the "three jades" were in the orchard again every night for a week; and they got such a taste of the grass, that it was hard to get them out. And at last, as they were trying to drive them out, one of the jades jumped the wall by the parsonage well, and, falling into the well, was killed. Mr. Green knew, that, under the circumstances, it was no business of his to pay for that horse; but he made up part of the loss to Mr. Hutchinson, and told him that he did it "to make him easy; and, if that end was not obtained, he should account his money thrown away."

That ministry pasture was hard of fencing, for what belonged to the parish as well as for the share of these neighbors. The matter came up in the parish meeting for very many years; and, if the work done had corresponded to the number and power of the votes that were passed, that field would have been walled in like the ancient Babylon. There have been no traces, however, within recent times, of such structures extending round it.

The diary abounds in marks of Mr. Green's affectionate interest in his church and in all his people. I will only cite further the following entries :—

"1702, Jan. 1. Cold. I at Study. Bray Wilkins dyed who was in his 92 year. He lived to a good old age and saw his children's children and their children and peace upon our little Israel. 2. The church here kept a day of prayer for ye outpouring of ye Spirit of God upon us and ours. Lord hear us. Old William Buckley dyed this evening. He was at ye meeting ye last Sabbath and dyed with ye cold (I fear) for want of comfort and good tending. Lord forgive. He was about 80 years old : I visited him and prayed with him on Monday and also ye evening before he dyed. He was very poor, but I hope had not his portion in this life." *

It would be pleasing to dwell longer upon these personal narrations, and upon the pastorate of this admirable man. He was the first minister that closed his life among this people. In the proper import of that term, he might almost be called the first pastor of the church. He died on the 26th of November, 1715, being forty years and two days of age. Reckoning from the time when he began his preaching, about a year before his ordination, he had completed the eighteenth year of his ministry upon the last sabbath before his illness.

The funeral sermon was preached by Joseph Capen, pastor of the church in Topsfield, and was afterward printed at the urgent request of the people.† He was buried in the Wadsworth Burying-yard.

There may still be made out upon the stone at his grave the inscription in Latin, of which the following is a translation : —

"Beneath this turf rest, in hope of a blessed resurrection, the remains of Reverend Joseph Green, A.M., deceased. For about eighteen years he was a most watchful pastor of this church : a man to be held in perpetual remembrance for the weightiness of his teaching, and the agreeableness of his manners ; who departed from this most laborious life on the fifth day before the month of December, A.D. 1715. He had just completed his fortieth year."

There was also written, by Rev. Nicholas Noyes, this not very elegant epitaph : —

> "Under this sorry heap of stones
> Rich treasure lyes, *dear Joseph's bones:*
> *From Salem Village,* Christ will move
> Them to His Salem that's above.—

* The wife and daughter of William Buckley had been imprisoned during the witchcraft prosecutions ; and the family were impoverished by the costs unjustly laid upon them. See Mr. Upham's History, vol. ii. p. 199.

† In a prefatory note by Increase Mather, printed with this sermon, he speaks of the people as "honoring themselves in the Love and Honour which they have expressed to their deceased Pastor:" and adds, "I am informed that they are the Publishers of the Sermon Emitted herewith."

When the Last Trumpet gives its sound,
The Saints will Start from under ground,
Be Changed and Mount, with one accord,
To Meet with their Descending Lord."

There is extant, too, an " Elegy" of considerable length, and nearly equal poetical merit, composed by Mr. Noyes upon the same occasion, of which I give the opening lines : —

" In God's House we of late did see
A *Green* and growing Olive Tree.
'Twas planted by a living spring
That always made it florishing :
Filled it with Sap, and Oyley Juice,
That Leaves and Fruit and Light produce ;
An holy Tree, whose very wood,
For Temple use was choice and good.

. . . . . .

But now alas, we weep to see
An Empty Place where stood that Tree :
That Green and lovely Tree, whose sight
Has blessed our Eyes with much delight,
For his good Nature and his Grace
Both visible were in his face."

A more interesting memorial is the minute in the Church Book, by Dea. Edward Putnam : —

" Then was the choyces flower and grenest olif tree in the garden of our Lord hear cut down in its prime and florishing estate at the age of forty years and 2 days, who had ben a faithfull ambasindor from God to us 18 years, then did that brite star seet and never more to apear her among us : then did our sun go down and now what darkness is com upon us ; put away and pardon our Iniquityes o Lord which have ben the cause of the sore displeasure and return to us again in marcy and provide yet again for this thy flock a pastor after thy one hearte as thou hast promised to thy people in thy word one " (on) " which promise we have hope for we are called by thy name. o leve us not."

Thus he passed away from the people and the service of his choice. The work he wrought has endured ; and his memory is blessed. I am slow to leave this chapter of our history. His life will be among the treasures of the church in all its coming years. For him, having been faithful in these few

5

things here committed tò his charge, he has long since, we trust, by the welcoming and rewarding Lord he loved, been made "ruler over many things."

It was a little more than a year and a half before a successor was established. The people voted distinctly that they would "hear more than one minister,"—a principle which I believe they have followed since on some like occasions. On the 7th of August, 1716, the parish gave a call to Mr. Peter Clark. Some negotiation followed; and they began to grow impatient at the delay, until, on the 3d of December, they renewed the offer, with specifications of what they would do for him, and added that "we expect a positive answer, and no more proposals." Mr. Clark, however, took his own time; and though he began his regular preaching earlier, he was not ordained until June 5, 1717. On the sabbath before he had been admitted as a member of the church upon a letter of dismission and recommendation from the church in Bridgewater.

He received ninety pounds salary, with an equal additional sum at first as "settlement," and the use of the ministry house and lands. This ministry house was much out of repair; and, as he had doubts about occupying it, he was authorized to let it out if he pleased; "Provided he Lett it to shuch men as will not Damnifie ye house."

The new minister was a native of Watertown, a graduate of Harvard in the class of 1712, and was about twenty-five years old at his settlement. He married Deborah Hobart of Braintree, Nov. 6, 1719.* He continued in the pastorate of the church for a period of almost exactly fifty-one years, unto his death, which occurred on the 10th of June, 1768.

* Peter Hobart, the father of Deborah, removed to Salem Village some years later, or about 1730. He bought land of Robert Hutchinson, and occupied perhaps, for a time, his house. But soon after, and using, it may be, portions of the old building, he put up, upon Hobart Street, which is named for him, the house now owned and occupied in part by his descendants, the family of Perley Clark. The wife of John Hook, jun., and the family of Benjamin Millett, are also among the descendants of the Clark and Hobart families by this marriage.

Mr. Clark was a man very unlike his predecessor, and yet well fitted to serve the people among whom he came. He had a sharp and vigorous mind, with a taste for theological discussions. He has left numerous published discourses and essays, largely upon points of controversy, and amounting in all to several volumes.*

His sermons are forcible, and sometimes eloquent ; always exact and sharp in division, and divided, after the fashion of the times, at every divisible point ; and in length it would seem unutterable.

Two of these discourses have lately been re-preached in this pulpit ; or such portions of them as this people — not otherwise altogether unused to experiences of grim endurance — were able to receive. The time occupied was fifty minutes ; and of one, and nearly the shortest that could be found, about one-half was used ; of the other, which I think must have been of a full average length, not more than one-third. And through such spaces did this disciplined people sit even in the cold of winter.

Mr. Clark had a purpose in these full-grown sermons, whatever it was, and was appointed to make them not shorter. It is related of him that at one time the people, having doubts upon this very point, caused him to be waited upon by a delegation with the inquiry whether he could not shorten his sermons. But he answered, No: any of the people might

---

* There are now extant of Mr. Clark's publications, two volumes, of 158 and 453 pages respectively, in defence of infant baptism ; the first in reply to " Mr. Walton," the second to Dr. John Gill. Also a Summer Morning's Conversation, in defence of the doctrine of original sin, with an appendix ; followed by a second treatise on the same subject. And of sermons, one preached at the Lecture in Boston, Feb. 13, 1734 ; an Election Sermon, May 30, 1739 ; two sermons preached at Salem Village on the General Fast appointed on the Occasion of the War, Feb. 26, 1741 ; one preached at the Lecture in Watertown, Sept. 10, 1743 ; another on a like occasion at Topsfield, in June of the same year ; an Artiilery Election Sermon, at Boston, June 7, 1736 ; a Convention Sermon, in Boston, 1745 ; a sermon in this place before the Men enlisted for the War, April 6, 1755 ; another, Dec. 15, 1757, before a Society of Young Men in the North Parish, in Danvers ; and the Dudleian Sermon, in 1763, which I have not seen ; also, a Right Hand of Fellowship, given at the ordination of Mr. James Diman in Salem, May 11, 1737. There may probably be others.

freely leave when they judged they had heard enough ; but the sermons could not be shortened. An examination of these sermons as to their laying-out may lead us to wonder, indeed, that they should have ended even where they did ; since by the like method some of them might easily have been continued to the present time. There was also that in their arrangement which must have been peculiarly trying to the youthful or the inexperienced mind, by the difficulty of distinguishing in advance between the veritable and accomplished end, and the many awakening but illusory " finallies " by which it was fore-run. While passing out upon one of the branches of his argumentation, it could have been only the most thoroughly instructed sense, if any, that might not have judged him to be putting his hand upon the topmost twig of the tree, whereas there should be found still remaining three and twenty corresponding and loftier limbs, each to be gone out upon to its final leaf, before the central summit could be reached.

I give as a specimen of this style a diagram exhibiting the plan of one of Mr. Clark's sermons ; the same having been " preached at the Lecture in Boston, Feb. 13th, 1734.* It is said to have been published, " with enlargements and additions, at the request of several of the hearers." But these enlargements, whatever they may have been, do not make it an unfair representation of his discourses, saving that it may be somewhat longer than any of the others that have been preserved. I give the divisions and numbers only, without setting forth the various heads.

---

* The volume from which this is taken is made up of sermons printed at different times, and bound together. Five of these sermons are by Mr. Clark. One is by Benjamin Colman, D.D., and one by Joseph Sewall, D.D. ; and these were also preached " at the Lecture in Boston."

This sermon bears the imprint, " Boston, N.E. Printed by S. Kneeland and T. Green, for D. Henchman in Cornhill, MDCCXXXV." This S. Kneeland, in 1739, was " printer to the Honourable House of Representatives." And, in 1741, the office of Kneeland and Green was " in Queenstreet over against the Prison."

The book is the property of John A. Sanborn of Charlestown, a descendant of Mr. Clark.

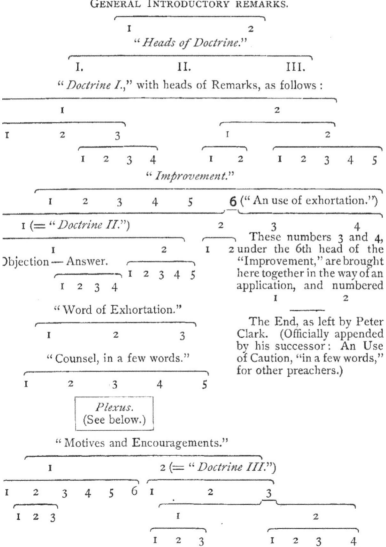

"The Necessity and Efficacy of the Grace of GOD in the Conversion of ι Sinner, Asserted and practically Improved : chiefly for the Direction and Encouragement of the Unconverted to pray for Converting Grace."

Jer. xxxi. 18, latter clause.

' *Turn thou me, and I shall be turned; for thou art the Lord my God.*"

Exposition of the text, with observations, "first" and "secondly," ollowed by

GENERAL INTRODUCTORY REMARKS.

1 2

"*Heads of Doctrine.*"

I. II. III.

"*Doctrine I.*," with heads of Remarks, as follows :

1   2

1 2 3 1 2

1 2 3 4 1 2 1 2 3 4 5

"*Improvement.*"

1 2 3 4 5 **6** ("An use of exhortation.")

1 (= "*Doctrine II.*") 2 3 4

1 2 1 2 These numbers 3 and **4**,

Objection — Answer. under the 6th head of the

   1 2 3 4 5 "Improvement," are brought

1 2 3 4 here together in the way of an

       application, and numbered

"Word of Exhortation." 1 2

1 2 3 The End, as left by Peter Clark. (Officially appended by his successor: An Use of Caution, "in a few words," for other preachers.)

"Counsel, in a few words."

1 2 3 4 5

> *Plexus.*
> (See below.)

"Motives and Encouragements."

1   2 (= "*Doctrine III.*")

1 2 3 4 5 6 1 2 3

1 2 3 1   2

    1 2 3 1 2 3 4

          1 2 3

The first head of "doctrine," the preacher observes, is to be mainly dwelt upon ; and the second and third are to come in by way of "inference and application." They are, indeed, disposed of in a truly wonderful manner by the sixth very extraordinary head, or little horn, in the "Improvement," called "an use of exhortation," which waxed exceeding great, and by which both of those capital stars of doctrine were cast down to the ground, and stamped upon.

There is also a very peculiar arrangement, marked in the plan as a *plexus*, which I cannot in a few words, or by any diagram, convey clearly to the mind, even if I do myself adequately comprehend it. It appears to be an instrument for the collecting and braiding together of such lines of thought as may, from any quarter, be laid hold of, with a view to bringing them forth in new and unlooked-for directions. But I do not recommend its general use.

The whole number of divisions, as actually marked in the sermon, is eighty-four. If the analysis presented is not perfectly plain, I believe the student of the original document will find few "motives and encouragements" to attempt any "improvement" upon it. If the author of the discourse had spent as much time, to begin with, in making his plan, as I have spent in trying to make out what plan he may in fact have made, he might so have made a plan which I could have made out in as little time as it probably took him to make the plan he did make.

But, however, these sermons are far enough from being contemptible. The signs of strength are upon them ; and their faults are largely due to the habit of the times. Mr. Clark was reckoned among the most powerful preachers in the Colony. These were "great sermons." And it is pleasant to reflect, that the Boston people of those days had some mental exercise and some solid instruction, at least when such country ministers dropped in occasionally upon them.

Mr. Clark was noted, moreover, as a man disposed to keep abreast with his age ; and, withal, as somewhat less tenacious than the most of his associates, with respect to the received forms of theological belief. Yet I am persuaded he may safely be thought of as "sound"

Mr. Clark's strong will, of which there are many traces, might sometimes have brought him into difficulty but for a strong good sense, which, in most matters, kept it under control. He was in repute for force of character and power of accomplishment in his household, as well as throughout the parish, and in the Colony. It is related of him, that, during a summer of excessive drought, the neighboring ministers had made an arrangement for concerted prayer for rain, into which, for some reason, Mr. Clark had not entered ; and his people blamed him for standing thus, as it seemed, aloof. Upon their coming to him with complaint, he told them that on the next sabbath he would pray ; which he did, — a copious rain immediately following. Whereupon his negro man observed, that "he knew that when Massa Clark took hold, something would have to come."

A bell was put upon the meeting-house for the first time, in 1725 ; the money for its purchase being raised mostly by subscription. It weighed 326 pounds. The bell-rope came down from the "turret" above to the middle of the broad aisle, where the sexton stood. John Britain, the sexton, soon after had permission to move his own house to a spot near by. It was set toward the present road, a little to the south-west of the south-western corner of the meeting-house, as it now stands ; and remained there for many years. This building afterward, as I think, became the property of the parish, and was called "the Parish house," and was kept for the occupancy of other sextons. The bell itself continued in use nearly through the century.

In 1727 there occurred an earthquake of great violence for this part of the world. The account of it, as given by Mr. Clark, is as follows : "On ye 29th Day of last October, Being Lord's Day, at night, between 10 & 11 o'clock, y^{re} happened a very Great Earthquake, accompanyed with a terrible Noise and Shaking w^c was greatly surprising to ye whole Land. ye

Rumbling Noise in ye bowels of ye Earth with some lesser trepidation of ye Earth, has been Repeated at Certain Intervals for Divers weeks after."

The Lord, at this time, was in the earthquake. A special day of prayer was appointed. A revival of religious interest followed, and many were added to the church.

The handwriting in which this entry is made is very peculiar, and suggests irresistibly that the rumbling and shaking must have been still going on when he wrote. The record, indeed, for those many years, is not greatly different; so that we are led to question if "some lesser trepidation of the earth" did not continue through Mr. Clark's whole ministry. Mr. Green's style of recording, it should be said, was not much superior. And for my immediate predecessor I will not speak. Mr. Upham has been led to remark somewhat at length upon the fine penmanship of the first four ministers of this parish; but he proceeds no further. The style did not return, unless in part with Dr. Wadsworth. And so it seems that the church, despairing of being ever again provided with a minister by whom its records could be legibly kept; or fearing, perhaps, remembering its early fortunes, to engage such a minister, — has of late years elected a clerk from among its lay members.* This arrangement, however, it is important to observe, was made before the settlement with you of the present pastor.

Petitions began about this time to be presented from the people at " Will's Hill," now Middleton, asking leave to withdraw, and form a separate organization. The men of the Village were not pleased with this proposal, and were disposed " to consider of it until a convenient time." But its reasonableness and necessity were soon apparent. The town of Middleton was incorporated in June, 1728; and the church was organized, apparently, October 22, 1729. The ordination of Mr. Andrew Peters, the first pastor of the church in Middleton, took place Nov. 26 of the same year.† Ten days

* Mr. Edward Hutchinson.

† Mr. David Stiles of Middleton informs me that Mr. Peters was styled

previously the Village church had chosen its two deacons, with Ezekiel Cheever, messengers to the council, and had given letters of dismission, and recommendation to the new church, to the persons whose names here follow: Henry Wilkins, Daniel Kenny, Jonathan Fuller, Joseph Fuller, Isaac Wilkins, Ezra Putnam, Edward Putnam, Benjamin Wilkins, Sarah Fuller, Mary Fuller, Sarah Putnam, Elizabeth Putnam, Mary Wilkins, Mary Kenny, Susanna Fuller, Elizabeth Nichols, Mary Wilkins, Hannah Carril, Margery Wilkins, Eunice Lambert, Elizabeth Eliot, Penelope Wilkins, Susanna Fuller, and Susanna Hobbs, — twenty-four in all.

The residence of Edward Putnam fell within the bounds of the new town; but the person thus mentioned was not the deacon, but a son of the same name, and who afterward sustained the same office at Middleton. The venerable deacon himself did not remove his connection from the church in whose welfare he had been so long and so deeply interested.

The ministry house, through all these years, had been mended chiefly by votes, which were not able much longer to make it serviceable. At a meeting held on the 17th of January, 1734, it "was put to vote to see if the Inhabitants would build a new house;" and "it passed in the negetive." A motion to give Mr. Clark three hundred pounds, and let him build a house for himself, was disposed of in the same manner, — which, indeed, was a very common mode in those days of "passing" votes. It was then voted that "we will demollesh all ye Lenture behind ye parsonage house, and will build a

"pastor" on the 22d of October, — which means that he was thought to be as good as settled. But there is a more curious discrepancy as to the date of the ordination. It was voted, as appears by the Middleton records, that the ordination should be on the second Wednesday of November, which fell upon the 12th. But the Village church, on the sabbath next *after* that day, or the 16th, chose its messengers to the council called for Nov. 26. There is no reason at all to think that either record is incorrect. The ordination may probably have been postponed; but neither account gives any mention of it; and, between Mr. Stiles and the present writer, the thing cannot be settled. My inference is, *that discrepancies, not flatly contradictory, but unexplainable, between any two of the much more ancient scriptural records, are* NO PROOF THAT BOTH OF THEM MAY NOT BE, *so far as they go, accurate and trustworthy.*

new house of three and twenty feet long and eighteen feet broad and fifteen feet stud with a seller under it and set it behind the west Room of our parsonage house." This supplementary house was accordingly built, running back to the rear of the west end of the main building, toward the north ; and in this new building Mr. Clark appears to have had his study.

From 1735 to 1766 there is a break in the parish records, occasioned by the loss of the volume covering that period. The book was destroyed by the burning of a house in Putnamville.* But, besides the unbroken records of the church, we have also the book of the parish treasurer, with his accounts, covering this space.

The organization of the town took place within these years. Danvers was incorporated first as a district, Jan. 28, 1752.† This did not give the right of sending a representative to the General Court ; and the form of proceeding had been chosen to that end, since the English Government was slow to admit any increase in the weight of popular representation. Upon the 16th of June, 1757, an act was passed completing the organization as a town.

The first town or district meeting was held on Wednesday, the 4th of March, 1752, at the Village meeting-house. Daniel Eppes, Esq., was chosen moderator ; Daniel Eppes, jun., clerk ; James Prince, treasurer ; and Daniel Eppes, jun., Capt. Samuel Flint, Deacon Cornelius Tarbell, Stephen Putnam, Samuel King, Daniel Gardner, and Joseph Putnam, selectmen. The town of Danvers, as thus constituted, embraced, along with the Village, the territory lying toward the south and

---

* Then called Blind-Hole.

† The origin of the name Danvers, as applied to this town, is involved in much obscurity. There was an English family of the name of Danvers. The word itself is " De Anvers," or Antwerp, according to the French pronunciation. The occasion of its being fixed upon this town is not clear. I am disposed, on the whole, to agree in opinion with Deacon Fowler, who says, in an article lately printed in " The Danvers Mirror," " I have but little doubt that our town, in some way not yet discovered, received its name from Sir Danvers Osborne, Bart., the unfortunate Governor of New York, in 1753." As to the " way not discovered," I think it must have been through Lieut.-Gov. Phips.

south-east to the present boundary of Salem, and then known as the Middle Precinct. This precinct or parish had been established for the maintenance of preaching in 1710, and was the third parish in Salem. After the formation of the new town, it became known as " the South Parish," which was often shortened into "the South." After a union of a hundred years, by a division of Danvers, this became in 1855 a distinct town, with the name of South Danvers, which name was again changed, in 1868, to Peabody.

It should be borne in mind, however, that not all of the territory now belonging to Peabody was embraced in the former " Middle Precinct ; " since, as has already been stated in another connection, a large section in the north-western part of the present town of Peabody was included within the original limits of the Village parish. The people of this section, it may be observed, maintained their parish relations with us, for the most part, after the incorporation of the town of Danvers, and until a comparatively recent period. They have now a sabbath-school and a meeting of their own, with preaching for one-half the day, in the commodious school-house lately erected in that neighborhood ; and it is hoped that a church may at no distant time be organized.*

The region at " Skelton's Neck," " New Mills," or " Danvers-Port," became first formally associated with the old village at this time of the incorporation. Its inhabitants had been

---

* An active part in this matter has been taken by Capt. Thomas Flint and his family, descendants of that Thomas Flint who was upon the first Village parish committee. The Flint lineage runs thus : Thomas, coming from Wales, in 1642, and settling in Salem Village in 1654 ; Capt. Thomas, concerned in the organization of the parish, builder of one of its meeting-houses, and fighter in King Philip's war ; Capt. Samuel, active in the separation of the town from Salem ; Capt. Samuel, son of the former, and a hero of the Revolution ; Major Elijah ; Capt. Thomas of the sixth generation, now living, with children and grandchildren about him.

Capt. Flint still keeps the old family homestead ; and the house has been of late repaired and greatly improved. Two hundred and nineteen Thanksgiving dinners have been eaten beneath its roof.

But just as these pages are passing through the hands of the printer, I have to add the sad and closing record of this ancient mansion, which has been totally destroyed by fire, June 16, 1874.

before among " the Neighbors " who had contributed somewhat to the support of the Village ministers. And some of them have been accustomed to meet with us until the establishment, lately, of the Maple-street Church, at the Plain.

The lost volume of the parish records was undoubtedly much occupied with details of efforts made looking towards this separation from Salem, and the establishment of the new town. Signs, indeed, of this movement are to be found long before, and upon the records which still remain to us.

In 1757 action was taken by the church for regulating, in some particulars, the mode of admitting its members. It was declared to be the purpose of the church, as it had been its previous practice, to admit none to its communion but such as had " some competent knowledge of ye main Doctrines of Christianity, and who appear to a judgment of Charity, Persons of a pious Disposition, or who shall make credible profession of Repentance toward God and Faith toward our Lord Jesus Christ." It was provided that public relations of experience should not be insisted on, — which, indeed, the rules had not before made indispensable ; and there was adopted a " Confession of Faith," to be assented to by such as should unite with the church. This is the first appearance of " a creed " upon our records. The church had been organized by the adoption of a covenant, with its doctrinal basis in a general reference to the Boston Confession of 1680. Whether the confession of faith at this time adopted was written by Mr. Clark, I have no means of knowing ; but, meeting with no other like it, we may infer that it is his.

It is broad in its terms, as will be seen, and does not dwell upon the minuter points of doctrine. It differs but slightly from the Confession now in use ; and, in so far as the variations have been made by the omission or modification of words here employed, I have indicated them by brackets in the copy which follows, and which I give without the ancient spelling.

(1.) [A B, You do seriously and solemnly purpose to] believe in one Eternal, Almighty God, the Father [the] Son and [the] Holy Ghost, who made the world by His power, and governs it by His providence, [and who is the Redeemer of the fallen world by His Son Jesus Christ.]

(2.) [You] believe the Holy Scriptures of the Old and New Testament to be the Word of God, and adhere to them as the only perfect rule of faith and practice.

(3.) [You] believe that our first parents fell from that state of integrity, honor, and happiness in which God at first created them, [and all mankind in them, by their transgression in eating the forbidden fruit, and thereby] involved themselves and all their posterity in a state of sin and death. (The present form substitutes for the lines in brackets the words, "and that upon their eating the forbidden fruit, they," &c.)

(4.) [You] believe that God, in compassion to the sinful, perishing state of mankind, foreordained, and in the fulness of time sent, His only begotten Son to be the Saviour of the world. (The 4th and 5th are united in the present form.)

(5.) That Jesus Christ, the Son of God, in compliance with His Father's will, took upon Him the nature of man, and therein humbled Himself in His obedience unto death, for our redemption.

(6.) That He rose again the third day and ascended into heaven [as our victorious Redeemer,] and sitteth at the right hand of God, making intercession for us, and [having] power given Him over all things in heaven and earth. (The present form has "as" after "again," "ther" before "sitteth," and "that He hath" for "having.")

(7.) That He [sustains and] executes the three-fold office of Prophet, Priest, and King, [to His church.] (7 and 8 now united.)

(8.) That in the exercise of His office as Redeemer, and [of the] fulness of power committed to Him, He has published His Gospel covenant, requiring faith and repentance of sinful men in order to pardon and salvation. (The present form has "man" for men," with some changes in the particles.)

(9.) [You] believe the Holy Spirit is given through the merit and intercession of Christ, to make application of his purchased redemption to men's souls; and that His gracious influence is necessary to a life of faith and obedience. (The present form has "the souls of men," and inserts "new" before "obedience.")

(10.) That Christ hath instituted a gospel ministry, and the two sacraments of Baptism, and the Lord's Supper, as the outward means of the application of Redemption, to be observed in His church till His second coming. (In the present form "has" is used for "hath.")

(11.) [You] believe in another life after this, and that Christ will come again, and raise the dead and judge the world, and that we must all appear before the judgment seat of Christ.

(12.) That at the last day the wicked shall be adjudged to everlasting punishment, and the righteous to life eternal.

(In the present form, 11 and 12 are brought together. " Appear again to " is put for "come again and," "his judgment seat" for "the judgment seat of Christ," and "will" for "shall." Each paragraph now begins with "we," referring to the church; and "Finally" is prefixed to the concluding sentence.)

It may be here observed that the records of the church, through all the middle and the latter part of the eighteenth century, afford evidence, in the acknowledgments that were made upon the admission of members to the church, of the prevalence of immorality in the community to a much greater extent, as I must think, than at the present time. In comparison with that particular period, and in this respect, the age we have fallen upon is not degenerate. And within the same limitations, the observation may be extended, I think, throughout the most of New England.

As his half-century of ministerial labor drew to a close, Mr. Clark began to feel the infirmities of age. He was sometimes obliged to stop for a time in the midst of the sabbath service; and on such occasions the deacons would go forward to offer him assistance. He was inclined at first to be displeased with this, and would give them to understand that he could judge for himself what needed to be done. But he was approaching those bounds which the most determined resolution cannot pass. With the opening of the year 1768 he was unable longer to discharge the duties of his office; and a supply for the pulpit was procured by the parish committee.

There presently arose a question as to the payment he should receive under this condition of things. His original salary had been ninety pounds; but, through changes in the value of the paper currency, as was affirmed on the part of the parish, it had come to pass that sixty pounds would then buy as much silver as the ninety pounds would formerly have done. The smaller sum, therefore, as they claimed, was the amount really due; and though they had, in fact, up to that time, paid the full ninety, yet they had done it, they said, as of grace and not of debt. And now, unless Mr. Clark would procure a supply for the pulpit, they were unwilling to continue what they looked upon as a gratuitous payment. A delegation was sent from the parish meeting to learn distinctly their pastor's mind. They had no difficulty in discovering precisely what it was. They put to him two questions : What sum of money should he receive ? He answered, Ninety pounds. Had he thought of supplying the pulpit ? And he answered, No. But the people held also to their opinion. The affair attracted considerable attention ; and some person caused to be printed, in a paper published by " Messrs. Green and Russel," a communication, misrepresenting, as was thought, the action of the parish. A committee, consisting of John Nichols, Dr. Samuel Holten, John Preston, Archelaus Putnam, and Archelaus Dale, was appointed to prepare a reply, which is found at length upon the records, and which they were instructed to have forthwith printed. The death of Mr. Clark, which soon occurred, did not cause the matter to be at once adjusted. Dr. Samuel Holten, Lieut. Archelaus Putnam, and Archelaus Dale were appointed a committee to settle it with the executors ; which thing they found not easy to do. The business, however, seems to have been prosecuted with good temper on either side. The committee at one time offered to pay the sum in dispute " as a gift ; " but the executors declined to receive it on those terms ; and the parish also shortly refused to allow more to be offered than was recoverable at law. The question was not settled until nearly three years later, when the executors offered to take whatever the parish might choose to pay ; and the parish paid, that is for the few months only that were in question, upon the basis of sixty pounds. I wish they had paid the larger sum : I wish, also, that Mr. Clark had chosen at first to receive only the smaller.

The views of the people were modified somewhat by the fact that Mr. Clark was possessed of a very handsome estate himself, — " one of the best in the parish," it was termed. He had property by his wife, and probably, also, in his own right by inheritance ; and he was thrifty withal. As to the legal merits of the controversy, the committee were very clear about it in their own minds ; but, though one of them was no less a

man than Dr. (or Judge) Holten, yet I do not immediately
conclude that Peter Clark did not know what he was about.
For the ground of moral right involved, and making no account
of the pastor's illness, it is to be remembered that silver itself,
which the committee proposed to make the sole basis of
measurement, had been falling in value through all that period,
as it has been for centuries ; and that perhaps the purchasing
powers of silver in 1768 and in 1717 were not, in fact, so nearly
equal to each other as the corresponding powers of the paper
money may have been.

Nothing of all this, however, should be thought of as seriously affecting the feelings of the people towards their pastor.
The venerable and sturdy man was respected and honored by
his parishioners to the last of his life, and sincerely mourned
by them at his death.

His burial was in the Wadsworth Yard, by the grave of his
wife, who had died three years before.

The account, in the church records, of his funeral, contains
in the midst of its solemnity, a most singular statement :

Now it has Pleased God in his holy Providence to Take away from us
our Dear and Rev⁴ Pastor by Death Mʳ Peter Clark, who Departed this
Life June ye 10, 1768 — in ye Seventy Sixth Year of his age and on ye 15th
Day was his funeral. itt was attended with Great Sollemnity, his Corps
was Carried in to ye Meeting-house a prayer made by ye Rev⁴ Mr.
Diman of Salem a Searmon Delivered by the Rev⁴ Mr. Barnard of
Salem from Galatians 3 Chap. 14 verse. Then Removed to his Grave with
ye Church walking before the Corps assisted by 12 Bears, with a great
Concours of People following. after his Enterment Left his Deacᵗ Body
in ye Dust for worms to feed upon which we Took So much Delight and
Satisfaction in he is gone who has been so faithfull in ye ministry among
this People (the number of fifty one years) now he is gone, Never to see
his face no more in this world no more to hear the Presious Instructions
and Examples out of his mouth in Publick or in Private any more that ye
God of all grace would be Pleased to Sanctifee this great and sore bereave-
ment to this Church and Congregation for good and in his own Due Time
Give us another Pastour after his own heart to feed this People with Truth
Knowledge and Understanding that this Church may not be Left as Sheep
without a Shepherd. but for these things God will be inquired of ye O
house of Israel to do itt for them.

The entry is in the writing of Dea. Asa Putnam. And, despite the slips it may contain, it is in a strain of mingling personal affection towards his late pastor, and of pious solicitude and trust concerning the church, that conveys a pleasing impression respecting the man himself that placed it there. Other pages of the book confirm it. And I am led here to bear testimony concerning the Christian worth and helpfulness of the men who have held that office in the church through all its history. There have been cases in exception. But, from Nathanael Ingersoll and Edward Putnam to those now living, these deacons, for the most part, have been men who have honored their office, and have contributed their full share to the promotion of the peace and prosperity of the church. And I will add my belief that throughout all our churches, there is no more reason, in general, for any complaint to proceed from the pastors respecting these deacons, than there would be for a reversing of the order of complaint, and the making it turn in the opposite direction.

After the death of Mr. Clark, the parish was for more than four years without a minister. Troubles threatened to arise with respect to one, Mr. Amos Sawyer, who preached as a candidate, and in whom many of the people were greatly interested. A call was given to him to become pastor of the church and the parish. But there was a minority sharply opposing. Mr. Sawyer declined somewhat doubtfully. In his letter dated at Reading, April 22, 1769, he says, " I am heartily grieved that there are so many respectable persons among you that are dissatisfied with, and are not sensible of profiting by, my preaching. But, as I esteem them men of reason and religion, so I can't but suppose, that, were they entirely disinterested persons, they would judge as other disinterested persons do;" (!) "that, considering the great majority for my settlement among you, I should not be justified in refusing, if every thing else was agreeable." And he goes on to add that the " encouragement" offered is too small for

6

his support. The cooler-headed men among the people may not have had their zeal in his behalf stimulated by the remarks which I have quoted. The parish, however, made him another offer, though only changed from the first by the striking-out of a clause which their experience with Mr. Clark had led them to insert, providing for some deduction from the salary in case of his inability to supply the pulpit. It was understood within a few weeks that Mr. Sawyer was ready to accept the offer; and a call was issued for a church-meeting, to be held early in September, to take measures for his ordination. But there were wise men among the people, upon whom the lessons of the past had not been lost. The church, immediately after the death of Mr. Clark, had chosen a standing committee of five, consisting of John Nichols, Capt. Elisha Flint, Dr. Amos Putnam, Lieut. Archelaus Putnam, and Dea. Asa Putnam; to whom Dea. Edmund Putnam and Dr. Samuel Holten were soon joined; and to whose care the interests of the church in the settlement of a pastor were in some manner intrusted. This committee now exerted itself with vigor and good judgment to guard against any rupture. They secured a stay in the proceedings for an immediate ordination, and an agreement by both parties in the church to submit the whole matter to a council, and to abide fully and heartily by its decision. A parish meeting was called to act in concurrence, when the business was suddenly and sadly ended by Mr. Sawyer's death.

Deacon Asa Putnam made this minute upon the records of the church : —

"After a few Days sickness Mr. Amos Sawyer Departed this Life ye Twenty first Day of Sept. 1769: and was Decently Buried ye 23, in the 26th year of his age — We ought to Eye the hand of God in his Providence in ye Removing this our Elect Pastour from us so soon after ye Death of our Late Minister ye Revd. Mr. Clark. And that we may be Deeply Humbled before God for the frowns of his Providence toward us, and that we may be Looking unto him for his Divine Presence and assistance to be with us in our Proceeding in Re-setling ye Gospel Ministre with us again, and that ye God of Peace would Direct our Steps for us so that we may walk in Love, Peace, and Unity with one another, and that the God of all Grace would in his own Due Time give us a Pastour after his own Heart to feed us with Knowledge and Understanding that itt may be for the Glory of his Great Name."

An invitation was given to Mr. Joseph Currier, in the spring of 1771, to take the vacant office. But the salary was not satisfactory, nor the people wholly united ; and Mr. Currier answered in a short and sensible letter, declining to come.

The pay given to the ministers employed at this time was usually one pound, six shillings, and eight pence, for a sabbath's preaching. They were provided for at the expense of the parish, by Sarah Clark, daughter of the late pastor. Two days of fasting were observed ; and the help of some of the neighboring ministers was engaged "to carry on the work of the day." On one of these occasions Sarah Clark was paid two pounds, five shillings, and four pence ; and on another a sum only a little less, for entertaining these ministers. The number is not stated ; but it was usually two, or not more than three. Not belonging to the parish, doubtless, they did not consider themselves bound to fast ; and we may hope they carried on the work of the day at the meeting-house with a vigor corresponding to that which they must have exhibited in some other directions.

Parish meetings were held during these years, upon an average, about once a month. They were very frequent, indeed, through the whole century, and beyond it. Little discretion was allowed to the parish officers, especially in any thing involving the expenditure of money. The standing committee would have been very slow to have paid out a dollar without express warrant for doing it from a legal meeting of the inhabitants. They would have been much slower still in getting that dollar back again into their own pockets, if they had so paid it out. Parish meetings were called, therefore, upon slight occasions ; as to see if the people would have preaching on Thanksgiving Day, or to see if "a Law Book" might be bought ; there being in either case no other business. The labor of the parish clerks was great. They more than once applied .for pay ; but they got slight "encouragement." Archelaus Dale makes note, on the day of the annual meeting in March, 1773, " N.B. this Day I Rec^d one Pisterene of Dr. Holten, and another of Mr. Benj. Russel jun. as a Gift for my last year's Service as P. Cler." He did his work well, and earned more money.

They looked sharply, too, in these parish meetings, after all that their committees had done. Nothing is more common than an article in the warrant for "calling to account" some committee concerning its expenditures, and as to any "overplush of money" in its hands. No parish officer, I venture to say, could ever have kept in peace one penny of any such "overplush." And the whole sum ever lost to the parish, by any peculations or misdirection, or "irregularity" of any description whatsoever, on the part of those handling its money, could never, I am sure, have amounted to so much as Archelaus Dale's two pistareens.

We know a little of what our New England towns, with their open meetings for the settlement of all business, have done for us as a people. The old parishes were institutions of a like order. And in this one the roots of liberty must have spread, summer and winter, perennially. In all this matter, if they may then perhaps have been over-careful, we are now throughout the country swiftly growing to be too careless; and the danger is all in the direction in which we are tending, and not in the other.

But now the "Due Time" that had been prayed for was at hand. Early in the autumn of 1772, Mr. Benjamin Wadsworth, who had preached for several weeks during the summer, was called to a permanent settlement. The vote was unanimous in the church; and although in the parish all did not at first concur, yet there was no active opposition; and the agreement among the people shortly became general and substantially complete. The salary was to be ninety pounds, with one hundred and sixty pounds "settlement," and the use of the parsonage. The parsonage house and land had been rented in the years just before for between five and six pounds.

An ordination was a great matter in those days; and it might well be so here, where it occurred but twice in a century. The appointments made were elaborate. Enoch Putnam, Samuel Holten, and Archelaus Putnam were chosen to provide entertainment for the council. It is a curious illustration of what has just been said of the responsibility of these parish officers, that, on this occasion, the committee being only authorized to provide for the council, a subsequent meeting was warned and held for the sole purpose of seeing if any entertainment might be made for "any of the Clergy or other Gentlemen" who would be likely to attend, though not members of the council.

Eleven men — Richard Whittredge, jun., Aaron Putnam, Elisha Putnam, Archelaus Dale, Gideon Putnam, Joseph Brown, Jacob Goodale, James Prince, jun., John Preston, John Hutchinson, and John Very — were chosen a committee to take charge of the meeting-house. They were instructed to keep the deacons' seat, the three foremost front seats below, the two foremost side seats below, and the women's great pew, for the council to sit in ; to keep the two foremost seats in the men's front gallery for the members of the church ; to keep the women's front gallery for the singers ; and to brace the galleries well. They were to open the doors before the council came, and "to do their endeavor to Clear the way for the Council and Church to get to their Seats." They had charge also "to keep the Beems clear, and not suffer any Person to go up inside of the Roof."

This may bring before us a vivid picture of the old meeting-house. It was the house of 1701, — too small for such a gathering, and with the beams and timbers of the roof open to view. There was much timber, withal, in that roof ; so that it was called "the Danvers wood-lot." Ascending from the galleries, we may see the youths perched like fowls among these beams and braces ; and may hear, belike, — for of such things the report has come down to us, — their not always most fitting responses in the midst of the solemnities. Bating the misbehavior, we may be allowed to hope that on this day there was here and there a lad that eluded the whole body of the eleven, and kept his post aloft, hard by the rafters.

Of the ordination services the clerk has left us a memorandum, which indicates his sense both of the importance of the occasion, and of propriety in the use of titles.

"North Parish in Danvers, December ye 23ᵈ 1772. This day (Agreeable to a Vote of the Church in Said Parish at their Meeting ye 19ᵗʰ of November last, with their Then Elect Pastor Mʳ Benjᵃ Wadsworth (But now the Revᵈ Mr. Benjᵃ Wadsworth, Pastor of said Church and Congregation in said Parish) being Present and Consenting thereto, with the Concurrence of the Freeholders and other Inhabitants of said Parish at their Meeting the 4ᵗʰ Day of December Instant) was solemnised as a Day set apart for the Ordination of the said Mr. Wadsworth to the Pastoral Charge of said Church and Congregation. The Revᵈ Mr. Holt of the South Parish in said Danvers Opened the Solemnity with Prayer. The Revᵈ Mr. Robbins of Milton preached.* The Revᵈ Mr. Morril of Wilmington Prayed and Gave the Charge. The Revᵈ Mr. Sawin of Wenham made the Conclusive Prayer, and the Revᵈ Mr. Smith of Middleton Gave the Right Hand of Fellowship — Recorded by Arch. Dale, P. Cler."

The day was unusually warm and pleasant for the season, so that the windows of the meeting-house were opened. There was a gathering of people from all the surrounding region. The houses of the inhabitants were opened for their entertainment. There are reports still current of the social festivities that were held in the different households.†

---

* From Eph. ii. 17.

† A company of people from Andover spent the night in a dance at the house of Mr. John Preston, where Mr. Charles Peabody now lives; and one of the young men, climbing the well-pole, and being in more ways than one elated, crowed at the dawning of the day. In another place a man wore out a new pair of boots in the same manner upon the sanded floors, — from which the inference is, that there was fraud in leather-work before our days. Yet more incredible is the story of the cracked plastering still shown at the house of the present Dea. Putnam, beneath the chamber occupied by Mr. Wadsworth himself as a boarder; which thing, as commonly explained, I refuse to believe, or further to narrate; nor is it needful. The crack may well be there. To a judicial and philosophic mind it is but natural to observe that the young minister may have had classmates and other student friends in his room, with much not immovable weight on the floor. One of them probably fell with a heavy load of wood for the fire.

The people of the parish, at all events, were well satisfied with the proceedings of the day. Among the papers of Judge Holten, in the possession of Mrs. Philemon Putnam, there is a minute made by him with respect to the ceremonies, which ends with the statement that "The utmost Decency was preserved through the whole of the Solemnity, and the Entertainment consequent was generous and elegant, reflecting great Honour upon the Parish." *

It will be seen that the settlement of Mr. Wadsworth took place almost exactly one hundred years after the first organization of Salem Village. The old name had been dropped from official use. The population had more than doubled. There were one hundred and fifty families within the parish. The

---

* Judge Holten has left a memorandum of some of the items of expense for this reputable entertainment, which I transcribe in part : —

	£	s.	d.			£	s.	d.
Pd Dr. Rust for wair.........	3	19	0	Pd John Crowel 2 Days work	1	17	0
" the Tin man.............	3	0	0	" John Hayward 1 Do.....	1	0	0
" Grant for wair..........	6	15	0	" Benj Gifford one Days			
" Whittemore for Do......	2	0	10	work.................	1	0	0
" Buxton for Sugr.........	7	10	0	" for Bisket 45s...........	2	5	0
" for Malt................	0	7	6	" Phebie Pease	0	9	0
" for Rum................	0	8	0	" Widw Hayward.........	1	16	0
" at Salem wine sugr.......	4	0	0	" Prudence...............	0	11	3
" for Fowls...............	9	1	10½	" About 2 Cord of wood...	9	0	0
" for 5 fowls wt 11¾........	1	9	4½	" Grant for sum Coton (?)*.	3	0	0
" 4 Gees wt 34, Cross......	3	8	0	" For my own time and Trou-			
" one Flower Barrel.......	0	1	0	ble about a fortinet....	38	17	0
" 3 Gees wt 25 half........	3	3	9	" Journey to Gloucester....	6	5	0
" 2 Gees.................	1	13	0	" Pork, Beef, Salt (?) and			
" for Fowls...............	0	10	0	Rye and Ingun meal...20	20	17	0
" for Turkeys.............	8	14	0	" Miss Clark for one day..	0	7	0
" Cake...................	1	10	0	" Syder about half a Barrel.	0	15	0
" about one Ton of Good				" Cheese.................	1	5	0
Hay...................25	25	0	0	" New England Rum......	0	16	0
" 1 Barrel and one small Cask	1	15	0	" Miss Kelly for Butter....	3	12	0
" Buxton 7 Days work.....	5	6	0	" Also to Sundry Persons.105	105	13	6½

The total expense, deducting for the value of what was left in hand, was £212 12s. 9½d.

This was in "old tenor," or "inflated currency," of which our fathers saw enough.

The relative cheapness of "Syder" may be noticed, and also the small quantity of any intoxicating drink that was purchased.

* I suppose it is meant for "some cotton."

assessor's list had increased from 94 names in 1681 (nine years after the organization) to 186 ; and this notwithstanding the cutting-off of Middleton.

Mr. Wadsworth was the son of a deacon in Milton, and was born July 18, 1750. He was a Christian from early years. He graduated with distinction at Harvard in 1769 ; taught for a year ; studied theology at Cambridge ; and, with Rev. Mr. Williams of Weymouth, was licensed to preach in the spring of 1772 ; and was ordained here, as we have seen, a few months later, and while he was in his twenty-third year.

He was received as a member of this church on the day of his ordination, by a letter from the church in Milton, which Nathanael Robbins the pastor had brought. He married Mary Hobson of Rowley ; and he was also married a second time, to Mary Carnes of Lynn, who survived him. Forty-four years after his settlement, he received from Harvard the degree of Doctor of Divinity. But I shall apply the title to him without waiting for that time ; since it is fixed in common use upon his name, and since the matter of the doctor must have been growing within him from the first.

The mention of the setting-apart of seats for the singers upon the ordination day is the first notice which I have observed in the records of any special provision for that branch of public worship. The singing before was congregational, whatever else it may have been. The hymns, in the scarcity of books, were " deaconed,"—that is, read line by line, or by couplets, by the leader ; and all joined as they were able, and some beyond their ability. This custom was continued by the church at the communion, after it had been given up in the usual sabbath service. Shortly after the ordination, if not from that time, there was a choir. For within a little more than a year, " at the desire of a number of the Inhabitants," they had a permanent seat assigned them in the front gallery. The movement was set afoot, no doubt, by the new minister, and the other young people with him. However, the choir were not to be allowed to have the first seat in the gallery, but were put back into the second and third seats, while a goodly and sober and well-behaved row of matrons — the wives of Tarrant Putnam, Asa Prince, Eleazer Goodale, Joseph Dwinel, and Richard Whittredge — sat in the front seat before them. It ought not to have been thought that these spirited young singers could rest in such a position. They straightway asked for and obtained liberty " to Build up the second and third seats in the front gallery in Banisters upon their own Cost for their Convenience to sit in."

There must be a new singing-book withal ; for things were no longer to be behindhand in this parish. And shortly, that is, early in January, 1775, it was voted that " Doctor Watses version of the Psalms with the three Books of hymns," should be used in the congregation. I suppose the old " Bay State " hymn-book had been in use before.

A movement was started also, and a little earlier, to build a new meeting-house ; but it came to nothing. It was not· strange ; for the shadow of the great War of Independence was beginning to fall upon them. There was likely to be other use for what money they might have to spare ; and scope was offered for all the energies of the young and the old.

No town in the State, it is believed, entered into the Revolutionary struggle with more of heartiness and unanimity than Danvers. And none, in proportion to its population, furnished to the Continental army a larger number of brave and distinguished soldiers.

Of this parish, besides Gen. Israel Putnam, who left the place when he was but a young man, there were: Gen. Moses Porter, in the artillery, distinguished at Bunker Hill and throughout the war. Col. Enoch Putnam, grandfather of Mrs. John Preston, and living until within the present century upon the place now owned by William A. Lander, Esq., not far from " Beaver Brook." Col. Jeremiah Page, grandfather of Dea. S. P. Fowler. Capt. Samuel Flint, of the bravest at Lexington and Bunker Hill, slain in battle during the campaign against Burgoyne. Capt. Samuel Page (son of Jeremiah); Capt. Jeremiah Putnam, Capt. Asa Prince, at Bunker Hill and Ticonderoga; Lieut. Moses Prince, Lieut. Stephen Putnam, Lieut. David Putnam, Ensign Tarrant Putnam, Dr. Amos Putnam, Levi Preston, Asa Tapley, and many others.

The military titles attached to the names of these persons were gained and borne during the war (unless as to one or two of those last named) ; except that Gen. Porter remained in the army, and rose to the rank he finally held after the return of peace.

Business with respect to the prosecution of the war was mainly transacted in the town-meetings. Yet matters of this kind came sometimes before the parish. A committee was appointed in one instance to procure the enlistment of soldiers at the parish expense. This must have been without legal right ; and the authority was soon withdrawn. Obligations, however, had been contracted, which the parish had afterwards some trouble in discharging.

That business of this kind should ever have been brought forward in such a meeting, shows the extent to which, for a long period of years, the parish had been looked upon as almost identical with a town. Another instance of the same sort may be mentioned as occurring a little before, in 1772. There had been an agreement between the two parishes, previous to their being set off, from Salem, to the effect that town-meetings should be held alternate years in each parish ; and this had been violated by the selectmen. The matter was forthwith taken up in a parish meeting, and a committee appointed to appeal to the General Court for a remedy, which they did successfully. It may also be noticed in the same connection, that in 1783 the parish voted in favor of a division of the town, and the organization of the northern portion by itself. But the movement was not followed up.

More exactly in the line of parochial business were the measures taken for the relief of the poor in Boston, in the winter and spring of 1775. A committee was appointed, consisting of Capt. John Putnam, Lieut. Enoch Putnam, Ensign Archelaus Dale, Capt. William Putnam, Francis Nurse, Capt. Nath. Pope, and Capt. Samuel Flint, to gather a contribution. Enoch Putnam was instructed to carry it to Boston, and deliver it "to the Committee of Donations in the town of Boston, in the name of the North Parish in Danvers." He made report that he "delivered 8 pair of men's shoes, 2 pair Boys', 8½ yards of Check, and 2 skeins of thread and one pair of moose-skin Breeches, also the sum of twenty six pounds fifteen shillings and four pence Lawful money to said committee."* The names of the contributors, and the sums they gave, are recorded at length by the clerk.

Soon after the close of the war the attention of the people was called again to the necessity for home improvements.

The buildings of the parsonage, but not the land, had been given to the minister soon after his settlement; and he had been able thus far to make use of them. But the house was becoming unsuitable for further occupancy; and in 1784 the question arose of building a new one. The burdens of the war, however, were still felt to such a degree that this was not thought advisable. The matter was arranged by the parish making a gift to Dr. Wadsworth, of an acre of land, bordering upon the road, for a house-lot. And upon this lot, the bounds of which may now be traced, he built for himself, about twenty rods west of the old site, the spacious house which is still standing, and which is now owned by the heirs of the late Caleb Prentiss. He had received property with his wife, and was thus able to do it.

The newer section of the parsonage house, that is, the building put up as an addition in 1734, was sold, as I suppose, by Dr. Wadsworth, and was removed to the neighborhood of the

---

* Mr. Hanson, in his history, gives the date of this contribution a year later, as nearly as can be told, and says it was "for the army besieging Boston." There *was* no army then besieging Boston. But the business of the place was suspended, as the war was about to break out; and there was suffering among the patriot inhabitants.

school-house in No. 6,* where it still stands, in a condition next
to ruinous, and occupied by hay; squashes, old barrels, and pigs.
It will thus be seen that this building, contrary to a report that
has had some currency, was not in reality any part of the
original parsonage, and was never occupied by Mr. Parris or any
of his witches.   It was not in existence until nearly forty years
after he had left the place ; and it has no other flavor of witchcraft upon it than what it may have absorbed in standing for
half a century in contact with the older and once infected
building.†   It has, however, interesting associations from its
having been so long occupied by the ministers of the parish.

The original parsonage was demolished by Dr. Wadsworth
probably about the time he built his new house.   There is a
tradition, coming through Mr. Moses Prince, which, I think,
may be depended upon, to the effect that certain materials
from the old house were used in the construction of a low
building or shed, running back to the rear from the Wadsworth
house, and which is still standing.   There are boards now in
sight in this building which have upon them mouldings and
other marks indicating that they once belonged to what was
meant for good work.   These boards, if any thing, are bewitched.   By the favor of Mr. Henry Prentiss I have come
into possession of one of these boards, some part of which I
have here with me, and which will be laid up as a relic in the
present parsonage, in the hope that there may never be any
more wood in this parish of the same sort.‡

* The " District System " has lately been abolished by law (1869) ; but the
old designations are still in use for convenience.

† Mr. Hanson has given, in his history, a view of the building now standing as
of "a portion of the old Parris House."   John W. Proctor also was misled in
the same manner, though he speaks less confidently, and only as from report.
But the measurements are conclusive.   The present building corresponds to the
dimensions of the addition of 1734, while it bears no likeness to the original
house of 1681, or to any practicable section of it.   The difference in height to
the plates, for one item, is three feet.   Due inquiry would have shown, too, that
the more trustworthy tradition does not identify the buildings ; while the fact
of the removal of the present structure from the old site will readily account for
the mistaken notion of some concerning it.

‡ There are perhaps those who do not know the test for bewitched wood.   It

MEETING-HOUSE OF 1786.

In 1785 it was resolved to build a new meeting-house ; and
Dea. Asa Putnam, Phinehas Putnam, Aaron Putnam, Ezra
Upton, Amos Putnam, Esq., Gilbert Tapley, Ezra Johnson,
Col. Enoch Putnam, and Nathanael Pope were chosen a committee to prepare a plan. A building committee was subsequently appointed, consisting of Dea. Asa Putnam, Capt.
Joseph Porter, Col. Enoch Putnam, Gideon Putnam, Stephen
Putnam, Ezra Upton, and Phinehas Putnam. There was delay
in beginning, as is usual. The timber was mostly furnished
within the parish ; and as to money, it was not easy to
agree how it should be raised. The building was erected in
the summer and fall of 1786, and was used during the winter
following, but was not finished till the spring of the next year.*

This house of 1786 was 60 feet long by 46 feet wide, and
with posts. 27 feet in height. There was a steeple at the
northern end, 14 feet square at the base, and, as Dr. Wadsworth says, "well-proportioned ;" and at the other end was a
porch 12 feet square. The house was painted, as neither of
the others probably had been. Whatever the original color
may have been, upon its being re-painted, in 1803, the body of
the house was made of a yellow stone color, with the "cornices,
weather boards, window frames and sashes" white. The cost
was about 1606 pounds ; or, according to Dr. Wadsworth,
"about five thousand six hundred and sixty-six dollars." He
adds, concerning it, that it "was a neat piece of architecture,
handsomely finished, and exhibiting a pleasing appearance."
(See accompanying cut.)

The pews were built under the direction of the parish, and
were sold at auction ; which was the beginning here of the
system of private ownership in pews, saving as certain indi-

---

should be hung up with the top (as it grew) downward, in the north-eastern corner
of a fireplace, from St. Michael's Day to Ash-Wednesday ; and then be laid,
without approach of moisture, and with a form of words which I shall not tell to
those that do not know it, upon a bed of red-hot alder-wood coals. If it does not
take fire while one can run thirteen times around the house, turning to the left,
and the heat being kept up, it is bewitched. This wood which I have in keeping has never taken fire.

* Certain posts in the barn built by Dr. Wadsworth at the rear of his house are
supposed to have been in the old meeting-house of 1701, then torn down.

viduals had before had liberty to build pews or seats for themselves.*

* There were 63 pews on the floor, and 25 in the gallery. The following is an account of purchasers, and of the sums paid. This list, with those corresponding for the later meeting-houses, has been made out by George Tapley, treasurer of the parish.

It appears, however, that some of the pews thus bought were not paid for: so that these names do not indicate with exactness the actual ownership and occupation of the house.

ON THE FLOOR.

No.	£.	s.	d.
1. John Andrew	18	12	0
2. Aaron Putnam	20	8	0
3. " "	22	10	0
4. Levi Preston	19	4	0
5. Nathl. Pope	24	18	0
6. Israel Putnam, 3d	19	10	0
7. Capt. Wm. Towne	24	0	0
8. Amos Buxton	16	10	0
9. Allen Putnam	15	0	0
10. Joseph Porter	22	16	0
11. Zerubabel Porter	23	2	0
12. Archelaus Rea	24	6	0
13. Israel Putnam	19	16	0
14. Enoch Putnam	25	10	0
15. Archelaus Putnam	29	4	0
16. Jesse Upton	20	14	0
17. Joseph Putnam	26	8	0
18. Danl. Putnam	24	18	0
19. Ebenezer Brown	24	6	0
20. Benja. Russell	22	4	0
21. Ezra Batchelder	23	2	0
22. Wm. Whittredge	15	18	0
23. Saml. White	16	4	0
24. John Preston	20	14	0
25. Jesse Upton	23	2	0
26. Elijah Flint	24	6	0
27. Joseph Porter	20	2	0
28. Wm. Whittridge	22	10	0
29. James Prince	20	14	0
30. Benja. Putnam, jun.	15	18	0
31. Gideon Batchelder	21	18	0
32. Asa Tapley	18	6	0
33. Matthew Putnam	23	2	0
34. Phinehas Putnam	24	12	0
35. Saml. Holten	24	18	0
36. Stephen Putnam	24	18	0

No.	£.	s.	d.
37. John Walcott	18	18	0
38. Saml. Page	21	18	0
39. Symon Mudge	19	4	2
40. Wm. Putnam	18	12	0
41. Zadock Wilkins	21	12	0
42. Asa Putnam	19	4	0
43. Nathaniel Pope	15	6	0
44. John Smith	18	0	0
45. Andrew Nichols	17	14	0
46. George Wiatt	15	0	0
47. Amos Tapley	21	12	0
48. Eleazer Putnam	23	8	0
49. Thomas Towne	15	18	0
50. Joseph Porter	18	6	0
51. John Hutchinson	17	14	0
52. Joseph Dwiniel	16	10	0
53. Timothy Fuller	19	10	0
54. James Goodale	22	4	0
55. Wm. Giffords	18	18	0
56. Hennery Putnam	19	10	0
57. Widw Mary Cross	23	8	0
58. Gideon Putnam	23	14	0
59. Not sold.			
60. Benja Putnam	20	2	0
61. Jesse Upton	20	14	0
62. John Kettell	20	2	0
63. David Putnam	21	6	0

IN THE GALLERY.

No.	£.	s.	d.
1. John Sheldon	6	6	0
2. Timo Putnam	6	18	0
3. George Wiatt	6	0	0
4. Archel Dale	4	4	0
5. Elisha Putnam	4	10	0
6. Willm Goodale	5	8	0
7. Aaron Putnam	4	16	0
8. Nathan Cheever	6	0	0

The old bell of 1725 was hung upon this church; but it was exchanged in 1802 for a new one, weighing 674 pounds, and costing (for the bell alone) $299.56.

Joseph Verry, who was also parish collector the same year, rang this bell, and performed the other duties of sexton, for the sum of twelve dollars. There are upon the books many copies of the contracts entered into by the parish committee with the sexton. Job Holt held the office for a considerable term of years near the end of the last century. He received ordinarily six dollars, besides the use of the parish house and garden; but these last were of small account. The duties of the sexton were to ring and toll the bell on days of public worship, and for some years also at nine in the evening of each day; to sweep the meeting-house once every month, on the week before the sacrament; to shovel the snow from the steps and the horse-blocks, and from the paths to the roads; and to keep the yard and stables clean and in good order. There was no care of fires or lights.

But the geese in those days, and for a long time, gave these sextons much work, and the people much annoyance. The sexton was required and expected to keep them diligently from the meeting-house. In this respect the duties of that post have become less laborious; and for many years past the geese have kept away mostly from this meeting-house of themselves.

At not far from this time, probably in 1794, was established the "Danvers Social Library." It was owned in shares by

No.	£.	s.	d.	No.	£.	s.	d.
9. Joshua Dodge	4	4	0	19. Nathan Putnam	4	16	0
10. Ebenezr Goodale, Jun	6	18	0	20. Gilbord Tapley	6	12	0
11. Ebenezr Kenney	6	12	0	21. Philip Nurse	4	10	0
12. Benja Nichols	4	10	0	22. Israel Putnam	4	4	0
13. Amos Tapley	6	18	0	23. Jethro Putnam	6	12	0
14. John Kettell	4	10	0	24. Solomon Wilkins	5	2	0
15. Andrew Nichols	5	2	0	25. Nathan Page	6	0	0
16. Timothy Fuller	6	6	0				
17. John Prince	4	16	0		£1,425	12	0
18. Jesse Upton	5	14	0				

different individuals, and the books were loaned to share-
holders. It was kept at times at the house of Benj. Chase, at the
place owned by the late Elijah Pope ; and also, probably, at
Judge Holten's.* · This institution did not prove permanent ;
hardly continuing above twenty years. A few of the books
have been lately presented to the " Ministerial Library " of this
church. So far as we may judge by these, the people were not
harmed by light or " sensational " reading from this library.
They had, rather, " Mason on Self-Knowledge," John Newton's
Hymns, Blair's Sermons, and the like.

In 1801 the old " Parish House," before referred to, and in
which the sextons had usually lived, was sold and moved away.
Judge Holten gave for it $15.50, and $2.75 for the stones
under it and around the garden ; and Matthew Putnam paid
$1.30 for the " parish well-crutch." I suppose this to have
been the house that was moved upon the meeting-house
ground by John Britain seventy-five years before. The land
was levelled, and the old well· covered and finally filled up.
The west side of the meeting-house was becoming of more
account now, with the new roads made or contemplated.

The present arrangement of horse-sheds dates from about
this same time. There were no sheds before at the south of
the meeting-house. The old sheds, or "Stalls," had stood
upon the east side and quite near the meeting-house, with
some scattered groups apparently toward the west and north.
In 1803 additional land was purchased upon the east, of Major
(afterward General) Ebenezer Goodale, by a company formed
for the purpose. The old sheds were removed, and the land
levelled ; and new sheds were erected, nearly as they now are,
upon the east and south sides, forming a right angle at the
south-east corner. The south row was set upon land belonging before to the parish, and given for that use in consideration of the enlargement of the open space at the east. The
" horse-blocks," less needed now with the increase of car-

* The book-case belonging to this old social library is now in the south-
western room of the basement of the meeting-house.

riages, and interfering with the new arrangements, were removed. They had stood, one towards the north, the other to the south-west, of the meeting-house.

These improvements were scarcely completed when the parish was called upon to restore its meeting-house, suddenly destroyed by fire on the morning of the 24th of September, 1805. The minute by Jonathan Porter, jun., parish clerk, is as follows : " Before the dawning of the day the meeting-house was discovered to be on fire, and was soon burnt to the ground in a short time. It was supposed to be set on fire by some incendiary ; and a man by the name of Holten Goodale was the suspected person, who was accordingly arrested the same evening, and, after examination the next day, was committed to prison. But, having his trial at the next session of the Supreme Judicial Court that was holden at Salem, he appeared to be an insane person, and was therefore sentenced to receive no punishment but that of confinement as a lunatick."

Dr. Wadsworth states that there were lost, of the sacramental furniture, eight silver cups of the value of twenty-five dollars each, "one of which was presented to the church by Judge Lindal, and the rest by particular members." * There were also other vessels of pewter ; and he adds, " Some silver, though not sufficient for one cup, was found among the ruins : but the full quantity of pewter remained, — a circumstance which renders it highly probable that the house was robbed of most of the plate before it was set on fire." That the plate was stolen there can be no doubt. It was kept beneath the pulpit ; and most careful search was made to recover the materials, with only the partial success just mentioned. Other persons than the one arrested were

* Judge Timothy Lindal had lived in the middle of the preceding century, at the foot of what is named for him " Lindal Hill," and in the house now occupied by Richard Flint. He was often representative from Salem to the General Court, and sometimes speaker of the House of Representatives. He was Justice of General Sessions and of Common Pleas. He died Oct. 25, 1760. See Felt's " Annals of Salem."

concerned in the crime ; and his connection with it was of but small account. There were those upon whom suspicion fell violently and persistently ; but, as no decisive evidence could be brought forward, judicial proceedings were not attempted against them. And their names will not now be mentioned.

The parish had been prospering, and was now strong in resources and in spirit. The standing committee — Amos Tapley, Asa Tapley, and Jonathan Porter, jun. — issued on the day of the fire a warrant for a meeting to be held on the 4th of October, at the house of " the widow Eunice Upton, inholder." The fire was on Tuesday, — the meeting on Friday of the following week. Israel Andrews was chosen moderator ; and the meeting was adjourned to the neighborhood schoolhouse, a quarter of a mile towards the west.* " After a pathetic and well adapted prayer by Rev. Mr. Wadsworth," it was voted to rebuild the meeting-house on the same spot. And on motion of Eleazer Putnam, Esq., a committee — consisting of John Fowler, Capt. Hezekiah Flint, Capt. Levi Preston, Amos Tapley, and Amos Pope — was appointed to report plans. It was subsequently determined that the building should be of brick, and should have " a Tower and Dome." The contractors were " Col. Ebenezer Goodale and others ;" and the superintending committee, John Fowler, Capt. Levi Preston, and Amos Tapley.

The size was sixty-six feet by fifty-six, with a height to the eaves of twenty-eight feet. And the tower, according to Dr. Wadsworth, was " sixteen feet four inches square, having two wings, crowned with a cupola, and terminated with a vane ninety-six feet from the foundation."

Unlike the three earlier houses, this, like the one now standing, was set fronting toward the west or south-west, upon " the great road leading from Andover to Salem." The corner-stone was laid on the 16th of May, 1806 ; and the build-

---

* The inn was where Deacon Hutchinson now lives. The schoolhouse then stood to the northward, at the foot of the hill, and across the road from the present site, and upon what is now a small, open, triangular space included between the branchings of the roads at that point. It was a one-story building, smaller than the present schoolhouse.

THE BRICK MEETING-HOUSE.

ing was ready for use late in the fall of the same year. The
cost was not far from twelve thousand dollars. And the bill
included a bell to replace the one that had been melted, costing $444.75, and weighing 1,116 pounds; which is the bell
now in use. There were no arrangements as yet for warming
the building. Fifteen years later stoves were put in, which
had been bought by subscription.

The new edifice was thought to be a good one. And, as the
use of such a material for a building of that kind was not
common in country places, this "Brick Meeting-House" became an object of distinction, and was a noted landmark for
the region about it.*

* There were seventy-six pews on the floor of the brick church, and thirty
in the gallery. The purchasers of pews, and prices paid, are as follows : —

No.	ON THE FLOOR.				
			29	Levi Preston	185 00
1	Ebenr Dale	$146 00	30	Benajah Collins, Esq.	130 00
2	Hezekiah Flint	176 00	31	Jesse Upton	175 00
3	Elijah Flint	182 00	32	Benja Chase and Jos Flint	141 00
4	Joseph Putnam, 3d	209 00	33	Samuel Page	190 00
5	James Putnam	172 00	34	Ezra Batchelder	188 00
6	Saml. Fowler, jun.	230 00	35	Ebenezer Brown	128 00
7	Matthew Putnam	174 00	36	Amos Tapley	170 00
8	Jos and Jesse Putnam	228 00	37	Asa Tapley	152 00
9	Nathaniel Putnam	193 00	38	Jos. Hutchinson	98 00
10	Aaron Putnam	208 00	39	Not sold.	
11	George Ingersoll	146 00	40	" "	
12	Jonathan Shelden	110 00	41	Benja Putnam, jun.	$100 00
13	Benja Russell, jun.	129 00	42	Seth Putnam	150 00
14	Geo. and Saml. Small	105 00	43	Amos Putnam, jun.	150 00
15	Amos Buxton	60 00	44	John and Jesse Hutchinson	136 00
16	Zadock Wilkins	63 00	45	Simon Mudge	176 00
17	David Putnam.	102 00	46	John Gardner	180 00
18	Peter Cross	100 00	47	Allen Nurse	144 00
19	Caleb Prince	101 00	48	William Goodale	183 00
20	Samuel Towne	131 00	49	Eleazer Putnam, Esq.	139 00
21	Jos & Jona Porter, 3d	169 00	50	Samuel Holten, Esq.	175 00
22	Eben Putnam	181 00	51	Israel Andrew	183 00
23	Caleb Oakes	228 00	52	Elijah and Amos Pope	186 00
24	Peter Cross, jun.	181 00	53	Andrew Nichols	173 00
25	Mehitable Putnam	240 00	54	Stephen Putnam	169 00
26	John Fowler	166 00	55	Ezra and Moses Putnam	156 00
27	Israel and Danl. Putnam	213 00	56	John White	153 00
28	John Preston	185 00	57	Samuel Holten, Esq.	141 00

The first sabbath of meeting in the new house was November 23, 1806; and the dedication services were on the Thursday preceding. Dr. Wadsworth's sermon at the dedication was printed, and has been already referred to. It will be of interest to make some quotations from it, both for the subject matter, and to show how it was handled. The opening is as follows : —

"*Christian Brethren and Friends*, — Assembled for the religious dedication of this new temple to Jehovah, what mingled emotions, what conflicting passions, what mournful reflections and joyful congratulations, does the occasion inspire!

"Retrospection calls up the most painful sensibilities by reviving in our minds the gloomy morning of the 24th of September, 1805, when this very spot on which we worship exhibited a sacrilegious conflagration*

58 Peter Putnam	130 00	7 Not sold.	
59 Not sold.		8 " "	
60 Jonathan Walcut	109 00	9 " "	
61 Amos Flint	76 00	10 Andrew Nichols	43 00
62 Not sold.		11 Jesse Putnam	48 00
63 " "		12 Zadock Wilkins	43 00
64 Nathan Smith	76 00	13 William Towne	43 00
65 Porter Putnam	106 00	14 Caleb Clarke, jun.	40 00
66 Not sold.		15 Not sold.	
67 John Joselyn	130 00	16 " "	
68 Amos Mudge	143 00	17 " "	
69 Abel N. and Levi Preston		18 " "	
and Ebenr Berry	153 00	19 " "	
70 Jona. Kettell, Geo. Osgood,		20 " "	
and Jeremy Hutchinson	157 00	21 " "	
71 Samuel Page	160 00	22 Job Goodale	36 00
72 Moses Endicott	194 00	23 Amos Tapley and Sarah	
73 John Endicott, jun.	196 00	Upton	51 00
74 Ebenezer Goodale	200 00	24 John Hutchinson, jun.	45 00
75 Not sold.		25 John Fowler	59 00
76 Gideon Putnam	133 00	26 Timothy Fuller, jun.	40 00
		27 Elijah Flint and Eler.	
No. IN THE GALLERY.		Putnam	42 00
1 Jasper Needham	$43 00	28 Ebenr Goodale and Israel	
2 Asa Hutchinson	42 00	Cheever	56 00
3 Richard Butler	43 00	29 Jesse Hayward	47 00
4 Elijah Pope and Perley		30 Bartho Demsey	49 00
Goodale	50 00		
5 Israel and Danl. Putnam	43 00	Total,	$11,436 00
6 Not sold.			

* I omit the capitalizing, and for the most part the italicizing, of words, which things were more common then than now.

scarcely paralleled in history. Roused from our slumbers at about four o'clock, by a transient passenger, with the alarm of fire, a dismal spectacle presented to view, — *the house of God wrapped in flames.* Consternation seized us. What majesty of desolation when a superb column of the raging element encircled and ascended the lofty steeple ! Who at that moment could credit the testimony of his own senses ? But, alas ! in one sad hour " our holy and our beautiful house, where our fathers praised God," was reduced to ashes. Whose eye could witness the melancholy scene, and not melt to tears ? — whose heart, without being overwhelmed with grief ! What solemn sentiments crowded upon our minds, who were spectators ! what lessons of wisdom did it seal to our souls ! Impressions surely it could not but leave, which time can never erase. . . . The rising luminary of day, as if conscious of the indignity offered its Maker, lowering, frowned on the atrocious deed ; and the circumambient clouds dissolved in tender sympathy.* Strangers walked in pensive silence over the dreary waste, and paid the affectionate tribute. At such wanton destruction humanity revolted ; while virtue, piety, and the friends of Emmanuel wept. Hell exulted, but Heaven pitied ; and Gabriel's lyre struck a mournful string.

" That was the memorable day of our Zion's distress. Every countenance was fallen, and every heart sad. Deprived of our house of worship, dark was the opening scene and discouraging the prospect.

" During a tedious interval, rather exceeding one annual revolution, we assembled in a humble place of worship [the school-house] and, unwilling to hang our harps on the willows, there tuned the sacred song.

" But, blessed be God ! the scene is happily changed. This day's smiling sun lights up joy in our hearts. *Zion's ruins are repaired.* From

---

* This is not quite a fair specimen of Dr. Wadsworth's style ; but it shows fairly its point of weakness. The doctor loved long words and a majestically sounding sentence. This, too, was a peculiarity of that age. There were few writers or speakers of the period immediately following the Revolution that were not more or less inclined to a certain stateliness and sonorousness of language, that was liable to pass into turgidity. Any one familiar with the pamphlets and the speeches of that period could hardly fail to recognize one of them that he never had met with before, upon hearing a few sentences from it. It would be curious to trace the cause of this peculiarity. It had to do, no doubt, with the youth of the nation, and with the anniversary of our independence, and with the Bird of Freedom that was wont then to spread wide his wings above us. But there were other causes. This style is said not to be wholly lost in our day. It is understood, too, that young men in all ages may be able to reproduce it. But the doctor was old enough at this time to have lightened his page somewhat of those " circumambient " adjectives, and to have suffered the clouds themselves to weep, if they must do any thing, rather than " dissolve in sympathy." But, as I have said, this is not quite a fair sample. The doctor wrote best, as many other persons have done, when he did not think of writing well.

the ashes of the former this spacious temple rose, a recent memorial of your zeal for religion. In devout acknowledgment we may say, 'This is the Lord's doing ; and it is marvellous in our eyes.'

I will also add some paragraphs containing very appropriate remarks upon the manner in which the people of the parish had conducted themselves in this emergency : —

" The destruction of property could not but be severely felt ; but it was the *divine displeasure*, we trust, that most deeply affected our hearts. Awakened to serious attention, and indulging penitential reflections, we humbled ourselves "under the mighty hand of God," by fasting and prayer.* In the midst of judgment he remembered mercy, heard our supplications, compassionated our afflicted state, cemented our union ; and inspired a noble resolution with one heart and one voice to rebuild, and on a scale worthy a wealthy and flourishing people, with more durable *materials*, and on a broader *base*. Instead of sinking into discouragement, or crumbling into parties, one accommodating spirit seemed to pervade the whole. Calm and deliberate were your discussions on the subject ; and your deportment has been like a band of brothers in affliction. The unanimity, regularity, and vigorous exertions which have marked your proceedings reflect honor on your Christian character. In all your decisions there has scarcely been a dissenting vote. This is acting worthy the descendants of a pious ancestry, and exhibiting an illustrious pattern for posterity. Should controversies and animosities ever begin to kindle among them, let them call to mind their fathers' pacific virtues, feel the tender reproof they administer, blush for their degeneracy, and rouse to imitation. . . .

" To hearts glowing with holy ardor in so good a cause, how reviving and animating are sentiments like these ! Your public spirit, your pious zeal, your united efforts, the world admire, the friends of religion applaud, ministering angels witness with pleasure, and God himself will graciously remunerate. Imagination is ready to paint the departed spirits of those who have been trained up here for glory, as granted the indulgence of the day, and mingling joys and praises ; while the great Adversary, and enemies to religion, experience an infernal disappointment. Pious posterity will rise up, and, while they enjoy the spiritual privileges of this house, revere their fathers' memory, and call their dust blessed. And you yourselves, when in heaven, should you obtain admission there, will reflect with sublime satisfaction that you rebuilt the house of God on earth, and left the sacred legacy to your children, to educate them in Christian faith and holiness for the same world of glory."

* The 26th of December, after the fire, had been kept by the church as a special day of fasting.

These sentiments were assuredly befitting to the occasion. And for the "pacific virtues" of the men of that time, as they appeared throughout this proceeding, they were worthy of all the commendation which the pastor of the church bestowed upon them.

The parish received a welcome accession of strength at this time, by the incorporation with it of a number of families and estates, mostly from that part of the town now known as Danvers-Port. This district, not being included in the original limits of the village, had heretofore belonged with the Middle Precinct, or South Parish. A considerable number of the inhabitants, however, had worshipped here; and some of them had been pew-owners in the meeting-house just destroyed. They had repeatedly endeavored to remove their connection from the South Parish; but the people there had not consented, regarding themselves as no stronger in the matter of property than the North Parish, even while they retained that neighborhood. But, previous to 1805, the South Parish had given up the raising money by assessment upon estates, and had laid a tax instead upon the pews in its meeting-house. It had grown also to be abundantly strong. There was thus an opportunity for the people of the Port to be brought here. Accordingly, as Dr. Wadsworth has stated it, "ten respectable characters, with their families, . . . immediately after our meeting-house was consumed, voluntarily came forward, and generously offered to join us, and bear their proportion of the expenses which might ensue." And in the winter following, at the session of the General Court, they were transferred, with their estates, to this parish for so long a time as the act empowering the South Parish to tax its pews continued in force. This act of transfer bears date March 8, 1806, and is signed by Timothy Bigelow, Speaker of the House; H. G. Otis, President of the Senate; and Caleb Strong, Governor. The ten "respectable characters" were Samuel Page, John Endicott, Moses Endicott, Nathaniel Putnam, Samuel Fowler, jun., Caleb Oakes, William Pindar, Jasper Needham, John Gardner, jun., and Amos Flint.*

In these families the parish had, through that and the following generations, some of its most active and liberal supporters.

Some reference may here properly be made to the system of roads in our town, which underwent great change at about this period.†

The original road from Salem to Andover, crossing the brook at " Hadlock's Bridge," near where the carpet-factory now stands in Tapleyville, followed the line of Pine Street to the corner by the house of S. Walter Nourse ; thence turning upon Hobart Street, — which is the " old meeting-house road," — it passed westerly to the Ingersoll corner, by the present meeting-house, and thence along the line of Center Street, past the house of Joel Kimball, and keeping what is now an almost untravelled road to the " Log Bridge " over the Ipswich River, nearly half a mile west of the place now occupied by Charles Peabody. From this point it made away towards " Will's Hill " and Andover.‡

* The three men last named were from West Danvers (now West Peabody).

† I had at first intended to trace somewhat fully the laying-out of these roads from early times ; but after further meditation — not without some discernment of the real nature of the subject — I have determined that the men and women of the seventeenth century may have liberty in imagination, for any hinderance from me, to travel over the whole of this parish at their own pleasure ; which is pretty nearly what they did do, in fact.

There is printed, with the annual " Statement of Accounts " of the town for 1873, a report submitted by a committee for the "Re-Survey of Highways," consisting of Wm. Dodge, jun., Andrew Nichols, S. W. Spaulding, Andrew M. Putnam, and C. H. Gould, which contains much valuable information. But this report gives dates only, for the most part, of the laying-out of roads by the selectmen or the county commissioners in comparatively modern times, while it is often only some change or re-location of a much older road that is thus designated. As to these older or original paths of travel, the report is of little use ; and it gives, in fact, but a single date of the seventeenth century.

It is to be hoped that Mr. Nichols, who has the materials well in hand, may give a fuller account of the whole matter ; and I wish him much comfort in the business.

‡ There is uncertainty in the mind of Moses Prince as to the exact location of

At a little distance beyond the present schoolhouse upon Center Street, and turning southward, is one of the most ancient roads, leading near to the house of Zephaniah Pope ; and thence, little used, and closed mostly to travel, passing by the house of Nathanael Pope to the place which has been owned from early times by the Goodell Family ; and thence bearing away originally to Reading and Medford Bridge and Boston. This is "the old Boston Path." It saved some crossing of ferries. And, though the "Ipswich Road" was the greater thoroughfare, yet travellers from Boston or the neighboring towns, according to the point they wished to reach, came often by this path, on their way to the northern settlements.

The present road from the meeting-house to Tapleyville, by Center and Holten Streets, was opened not far from 1725 ; though it may have been used as a private way, in some part, before.

The road across what is termed the "Judge's Hollow," to the Plain, being the easterly part of Holten Street, dates from 1793. But Holten Street was relaid in parts, straightened at what had been a great bend to the northward from Tapleyville to the crossing of the brook in the hollow, widened, and greatly improved along its whole course, in 1837. Great improvements have also been made along the causeway at the crossing of the brook within the last four or five years, and during the present year (1874).

Collins Street was opened in 1808 ; and there was at the same time a widening and straightening, with a general improvement, of Center Street along its entire length. Judge Holten was active in securing these changes. The location of the road as it passes the meeting-house was materially altered at this time, its course having been before much nearer the house.

The "Andover Turnpike Company" was chartered the same year, and the road was built not long after. It was no doubt in

this road for some distance beyond the "Log Bridge." But for my part, having seen it, if not beyond the original bounds of the parish, yet safely across the "Great River," I do not care where it went.

part, this movement for another route from Salem and the South Parish toward Middleton and Andover, that stimulated the effort to put in better condition the line by the Center, in connection with the laying-out of Collins Street.

Dayton Street was widened from near the house of Charles Peabody to Center Street in 1837, and extended to the Middleton Line in 1854. Of its earlier history I know nothing. The way must have been open long before; though this was not among the early roads.*

A charter, meanwhile, had been given in 1803 for a turnpike leading from Newburyport to Boston, passing through Danvers about a mile west of the meeting-house. This road, now Newbury Street, — straight for the most part, saving as it bends upwards and downwards, — was built with great labor, and opened about 1806 or 1807. It was much used during the war of 1812 in the transportation of military stores eastward. But it did not succeed, so far as was expected, in drawing the travel from the older routes nearer to the sea-shore, which, though longer, were less hilly, and had the advantage of passing through the larger towns. The opening, at length, of lines of railroad caused it to be of little value, except for local traffic.

The turnpike system, which had its use in its day, has been long since abandoned in Massachusetts; and the roads so built are all, with possibly some rare local exceptions, open, without toll, to public use.

Returning to the meeting-house, and passing eastward upon Hobart Street, we come, at the corner of Forest Street, to what was the old " Boxford Road." Tradition reports that it kept the

---

* There was an early road, now closed, running from near the " Log Bridge " over the hill eastward, through the place lately owned by Peter Putnam, crossing the turnpike near the pine-trees, and thence to Beaver Brook and to Putnamville. (By "Beaver Brook," as designating a point of location, I mean the neighborhood of the railroad station of that name.) There was also an old road, though by no means one of the earliest, from a point farther north, — that is, from near the place now occupied by Joseph Towne, the old neighborhood of Dea. Edward Putnam and Thomas Putnam the clerk, — running south-easterly over the hill, past the house now occupied by William Putnam, to Dayton Street.

line of an Indian trail leading toward the valley of the Merrimack, at North Andover and Haverhill. It followed, in general, the course of what are now Forest and Nichols Streets, crossing the Newburyport Turnpike by the house now occupied by Edward Wyatt; passing the house of Henry Verry, whose fine maple might not then have served the traveller for a staff; ascending the hill to the north-west by a way not yet quite closed up with brushwood, and leading thence across the Ipswich River to "Rowley Village," or Boxford, or, bearing more to the right, to Topsfield. From the hill beyond the place of Henry Verry, a path led also westerly toward Middleton.

Returning to Beaver Brook, and to the intersection of the road before described, from the "Log Bridge," we find a path leading in at the lane by the house of David M. Guilford, turning east by the houses of Jacob E. Spring and of Wm. A. Lander; and, crossing thence to Putnamville, entering upon what is now Locust Street by the lane south of the house of I. H. Putnam; and also by a branch, passing to Wenham, north of the Great Pond. Travel from the meeting-house to Wenham and the towns beyond might take either this or the "Ipswich Road."

Returning thus again to the neighborhood of the meeting-house, at the intersection of the "Boxford Road" with the present Hobart Street, we may conclude that the line of the Boxford road was continued past the spot where Joseph Hutchinson once lived, and across the fields to the neighborhood of "Hadlock's Bridge." A branch may also have led to the right, toward the house of Joseph Holten, at the place now owned by the family of the late Isaac Demsey, and thence south-westerly across the meadows.*

* Far it be from me to speak with any confidence concerning the origin, direction, or final destination of any of these roads — if there were any — passing to the rear of the present meeting-house. There are bounds to all human knowledge, though to the patience of a minister there be none. If any one wishes to know any thing more about these roads, he may go to Moses Prince or Wm. P. Upham, Esq., of Salem. He need not come to me.

It should be remembered, however, that the greater part of these early roads were at first mere paths through the woods, from house to house. They might

It will be seen that the first meeting-house, near the corner made by Hobart and Forest Streets, was upon a site more easily accessible from all directions than might now be thought.

Proceeding again toward the eastern portion of the town, we find from the earliest times the "Old Ipswich Road," already described in connection with the boundaries of Salem Village. This was a State or Colonial road, designed to facilitate intercourse between the scattered settlements along the coast. It was laid out by the General Court in 1643, though doubtless the path had been used before.

Sylvan Street, leading from Ash Street, by the mills of Otis F. Putnam, and past the Peabody Institute, to the Town-House, was opened in 1842; being, in effect, a straightening of the Ipswich Road.

The road along High and Water Streets, from the Plain to Crane River at the Port, was opened in 1755, and re-located in 1802. The continuation of this road from Crane River, by Water Street, to the North Bridge in Salem, was made in 1761; this part of the line being also re-located in 1802. Previous to the opening of this Crane River route, the Ipswich Road was the only highway leading toward Salem; and, indeed, the population in the neighborhood of the Plain, or between the Plain and the Port, having need of any other, was but small.

Liberty Street, with its bridge over Porter's River, dates from 1803.

Locust Street occupies, in general, the track of an old "Topsfield Road." It was re-located in 1807; the bounds be-

---

be foot-paths, horse-paths, cart or sled paths. They could·be laid out wherever a man could drive his sled, or ride or lead his horse. And as the most common mode of travel, where any beast was used, was upon horseback, these ways were often called "bridle-paths." Now, therefore, in any matter of dispute concerning an ancient road, there is nothing safer than to conclude that there was probably once a bridle-path somewhere in that neighborhood. This is my belief in the present instance.

Furthermore, across the most of these roads there were gates or bars in passing from field to field.

ginning from near where the flag-staff now stands, at the Plain, and in front of the post-office.*

North Street, running north-west from Locust Street, passing to the south of the house of Samuel Wallis, crossing the turnpike, and reaching away into Topsfield, is an old road, relocated in 1785.

The road from the old Judge Lindall place upon Locust Street (now occupied by Richard Flint) to Beaver Brook, along the lines, in part, of Poplar and Maple Streets, was opened in 1793. Travel that way had gone before by Hobart and Pine Streets, passing the corner at the place of S. Walter Nourse. The continuation of Maple Street from Beaver Brook, past the house of Dea. Wm. R. Putnam, to the intersection with Preston Street by the house of S. B. Swan, and making now the main line from the Plain to Middleton, was effected in 1813. The travel before had been by Nichols Street (the Boxford Road) and Preston Street; which latter is also an old road, though relaid in 1811, as part of the "Dyson Road," running from Beverly to Middleton.

Another old road through this neighborhood came from the region of the "Indian Bridge," on the main road now leading to

---

* Mr. Nichols is of the opinion, that, until a comparatively recent period, there was no road along this part of what is now Maple Street and the main street of the Plain's Village. But in this opinion I do not quite concur; holding, at least, to the great moral principle of the bridle-path, already laid down. Mr. Upham brings the early Topsfield Road down to meet the Ipswich Road, nearly as at present. And this seems most probable; though of the alleged lack of reference to such a road in deeds of land I can give, perhaps, no clear account.

There is a mystery, also, hanging over the end of the "old meeting-house road" at the Plain. It seems difficult to find it. It may have been swallowed up in the gravel after crossing the brook, like an African river in the sands; and, having thus come to such an untimely end, it may really have *had* no end at all. But this is not my belief. Mr. Upham holds that it kept the present line of Hobart Street to Maple Street, near to the station of the Newburyport Railroad. Mr. Prince concurs. The idea is a natural one. But Mr. Nichols dissents. He inclines rather to think, that, after crossing the brook, the road may have borne more to the right, toward the old place of Nathanael Putnam (the "Judge Putnam" place, now owned by Otis F. Putnam). I allow that it may have done both, — at least by a path. And, if my great healing principle of a bridle-path is not in this case accepted, I do not see why there must not be a war. But, come what may, I shall have no part in it, — not even if the "old meeting-house road" should be devoured throughout its entire length.

Middleton ; bore southward, past the old houses of Dea. Edward and of Thomas Putnam ; thence skirting Hathorne Hill on the north, near the line of the Essex Railroad, it came down to the rear of the house of Dea. Wm. R. Putnam, crossed the present road, made up the avenue to the house now owned by John M. Putnam, and went over the meadow to the Boxford Road, or Forest Street, near by the house now owned by Dean Kimball.*

The sketch thus roughly drawn may, I hope, convey some idea of the earlier arrangement of our roads, and of the great changes and improvements that have been made upon them.†

The first movements of the temperance reformation in our town date from the latter part of the ministry of Dr. Wadsworth. There had been a great increase of intemperance here and throughout the country, beginning with or soon after the war of the Revolution, through the enlarged production and use of distilled liquors. The evil reached a prodigious height during the first quarter or third of the present century. A society, the first in the country, was formed in this State in 1812, for the purpose of arresting the mischief. Dr. Wadsworth and Judge Holten were among the original members. An auxiliary society was formed in Danvers the next year. Dr. Wadsworth delivered an address before this society in 1815, which has been preserved in print.

---

* The part of this road last mentioned would be of use at the present time. Mr. Nichols tells me that nobody knows when, if ever, it was discontinued ; and I do not know.

† I feel less confidence in the accuracy at every point of this account of the roads than I do with respect to most other parts of this history. The mistakes, however, which may appear are few in number compared with those that I might have committed had the subject been followed into more of detail. I have kept to myself, be sure, the knowledge of much ignorance. Altogether, when one considers what journeying we have already had over the crooked ways the fathers made, he will not, I trust, think it unfit that we should proceed, without further delay, upon the temperance reformation.

It is well known that the temperance movement was not at first planted upon the basis of total abstinence from all intoxicating liquors not prescribed by a physician. The address of Dr. Wadsworth, accordingly, did not distinctly lay down this principle : yet it came but little short of it, and was such an address as the most thorough temperance man of the present day might give with little risk of being thought behind the age. He rebukes the prevailing " custom of treating friends and visitors with spirits," of furnishing it at funerals and other public occasions, and of supplying it to hired laborers. He says to the young, " Have the magnanimity to be singular when virtue requires it. Studiously avoid the snare of evil and vain company. And particularly guard against the use of spirituous liquors. Your blood circulates too freely, and your spirits flow too briskly, to require such stimulants. Those who never taste never crave ; and, where there is no appetite, abstinence is no mortification. As you value your virtue, your respectability, and your usefulness in the world, maintain your innocence." It is altogether an excellent address, and presents the arguments covering the whole subject with a fulness and force that leave little to be added.

This period must not be passed without some reference, beyond the occasional mention of his name, to Doctor or Judge Samuel Holten. All things considered, he was the most remarkable man the town has ever produced. He occupied very numerous and important public positions through a long period of years. He was more influential among his townsmen, if not throughout the neighborhood, in all public affairs, than any other man has ever been ; and he was worthy of his influence and his distinction. There ought to be prepared for popular use and instruction a fuller account of his life than could with propriety be furnished in this sketch of the parish history. I will give here only the outlines, drawn largely but not wholly from the discourse preached at his funeral by Dr. Wadsworth, Jan. 5, 1816.

Samuel Holten was born June 9, 1738. He was the son of

8

Samuel and Hannah Holten, and great-grandson of Joseph
Holten, an early inhabitant of the village. His parents lived
then in a house, not now standing, built by his grandfather
Henry, and called " the Holten Hotel." It was situated at the
south-west of the meeting-house, upon an old road, or at the
least a path, near the line of what is now Prince Street, leading from Center Street to the line of the Newburyport Railroad,
and not far from where the house of Artemas Wilson now
stands.

It was purposed to send him to college ; and he spent four
years at study in the family of Peter Clark. But at twelve
his health failed, and this plan was given up. His hearing
was permanently impaired, and he was never afterward strong.
But, being after a time somewhat recovered, he went to study
medicine with Dr. Jonathan Prince.* He made rapid progress ;
and when he was eighteen years old, Dr. Prince told him he
was qualified to set up for himself. He practised for a short
time at Gloucester, and then returned to this place, where he
continued to follow his profession — though very much interrupted after the first few years — until about the time of the
breaking-out of the Revolutionary war, when he left it altogether. In his thirtieth year he was chosen representative to
the General Court. He entered among the first, and with zeal
and energy, into the preparations that began to be made for
resistance to the encroachments of the British power. He
was a member of the Provincial Convention of 1768, called,
without authority of the royal government, by a Boston town-
meeting.† He was also in the Provincial (State) " Congress "

* Dr. Prince was a man of note in his profession, with a wide practice in this
and in the neighboring towns. He lived upon the southern slope of Hathorne
Hill, near Newbury Street, at a spot now marked by a cluster of pines. The
house has been moved away, and is the one now occupied by John Hook, sen.
Dr. Prince practised medicine for twenty-five or thirty years, until his death,
which occurred in 1753. He was the father of Capt. Asa Prince of Revolutionary memory.

† Dr. Wadsworth says "the Provincial Convention which was in session
when the British troops first landed in Boston." This is nearly true. The
convention met on the 22d of September, adjourned on the 27th, I think ; and
the regiments from Halifax came on the 28th.

Judge Holten was chosen, through all these years, to represent the town

of 1775 ; and was an active member of the general " Committee of Safety ; " and a major in the First Essex Regiment, though not a military man. He was a member of the executive council under the provisional government ; and these affairs soon occupied all his time.

" In 1777," says Dr. Wadsworth, " Judge Holten was one of the delegates from Massachusetts who assisted in framing the *Confederation* of the United States at Yorktown. The ensuing year he was for the first time chosen a delegate in the American Congress, and annexed his ratifying signature to that constitution of government. . . . And so high did he stand in the esteem of that august body, that they elected him President of Congress, and thus promoted him to the first seat of honor in his country." * He was five years in Congress under the Confederation, and two years under the Federal Constitution. Ill health alone prevented his continuing longer at the seat of the general government. He had been, meanwhile, five years a member of the State Senate, and twelve years in the Governor's Council. He had also, according to Dr. Wadsworth, been appointed, in 1776, one of the judges of the Court of Common Pleas for his native

---

wherever it was thought that he was most needed. And it is a signal mark of the esteem in which he was held by his townsmen, that their choice of him was usually unanimous.

* I give these sentences in Dr. Wadsworth's words, as being unable myself to determine precisely what may be meant. The articles of confederation were framed by the " American Congress " itself, and the work was completed in November, 1777 ; while Judge Holten is said, and truly, to have been first chosen a member of Congress in 1778. His first appearance in that body was on Monday, June 22, of that year. His name is in the list of those ratifying the articles soon after ; but I think he did not assist in framing them. The "Yorktown" here referred to is the town of York in Pennsylvania. [See Journal of Continental Congress, Sept. 27, 1777.]

That Judge Holten was at one time the presiding officer of the Continental Congress, is fixed in all the local histories and traditions, and I do not doubt the fact ; but it is nearly, and as I think quite certain, that he was never elected its "President." John Hancock and Nathaniel Gorham were the only Massachusetts men holding that position. But "chairmen" were occasionally chosen in the temporary absence of the president. This, I think, must have been the post which Judge Holten at some time occupied. But the date, in looking over the volumes of the Journal, which are almost without an index, I have not yet lighted on.

8

county, performing the duties of that office about thirty-two years, and presiding half that time. And "he was Justice of the Court of General Sessions of the Peace " — whatever that may have been — " thirty-five years, and Chief Justice of the same fifteen."

In 1796 he was appointed judge of probate for Essex County, which post he held until 1815. And moreover, to fill up somewhat his time, he was, upon occasion, selectman, town-clerk, and assessor ; twenty-four years town-treasurer ; and for nearly half a century treasurer of the parish. And furthermore, lest for lack of some business he should fall into evil habits, it was usual to appoint him as arbitrator in cases of difficulty, and to call upon him to settle disputes of all sorts.

For this latter work he had a happy faculty. In the affairs of the parish, matters of weight or difficulty or delicacy were intrusted to committees of which he was usually a member ; and his hand appears in the result. It would be clear from the parish records, if nothing else were known of him, that a man of a comprehensive and liberal mind had laid hold upon these affairs of business.

Dr. Wadsworth describes him as in form majestic, of graceful person, "his countenance pleasing, his manners easy and engaging, his talents popular, his disposition amiable and benevolent, and of good intellectual powers." He was not a brilliant man, and perhaps not a great man in ability for any one line of action ; but he was great in capacity for general accomplishment, in balance of mind, and in the easy and regular and effective working of all his faculties upon whatever · service they might be employed. He was faithful, too, in every trust, — a man of unswerving integrity, and always to be relied upon.

He was also a man of Christian principle. He had the instruction of pious parents from childhood, and had been early impressed with serious things. It is a suggestive fact we learn of him, that when he was seventeen years of age "he joined a religious society of young people, and was a zealous promoter of it." He made profession of his Christian faith, and became a member of this church, Feb. 4, 1759, — a little

before he was twenty-one years old. He did not afterward forget his religion in the hurry of business. "Whether at home or abroad, he was a constant attendant upon public worship and ordinances, notwithstanding the disadvantage under which he labored of hearing but a part of the services." *
In his last illness he observed to his pastor, that it was a happy circumstance that his mind was settled in religion before he was called abroad in the world : otherwise, meeting with so many avocations, and mixing with such different companies, he should have been in danger of remaining unprincipled all his days. I record here his words in the hope, that, by this weighty testimony from a man of years and wisdom and honor, other young men of this town, of the present and in future time, may be led to seek with promptness for themselves this best and only sufficient security for a life guarded from evil, and directed toward the welfare of mankind and the final approval of God.

Judge Holten passed away from the world in the rest of faith, declaring of the great Christian atonement, " It is the foundation of all my hopes."

Judge Holten's homestead, and his residence for the greater part of his life, was not upon the spot where he was born, but at the branching of the roads about a fourth of a mile below the meeting-house, toward the south.† " Holten Street" extends from it through Tapleyville, to the Plain. And to the left of the street, as it enters Tapleyville, is the " Holten ·

---

* " But I should do injustice to the memory of Dr. Holten if I failed to bear testimony to the highest and noblest part of his character : I refer to his Christian piety. He was a man who revered the word and the institutions of God. He was constant and devout in his attendance on divine worship in public and in private life. He was ever alive to the interests of 'pure and undefiled religion,' cheerfully bearing a large share in the support of all Christian institutions, and adorning the profession of his Saviour's name by a life which exhibited in beautiful consistency the Christian virtues and Christian graces, during the whole period of fifty-six years for which he was a member of the church." — REV. ISRAEL W. PUTNAM, *at the Centennial Celebration,* June 16, 1852.

† This house, which before belonged in the Holten Family, was reconstructed and built in part anew either by Judge Holten in his younger life, or by his father, who removed with his family to this place in 1750. It is still standing,

cemetery," which is a gift, in part, from Judge Holten to the neighborhood.

The " Holten High School,"* established by the town in

and is owned by Thomas Palmer.   The spot is often called "The Adams Corner ; " having been long the residence of Israel Adams, whose wife was a granddaughter of Judge Holten.

The late Mr. Philemon Putnam, whose gentlemanly qualities are well remembered among us, was a grandson of Judge Holten ; and the house in which he lived, and which is still occupied by his family, belonged, or the land about it, to Judge Holten's estate.

There is also another grandson of Judge Holten, Capt. Hiram Putnam, now living at Syracuse, N.Y.

* The first session of the Holten High School was held in the spring of 1850, in a room temporarily provided for the purpose.   The salary given to the principal was $750.

The following is a list of the teachers of the High School : —

PRINCIPALS.

JOHN P. MARSHALL (now Professor in Tufts College), May, 1850, to November, 1851.

AMBROSE P. S. STEWART (now Professor in ——— College, Ill.), January, 1852, to October, 1853.

NATHANIEL HILLS (now Principal of High School in Lynn), December, 1853, to June, 1865.

JOHN C. PROCTOR (now Professor in Dartmouth College), August, 1865, to March, 1866.

REV. JAMES FLETCHER (now Principal of Lawrence Academy, Groton), April, 1866, to March, 1871.

O. B. GRANT, April, 1871, to May, 1872.

M. O. HARRINGTON, May, 1872, to November, 1873.

A. W. BACHELER, December, 1873.

ASSISTANTS.

CLARA S. FLINT, during some part of the years 1855 and 1856.

SUSAN SMITH, April, 1860 to June, 1865.

MARY J. THAYER, August, 1865, to March, 1867.

L. A. LORD, April, 1867, one term.

CLARA H. HAPGOOD, August, 1867, to fall of 1868.

(MISS EMMA FELLOWS taught in place of Miss Hapgood, for part of the fall term of 1868.)

HENRIETTA LEAROYD, December, 1868, to March, 1869.

CLARA H. MUDGE, May, 1869, to May, 1871.

LIZZIE S. MERRILL, part of spring term, 1871.

FANNY H. HATCH, August, 1871, to July, 1872.

SARAH F. RICHMOND, August, 1872.

1850, presents in its name another and befitting memorial of this eminent man. The pupils in it, and all our youth, might study with profit the character and life of the person whose name it bears.

There are traces, I think, still to be found of the influence of Judge Holten upon this community. It might be possible, perhaps, to prepare some such fuller account of the man, with incidents of his life, as should restore him to the popular memory, and prolong his power for good among us. It is due to him, if it may be done. It would be assuredly profitable to us. It is a high style of manhood, apt to be rare, and certain to be always needed.

In 1818 a sabbath school was organized in connection with this church. (See Appendix E.).

Dea. Samuel Preston was the first superintendent. The following is a list of the first members of the school, as nearly as can now be ascertained :—

Eben G. Berry,	Daniel Carleton,	George Floyd,
Thomas Flint,	Benj. Flint,	Kendall Flint,
Elbridge Guilford,	Elijah Hutchinson,	Benj. Hutchinson,
Elisha Hutchinson,	Josiah Mudge,	Samuel P. Nourse,
Daniel E. Nourse,	Jonathan Perry,	Jasper Pope,
Zephaniah Pope,	Elijah Pope,	Amos Pratt,
Moses Prince,	Putnam Perley,	Joseph Porter,
David Porter,	William Preston,	Ebenezer Putnam,
Augustus Putnam,	Edwin F. Putnam,	Gustavus Putnam,
Stephen Putnam,	Daniel F. Putnam,	Ahira H. Putnam,
William R. Putnam,	Andrew M. Putnam,	Francis P. Putnam,
Cornelius Roundy,	Eben Swinerton,	David Tapley,
William Walcott,	David Wilkins,	John Martin,
Amos Cross,	Simeon Putnam,	Benjamin Moulton.
George Smith.	James Swinerton.	

Almira P. Batchelder,	Maria Goodale,	Elizabeth Batchelder,
Mehitable Berry,	Eunice Hutchinson,	Elizabeth Chesley,
Hannah Cross,	Clarissa Morse,	Betsey Dale,
Hannah Dale,	Catherine Mudge,	Mehitable Dwinell,
Eunice Evans,	Mary Balch,	Mary Flint,

Sally Guilford,	Phebe Pope,	Mary Ann Putnam,
Augusta Jocelyn,	Ruth F. Prince,	Ruth Parker,
Sally Morse,	Polly Putnam,	Nancy Smith,
Polly Batchelder,	Harriet Putnam,	Salina Wyatt.
Betsey Cross,	Sally Putnam,	Abigail Phelps,
Lydia Dale,	Dolly Smith,	Mary Perry,
Lavinia Evans,	Mary Wilkins,	Charlotte Prince,
Rebecca Fowle,	Mary Sheldon.	Lydia Putnam,
Clarissa Hutchinson,	Ruthy Nourse,	Catherine Putnam,
Mary Jocelyn,	Elizabeth Phelps,	Polly Putnam, 2d,
Sophia Moulton,	Eleanor Plumer,	Mary Roby,
Pamelia Nourse,	Eunice Pope,	Narah Swinerton,
Polly Nourse,	Eunice Prince,	Lucinda Wyatt.
Mary Phelps,	Emma Putnam,	

Of the persons thus named, a few may not perhaps have been members of the school until some months after its opening.

The school thus established has been continued with great interest and profit to the present time.

In 1819 a parish meeting was called for what may appear to us a singular purpose, as expressed in the following article, which was the only one in the warrant: "To choose a moderator :— to see if it be the minds of the Inhabitants that the Rev. Doct. Wadsworth Read a Portion of the scripture at the opening of the meeting at such times as he shall think proper." It was voted that the doctor might do it, both on the sabbath and on "all other Publick Days as in his opinion shall be to the advantage and benefit of the hearers."

The habit of the Puritans in this matter may not be understood by all at the present time. The Puritan studied the Bible as much, at the least, as we do. But he meant to keep clear of every thing that might savor of formalism, or that might ever lead to it, even in the use of the Bible. If the Bible were read in the ordinary sabbath service, and without a free commenting upon it, it might easily come to be done as a mere matter of routine, it was thought, without spirit or present purpose in it. And it might readily enter, along with the reading of set prayers, and the singing of appointed hymns, into the prescribed order of a heartless service. Of such mockery the Puritan would have nothing. So it became usual, in the early New England churches, to read the Bible only in connection with copious comments or explanations, "giving the sense." It was "dumb reading" where these were omitted. But this expository reading, taken with the great length of their sermons and their prayers, must doubtless have become tedious. And for this reason apparently, and because, too, the sermons themselves were largely scriptural, the reading came in many instances to be dispensed with altogether. How far this was done, is a matter with regard to which there is a difference of opinion among those that should be qualified to judge. My belief is, that, with the majority of our churches, the public reading of the Scriptures was dropped during some part of the last century. It has been gradually and universally restored with the prevalence of the better judgment, that a service of such propriety and of such clear and positive good should not be given up for the fear only of evils that are but distantly and doubtfully connected with it.*

And so the long and peaceful ministry of Dr. Wadsworth drew toward its close. His health had been remarkable; and he had never, for more than four or five times, been unable to perform the ordinary duties of the sabbath, until near the end of March, 1825. At about that time began the illness which terminated with his death on the 18th of January in the following year. His age was seventy-five years and nearly six months; and he had been pastor of the church fifty-three years and twenty-six days. Of all the members of the church at the time of his settlement, two only remained, — Hannah Goodale and Lydia Putnam. They were of the young women

---

* It is worthy of notice, that the English Puritans did not commit this inadvertence. In the Directory for Public Worship, prepared by the Westminster Assembly, and afterward approved by the Parliaments both of England and Scotland, it is advised that a chapter should always be read from the Old Testament and from the New.

then for whom those gallery seats had been kept in the old meeting-house at the ordination ; or perhaps they sang that day in the choir. The funeral service was held five days later, on Monday of the next week ; and the sermon was preached by Rev. Samuel Dana, pastor of the First Church in Marblehead.*

The following is the minute made by Eleazer Putnam, Esq., in the records of the church : —

" Rev. Dr. Wadsworth deceased on the 18th of January, A.D. 1826, after a severe illness of ten months. He retained his reason to the last moments of life. He has enjoyed a long and peaceful ministry amongst us. His funeral was attended the 23d inst. by a large concourse of people. The services were solemn, and very appropriate. Rev. Mr. Green addressed the Throne of Grace. Rev. Mr. Dana preached. Rev. Dr. Woods made the last prayer. *Blessed are the dead which die in the Lord.*"

The burial of Dr. Wadsworth was in the cemetery which bears his name. This was an ancient burial-place, originally set apart to that purpose by the Putnam Family ; and though always heretofore belonging to private owners, yet much used by the public, and containing probably more of the graves of those of the earlier generations than any other in the town. This yard Dr. Wadsworth had purchased, during his sickness, of Jonathan Perry ; and had conveyed it to the parish, to whom it still belongs.

Here also is the grave of Mary Hobson, the first wife of Dr. Wadsworth. And it may be interesting to notice, that near by is the monument which he had caused to be erected " In memory of Phebe Lewis, who died Jan. 10th, 1823, aged 49 years ; " and whom he styles " a bright example of integrity and fidelity," and " an ornament to the Christian profession." This Phebe Lewis was a colored woman, a daughter of Han-

---

* From a printed copy of this discourse I have drawn some of these items. For many of the particulars making up the brief personal sketch which is to follow, I am indebted to Dr. Braman, concerning whom it is a matter of much regret, that he might not himself have prepared this account of his predecessor, not to say also this entire publication.

nibal Lewis of Lynn. She had been brought up in the family of Dr. Wadsworth as a servant, and had been for sixteen years a member of this church. Each of the two pastors next preceding had had a corresponding member of his household; and those earlier servants had been "slaves," but the yoke of bondage rested but lightly on them.[*]

Dr. Wadsworth was a man of fine personal appearance, and with the bearing of a thorough gentleman of those days. He is described by the late Judge Samuel Putnam, as "of great bodily vigor, with limbs finely proportioned; about five feet ten inches in height, with a handsome and florid countenance." [†] But there are those of yourselves with whom the figure of this former pastor is still familiar. " I can see him now," says Dea. Samuel Preston,[‡] "precisely at the minute

---

[*] Slaves in Massachusetts were never numerous. They could testify in the courts, serve in the militia, hold property, and be members of the churches. And none were ever *born* to be slaves by law. See PALFREY's *History of New England*, vol. ii. p. 30, note.

[†] Samuel Putnam, son of Dea. Gideon Putnam, occupied the place now owned by Otis F. Putnam, upon Holten Street, just beyond where it passes, by a causeway, through what is still known as "the Judge's Hollow." He was an eminent lawyer, and a solid man. For more than twenty-five years he was a judge of the Supreme Court of the State. He removed his residence from Danvers to Salem; but he kept his pew and paid his tax here so long as Dr. Wadsworth lived, if not somewhat beyond that time, as a mark of his interest in the parish, and his respect for its pastor.

[‡] In the Salem Village Gazette, "published at the Fair of the First Church in Danvers, holden at Village Hall, Dec. 8 and 9, 1869: editors, Augustus Mudge and George Tapley," — vol. i. No. 1.

The pews in the house of 1786 were all square, so that many of the audience sat facing the aisle, or the doors at the entrance. It was easy thus for the minister to notice persons in the congregation as he passed up the aisle

The seats in these pews were hung with hinges, that they might be lifted up for convenience of standing in time of prayer. And Dea. Preston, in the same connection, goes on to say, "This plan was continued a long time in the brick house, even after Mr. Braman was settled. The seats made a great noise when they were all being let down together; sometimes it was like a volley of musketry. At one time a Southern merchant, a Philadelphian, and a customer of mine, was passing the sabbath with me, and I invited him to go to church. It was in Mr. Braman's time; and, as we were returning, he said, 'Well, you have reason to be proud of your minister, but what was that *clapping* for after the prayer?' I told him it was merely letting down the seats, and had no particular meaning. 'Ah! that's it,' said he : 'I thought it was meant for *applause.*'"

appointed, with a dignified step passing up the broad aisle, dressed in surplice and band, cocked hat in hand, the curls of his auburn wig gracefully waving over his shoulders ; slightly recognizing the powdered dignitaries, such as Judge Holten, Judge Collins, and others, as he passed ; ascending with an agile step the stairs of his high pulpit, and taking his seat under the huge canopy or sounding-board which hung suspended over his head."

The doctor was formal and ceremonious, but courteous without exception to all, and warm and kindly, withal, at heart.   He kept his position, as the manner of those times was with ministers, a little apart from his people.   The children looked upon him with a kind of awe ; and the feeling extended to his family, and the house in which he lived.   The lad who drove his cows to their pasture was not expected to enter the yard by the front way.   He could keep persons at a distance from him, whenever he chose to do so, with wonderful civility and ease.   He was reckoned by many to be reserved ; and he was so with many, but not with his intimate friends.   In his intercourse with his brother ministers he was often facetious and witty ; which may be thought a singular circumstance. But even with his fellow ministers he was understood to be a person of dignity.   By one of them, Mr. Huntington of Topsfield, it used to be said that "when any of the brethren called upon Dr. Wadsworth, they were civil enough," but when they came to his house "they threw in their saddles at the front door."   The former part of this only should be believed.

In the management of his worldly affairs the doctor was prudent and methodical.   He had a faculty for business ; and he was shrewd at a bargain, sometimes to a degree beyond what was most suitable.   He was skilled at a trade ; and my informant has added, in a sentence the peculiar humor of which will sufficiently reveal its origin, " I suppose he did not mean to be dishonest ; but men not used to making a bargain, in trading with him were liable to fail."   But, if there was here some slight blemish, it need not be dwelt on.   The doctor had occasion enough, in all the later years of his ministry, to be economical and prudent, with his salary of but three hundred dollars, and some occasional gratuities. He often made representation that his support was inadequate; and it may be that in this single particular, considering the change of times during the long period of his settlement, the parish had not been altogether just toward him. If, therefore, one of these parishioners, in dealing with his pastor, did now and then "fail," it may perhaps have been only by a delicate turn of retribution.

Dr. Wadsworth, as a matter of course in those days, was upon the school-committee of the town; and he had a habit in this connection, which I must unqualifiedly condemn, of expecting the other members of the board to carry him when he went away upon school-business. He was persistent, too, in this, as he was apt to be in other things. He called once at Major Flint's to get his horse for such an errand. It did not happen to be convenient for Mr. Flint to spare the animal. Whereupon the doctor pressed it the more earnestly, saying, "The more difficult and inconvenient it is for you to lend me the horse, the more merit there will be in the act."

Of Dr. Wadsworth's sermons we have had some taste already. And, though they may have been in style sometimes too far elaborate, ornate, and stately, yet they were well studied, clear, and instructive.*

---

* The following is a list of Dr. Wadsworth's publications: —

Sermon upon the Annual Thanksgiving in 1795; and in 1796.

Eulogy upon Gen. Washington, Feb. 22, 1800.

Sermon at the Dedication of the Brick Meeting-House, Nov. 20, 1806.

Sermon before the Bible Society of Salem and Vicinity, April 19, 1815.

Sermon before the Society for "Suppressing Intemperance and other Vices," in the Brick Meeting-House, June 29, 1815.

Sermon at the Installation of Moses Dow at York, Me, 1815.

Sermon at the Burial of Hon. Samuel Holten, Jan. 2, 1816.

Sermon before the "Charitable Female Cent Society" of Danvers and Middleton, in the Brick Meeting-House, Nov. 7, 1816.

Sermon on Account of the Death of Bethiah Sheldon and Benjamin H. Flint, Nov. 19, 1820.

Sermon at the Funeral of Rev. Manasseh Cutler, at Hamilton, 1823.

Sermon at the Ordination of Josiah Babcock, Andover, N.H.

A charge at the Ordination of Israel W. Putnam, March 15, 1815.

There is also a Charge at the Ordination of S. Gile; and a Right Hand at the Ordination of D. Storey, of which I have no further knowledge.

He was conservative in all his tastes and habits, and did not enter readily into new methods. He introduced the observance of the monthly concert near the end of his ministry, held in the afternoon of Monday ; but there were at that time no other prayer-meetings. The weekly meeting on Friday evening dates from the settlement of his successor. The service of public or social prayer by the brethren of the church had fallen, indeed, considerably into disuse at this period ; so that at the establishment of the sabbath school there was some difficulty in finding persons who were willing to offer the opening prayer.

But, if Dr. Wadsworth had the weaknesses of a conservative temper, he had also its strength. He was steady and judicious in his work. He did little that ever needed to be undone, either by himself or by any one else. He was a lover also of peace, and had wisdom to maintain it. He was able in his own life to illustrate, in a good degree, the principles of the religion he taught. He exhibited remarkable patience and calmness in the midst of difficulties, and resignation in times of trial. He had a steadiness of devotion and of trust, the power of which was not lost upon his people. And thus, if in its later years his ministry failed somewhat in general and marked popular effect, it did not lack in thoroughness and beauty of impression upon those that cherished its influences. It was long afterward to be noticed that among those whose lives had been moulded by his ministry, there was to be found a rare and admirable type of Christian character.

It was during this pastorate that the great Unitarian division occurred in Massachusetts. Dr. Wadsworth remained distinctively and strongly upon the old orthodoxy, and yet without entering much into controversy respecting it. At the close of his ministry the new views had spread to a considerable extent in the parish, and there was some danger of division. The solid preaching and judicious management of Dr. Woods of Andover, who supplied the pulpit for a considerable time during the illness of Dr. Wadsworth, and who took some special interest in the welfare of this church, had a decided effect in warding off such a rupture. This is the testimony of Dr. Braman. It ought to be added that both these things, the strong preaching and the wise management in this regard, were continued under the new pastor who soon succeeded to the vacant post.

I have been further informed, by the same authority upon which rests the statement concerning Dr. Woods, that those persons themselves who had been influenced by the new beliefs, and who were desirous of changes to be made in that direction, exhibited, for the most of them, on their part, a commendable spirit of moderation, and a readiness to yield for the sake of peace. And I am glad here to record this testimonial in their behalf.

Milton Palmer Braman was the son of Rev. Isaac Braman and Hannah Palmer Braman of New Rowley, now Georgetown. He was born Aug. 6, 1799; was graduated at Harvard in 1819, and at Andover Theological Seminary in 1824.

He had preached in the place before the death of Dr. Wadsworth; and within five days after the funeral a warrant was issued for a parish meeting to consider the question of his settlement in the ministry. The meeting was held on Tuesday, Feb. 7, and the people were found to be of one mind in favor of the proposition; and they offered a salary equal to about seven hundred dollars besides the use of the parsonage land.

It is an interesting circumstance, indicating both the promptness of the movement and the heartiness with which it was made, that upon the church record, immediately after the memorandum already quoted respecting the decease of Dr. Wadsworth, and as part apparently of the same entry, there are added the lines: " O that the Lord would give us thankful hearts for His goodness in sending us one of His servants whom we trust will feed his flock in this place with the sinsear milk of the word; and has so far united our hearts in Christian charity as to accept of him; and that his heart is inclined to labor amongst us."

The ordination took place on the 12th of April. The opening prayer was offered by Rev. Israel W. Putnam of Portsmouth.* The sermon was preached by the father of the pas-

* Israel Warburton Putnam was the son of Eleazer and Sarah F. Putnam, and was born Nov. 24, 1786. His father, "'Squire Eleazer," as he was commonly called, — though with the name often shortened from this, — lived at the place now owned by S. B. Swan. He was a man of capacity and of note in the parish and the town. He was clerk of the church in the interval after the death of Dr. Wadsworth; and he has left upon the book as fine specimens of the work of a recording officer as can readily be found.

The young man, his son, having become fitted for college, not without the exercise of vigor and the practice of economy, entered at Harvard in 1805. Becoming involved there in the great "bread-and-butter rebellion," he removed to Dartmouth; wresting his certificate of regular standing from the Harvard faculty by force of law, and graduating with credit in 1809. He then entered upon the study of law at Salem, with his relative and friend Judge Samuel Putnam. But becoming decided in his hopes and purposes as a Christian, in connection with the ministrations of the elder Dr. Worcester, and through the Christian friendliness especially of Dr. R. D. Mussey, he afterward determined to become a preacher. Toward this conclusion his father helped him, when others, and the Andover professors among them, doubted. He graduated at Andover in 1814. In March of the next year he became pastor of the First Church in Portsmouth, N.H. The charge to the pastor, on this occasion, was given by Dr. Wadsworth, who was also moderator of the council. The spread of Unitarian sentiments in the parish had made the position one of great difficulty. Mr. Putnam discharged its duties with fidelity and with excellent judgment. After a successful ministry of twenty years, having a wish to promote the union of another church in Portsmouth with his own, he resigned his pastorate. Shortly after, in October, 1835, he was installed at Middleborough in this State. Here he continued to the end of his life. But in 1865, having completed fifty years in the ministry, he desired to be relieved from its labors; and a colleague was soon after settled. He died at Middleborough, in the fulness of age, May 3, 1868..

He was a wise and good man.

The sermon at his funeral was preached by Dr. Henry M. Dexter of Boston. And from a printed copy of this discourse, which has the merit, rare on such occasions, of setting forth little or nothing that is not true, and which is a model of its kind, I have gathered the main facts given in this note. The Congregational Quarterly for October, 1868, contains also a somewhat fuller sketch by the same hand. But memories of Dr. Putnam are fresh also and fragrant in his native town. He took a lively interest in all that belonged to this place, and he had a special love for this ancient church. Had his life been prolonged to the present time, there could have been no one whose contributions would have added more of value to this occasion than his.

I have myself the most pleasing recollections of the venerable man, and could have wished to have known him more.

Dr. Putnam had a sister, Miss Betsey F. Putnam, who was afflicted with deafness for many years, but who maintained to a remarkable degree an intelligent and a genuinely Christian interest in all that went on around her. The later years

tor. The consecrating prayer was by Rev. Mr. Briggs of Boxford ; the charge — to the pastor, as I suppose — by Rev. Mr. Walker of the South Parish ; the right hand of fellowship by Rev. Mr. Boardman of Boylston ; and the concluding prayer by Rev. Mr. Perry of Bradford.

Mr. Braman married, Nov. 15, 1826, Mary, daughter of John Parker of East Bradford, now Groveland. There being at this time no parsonage, they occupied part of the Adams house, at the corner below the meeting-house.

Of the distinctively personal characteristics of the pastorate thus established, I shall not speak at length ; both because the topic has been with propriety assigned to another, a son of the parish, and reared under Dr. Braman's ministry,* and

of her life she spent at Middleborough ; but she never omitted to provide for continuing her own contribution, in connection with this church, to the various benevolent objects that were presented.

Esquire Eleazer Putnam being thus brought to mind with his family, I am moved to record an incident which I have heard related along with the mention of his name, though its connection with him may possibly be apocryphal. I have been unable of late to distinguish the man from whom it was received. Mr. Swan declines distinctly to acknowlege or indorse it ; or would refer it, perhaps, to the Deacon Eleazer of an earlier century. But, while Mr. Swan thus speaks, history cannot be so be so thwarted and turned from its ends. And, though the father of this story, — who is not herein, I trust, the father of aught but the truth, — has abandoned it, yet I cannot suffer it to perish.

'Squire Eleazer had, therefore, in his family, a negro man, to whom, when he was himself away, the care of matters about the place was left. Being one day from home, an unscrupulous hog he had broke from her pen, and was found of the negro in the vegetable garden. To get her out was not easy ; for the creature would drive no better than a hog. The patience of the man — who had never been made to write a history of this parish — was spent. He went hard after her with a club, and hit her upon the head. The blow fell, unluckily, upon that spot whereat her vital principle as a hog was least defended ; and the usefulness of the beast in that capacity had there an instant end. The negro awaited with misgivings his master's return, and was at hand to tell him that the hog had been in the garden, he was plagued to get her out, she had eaten the cabbages and the squashes and the cucumbers. "Been in the garden !" cried the 'Squire, "eaten the cabbages ! Why didn't you *kill her?*" "Massa," said the man, beginning to recover again, we may think, that air of hopefulness and conscious worth that belongs with his race, "I DID, *sir !*"

* See the remarks of Rev. Hiram B. Putnam, in the account of the afternoon exercises.

because with most of you the man himself is freshly in mind; and since also these matters concerning him are not as yet, happily, among the subjects of history. His rare native endowments, his thorough scholarship, his keen and abounding wit, his logical acumen, his power in the pulpit, and his ample furnishing for every ministerial work, — these, we trust, may not for yet many years of his honored life have place with the topics of the past.

The " Half-way Covenant " was abolished by the church immediately after Dr. Braman's settlement. It had fallen somewhat into disuse before that time. But through the whole period, since its introduction during the ministry of Mr. Green, more than five hundred persons had " owned " this form of covenant.

The efforts of Dr. Wadsworth and his associates had not freed the community from the evils of intemperance. The mischief, indeed, was widely spread and deeply seated throughout the land. There is no reason to think that this parish was peculiarly infected with the vice. On the contrary, the people, taken as a whole, were in good repute for sobriety, according to the standards of that time; but the neighborhood at the Centre was then an exception. At this particular locality, the intemperate men outnumbered the sober. Dr. Braman dealt faithfully with the evil. His pungent sermons on the subject are still remembered, along with the flashes of humor with which they were enlivened. It is related of him that, on one occasion, having referred to the popular notion that strong drinks were able to give coolness or warmth, as either might be needed, he observed that, if these liquors had indeed any such power to afford heat, " it would be perpetual summer about this meeting-house."

The great temperance reformation, which had begun earlier, but with some lack of decision and vigor, was now ready to press its work throughout New England with more of thoroughness and force. It was entered upon with energy in this place; and its effects here were happy and permanent. For many years in the past, and to the present time, our community has been to a remarkable degree exempted from the ravages of this vice, with its allied mischiefs and miseries. But yet the evil is still such that constant watch must be kept upon it.

Early in Dr. Braman's ministry, the method of raising money for parish expenses underwent a total change. From early times in Massachusetts, parishes had been territorial; that is, all property lying within certain bounds had been taxed for the support of preaching and for other parochial charges. The limits of the parish were usually the same with the town; and the parish was thus, in fact, only the town acting in that particular capacity. This was different with us; since here from the first organization of Salem Village in 1672, there had never been the same bounds for the town and the parish. But the parish was a territorial one not the less; and persons and property within its limits were subject to taxation to meet all charges connected with the support of preaching. The preaching thus maintained had been in the Congregational order, though in many parishes in the later years by no means always "orthodox."

In the earlier periods this had been no hardship. The people of the Colony were nearly all Congregationalists by choice. Congregationalists owned the land absolutely. They owned it by grant from the English crown; by purchase, in part, from the Indians; and by actual occupation. Their legal title to exclusive possession was complete. The moral right seemed to them not less clear. The improvements, the public works, the institutions of society that gave value to the soil, were at their hands and of their creation. It was not strange, therefore, that the ecclesiastical system of the Colony should have been planted upon this foundation, and that it should have been upheld by laws laying contributions upon all the inhabitants. For this latter feature, indeed, there was not, probably, at that time a Christian people anywhere in the world that did not in like manner maintain by public law some form of religious worship and teaching.

9

With an enlarging population, and with the wider opening of the country on every side, the ideas of exclusive ownership were subjected to change. The practical working of the original parochial system became also a matter of grievance to an increasing number of individuals, who desired either to contribute to some other religious denomination or to none at all.

Relief was granted to the former class first. For a hundred years before the point to which this narration has been brought, there had been some provisions by which a man might have his parish tax remitted, or directed rather toward the support of preaching in some other than a Congregational church. But such provisions were made at first with reluctance, and were hedged about with difficulties. They grew gradually more broad and generous, until, from a period near the end of the last century, there was no serious legal obstacle in the way of any person's paying his assessment wherever he chose.*

Payment, however, in some direction might still be required. And it was not until the first third of the present century had passed, that the State let go altogether its purpose of furnishing some enforced support to the institutions of religion.

In this parish the last rate, or tax, was laid in 1828. For a few years after that time money was raised by subscription. In 1838 an act of incorporation was obtained from the legislature ; and that which since the organization of the town had been known as the North Parish, — the old first territorial parish of Salem Village, — became the "First Religious Society in Danvers." To this purely voluntary society, as to others like it elsewhere, the name of "parish" is still often applied, but with a wide departure from its original meaning.

Under the new arrangement, money for current expenses has been raised with us mainly by a tax upon the pews in the meeting-house, but in part also by subscriptions.

It is pleasant to note the change upon the parish records,

---

* These statements would need some modification if the subject were to be treated in fulness. What I have said is, of necessity, but general. Thus qualified, it will not be found untrue.

and the dropping out of the old familiar entry of the warrant issued to the collector, authorizing him, like the town collectors, in case of refusal or neglect to pay, to make "distraint upon the goods and chattels" of the delinquent; or, in lack of these, "to take the body of such person or persons so refusing or neglecting to pay, and him or them commit to the common gaol in the county, there to remain until he or they shall pay the same, or such part thereof as shall not be abated." The concluding clause was terrible chiefly in its sound; but it was out of its place, nevertheless, in all such records.

While the matter is thus before us, it ought to be said, that this maintenance by the State of religious worship did not rest in theory upon the benefits of a purely personal or spiritual nature, to be thus secured. A public advantage rather was aimed at. Nor was the end chiefly the strengthening of the church, as an institution, for its own sake. It was for the use of the church, and of religious teaching, towards the State itself. The State undertook to strengthen the church, that the church in turn might uphold the State. Thus understood, the purpose was legitimate, and was within the proper sphere of political action. The error withal was not in the belief that the influences of religion are essential to the well-being of society, — a conviction that we hold not less stoutly than our fathers; but in the supposition that these influences can be made more effective by the effort of society in a compulsory manner to strengthen them. The State has need of the church; but it cannot in this way help the church to be any more useful to itself. Religion has its own sources of power, which are not of this world. It is most strong when it draws nigh to them. It suffers loss if it turns to other reliances. It is apt thus to be enfeebled, and not invigorated by any union with the civil power.

The trial was made in New England under the most favorable circumstances; and a careful review of it will confirm this conclusion. Religion was wonderfully powerful in this land in the earlier periods. But there are no evidences that the attempted interference of the secular authority in its behalf ever added to its real efficiency. On the other hand,

there are the most certain marks of injury done to the cause
of religion, when the fruits of that policy had time to ripen.
Under the Providence of God we owe our liberty, and all our
public blessings, largely to our religion, so far free ; but
to this blemish upon it, we owe nothing, except it be the
thankfulness with which we may contemplate its removal.

For our own denomination, it may be added, that its strength
is in its freedom ; and that it suffered a peculiar injury through
this effort to give it special assistance.   Even in a pecuniary
point of view alone, and as to "orthodox" Congregationalism,
when we remember how many of these churches, early in
the present century, lost their share in their parish meeting-
houses, and parsonages, and were despoiled even of their own
church records and sacramental furniture, through this relation into which they had been brought with the towns, we
may conclude that such "assistance" did not prove highly
profitable.

In this particular locality, and from the history of our own
parish, it is certain that there were many vexations and an-
noyances arising from the system of general taxation for the
support of preaching.   And the business has been conducted
with much more of ease and comfort since that system has
passed away.

The year 1831 is memorable among us for a great revival
of religion, the most extensive and powerful that the place
has ever known.   A preaching service was held for four days
consecutively.   The whole community was moved, and yet
not in noisy excitement.   The thoughts of men were turned
in a serious and becoming manner to the care of their souls.
The Spirit of God was with them.   Numbers were led to
enter upon a new life of Christian love and obedience.   The
work with many was thorough ; and its results have been
happy and lasting.

There were added to the church, in the year 1831, twenty-
nine persons, most of them by profession ; and in the next
year, eighty-three persons.

Previous to these additions the church had been much reduced in membership. In 1828 there were reported, of male members, 25 ; of females, 75. A total of 100. Members living out of the town were of course included ; and as the counting of such is often uncertain, and as these have some appearance of being "round numbers," it is likely that the actual membership may have fallen a little short of one hundred.

In 1833 the number had risen to 195. Sixty years before, at the settlement of Dr. Wadsworth, the figures had been, of male members, 45 ; of females, 90 ; making a total of 135.

The business affairs of the parish were conducted at this time with a vigor that corresponded with, and no doubt in part resulted from, the enlargement and quickening of the church. After the death of Dr. Wadsworth, who lived in his own house, the want of a parsonage had again been felt. The old "ministry land" remained in possession of the parish, but with no buildings upon it.

There was a dwelling directly across the road, north-west from the meeting-house, which, for more reasons than one, it was desirable now to obtain. This was upon the place formerly owned by Dea. Nathanael Ingersoll. The property had passed through many hands. The deacon himself held it by a title covering only his own life, and by which he was not empowered to transmit it to any except his children. He had no children, save that he adopted into his family Benjamin Hutchinson, a son of Joseph Hutchinson, his neighbor on the east. As he drew near to the close of his long life, he appears to have forgotten the peculiarity of the title ; or, perhaps, he may never have fully understood it ; or he may have supposed that the formality of adoption met the conditions of the case ; and he undertook to convey the real estate to his adopted son. But this failed. The death of Dea. Ingersoll occurred not far from the beginning of the year 1719. The heirs at law, from the line of a former generation, took steps to recover the property. The lands which Dea. Ingersoll had given for the meeting-house, and the training-field, with others, were involved. These titles were finally settled. And the main property, including the homestead, passed, in 1733, by sundry conveyances, into the family of Samuel Ingersoll of Marblehead. The husbands of his daughters, as I suppose, Eben. Hawkes, and Samuel Pope, of Marblehead, conveyed it three years after to " Joseph Cross, of Salem, mariner." From him it passed to his son, Michael, who lived upon it ; and who transferred it by deed, in 1783, just before his death, to Nathaniel Pope.*

From the heirs of Mr. Pope it passed, in 1802, into possession of Ebenezer Goodale, commonly known in later years by his title of " General." Gen. Goodale occupied the place for about thirty years. He was a man of considerable capacity, and inclined to enter extensively upon business of various sorts. He made his mark in the neighborhood ; and not for good. His house was in some manner a tavern, and, of course, a place for the sale of strong drink, and of resort for men that liked it. And the general himself became one of his own customers, and he was a leader in many ways among the rest.† He carried on the business of a wholesale butcher. He had a group of slaughter houses, not sightly nor savory, upon " Watch-House Hill ;" and herds of sheep, hogs, and men, with habits commendable in the order in which they have been named, swarmed about the premises. As this establishment was so near to the meeting-house, and as its occupations were not varied for the better on the sabbath days, it became a source of great annoyance to the people of the parish. The habits of the patriarch himself did not improve with years ; nor did his business prosper. He mortgaged the place to Elizabeth

---

* Grandfather of the present Nathaniel Pope ; also of Jasper and Zephaniah, and of the late Elijah Pope.

† It is told of him, that at one period of his life, having occasion to reckon with the store-keeper, of whom he had his supplies for family and personal use, he objected to the account as too large, and asked for the reading of the items. The account began: " Rum, rum, tobacco, rum, tobacco, rum, rum, tobacco, rum." The general said they need read no further, — he guessed the bill was right.

Williams of Salem ; and, as he proved unable to retain it, she took possession. The opportunity had been waited for, and the property passed at once, by deed of date May 26, 1832, to " Moses Putnam, Samuel Preston, Gilbert Tapley,* and their associates, for a parsonage."

The old house of Dea. Ingersoll was standing in 1733. A new one, and that which is still upon the spot, was built probably within twenty years from that time. This second house, however, underwent extensive repairs and alterations upon

---

* This name first appears in the parish records about the middle of the last century. The spelling of the first name was often "Gilbord," with other like variations. A Gilbert Tapley, "house-wright," then of Salem, was married June 17, 1747, to Phebe Putnam. In August of the same year he bought for £2,010 (old tenor), sixty-seven acres of land, bounded by the Ipswich River, by lands of Amos Buxton, Joshua Swinerton, Ambrose Hutchinson, Wm. Small, and Ebenezer Goodale, and by a way, part of which is now "Buxton's Lane." The house, which was the original seat of the Tapley family in Danvers, stood near the Andover Turnpike, a little distance to the south-east from where Wm. Goodale now lives.

There was a Gilbert Tapley in Salem, a hundred years before, with Gilberts plentifully along the line between. But Mr. George Tapley, who has furnished me with this account, has not yet traced distinctly the succession. His is still engaged upon the matter ; and I cheerfully welcome him to some share in these delightful employments.

From the pair whose marriage has been given, have descended all of the name now living in this town, with many that have gone abroad, and with many others, also, of other names.

From Amos, the first of their eight children, we have the families of the late Aaron and Rufus Tapley ; and also a daughter, Mrs. Betsey Nichols, still living, the mother of Capt. Amos Pratt.

From Asa, the sixth child, there are of the Tapley name, now living in the parish, and heads of families, Col. Gilbert, with his son, Gilbert Augustus ; the sons of the late Daniel, George, and Charles, with Herbert S., son of George ; and Col. Jesse. And of this branch of the family there are many in the parish now bearing other names.

The memory of the present Gilbert Tapley has brought down to us an incident from the life of his grandfather, the original Danvers Gilbert, illustrative also of those times, which I tell as it has been told to me. When he was but four years old, he was standing by his grandfather's knee, and the old man said to him, "Gebbard, I will show you how to make a cider-tap. First, make it four square, and tapered to a point ; then cut off the corners, and make it eight square ; and then any fool can round it off and make a cider-tap." The value of the direction for the matter in hand, no one may gainsay ; but it could hardly have had any special significance in the childhood of one who was to be so stout an enforcer of the "prohibitory law."

its coming into possession of the parish. An addition was made along the whole length at the rear, by which the thickness or width of the main building was increased. Thus remodelled and improved, it was first occupied by Dr. Braman on the 8th of January, 1833 ; and it has furnishèd a comfortable home for the family of the parish minister to the present time.

Of the several pieces of land belonging to this Ingersoll estate, at the time of its purchase, there was permanently retained by the parish only that portion to the north from the meeting-house upon which the buildings stood, and which was bounded by Center, Hobart, and Forest Streets, and by the old ministry land.

The money for this purchase was raised by contribution ; and the chief contributors were Mrs. Mehitable Oakes, widow of Caleb Oakes, and her daughters.* These persons received the thanks of the parish for their "very liberal donations."

At about the same time Moses Putnam, Gilbert Tapley, and Samuel Preston also bought what was called the "Rea lot," lying at the east of the meeting-house, for the purpose of confirming a doubtful title to the land purchased thirty years before for the horse-sheds. The field passed into the hands of the parish, but was soon disposed of.

In 1832 there was formed the Ladies' Benevolent Circle, originally styled "The North Danvers Female Benevolent Society," of which Mrs. Braman was the first president, and Miss Susan Putnam the secretary. The primary object of this society at first was, the relief of the poor by aid in the furnishing of clothing. The purpose of charity in some form towards the poor, it has never forgotten ; but it has turned its helpful hand also toward many other good works, both at home and abroad. Scarcely any considerable parish enterprise has been carried on without its assistance in some form. Its yearly boxes or barrels, well filled with clothing, and other valuable articles for domestic use, have carried gladness and comfort into many households of our home missionaries, in

---

* The daughters were Nancy and Mehitable. Of these, the last-named became the wife of Mr. John S. Williams of Salem. She was a member of this church, and was dismissed by letter to the Crombie-street Church in Salem.

Massachusetts and at the West. And the letters that have come to us in reply have been read among ourselves, not seldom with tears.

The meetings also of this Ladies' Circle, whether held with the different members, or, as often of late years, in the vestry of the meeting-house, have furnished the occasions for much pleasant social intercourse between the people of the parish.*

The want of a suitable place for prayer-meetings, and for other similar purposes, began to be felt as such meetings became more frequent. The meeting-house had but one room ; and that much too large for these uses. In 1834 arrangements were made for building "a vestry or chapel." An association was formed of persons who took such number of shares in the work as they pleased, at five dollars each. The Ladies' Society took ten shares ; the choir of singers, eight. The building was to be used for religious meetings ; for meetings of the sabbath school, and of all benevolent societies ; for singing schools, and meetings of the choir, and for "a high school." This "North Danvers Chapel Society" was organized by the choice of Samuel Preston, Gilbert Tapley, and Matthew Putnam, as standing committee ; with Samuel Preston for secretary and treasurer. Samuel Preston, Jesse Putnam, and John Preston were chosen a building committee. The chapel was put up the next year upon a site where traces may still be

---

* There had been an earlier organization somewhat similar, dating from 1816, and styled "The Danvers and Middleton Society for Promoting Christian Knowledge and Piety." I am not able to give a very exact account of this society, though some of its records are still in existence. It was before this society, undoubtedly, that Dr. Wadsworth preached the sermon, now extant, of Nov. 7, 1816 : on the title page of which publication it is called the "Charitable Female Cent Society in Danvers and Middleton."

Fifty cents a year was paid by each member ; and collections were also systematically taken, and forwarded to the parent body, which was styled "The Massachusetts Society for Promoting Christian Knowledge." The remittances for the first year amounted to $88. And there were 142 members. The meetings were held only annually. I do not know how long it continued in existence. It is worthy of notice, chiefly as showing the rising spirit of interest in benevolent operations at that period, and as a kind of forerunner of the present Ladies' Society, and also of such organizations as the "Woman's Board of Missions."

seen, on the parish grounds, a little to the east of the parsonage, and fronting upon Hobart Street. It was a one-story
building, forty feet by twenty-six, raised upon an embankment,
with a basement or cellar beneath it, upon which lower level
was also an entry-way, with passage from it by stairs to the
main room. This embankment was raised by the singers,
who discharged thus their subscription to the stock.

The chapel served for many years all its intended uses ;
including at different times that of a place for a private or
"select" school. In 1864 changes upon the meeting-house,
which would make it no longer needed, being in contemplation,
the chapel society surrendered it to the parish, the parish passed
it into the hands of its committee of repairs, its value went
afterwards into the new rooms beneath the present house, and
the chapel itself, in 1871, was sold to Mr. George B. Martin, and
by him removed to the rear of his residence, where it remains
in use as a carriage and store-house. If the embankment be
now the property of the singers, and if that Orphic lyre, by
which the stones might be moved, is still in use among them,
there will be no objection on the part of the parish minister
to their practising with it upon that very spot.*

Scarcely had the chapel been finished before a certain
cracking and settling of the walls of the Brick Meeting-house,
which had for years been noticed, became too serious, it was
thought, to be longer neglected. The building was adjudged
unsafe. In 1838, immediately upon the acceptance of the act
incorporating the society upon its new basis, as already mentioned, measures were taken for the erection of a new house.
The old house was demolished, The work on this building,
specially at the foundation, was not supposed to have been
done in the most orthodox fashion ; nor were the bricks re-

* May 27, 1874. By a company of working men of the parish, including the
minister, this embankment has been levelled, and what remained of those un-
counted stones removed and set for the foundation of a side-walk along Hobart
Street, by "the ministry pasture." The work was done in much good-will ; but

"With other notes than to the Orphean lyre."

garded as of the soundest quality. But when it was undertaken to pull it down, it was found that there had gotten in
some way more of Calvinism into that meeting-house than
had been thought for. If it had been let alone it might doubtless have stood to this day. But this was not apparent before
the trial was made ; and the " young men," as they are styled
upon the parish records, who were most efficient in pushing
forward the new work, are still to be commended for judgment as well as spirit.

The vote, in fact, was unanimous. Jesse Putnam, Samuel
Preston, William Preston, Nathaniel Pope, Peter Cross, Daniel
F. Putnam, and John Preston, were chosen as building committee. A year later Nathan Tapley was chosen to fill the
place made vacant by the death of Daniel F. Putnam. Levi
Preston was master carpenter. The work was done by the
day ; and this time, beyond a doubt, it was strong and
thorough. The cost was about twelve thousand dollars.

The dimensions of the building then constructed, and still
standing, are 84 feet in length, by 60 in breadth.

The pulpit, as originally built, was high, and enclosed in
front. It was lowered, and put in its present form, in 1864.*

The new house was built with a basement story, in which
was finished one large room for a sabbath school and for other
public uses. This was named VILLAGE HALL. The designation, though still in use, appears of late to be growing somewhat less familiar. It is desirable that it should be preserved.
It was designed, no doubt, to commemorate the ancient *Salem
Village.* And it is nearly all that now remains to us of that
locally historic title.

The house was dedicated Nov. 21, 1839. The sermon, by
Dr. Braman, was from Titus i. 3 ; and was an elaborate and
very able presentation of the power of " the preached gospel,
considered in relation to the obstacles to its success and support."

---

* Of the pillars that stood in the front of the original pulpit, by the doors on
either side, one is now preserved in the present vestry. In the same room is
also a book-case made of the pulpit materials, and having upon it one of the
pulpit doors.

Subjoined is also a plan of the audience-room, with the number and valuation of the pews, and the names of the present owners, but with no note of pews rented.

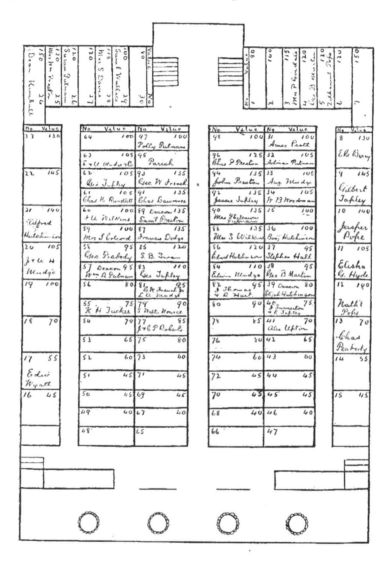

Mention should be made among these signs of vigor and growth, of the establishment, somewhat later, in 1848, of the "Ministerial Library." Some suggestion in "The Boston

Recorder" had taken root in the mind of Dea. Ebenezer Putnam ; and to him we owe the founding of the library. Sixty dollars were appropriated at first by the church for the purchase of books. Sums, varying from ten to twenty-five dollars, have been added annually. The library, designed for the pastor's use, is the property of the church ; and it numbers now somewhat above two hundred volumes. Saving a few that have been received by gift, and, indeed, including some of these, the books have been chosen with care ; and the collection is of great and increasing value. A like method might be followed in many other of our country parishes, to the great advantage of all concerned.

It is the purpose of the present pastor to collect and deposit in this library, as far as they can be procured, the printed sermons and other published works of his predecessors, and whatever further memorials of them he may be able to discover. The universal helpfulness of the Ladies' Circle, it should be added, has shown itself with respect to this library also, in the furnishing of valuable cases for the books.

In the early part of his ministry, and for many years, Dr. Braman suffered from ill health. In 1840 he proposed a dissolution of the pastoral relation on this ground. But he was persuaded to take leave of absence from his work instead. He spent several months in Europe ; and found benefit with rest and change ; but especially by the slow and stormy passage in a sailing vessel, through which he underwent, as he judged, something like renewal.

The period of the great discussion upon American slavery was just opening ; and when the doctor came back to his parish, strengthened from the perils of the sea, it was to encounter some waves of the political tempest upon the shore. Dr. Braman himself regarded slavery as an " atrocious system," — " an abominable system of oppression and mischief," — " one of the heaviest curses that ever afflicted man or provoked

Heaven." *   But he did not approve of the particular measures
that some were ready to adopt for its removal.   His course in
declining to give from the pulpit certain political notices led
to the passage by the society, in 1841, of the following vote :
" Resolved, that our ordained minister does, and of right ought,
to stand before his people in the discharge of the duties of his
office in a free and independent pulpit ; that we approve the
stand he has taken in the communication read to us yesterday,
so far as relates to the giving of notices ; and that we adopt
the same as the rule by which we wish him to be governed
while God shall spare him to labor amongst us." The resolution was adopted by a vote of fory-three to five.

In 1843, and again in 1845, Dr. Braman renewed his request for a dismissal.   At the time last named it seemed
likely that his purpose to leave could not be shaken.   The
parish voted a reluctant assent.   The doctor himself preached
a parting sermon, to which the memories of his hearers have
not yet bidden farewell.   But the strong desire of the people,
supported by the unanimous advice of a mutual council, prevailed at length, and happily, to secure his continuance in the
ministry.

The period through which we are passing was one of great
prosperity for the business interests of Danvers ; and the
modern growth and development of the town may date from
about these years.

The shoemaking industry, now one of the leading interests
of the town, had been planted in the place from near the beginning of the century.†   Before that time shoes had been
made only for home use.   But new markets were opening ;
and the men of Danvers had the sagacity and energy to enter
upon them.   Caleb Oakes and Moses Putnam were prominent

---

    * Discourse on the Annual Fast, 1847, p. 21.
    † The materials under this head were furnished and arranged chiefly by Mr.
Augustus Mudge.   For a fuller statement of the growth of the shoe-trade in
Danvers, see Appendix C, prepared by Mr. Edwin Mudge.

among the early manufacturers. The goods made were mostly of the coarser sort, for the Southern slaves. They were sent chiefly in coasting vessels; but, during the war of 1812, they were carried to some extent by horse-teams fitted out from this place. Col. Gilbert Tapley, and others now living, were once engaged in this variety of commerce. At first the fastening of the sole upon the shoe was always done by sewing. Within twenty-five years some experiments were made in the use of wooden pegs; and machines began soon to be thought of for that purpose. Dea. Samuel Preston obtained the first patent ever granted for a pegging-machine. The document, signed by Andrew Jackson, bears date March 8, 1833. This machine was arranged to put two rows of pegs upon each side of the shoe at the same time. It did not come into general use; but the principle involved is found in all later machines.

The manufacture was not carried on in this part of the parish, now known as the Center District, until about 1835. James Goodale, Otis Mudge, and others, began then to make ladies' and children's shoes of a finer grade, sending them to Boston for distribution from that point. This was done at first on a small scale; but the business has since greatly increased. In 1854 there were in the town, within its present limits, thirty-five firms engaged in this business, making annually 1,562,000 pairs, valued at $1,072,258, and giving employment to about 2,500 persons, — men and women.

The use of machinery in the work has increased year by year; though the most radical changes in this respect date from about 1860. Machines are now employed at almost every step. The manual labor required has been reduced one-half. This general introduction of machinery has tended to the concentration of the business in large places, and large shops; and in so far the effect is unfavorable, as compared with the older and simpler methods, which allowed the workman to remain in his own house. Production being also carried on with greater rapidity, the workmen are usually left without employment for considerable periods in each year. This very great evil may not prove to be of necessity involved in the system; and it is to be hoped it will not be permanent.

Danvers shoes have always borne a good reputation in the markets of the country ; and they have in general deserved it. But this is only comparative. As minister of the parish, I will not affirm that they are as yet, in all cases, constructed upon no other than Christian principles.

The modern village at the Plain may date, in its beginning, from about the year 1830. It suffered a severe check by a great conflagration on the 10th of June, 1845. The opening to that point of the Essex Railroad, leading from Salem to Lawrence, July 4, 1848, aided opportunely in its recovery and in its subsequent rapid growth. The road from Newburyport and Georgetown through Danvers to the line of the Boston and Maine Railroad, at South Reading, now Wakefield, opened for public travel in June, 1855, assisted in the same direction.

That portion of the town has continued to grow in population and in relative importance. There have been set the various public buildings and institutions that belong with the centre of a town. The First National Bank, formerly the Village Bank, was established in 1836. The present building was erected in 1854. The Savings Bank, kept in the same rooms, was established in 1850. The Town Hall, in which are also the rooms occupied by the Holten High School, was built in 1854, and was first occupied at the annual meeting, March 5, 1855.

In the same building there was opened, in 1857, the Danvers branch of the Peabody Library. This library, the gift of George Peabody, Esq., a native of Danvers, and afterward a banker in London, whose large donations in money have made his name memorable, was first established in South Danvers. His birthplace had been in that portion of what was then the undivided town. As the library thus placed did not accommodate the inhabitants at the North, arrangement was made for this branch. Subsequently large additional sums were given by Mr. Peabody ; and the institutions in the two towns were made independent, each of them being liberally endowed. The present building of the Peabody Institute, upon the Park to the south of the Town House, was erected in

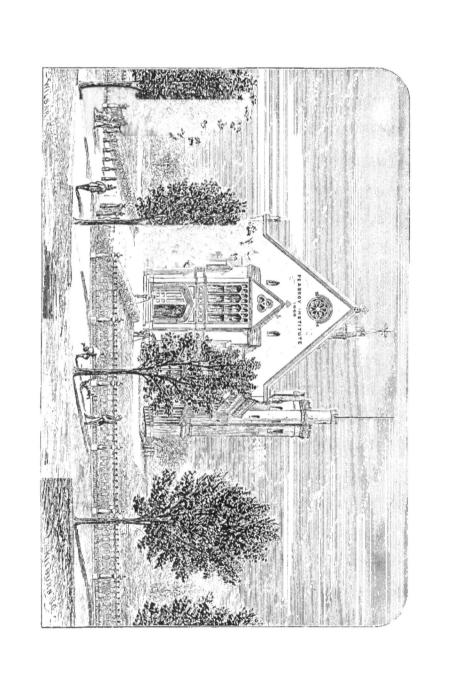

PEABODY INSTITUTE
1869

1869. The library now contains about seven thousand yolumes. The building has also an audience hall, in which courses of free lectures are given each year. The permanent funds of the Institute amount to about sixty-six thousand dollars.

With the growth of this village at the Plain, and the establishment there of a new centre of the town, the relative importance of the former and original centre has diminished, and it cannot be expected that it will ever be restored. We take, therefore, this period of twenty or thirty years now under review, having its middle point between the years 1840 and 1850, as a kind of transition period in the history of Danvers. Before this time, and for two hundred years from its first settlement, the territory had been known as the Farms, the Village, or Salem Village, or the North Parish ; and its public centre and place of gathering had been at or near the spot where the meeting-house now stands. The seat of business was then removed. The ancient names, ceasing to have significance, were dropped from use. They are now rapidly passing even from memory. And so swift are these changes with the changing generations, that but a small proportion, it may be thought, of the present inhabitants of our town have any distinct knowledge of that earlier and original order of things which characterized by far the greater part of its history.

This church and society, with its records and its name, is now the chief remaining memorial of all that former order and age.

With the increasing population at the Plain, there arose a desire for the establishment of public worship in that locality. Accordingly, at a meeting held in the schoolhouse, March 25, 1844, there was organized the "Third Orthodox Congregational Society in Danvers." Benjamin Turner, Samuel Brown, and Nathaniel Silvester were chosen standing committee ; and Moses J. Currier, treasurer and collector.* A meeting-

* These details are drawn mainly from an unpublished historical sketch, prepared by Dea. S. P. Fowler, for the twenty-fifth anniversary of the organization of the Maple-street Church.

10

house was erected the same year, upon the site now occupied. The first meeting was held in the basement, which was then named Granite Hall, Nov. 4; and the house itself was dedicated on the 22d of January following. The sermon on this occasion was by Rev. Lorenzo Thayer, who preached several months for the society. Meanwhile, the preliminary steps having been taken, a church was organized Dec. 5, 1844, with forty-two members.

"Most of these persons," says Dea. Fowler, "and many others who joined the church, were dismissed from the First Church in this town, of which Rev. Dr. Braman was then pastor." And he adds the filial and fraternal testimony, that, "Whatever of zeal and efficiency we may have shown in establishing and maintaining the ordinances of the gospel in this place, may be traced to the thorough teachings we received from the able and faithful pastors of the mother church."

Frederick Howe and Samuel P. Fowler were chosen deacons, the former having held the same office in the first church; and to them was added, in 1864, John S. Learoyd.

Rev. Richard Tolman, the first pastor of the church, was ordained Sept. 17, 1845. He resigned Nov. 8, 1848. To him succeeded, June 20, 1849, Rev. James Fletcher. The society had in these years its share of the difficulties belonging to a new enterprise, aggravated in this case by the losses in the great fire of 1845. On the 10th of July, 1850, the meeting-house, which had only in part been paid for, was burned by the act of an incendiary. A young man was convicted of the crime, and sentenced to the State prison for life; but nine years afterwards, having given signs of reformation, he was discharged at the petition of members of the society.

Steps were immediately taken to rebuild. And the house now standing was dedicated Sept. 17, 1851, the services being conducted by Mr. Fletcher. Three years later a clock was put upon the tower of the house. The society gained slowly but steadily in strength, and was at length, by the vigorous exertion of its members, and notably by the generosity of the late Moses Putnam, freed from debt. The church also grew in numbers. In 1857 the term "third" having lost its appropriateness by the division of the town, a change was made in name, and the titles became as at present, the "Maple-street" Church and Society.

Mr. Fletcher resigned his pastorate May 21, 1864. He was endeared by many admirable traits of character to his people, and was highly esteemed as a citizen throughout the town. After his dismissal, Mr. Fletcher was for several years principal of the Holten High School. He left this place, in 1871, to take charge of the Lawrence Academy, in Groton, where he now lives. Rev. William Carruthers was installed as pastor April 18, 1866. A revival was in progress at the time of his coming, as the fruits of which eighty persons were added to the church in that year by profession of their faith. Mr. Carruthers resigned March 28, 1868 ; and was subsequently settled at Calais, Me., where he still resides. Rev. James Brand was ordained as his successor, Oct. 6, 1869.*

The Maple-street Church had, at the beginning of the present year, 281 members. It has now outgrown the parent church ; but it can never grow, either in numbers or in efficiency, beyond the loving and Christian wishes in its behalf of the ancient body from which it sprung.

Some account may properly be given at this point of other churches now occupying the territory once embraced in this parish.

The Baptist church, at the Port, though a little outside the original lines, should not be omitted. This is the second, in point of age, in the town. The society was formed Nov. 12, 1781.† Rev. Benj. Foster was invited to preach for the

---

* From a later date it may be added that Mr. Brand left in the autumn of 1873, to become pastor of the First Church in Oberlin, Ohio. And also, that the meeting-house of this society has been of late entirely remodelled within, and somewhat enlarged.

† The materials for this sketch of the Baptist church were furnished to me chiefly by Mr. Francis Pope. After making out the leading items with difficulty from the records of the church and society, Mr. Pope fortunately learned of the "Sketch of the History of the Baptist Church in Danvers," prepared by Rev. A. W. Chaffin, and printed with the minutes of the "Salem Baptist Association" for 1855. By the courtesy of the clerk of the association, and by the favor of Mr. Pope, the minutes have been placed in my hands.

society ; which he did for about two years.* A meeting-house was built in 1783, and while Mr. Foster was still in the place. After his removal there was no resident minister for nine years, though preaching was had for most of the time. The church was organized with thirty-six members, July 16, 1793 ; and Rev. Thomas Green became, at the same time, pastor. Mr. Green resigned, Nov. 26, 1796, and the church was without a settled pastor until 1802. In May of that year Rev. Jeremiah Chaplin, afterward President of Waterville College, in Maine, became pastor. His prosperous ministry lasted for sixteen years. During the latter part of this period Dr. Chaplin had many theological students under his charge ; and among them were two of the early foreign missionaries, Wheelock and Colman. Dr. Chaplin resigned in 1818, and was soon after succeeded by Rev. James A. Boswell, who remained only to April 25, 1820. Rev. Arthur Drinkwater was installed Dec. 7, 1821, and remained until June 26, 1829. In 1828 a new meeting-house was erected. The old building was sold, and was subsequently removed to the Plain, where it is still standing.† Rev. James Barnaby succeeded to the pastorate in July, 1830, remaining until May, 1832. During his ministry the great religious revival of that period was felt in this society, and many were added to the church. Rev. John Holroyd followed him in the office in August, 1832, and continued in the pastorate until his death, Nov. 8, 1837. The church prospered under his charge. The next pastorate was that of Rev. E. W. Dickinson, from May, 1838, to Oct. 26, 1839. The next, that of Rev. John A. Avery, from February, 1841, to April, 1843. About this time several members of the church and society withdrew to form at the Plain "what was styled a Free Evangelical Society." Rev. J. W. Eaton followed in the pas-

* Mr. Foster was a native of Danvers, and a brother of Gen. Gideon Foster. He was a man of marked ability. He became afterward pastor of the First Baptist Church in New York City, where he died, in 1798, at the age of forty-seven.

† It is used by Mr. John A. Learoyd as a currier's shop. This building is said to have been thought infirm at its removal; but it has upon it at the present time a certain air of breadth and settlement in configuration, of such a sort that the eye of the beholder may not readily discern to what end it should ever fall down.

torate, from July, 1843, to August, 1849. The meeting-house of 1828 was burned, to the great loss of the people, on the night of Sept. 6, 1847. A new house, and the one now standing, was built the next year. Rev. A. W. Chaffin was ordained April 24, 1850. His labors were continued, with great acceptance to the society, until his resignation, April 26, 1862. Mr. Chaffin was highly respected, and had many warm friends throughout the town. The pastoral succession was continued as follows: Rev. Foster Henry, from Dec. 5, 1862, to May 1, 1865; Rev. Charles H. Holbrook, from Nov. 14, 1865, to Sept. 2, 1870; Rev. J. A. Goodhue, from Nov. 22, 1870, to May 1, 1872. Rev. G. W. McCullough, the present pastor, was ordained June 20, 1873.

The Universalist Society was organized in 1829. There had, however, been a partial organization from 1815, with only an occasional service. After its organization, meetings were held for two or three years in the old Baptist meeting-house, after its sale, and before its removal to the Plain. A meeting-house was begun in 1832, and made ready for occupancy by June, 1833. The present house, having the "Gothic Hall" in its basement story, was built in 1859. The pastoral succession has been as follows: Rev. F. A. Hodsdon, 1831-2; Rev. D. D. Smith, 1833; Rev. W. H. Knapp, 1834-5; Rev. Samuel Bremblecom, 1836-9; Rev. Asher Davis, 1840-41; Rev. D. P. Livermore, 1842; Rev. S. C. Buckley, 1843-5; Rev. J. W. Hanson, 1846-8; Rev. J. P. Putnam, 1849, to Nov. 30, 1864, the date of his death; Rev. H. C. Delong, 1865-8; Rev. G. J. Sanger, 1869. Mr. Putnam was for many years an active and valuable member of the school committee; and for two years representative of the town in the General Court. Mr. Sanger, the present pastor, is also (1873) the town representative in the Legislature.

The first Catholic service was held in Danvers, Nov. 1, 1854, at the house of Mr. Edward McKeigue. The officiating clergyman was the Rev. Thomas H. Shahan, now of Beverly, then pastor of the Church of the Immaculate Conception in Salem.

Regular services began soon to be held in Franklin Hall, and afterward in a chapel which stood on the south side of High Street, near the old cemetery. In 1859 the house first built by the Universalist Society was purchased; and, after an occupancy of several years, this building, having been greatly enlarged and remodelled, was dedicated anew by the Right Rev. Bishop J. J. Williams of Boston, April 30, 1871. Previous to 1864 pastoral duties were performed by clergymen from Salem. From Oct. 13 of that year, Rev. Charles Rainoni had charge of this parish, and also of the Catholic parish of Marblehead, having his residence in Danvers. In 1872 he removed to Marblehead, the parishes being separated, and his place was taken by Rev. Mr. O'Reilly; to whom succeeded, April, 1873, the present pastor, Rev. Joseph Haley.

This is styled Annunciation Church. The Catholic parish of Danvers includes the towns of Middleton and Topsfield; and it embraces a population estimated at more than 1,500.

Episcopal services were first held in Danvers, in the hall in the Bank Building, June 28, 1857; the Rev. George Leeds, then of Salem, officiating. The organization, under the title of the Calvary Church, took place April 14, 1858, the Rev. R. T. Chase being rector. The church building was consecrated by Bishop Manton Eastburn of Boston, May 25, 1859; and the incorporation of the parish was in October of the following year. Nearly the whole cost of this building was borne by Joseph Adams and E. D. Kimball; and to their liberality the parish owes its possession free of debt. There have been some vacancies in the pastoral charge. Mr. Chase held the position about four years; Rev. S. J. Evans about three years; and the present pastor, Rev. W. I. Magill, entered upon the place in June, 1872.

The Unitarian Society began its worship in the Town Hall on the first Sunday in August, 1865; the service being conducted by Rev. A. P. Putnam. The preaching was by various ministers, until the coming of Rev. Leonard J. Livermore,

April 1, 1867. A chapel was afterwards built on High Street, which was dedicated in 1871. The cost of this chapel, including the land, was about $13,000. Mr. Livermore was formally settled as pastor in 1872. The number of families connected with this society is now about fifty.

The Methodist Society began to hold its meetings during the summer of 1871, in Lincoln Hall, which had formerly been the schoolhouse in Tapleyville. Work was begun upon its meeting-house the next year ; and it was dedicated in the spring of 1873. The entire cost of the building was about $15,000. The society has had a rapid growth. Rev. Elias Hodge is now pastor.

There have also been occasional meetings of Swedenborgians for several years. These began to be held with somewhat of regularity in December, 1869, at the house of Mrs. Mary Page ; and in 1872 regular service was established at Bowditch Hall. There is no formal organization ; but the services are conducted by Rev. A. F. Frost, of the "Salem Society of the New Jerusalem Church."

In 1860 Dr. Braman began again to take steps looking toward the dissolution of the pastoral relation between himself and the people of the First Parish. In October of that year he sent a letter to the parish committee, giving the notice of six months required by the terms of his settlement, and proposing to resign his charge in the following spring. "I have reached," he said, "that time of life when I wish to retire from the labors which the ministry imposes on me, and when it is usually better to give place to younger men." The members of his congregation were far from concurring, either in this wish or opinion. At a meeting of the parish, resolutions were unanimously adopted, expressive of high appreciation of his "pastoral care, and teachings," and of deep regret at the prospect of his removal. Strong efforts were made to dissuade him from his purpose, but without success. He closed his ministerial labors, accordingly, on the last sabbath of March, 1861. Agreeably, however, to Dr. Braman's request, no council was called at this time ; and he continued, though only nominally, the pastor of the church, until the settlement of his successor. He was minister of the parish for but a little less than thirty-five years.

Dr. Braman removed to Brookline, and then to Auburndale, from whence he returned with his family to spend a few years in Danvers ; occupying the place upon the hill, east of the meeting-house, now owned by Mr. George H. Wood, and afterwards removing again, in 1868, to Auburndale, where he now resides.

The pastoral office remained vacant nearly two and one-half years. During this interval the meeting-house was painted ; and in the spring of 1863 a valuable organ was purchased, and placed within it.

The present pastor preached here for the first time on the 24th of May, 1863. He was called, with unanimity, by the church and parish during the next month ; and was installed on Wednesday the 2d of September of the same year.* He is a native of Conway, in this State ; and he had been pastor of the church in Saco, Me., for two years ending with December, 1861.

In 1864 a large part of the parsonage land was sold. There had appeared to be more than was needed. The portion disposed of lay mostly to the north-west of the land now belonging to the parsonage ; though a part of it was at the east, extending in that direction to Forest Street. The north-western

---

* Dr. Israel W. Putnam, D.D., was moderator of the council ; and the order of services was as follows : Opening prayer by Rev. George A. Bowman, Manchester, N.H. ; reading of the Scriptures by Rev. J. B. Sewall of Lynn ; sermon by Rev. Prof. D. S. Talcott, D.D., of Bangor Theological Seminary ; installing prayer by Rev. John Pike of Rowley ; charge to the pastor by the moderator ; right hand of fellowship by Rev. John S. Sewall of Wenham ; and concluding prayer by Rev. James Fletcher of Danvers.

and main division embraced nearly all of what had been the original gift, by Joseph Holten, for the use of the ministry. No part of this original "ministry land" is now owned by the parish, it is believed, saving only a narrow lane, just beyond the house of Mr. John Roberts, running in to the north-east from the main road toward the site of the first parish, or ministry house; and perhaps also a small strip at the north-eastern corner of the present parsonage land.

We may have some regret at this surrender of that ancient property. And from an early period in the history of the parish there have always been grave doubts with respect to both the moral and the legal right to sell this land.* On the other hand, it may be considered that the land still held by the parish is sufficient, or nearly so, for the uses required. For what remains, at least, it is to be hoped that it will on no account be transferred from its present ownership. It renders a permanent and very material aid in the support of a minister. It adds greatly to the comfort and attractiveness of the parsonage, as a home for his family, and gives a tendency thus to stability in the pastoral relation. The kind of man, too, needed for the minister of a country parish is most easily settled to stay, upon land. He has, and ought to have, some instinct of attachment to the soil. And with all that is now drawing men to the cities and large towns, our country parishes cannot afford to lose the counterbalancing value of these advantages which belong appropriately to them.

I desire to speak strongly on this point for the benefit of my successors, and of the parish itself in future times. The land that remains should not be sold, even if some minister were to wish it might be. Whatever might be true in exceptional cases, the parish would certainly lose something in a long course of years, by the giving up of its lands, as to the character of the pastors it could secure and retain.

---

* That Judge Holten shared in these doubts is certain, from a report made to the parish in 1784 by a committee of which he was a member, upon the proposal to convey this land to Dr. Wadsworth.

It is hardly necessary to add, that these lands about the parsonage are open to much improvement, not only in productiveness, but also in appearance. The judicious planting of trees, especially, in larger numbers, both upon the parsonage land and at some points about the meeting-house, would enhance the value of the place, and add much to the beauty of the neighborhood. For some neglect hitherto in this respect, the present occupant of the parsonage, pressed with many other engagements, must confess himself to be in part responsible.   .

This period of the history cannot be ·passed without some reference to the great war for the suppression of rebellion, and the maintenance of the Union, with freedom. The people of Danvers sustained their part in this contest with energy and determination, understanding the greatness of the interests involved. It was necessary only once, and that for but a little space in 1863, to resort to drafting in order to furnish the number of men required of us. The quota of the town was usually full, with a surplus to its credit ; and, throughout the last two years of the war, this was invariably the case. Five hundred and ten men of the inhabitants of Danvers, as nearly as I can now ascertain, enlisted for this war.

Shortly after the close of the war, measures were taken for the erection of a monument in honor of those who gave their lives in the contest. At the annual town-meeting in March, 1868, a committee was appointed to have the matter in charge, consisting of the following persons : Wm. Dodge, jun., E. T. Waldron, J. F. Bly, Wm. R. Putnam, Dean Kimball, Timothy Hawkes, George Andrews, Rufus Putnam, S. P. Cummings, Simeon Putnam, Henry A. Perkins, Josiah Ross, Edwin Mudge, and Daniel P. Pope. Nearly $3,000 was raised by subscription. Of this sum Mr. Edwin Mudge gave nearly half ; contributing to this purpose for two years his salary as representative of the town in the Legislature. The town added a somewhat larger amount ; making, in all, $6,298.20. The monument stands in front of the Town House. It is of

SOLDIERS' MONUMENT AND TOWN HALL.

Hallowell granite, 33¼ feet high, and 7¾ feet square at the base. It bears upon its front the inscription : —

ERECTED

BY THE CITIZENS OF DANVERS,

IN MEMORY OF

THOSE WHO DIED IN THE DEFENCE OF THEIR COUNTRY

DURING THE WAR OF THE REBELLION, IN 1861-65.

On the other sides are cut the names of ninety-five persons who died on the field of battle, or by wounds, or by sickness brought on in the war. The list begins with the names of Major Wallace A. Putnam and Lieut. James Hill.

The monument itself is a beautiful and appropriate structure. It was dedicated, with befitting ceremonies, Nov. 30, 1870.

There is here an organization of the soldiers of this war, styled " Ward Post, No. 90, of the Grand Army of the Republic," established June 21, 1869. Its purposes are to cherish the sentiments of patriotism and loyalty, to preserve the memories and associations of the war, and to furnish such assistance as may be needed to the families of soldiers. It holds its meetings weekly, numbers 150 members, and distributes annually in charities not far from $1,000.

It is our wish that these men, with their brethren throughout the land, — the survivors of the great contest, — may long enjoy the blessings they thus fought to purchase ; and our hope that these priceless institutions themselves, of justice and freedom, may withstand every coming peril, whether of war or of peace, and may survive for the nourishment and shelter of appreciating generations to the end of time.

The fiftieth anniversary of the sabbath school was commemorated with appropriate observances on Sunday, Aug. 9, 1868. Many members of the Maple-street sabbath school were present. A welcoming address was made by the pastor. Dea. Samuel Preston, the first superintendent, read a paper giving an account of the establishment of the school. Addresses were given by Rev. Samuel B. Willis, a former super-

intendent ; by Rev. Hiram B. Putnam, son of a superintendent ; and by Dea. John S. Learoyd, superintendent of the
Maple-street school.   Papers were also read by Dea. William R. Putnam, and Augustus Mudge, both superintendents,
the latter having held the post for twenty years ; and by
Edward Hutchinson, the superintendent then in office.

Particular mention was made on this occasion of two ladies,
Mrs. Emma Putnam Kettelle, and Mrs. Betsey P. Putnam,
who had been most efficient helpers in the school, through
nearly the whole period of its existence.   Mrs. Kettelle was a
teacher in the school from its first year.   And for more than
twenty-five years she was assistant-superintendent, having
charge of the younger portion of the school.   She died in
1867.   Mrs. Putnam was a scholar from the first, a teacher for
many years, and assistant-superintendent after the death of
Mrs. Kettelle.   Her own death occurred but a few weeks
before the anniversary, and while her thoughts were much
engaged in the preparations for it.

Measures were taken at about this time for the remodelling
of Village Hall, in the basement story of the meeting-house.
This hall, though reckoned good in its day, was unsuited to
the wants of the present time.   It was low, and deficient as
to light and air, and tending withal towards dilapidation.
The space, too, was insufficient ; since the entire western end
of the basement, now occupied by the two smaller rooms, and
amounting to about one-third of the whole, had been left unfinished, as bare cellar.   The chapel too, at the same time, had
gotten both out of date and out of repair ; and it was proposed,
by reconstructing the hall, to dispense with it altogether.

After much discussion as to the method that should be followed, and many delays, the work was finally entered upon in
1869, under the direction of a committee, consisting of Gilbert
Tapley, Edward Hutchinson, Augustus Mudge, Charles P.
Preston, and George B. Martin.   The side walls of stone
were in part removed ; the ground about the building was
lowered, to allow the enlargement of the windows ; the basement itself was deepened by further excavation, giving more

height to the rooms; and the interior was newly arranged and built, and furnished anew in every part. The expense was $4,150. This sum was raised in part by subscription, and in part by various other voluntary efforts, in all of which the ladies of the society bore their full share. The outlay has been amply repaid in the convenience and comfort of the rooms as we now have them.

The new hall was first occupied by the sabbath school on the 14th of November; and the first prayer-meeting in the vestry was held on Tuesday evening of the same week.

The walls of the main room in the meeting-house were frescoed the next year; and various improvements have also lately been made within and upon the parsonage buildings.

The population of Danvers, during this period of nearly two centuries and a half from its first settlement, has been stable and permanent to a somewhat remarkable degree. There has been comparatively little emigration to the West. Most of the early family names are still retained among us; and some of them have been greatly multiplied. There are many families occupying land that was owned by their ancestors at the settlement of the town, or not long afterwards.

The number of farms or homesteads, however, which have been kept in the family line with no break or interruption in the succession, is not so large. The following list, which may not be complete, nor wholly free from inaccuracy, embraces all that can now be traced. The comparison is given for convenience, with the proprietorship of Salem Village, as represented upon Mr. Upham's map for 1692; and it is made to follow the order of numbers which he has there assigned.*

8. Of Bray Wilkins's extensive lands, small portions are occupied by Luther Wilkins and by Mr. Higgins; and other portions also by other descendants.†

* This list was prepared chiefly by Dea. Wm. R. Putnam, Mr. Moses Prince, and Miss Susan Putnam.

† All the families of the Wilkins name in the parish, and indeed throughout the region, are his descendants.

20. The estate of Thomas Fuller, jun., in part owned by Jeremiah and S. Fuller, and by Augustus Estey, his descendants.

23. Of Dea. Edward Putnam's large homestead, the southern portion is owned by his descendant, William Putnam.

34. Benjamin Putnam owned in the north part of the village: a small portion is in the possession of Mrs. Samuel Wallis and Mrs. James M. Perry.

39. Mary, widow of Thomas Putnam, owned land that has descended to Francis P., John M., and William R. Putnam, and sisters.

41. Jonathan Putnam's farm, in Putnamville, is inherited by the children of the late Mrs. Nancy P. Boardman.

55. The farm near the paper-mill in Middleton, now owned by Sylvanus Flint, probably belonged to Capt. Thomas Flint in 1692; and it has descended from him to its present owner.*

59. John Buxton's estate, by intermarriage, has descended in the family to Asa and Robert Putnam.

60. That of James Smith has been transmitted in part to a descendant, Joseph Fuller.

71. The land of Joseph Hutchinson, jun., has descended to Elias Hutchinson and sisters.

79. Some of Nathaniel Putnam's large estate passed directly to the children of Judge Samuel Putnam. A small portion is now held by his son, Dr. Charles G. of Boston; other portions by Adrian and Otis F. Putnam, also descendants of said Nathaniel.

89. Some part of the estate of Joseph and Jasper Swinerton is owned by the family of the late Amos Swinerton. A large portion has also passed, by marriage, into the Pope family, and is now held by Nathanael, Jasper, and Zephaniah.

93. Of Benjamin Houlten's† land, some is now owned by the family of the late Philemon Putnam, his descendants.

111. Isaac Goodell's farm has been retained in the family, and is now occupied by Jacob Goodale and mother.

119. Capt. Thomas Flint's farm, in West Peabody, is now owned by his descendant, Thomas Flint.

130. The farm of Anthony Needham, jun., has passed by descent to Elias and Joseph S. Needham.

* This farm is marked upon Mr. Upham's map as belonging, in 1692, to George Flint. But Serg. George Flint, brother of Capt. Thomas, moved to Reading, according to the book of the Flint family, "before the year 1682." Agreeably to this, the name appears in the parish rate for 1681, while it is not in the corresponding list for 1689 (intervening rates gone). The present members of the family think he never owned this land; but upon that point I have no knowledge. That Mr. Wm. P. Upham should not hold accurately in memory every conveyance of land in this circuit of towns is, I suppose, conceivable; though this is the first indication I have ever seen of the fact.

† This is the ancient spelling. Judge Samuel wrote it without the *u*.

132. The land of Nathaniel Felton, jun., on Felton's Hill, lying partly within the parish, is now occupied by the heirs of John Felton.

142. George Jacobs, sen., owned near the present iron foundery; and some of the land is in the possession of descendants. This is within the bounds of the present town, but not of the Village parish.

The number of inhabitants within the limits of the present town of Danvers, in 1672, was probably not much above 350 ; and this was not far from one-fourth of the population of the whole town of Salem, to which it belonged, at that time. This is not to be confounded with the number in the Village parish, which embraced a larger territory. The first census of the State was taken in 1765 ; * the second in 1776. I give the population of Danvers, as returned in these years, and also in the United States census for 1790, and for each tenth succeeding year ; adding also, as marking the population at the time of the division of the town, and as covering the war-period, the enumerations by the State census of 1855 and of 1865.

1765	.	.	.	2,133	1840	.	.	.	5,020
1776	.	.	.	2,284	1850	.	.	.	8,106
1790	.	.	.	2,425	1855	.	.	.	4,000
1800	.	.	.	2,643	1860	.	.	.	‡5,110
1810	.	.	.	3,127	1865	.	.	.	5,144
1820†	.	.	.	3,646	1870	.	.	.	5,600
1830	.	.	.	4,228					

* Mr. HANSON, in his "History of Danvers," has twice stated the population of Danvers in 1752, the date of its incorporation as a district, at five hundred, or "about" that number. The village parish alone had that number seventy years before. There were more than three times as many. At the rate of increase from 1765 to 1776, the number for 1752 would be 1968. It was probably less. There were 326 resident tax-payers, — not 280, as Mr. Proctor by some mistake has said. The ratio of five would give 1630; which, as the list was made out, is not too high. Mr. Hanson and Mr. Proctor also put the population in 1783 at 1921 ; of which I can give no account.

† In 1820 there were but twenty-one houses on the line of road from the corner at the Plain, near the post-office, by Elm, Holten, and Center Streets, to the Newburyport turnpike. There was no other line more populous. And there was no village, as we now use the word, at that time in the town.

‡ The division of the town took place in 1855. The population of South Danvers, now Peabody, in 1855, was 5,348 ; in 1860, 6,549 ; in 1865, 6,051 ; and in 1870, 7,343. It will be seen that during the five years covering most of the war-

The valuation of the town in 1849 for the " North Ward," corresponding nearly to the town as at present, was $1,140,600 ; for the same limits in 1855, the last valuation before the division of the town, $1,561,100 ; and the next year, after the division, $1,809,650. The rate of taxation for that year was $\frac{78}{100}$ per centum. In 1860 the valuation stood at $2,290,200 ; and in 1865, at $2,268,625. But this decrease during the war arose from investments in United States Bonds, exempted from local taxation, and not included in the assessors' estimates. These investments, indeed, must have been made to a much larger extent than thus appears ; and the falling off in the valuation would have been greater, but for the nominal appreciation of values through the issuing of irredeemable paper-money. In 1872 the valuation was $3,296,950. The rise of values, as measured in the paper currency, had ceased during this period ; but the town assessors, in the mean while, had raised their appraisement upon certain descriptions of property, and specially upon real estate in the central districts ; and thus the increase in value, though in so far actual, did not in reality occur wholly within that period of years.* (See Appendix D.).

I will here make some statements in detail with respect to the organization and municipal arrangements of the town, which may be of interest at some future time.

The municipal year of the town dates from the annual meet-

---

period, Danvers barely held its own in population, while Peabody fell off nearly five hundred.

It may be noticed also, that the population of the town of Danvers, as now constituted, was nearly the same in 1860 with that of the undivided town twenty years previous.

The increase from 1855 to 1860 was in some part due to the enlargement of territory in 1857, by annexation of a district that had belonged to Beverly.

* In 1874 the valuation is $3,222,050. But this decrease is due, again, to an extrinsic cause ; the tax on bank-stocks held by non-resident owners being now collected and paid over to the towns by the State ; and the value of the stocks thus not appearing upon the books of the assessors.

ing held on the first Monday in March, at which time all town-officers are regularly chosen. For convenience, however, the financial year is made to close about two weeks earlier, in order that a statement of accounts, expenditures, and estimates may be prepared and printed for the use of the town at the annual meeting.

The amount raised by taxation for the year thus ending Feb. 15, 1873, was $44,888.96; and the rate of taxation on property $\frac{128}{100}$ per centum. There were expended in the highway department, $13,064.52, the outlay in this direction being somewhat larger than usual; for the maintenance of public schools, $12,821.37; for the fire-department, $3,615.97; and for the support of the poor, $3,512.81.

The number of public schools was nineteen, and the number of teachers employed twenty-four.

The town-officers for the same year were as follows: Moderator at the Annual Meeting, George Tapley; Clerk, A. S. Howard; Treasurer, Wm. L. Weston; Selectmen and Assessors, Wm. Dodge, jun., Henry A. Perkins, Joshua Bragdon; School Committee, W. Winslow Eaton, Geo. J. Sanger, Israel W. Andrews, John A. Putnam, John W. Porter, Chas. B. Rice; Overseers of the Poor, S. P. Fowler, Amos Pratt, Daniel Richards; Auditors of Accounts, Geo. Tapley, Jacob F. Perry; Road Commissioners, R. B. Hood, Ira P. Pope, Francis Dodge; Constables, Chas. H. Adams, Dennis W. Regan, J. C. P. Legro, F. W. Lyford, S. A. Merrill, F. A. Chase, Timothy Hawkes, Amos Prince, Richard Hood; Fire-wards, Timothy Hawkes, Geo. W. Bell, John. C. Putnam, Thomas Curtis, George Kimball; Health Committee, Ebenezer Hunt, W. W. Eaton, D. A. Grosvenor, P. M. Chase, Lewis Whiting, D. H. Batchelder, H. O. Warren, Joseph Merrill, Nathanael Bragdon; the first six of these being physicians.

There were also chosen three surveyors of lumber, eight measurers of wood and bark, one measurer of leather, one measurer and weigher of grain, one sealer of weights and measures, eight field-drivers, three fence-viewers, one pound-keeper, and three members of a " River Committee." But as many of these persons do not appear to have presented themselves to be qualified according to law, or to signify their acceptance of these trusts, I do not record their names; and thus, though by the fault of a part only, have they all failed of that undying remembrance to which they might otherwise have here attained.

Lists of certain church and parish officers will here be given. And for convenience of reference the ministerial succession, though already detailed, is placed with the rest.

MINISTERS. — *Stated Supplies.*

James Bayley, formally engaged Nov. 11, 1672.* Left about Jan. 1, 1680.

George Burroughs, engaged November, 1680. Left early in 1683.

Deodat Lawson, engaged February or March, 1684. Left in summer of 1688.

PASTORS.

Samuel Parris, ordained Nov. 19, 1689. Gave up work June 30, 1696.
Joseph Green, ordained Nov. 10, 1698. Died Nov. 26, 1715.
Peter Clark, ordained June 5, 1717. Died June 10, 1768.
Benjamin Wadsworth, ordained Dec. 23, 1772. Died Jan. 18, 1826.
Milton P. Braman, ordained April 12, 1826. Resigned March 31, 1861.
Charles B. Rice, installed Sept. 2, 1863.

The very unusual length of these pastorates, setting aside the first, cannot fail to be noticed. The parish had but four ministers for a period of 163 years. The terms of three of these ministers cover a space of 139 years, exclusive of the intervals between them. While the successive ministries of Mr. Clark and Mr. Wadsworth embrace together 104 years.

No minister in these two hundred years has ever left this parish at the call of any other religious society, to settle elsewhere. And only one minister has ever left its service at his own choice.

---

* This is the date of the first parish-meeting, and of the vote to provide for the payment of Mr. Bayley's salary. He may have begun to preach nearly a year earlier; but this is uncertain.

DEACONS.*

The person first named in this list, and perhaps also the second, had held an anomalous office "in the place of deacon," before the organization of the church in 1689; and both of them, though not at once formally inducted into the office, might be regarded as holding the position from that date.

1690. Nathanael Ingersoll, in office thirty years; died 1719, aged eighty-five years. He lived near the present parsonage, and left no children.

1690. Edward, son of Thomas, grandson of John Putnam, sen., was in office forty years. A record of his acceptance of the choice made, and of Dea. Ingersoll's ordination, was made by Mr. Parris, and can be found in vol. i. of Upham's "Salem Witchcraft," together with a sketch of the worthy man. His large homestead was in the westerly part of the village, near Ipswich River. His house stood near the one now owned by Joseph Towne, in Middleton. Died in 1747, aged ninety-four years. He had seven sons. His descendants living here are hereafter named. Among those scattered abroad was his grandson, Brig.-Gen. Rufus, who was distinguished as a military engineer and commander in the Revolutionary War; afterwards, as one of the first settlers of Marietta, and a founder of the State of Ohio. His great-grandson, Oliver, was the founder of the "Putnam Free School," Newburyport. Also among them was the late lamented Prof. John N., of Dartmouth College.

1709. Benjamin, son of Nathanael, grandson of John Putman, sen., in office nine years. Died 1714, aged 50 years. His home was on land now owned by Miss Goodhue, near the farm of Samuel Wallis. One son, Daniel, graduated at Harvard College in 1717; was settled in Reading, Mass., and there passed a long and useful ministry. Of his descendants, now connected with the society, are Mrs. Joseph Towne and daughters, Mrs. Samuel Wallis, Mrs. E. G. Berry.

1718. Eleazer, son of John 2d, also grandson of John Putnam, sen., was in office fifteen years. Died, "after a long illness," in 1733. His house stood on the spot now occupied by Mr. John Preston, Preston Street. His descendants in the parish are the children of the late Elijah Pope, sen. The children of the late Rev. Israel W. Putnam of Middleborough, and Samuel Putnam of Brooklyn N. Y., are also descendants.

1731. Nathanael, son of Dea. Benjamin Putnam, in office twenty-three years. Died in 1754. He lived near the house now owned by Otis F. Putnam, Holten Street. Many of his descendants are in New York and Brooklyn, and in Maine.

1733. Joseph Whipple, in office seven years. Died 1740. He lived at the foot of Whipple Hill, on the north side of the road from the Plain to

* This list of deacons was prepared by Miss Susan Putnam.

Middleton, near the present railroad bridge. The families of Mrs. John Preston, and of Adrian and Orrin Putnam, are descendants, now connected with the society.

1741. Cornelius Tarbell, in office twenty-one years. Born 1690. He lived in the now unoccupied gambrel-roofed house, corner of Pine and Hyde Streets. He had a large family, but it is not known that any descendants are in the parish: some are in Lynnfield.

1756. Archelaus, son of Dea. Nathanael Putman, in office one year. Died 1757. He lived in the house now occupied by Gilbert Tapley, in Tapleyville. Among his descendants in town are the families of the late Samuel Fowler and John Page. None in the society.

1757. Samuel Putnam, jun., in office five years. The record states that he, with his family, removed to Lunenburg, Mass., when in office; and he was dismissed from the church in 1762.

1762. Asa Putnam, great-grandson of Nathanael, sen., in office thirty-three years. Died 1795. He built and occupied the house afterwards owned by the late Jesse Hutchinson, on Newbury Street. Descendants now in the parish are the families of the late Asa Hutchinson and Dea. Elijah and Benjamin Hutchinson.

1762. Edmund Putman, also great-grandson of Nathaniel, sen., in office twenty-three years. Died 1810, aged eighty-six years. Lived where Augustus Fowler now owns, on the road leading from the Plain to Topsfield. His descendants in town are of the family of the late Elias Putnam, Esq. None in the society.

1785. Gideon, grandson of Dea. Benjamin Putnam, in office nineteen years. Died May, 1811, aged eighty-four years. Dr. Wadsworth's record says, "that having served the church almost twenty years as deacon, and being advanced in years, he requested to be exempted from the labors of the office, but did not make a resignation of the office itself." However, a successor was chosen. He lived on the site now occupied by Daniel Richard's store, corner of High and Elm Streets, on the Plain. The children of the late Judge Samuel Putnam are descendants, and reside in Boston and vicinity.

1795. Daniel Putnam, in office seven years. Died 1801, aged sixty-three years. His homestead is now owned (1873) by B. Augustus Peabody, near Ipswich River. The families of Nathanael, Jasper, and the late Elijah Pope are descendants, now connected with the society.

1802. Joseph Putnam, in office sixteen years. Died 1818, aged seventy-nine years. His home, on the south side of Maple Street, leading from the Plain to Middleton, is now owned by his grandson, John M. The families of the late Jesse Putnam and Allen Nourse are descendants. Some of the latter — Mrs. Elijah Hutchinson and children, and the family of the late Samuel P. Nourse — are now in the society.

1807. James Putnam, in office twelve years. Died 1819, aged sixty-nine years. He lived where the family of the late Asa Hutchinson now reside, corner of Holten and Collins Streets. No descendants now living.

1818. Jonathan Walcut, in office thirteen years. Died 1844, aged eighty-two years. He lived on the west side of Newbury Street, near the present farm of Jasper Pope; house not now standing. Mrs. George Tapley and family, and the children of Reuben Wilkins, are descendants, connected with the society.

1820. Eben. Putnam, great-great-grandson of Dea. Edward, in office eleven years. Died 1831, aged sixty-five years. He lived on a part of the large homestead of his good ancestor. The house is owned and occupied by his son William and daughter Polly, who are now connected with the society.

1832. John Thomas, in office twenty-nine years. Now living.

1832. Frederic Howe, in office twelve years. Now connected with Maple-street Church.

1845. Ebenezer, son of Dea. Eben. Putnam, in office three years. Died 1848, aged forty-two. Rev. Hiram B. Putnam and sister, of Salem, are his children. He lived on Dayton Street, leading from Newbury Street to Middleton, at the place now owned by Robert M. Peabody.

1848. Samuel Preston, in office thirteen years. Now living.

1861. Elijah Hutchinson,* now in office.

1861. William R. Putnam,† now in office.

STANDING COMMITTEES.

1672.	1700.
Lieut. Thomas Putnam.	Lieut. Jonathan Putnam.
Thomas Fuller, sen.	Benj. Hutchinson.
Joseph Porter.	John Tarbell.
Thomas Flint.	Benj. Putnam.
Joshua Rea.	Thomas Fuller, jun.

* The ancestry of the Hutchinson family has been traced back to Barnard Hutchinson, living in 1282, in Cowlam, Yorkshire, England. The first of the name in this country was Richard, who came in 1634. He brought with him his son Joseph, born the year before in England, and occupied the lands in the meadow and upon the hill, at the east, north-east, and north of the meeting-house.

The family connection springing from this stock is too large to be traced: I give only the single line toward the family of Dea. Hutchinson. From the first Joseph it proceeds, Joseph, Ebenezer, Jeremy, to Joseph; from whom we have Elijah and Benjamin; and from Elijah, as heads of families, Edward, Alfred, and Warren.

† The Putnam name has been borne from early times in this place by a much larger number of persons and households than any other. The line in this particular branch of the family runs back thus: William R., Daniel, Israel, David (brother of Gen. Israel), Joseph, Thomas, to the original John, coming from Buckinghamshire, England, in 1634.

1725.

Samuel Flint.
Joseph Fuller.
John Preston.
Nathanael Putnam.
Joseph Putnam.

1750.

Record missing. The names of the clerk and the treasurer for that year will be found in their places. Jonathan Putnam and John Preston were collectors.

1775.

Tarrant Putnam.
John Swinerton.
Cornelius Tarbell.
Abel Nichols.
John Preston.

1800.

Jonathan Porter, jun.
Levi Preston.
Elijah Flint.

1810.

Elijah Flint.
Asa Tapley.
Daniel Putnam.
Nathan Putnam.
Eben Putnam, jun.

1820.

Moses N. Putnam.

1820 (*continued*).

Jesse Putnam.
Amos Pope.

1830.

John Preston.
Nathanael Pope.
Nathan Tapley.

1840.

Jesse Putnam.
Samuel Preston.
Nathan Tapley.

1850.

Isaac Demsey.
Matthew Putnam.
Charles P. Preston.

1860.

Samuel Preston.
Augustus Mudge.
S. B. Swan.

1870.

Wm. R. Putnam.
W. B. Woodman.
Augustus Mudge.

1872.

Wm. R. Putnam.
Augustus Mudge.
George B. Martin.

1874.

Augustus Mudge.
S. B. Swan.
S. Walter Nourse.

The Standing Committee for a long time, saving for their power to call parish-meetings, were little more than assessors. In later years they have been expected to attend to the general interests of the parish ; and have possessed considerable discretionary authority.

CLERKS.

It does not appear who was the first clerk. The first four pages of the present parish record, which is a copy, are in the handwriting of Deodat Lawson, who certainly was not clerk. Thence, from 1674, the copy proceeds in the writing of Thomas Putnam. He appears soon to have been clerk; and there may have been none before him. He held the office, saving for five or six years, to 1699.

The list thenceforward, as nearly as can be gathered, is as follows, the figures indicating the date of appointment:—

Jonathan Putnam	 1700	Samuel Nurs 1724
Daniel Rea. 1702	Nathanael Putnam 1725
John Putnam 1703	Samuel Nurs 1726
Benj. Putnam 1705	Nathanael Putnam 1727
Jonathan Putnam 1706	Daniel Rea. 1729
Daniel Rea 1707	Joseph Putnam 1731
Edward Putnam 1708	Joseph Whipple, jun. . . . 1732
Samuel Andrew 1709	James Prince * 1734
Israel Porter 1710	Daniel Rea 1735
Joseph Putnam 1711	Joseph Whipple, jun. . . . 1736
Daniel Rea. 1712	John Giles 1737
Thomas Flint 1713	Jonathan Putnam 1738
David Judd. 1714	Samuel Holten 1740
Ezekiel Cheever 1715	Henry Putnam 1741
Thomas Flint 1716	James Prince 1743
Samuel Nurs 1717	Daniel Rea. 1745
Israel Porter 1718	Samuel Holten 1746
John Walcott 1719	James Prince 1747
Joseph Putnam 1720	Henry Putnam 1748
Jonathan Putnam 1721	Archelaus Putnam 1749
Samuel Putnam 1722	John Preston † 1750
Israel Porter 1723	Archelaus Dale 1751

* James Prince was a descendant of Robert Prince, one of the original petitioners for the setting-off of Salem Village. He was an active man in parish and town affairs, and was the first treasurer of the town. He lived in what is now the farm-house upon the place lately owned by Stephen Driver, and now owned by Jacob E. Spring. He was great-grandfather of Moses Prince and Amos Prince of the present time. The two connecting links were James and Amos; and James was brother to Dr. Jonathan.

† The Preston lineage runs thus: Roger, coming from England; Thomas, son-in-law of Francis Nourse of 1692; John, John, —— to Capt. Levi. Capt. Levi was father of the Levi by whom the present meeting-house was built; and from him we have also the family of the late Mrs. Mehitabel Preston Berry; John, with his son Charles P.; Dea. Samuel; and the family of the late William Preston, with others of the name not connected with the parish.

Harriet W. Preston, daughter of Dea. Samuel, is well known as the author

Gideon Putnam 1754	Jonathan Porter 1791
James Smith 1757	George Upton. 1793
Asa Putnam 1760	Zerubbabel Porter 1794
Richard Whittredge, jun. . . 1766	Jesse Upton 1795
Archelaus Dale 1770	Jonathan Porter, jun. . . . 1796
James Smith 1773	Hezekiah Flint 1806
Tarrant Putnam 1775	Israel Andrews 1806
Asa Putnam 1776	Elijah Flint 1807
John Preston 1779	Amos Pope 1820
Samuel Page 1781	John Preston, jun. 1822
Eleazer Putnam 1783	Daniel F. Putnam 1832
Daniel Putnam 1785	Wm. R. Putnam 1836
Zerubbabel Porter . . . 1787	F. P. Putnam 1837
Daniel Putnam, jun. . . . 1789	Rufus Tapley * 1838
Ebenezer Brown 1790	Augustus Mudge. 1866

It will be seen, that, as to the clerkship, the parish had for
a century the full benefit of rotation in office. The work was,
in fact, reckoned a burden, the clerk having no pay ; and it
was thus meant to be somewhat fairly distributed. For the
sake of the future annalist of the parish, it is to be hoped that
the former usage may not be restored, unless the historian
is to be also himself provided with a clerk.

TREASURERS.

Moneys belonging to the parish were at first in the keeping
of "the men chosen in the place of deacons." After the organization of the church, the business continued mainly in the
hands of its deacons, — the Standing Committee possibly
sharing somewhat in the responsibility, — until the choice of
a treasurer in 1720. Deacon Edward Putnam was the first
appointed to this office, the duties of which he had probably
discharged for many years before. From this time forward,
the list is as follows : —

of "Aspendale," "Love in the Nineteenth Century," of many German and
French translations, and notably of a fine reproduction in English of the Pro-
vençal poem, " Mirèio."

* Mr. Tapley held the office of clerk until his death, in the autumn of 1865.
He was also sexton for a long term of years. He took an interest in whatever
belonged to the house of God ; and his careful and conscientious discharge of
the duties of this not unimportant position is worthy of honorable remembrance.

Dea. Eleazer Putnam . . . 1722	Daniel Putnam 1778
Timothy Lindall 1723	Israel Putnam 1781
Capt. Thomas Flint 1724	Stephen Putnam 1783
Dea. Nathanael Putnam . . 1734	Col. Jeremiah Page 1785
James Prince 1738	John Kettelle 1786
Joseph Putnam 1744	Dr. Samuel Holten 1789
Henry Putnam 1752	Daniel Putnam 1816
John Preston 1753	Col. Jesse Putnam 1823
Archelaus Dale 1755	Israel Adams 1831
Amos Putnam 1760	Ebenezer Putnam 1835
Dea. Samuel Putnam . . . 1761	Nathanael Pope 1840
James Prince 1762	Sylvanus B. Swan 1854
Dr. Samuel Holten 1764	George Tapley 1870

Dr., or Judge Holten, was treasurer, in all, forty years, and held the office to the time of his death. Since 1840 the treasurer has also been collector.

SUPERINTENDENTS OF THE SABBATH SCHOOL.

Samuel Preston 1818	Ahira Putnam 1835
Porter Kettell 1820	Wm. R. Putnam 1836
Samuel Preston 1821	Ebenezer Putnam 1841
Nathan Tapley 1822	Moses W. Putnam 1842
Samuel B. Willis 1826	Wm. R. Putnam 1844
John Peabody	Ebenezer Putnam 1845
Porter Kettell 1829	Augustus Mudge 1848
Ebenezer Putnam . . . 1830–33	Edward Hutchinson . . . 1868
George W. Endicott . . .	Augustus Mudge . . Dec. 1873

CHORISTERS.

The first leader of singing, so far as is now remembered, was Mr. John Kettelle, who had charge of this branch of worship for many years, and who died in 1801.

To him succeeded Amos Prince, who resigned in 1816. Next, for a like space of fifteen years, John Preston, to September, 1831. Afterward, for shorter periods, Benjamin Henderson, William Preston, Elijah Pope, Rufus Tapley, Daniel Peabody (1843–45), William Preston (1846–50), George Tapley, Wyatt B. Woodman, John Swinerton ; and, from the spring of 1863 to the present time, E. P. Davis, who had also held the position at intervals, amounting in all to four or five years, previous to 1863.

Mention has already been made of the formation of the choir early in the ministry of Dr. Wadsworth, and about one hundred years ago. For a long time nothing was paid in any form for the singing. The singers had leave, as we have seen, to build their own seats in the meeting-house, at their own cost. After something more than fifty years, or about 1830, persistent efforts began to be made to secure a small appropriation of money for the use of the choir; with persistent opposition. The choir had permission in 1833 "to rent the end of the old singers' seats in the meeting-house," if they could, and apply the proceeds to the improvement of the singing. Money was at length voted. And of late years the Parish Committee has been authorized to expend such sums as might be needed, the amount being for chorister and organist usually not far from $200. Arrangements are also occasionally made for free singing-schools, which might well be held more frequently.

The harmony of this delightful part of public worship has not been interrupted, under its present management at least, by contentions among the singers, or by misunderstandings between the singers and the minister.

With respect to the number and order of meetings here held, it may be observed that the custom of holding two preaching services on the sabbath has never been departed from in this place; saving that very lately (1873), the monthly concert of the sabbath school has been held upon the afternoon of the second sabbath in each month. These concerts themselves, which had before been held in the evening, are of recent origin, beginning with regularity from June 14, 1857.

The third, or evening service of the sabbath, was not fully established until after the building of the chapel; although before that time meetings were frequently appointed at the different schoolhouses, and also at dwelling-houses. This evening service, as now conducted, is a missionary concert and prayer-meeting upon the first sabbath of the month, and at other times a prayer-meeting; except that recently " praise meetings," in which singing is made most prominent, have been held with something of regularity, upon either the fourth or the last sabbath of the month. The missionary concert began with the later years of Dr. Wadsworth's ministry, and was held on the afternoon of the first Monday of the month, at the schoolhouse in this district. Here also Dr. Wadsworth had his monthly Thursday afternoon lecture, occurring on the week before the sabbath of the communion. The sacrament of the Lord's supper was celebrated at that time, upon the first sabbath of each month; and this had been the prevailing, but not invariable custom from early times. From near the beginning of Dr. Braman's ministry, it has occurred on the first sabbath of each second month only, beginning with January. There is a lecture preparatory to this service on the Friday evening preceding.* And

---

* I have not been able to find exactly to what extent the old and famous New England "Lecture" was given in this place. There are, however, numerous traces of its occurrence; and I suppose it was observed from soon after the organization of the parish, with occasional interruptions, through most of the last century; and that it became finally, in some sort, merged in this "Preparatory Lecture." There was no relation between the two at first. The old "Lecture" was an institution by itself, and of renown in its day.

It was established in Boston, 1633, upon the settlement of Rev. John Cotton. Mr. Cotton appears to have brought it from Boston in England; but of its history there little is known. The fame and ability of the preacher, and the authority also of the government, soon brought it into great repute; and the observance was extended throughout the colony. It became, and continued to be for many years, nearly the most important meeting that was held. It occurred regularly on Thursday of each week, near the middle of the day; and it was.called at first the "Thursday-Lecture," or the "Fifth-day Lecture."

There was much exchanging among ministers for this lecture; and the "great sermons" were preached on these occasions. (Compare, as to this, the list of the publications of Rev. Peter Clark, p. 67, note.)

The attendance was for a time made compulsory, as it was also for the sabbath service. A man was fined in Salem, in 1649, 5s., and 2s. 6d. court fees, for absence. (Felt's "Annals," p. 180.) But such enforcement of the law was rare.

In Essex County, at the end of the 17th century, the lecture was held often on Wednesday, or on other days of the week, as might be convenient. And it did not occur of necessity each week; but it might be monthly, or with any other interval. Mr. Green often attended the Salem Lecture; and he held one in this place, as I think, once in six weeks, and on the week before the sacrament, which for a considerable time was administered at that rate of frequency. In this way I conclude it may with us, and probably elsewhere, have passed at

on this evening of every week besides, occurs the regular prayer-meeting of the church, open to all persons, and dating also from the early part of Dr. Braman's ministry. Since 1863 there has been held a regular meeting of the church, for business purposes, and also for social worship, once in two months, on the afternoon of the Friday before the communion, and upon the same day with the preparatory lecture. There is also held a "young people's meeting," upon each Tuesday evening. This meeting had its origin in 1857, and has been maintained, with only one or two brief suspensions, from that time.

Evening meetings, it will be observed, are of modern origin. The population, until within recent years, was too far scattered for easy assembling, except by day. Dr. Wadsworth, withal, did not approve of evening meetings, — a judgment for which he could probably have given reasons. The practice has its inconveniences, and possibly its evils, especially for young children. These inconveniences were greater then than now; while those changes in occupation, which have made it difficult to hold meetings in the afternoon, had not then taken place. At present the system is one of necessity and of great usefulness.

The number of church-members reported Jan. 1, 1861, was 156; in 1862 it was 143; and in 1863, it was given as

length into a service preparatory to the sacrament. But it did not take such a character for a long period.

The lecture was continued in Boston, upon its old footing, throughout the greater part of the last century, though with declension from its original honor. Even so early as 1715, "during a violent storm," the Chief Justice of the State was moved to count the audience, and found but sixteen women and two hundred men. It was suspended during the siege of Boston, and resumed on a day of triumph for the deliverance of the city, with the attendance of Washington and his officers. Of its later history there I am not informed.

There is an interesting discourse, of which I have made use, in the library of *the Congregational Association*, entitled "THE SHADE OF THE PAST: for the celebration of the close of the second century since the establishment of the THURSDAY LECTURE." By Rev. N. L. Frothingham.

175. But these figures are incorrect, since there were no additions to the church from 1860 to 1863. In 1863 there were twenty-four additions, mostly before the coming of the present pastor, and as the result of a considerable degree of religious interest that had prevailed during a period of six months, while Rev. William Crawford, now of Green Bay, Wis., was laboring in the parish. At the close of this year there were 155 church-members ; forty-three being males, and 122 females. Three years later, Jan. 1, 1867, the membership had risen to 202. This is a little larger that the number in 1833, after the great revival. And it indicates, undoubtedly, the largest membership ever reached by the church, — a number still much beneath that which it should attain, to hold its due relation to the congregation and the parish. The sabbath school was also then at its largest point ; the whole number of members amounting to 404, and the number present·on single sabbaths being nearly 300. The congregation had been much larger at a former period, just before the establishment of the society at the Plain. It averaged, however, at this time, upon pleasant sabbaths, about 400.

Since that time there has been a diminution in all these numbers. This is owing to a variety of causes. With respect to the church, it is due, primarily, to some relaxation in Christian zeal and fidelity, which we trust may not long continue. The very unusual prevalence of sickness and mortality in this part of the town during the last two years, by which nearly sixty persons have been taken from the parish, has also had a perceptible effect in diminishing our numbers. But the chief cause has been the establishment of the new Methodist church and society near by us at Tapleyville. This has drawn very largely from our sabbath school and congregation.

It has been the fortune of this society from an early period to be thus from time to time retrenched in extent and population, by the setting on foot of new enterprises : as having been originally a large territorial parish, it could hardly have been otherwise. First came the setting off of the new town and parish at Will's Hill, or Middleton. Then there was the loss of a large number of families upon our south-western

border, consequent, more or less directly, upon the establishment of the " South Parish " in Danvers, and the formation
ultimately of the new town of Peabody. A large section of
Salem Village fell within its boundaries ; and the inhabitants
there came gradually to be separated from us in association
and interest. This process is only now completing itself in
the permanent maintenance of a sabbath school, with a preaching service at West Peabody. Still later came the great
division at the organization of the Maple-street Church and
Society at the Plain. All these were territorial, and had
respect chiefly to convenience of attendance upon public
worship.

But other separations have grown out of diversities in religious belief and ecclesiastical practice. The agreement of
opinion in these points that marked the original population of
the parish, and of New England, could not be maintained with
the wider opening and continued growth of the country. It
was not to be expected, — perhaps not to be desired. Thus,
as already noted, there have been formed societies of Baptists,
Universalists, Roman Catholics, Episcopalians, Unitarians, and
Methodists. All of these, except the Catholic, have been
formed chiefly from the population once embraced within
this parish. The denominational diversity already arrived at
is so great, and offers so large a field to individual choice,
that we may suppose it will not be carried much farther in
the immediate future.

The old church and society, meanwhile, thus repeatedly
weakened, have rallied upon each occasion, and have gone far
toward regaining their full strength. So we may trust, by the
good hand of God upon us, it will be in the future. It is a
matter of wonder, as we review the history, not that the
society should have been thus weakened, but that, under all
these adverse circumstances, it should have remained so
vigorous.

The great change in the establishment of a new centre of
the town, at some distance from this point, has placed us at a
disadvantage to which we cannot be insensible. The growth
of business, and the increase of population, are in that direc-

tion, rather than with us. Public assemblies of every kind are more easily gathered there. Faithful and patient exertion will be needed to maintain this religious society in strength and efficiency. But the need there is of patience and fidelity may not prove in the end an injury to us. We have still a field to occupy. And we have abundant occasion to believe that the favor of God will be upon us in our efforts to sustain the institutions of religion upon this spot where they have for so long a time been planted.

It is worthy of mention, that, from an early period to the present time, there have always been persons connected with this organization who have been very active and efficient in promoting its interests. There has never failed to be found in the parish a succession of capable men, fitted to manage its affairs, and thoroughly engaged in their purpose to maintain and strengthen it ; and of women also, in all those important concerns that belong peculiarly to their charge, the like has certainly been true in these later years, if not from the first. It is to be hoped that the succession may never fail.

The hour admonishes me that this review of the history of our parish and church must end.* It is not, indeed, its deepest and most real history, that can, in this manner, be traced. The progress of life with man is not most truly down the course of the stream of time, as it runs in our view from age to age. It is across that stream, and upon the land that lies beyond. To that main land of life the members of all our earthly communities are swiftly passing. The history of a church, and of an order of Christian ministry, can only be

---

* The address, as given upon the day of the commemoration, followed the course of the parish history upon a closer and narrower line than in the enlargement, as here printed ; being substantially the same for such parts as were taken in hand. It occupied a little less than an hour and a half in delivery.

known by the aid it has rendered in the fitting of men for the journey toward it and the endless habitation upon it.

The work of a church in the present time, and in its influences on human society, may yet be of great and incalculable importance.   In these respects we may believe that the office of the church and the ministry of the word of God in this place have not wholly failed.   We find occasion, indeed, of warning, but far more of thankfulness and hope.   These centuries of this Christian society have passed like a day, heavy and darkened with storms on its early morning, but with many soon following hours of reviving sunlight.   It is far yet, we do not doubt, from the brightness of the perfect day.   Neither in the lives nor preaching of its members or pastors, has it ever arrived at the full ideal of the Christian state.   We recognize with thankfulness, as well as with humility, these possibilities and obligations of further attainment.   We rejoice in the higher standard ever before us in the word and life of the Son of God.   We think thankfully also of ourselves as only one among the many companies of those whose aim it is to honor and follow the same Lord.   We are gladdened by all the prosperity of our sister, our daughter churches, and in all the growth of the kingdom of God in the world.   We trust only that this our church may stand, with all these its friendly and helping companions around it, until that kingdom is set up in the fulness of its earthly grace and glory.

For what these gospel ordinances have here wrought, that is reaching already beyond the bounds of time, — we can only in part discern it.   The Christian faith has not failed here to make proof of its divine origin, and its power to the final salvation of the soul.   It has been heard and accepted in a penitence and love, and newness of life, that have their natural and befitting issue, by the power of God, in the perfect and everlasting righteousness of the redeemed.   There have gone from us in former times, we may not doubt, into the holiness and bliss of heaven, many of those whose names the most of us have never learned to speak.   Others, in the same hope, have left us but lately, whose names we might not need to speak, — Putnam, Preston, Lawrence ; and of these names more than one, and of others many, that might be added, — seeming yet scarcely to be separated from our communion on earth, and from these gatherings of our solemn and grateful commemoration. They will not return to us. It is in our most precious trust, that we may shortly be joined with them, and with the sacred assembly of which they form a part.

We stand with them upon the ancient faith, and in this tested hope of the Christian revelation. And thus to-day, with the memories here revived of all this fleeting past, encompassed by the failing generations of mankind, — and failing ourselves with them, — we keep this hope, which is not mortal, and which the wasting time has no more of power against than to make short the hours that withhold its fulfilment from us. The fathers and the mothers, and all that were before us, in their earthly succession are gone, as the grass of the fields they tilled : but THE WORD OF THE LORD still lives, with its color and blossom of endless promise on it ; AND THIS IS THE WORD WHICH HERE BY THE GOSPEL HAS BEEN PREACHED UNTO YOU.

12

DINNER, AND ADDRESSES FOLLOWING.

ADDRESSES AND LETTERS.

AT the close of the historical address, upon the day of the commemoration, after the singing of an anthem by the choir, Dea. Samuel Preston, chairman of the general committee of arrangements, and president of the day, made a brief welcoming address. He expressed the pleasure with which he witnessed the coming together, notwithstanding the unfavorable weather, of so many of our friends to join in the celebration of the two hundredth anniversary of this Christian society. He spoke of the interest with which he believed they had listened to the narrative of its early trials and struggles, as well as to the story of its later and more prosperous days. And, referring to the need they must feel of bodily refreshment, he invited them to proceed to the Village Hall, below, for that purpose.

Here the committee of entertainment, assisted by the ladies of the parish, had prepared a most elegant and beautiful repast. It is not believed that it could have been surpassed, even on the memorable occasion of the ordination of Dr. Wadsworth.

The storm abroad, in the mean time, was somewhat abating; and the assembly, which had been increasing in size from the opening of the morning service, had grown to be large as we returned, at two o'clock in the afternoon, to the audience-room of the meeting-house.

The president took the chair, and introduced the various speakers, whose addresses are herewith given in the order of their occurrence.* There was also singing at intervals by the

---

* These addresses are printed from MSS. furnished by the speakers in all cases, except where special statement is made to the contrary.

choir; and the reading of letters, of which further account will be given.

ADDRESS OF REV. JOHN PIKE, D.D., OF ROWLEY.

The object of this day is to remember the past. No man will here be. called an "old fogy" if he neglects the present, or even somewhat depreciates it, that he may magnify the days that are gone. Wendell Phillips would probably give one-half his earnings if he could always have such a day as this in which to deliver his celebrated lecture on the "Lost Arts."

The life of a people is closely associated with the character of its ministry. Hence it is natural for us to give a large portion of our thought to those ministers with whom your past has been honored. The history of your Clark is familiar to those who have kept themselves acquainted with the distinguished men of Essex County. I should like to have been present at the "winter evenings in Salisbury," and seen the downcast faces and mortified hearts which the argument he sent thither upon the "Doctrine of Original Sin" would naturally produce. The reputation of your Wadsworth is, that he was a florid writer, which was quite a distinction in an age when flowers were as rare in the pulpit as they are now abundant within and around it. With your last two pastors I have been personally and happily acquainted. They need no comment from me, being an "epistle known and read in all the churches" for intelligent thought and correct statements of Christian truth. I knew a clergyman who came from his study one morning with a long face and a distressed heart, and said to his wife that he wished there could be a pump invented to pump out ideas. The quick-witted lady replied that she thought the pump most wanted was one to pump them in. These ministers of yours have needed no machinery for either of these valuable purposes. Ideas lie in their brain as in their native bed; and the avenue through which they have gone forth to the world has been always forcible. The "trumpet" here has given no "uncertain sound."

The people of "old Salem Village" have been widely known. The exceptions to their honorable history ought to be charitably considered. Many who have criticised them severely have forgotten the saying, "There is no man that doeth good and sinneth not ; " and will find a hard fate if the Scripture should be fulfilled in their case, "With what measure you mete, it shall be measured to you again." Parris, your fourth minister, was probably no more to blame than Cotton Mather. He certainly entered into many of the transactions of "witch-craft," by a decree of the courts which he would not feel authorized to neglect. Witchcraft was a disease of the age, as common in the Church of England as in the Church of the Puritans. Clergymen, governors, judges, jurors, physicians, were so involved, that it is idle to separate one man, and make him a "scapegoat" for the rest. Their strange course has, at least, this charitable solution : that they reverently bowed to the word of God ; and, not detecting the line which He who "spake as never man spake" had drawn between the ceremonial and moral of the old dispensation, were left to certain acts which the pious heart generally will disown, and which they soon disowned themselves. Our Puritan ancestry have not been perfect ; but they have certainly been the fountains of as noble a government, and as pure a religion, as the earth ever had. Their modes of life will sometimes be trifled with as simple, and sometimes condemned as doubtful. But because they wore uncouth garments, and laid out their villages so that modern taste cannot correct them, and built their houses fronting toward the fields, and with a roof running so low that they had hardly a "sky-light" view of the passing traveller, and preferred their sanded rooms to a carpeted parlor, and the shining pewter upon their walls to our elegant mirrors and rich pictures, I will never forget the noble minds and pure hearts that those villages contained and those roofs covered ; which, like the stream from Ezekiel's temple, might seem at first view only ankle-deep, but which soon swelled into a river, that no one could pass, and filled the earth with verdure and fruitfulness.

The age in which we live has been called "fast ; " and certainly the epithet is deserved.   Every one is on the wing ; and but few stop to inquire what we are gaining, and what we are losing.   The Germans used to say that there was always a clearing or breathing-time after every new school of philosophy, in which they summed up the gains and losses.   When will the breathing-time of America come, that we can sit down quietly to inquire what we have gained by our speculations in philosophy and religion?   Dead matter seems to engross the attention of the world.   Perhaps the day may come when the Psalmist's expression will be more fully realized, that we are "fearfully and wonderfully made ;" and Galen's idea more deeply felt, that "the human frame is a hymn to the Almighty ;" and Pope's sentiment more closely sympathized with, "The proper study of mankind is man."   When the happy day arrives, that God is placed far above and beyond the earth upon which we tread and the skies upon which we look, and every scientific man will be ashamed to suggest that this wonderful universe has originated from the unthinking movements of its own globules, and that the men upon it, once said to be a little lower than the angels, are only the development of brutal form, thought, and feeling, — then will the saying be realized again, "The morning stars sang together, and all the sons of God shouted for joy."

ADDRESS OF ALLEN PUTNAM, ESQ., OF BOSTON.

My invitation to say a few words here to-day involved a hint that personal reminiscences of this spot and its appendages would be acceptable.   I shall comply in part.   To avoid the danger of duplicating what other gleaners on the parish common might bring before you, I sent memory off on a solitary stroll to see if she couldn't pick up something which no one else would be likely to find.   She soon brought back this experience.

Once upon a time my sister Emma, two years older than myself, was led over to this spot by the "hired help" in the family ; and she took home and gave to me the most sparkling gems my young eyes had ever seen.   Memory beholds them now, sparkling just as brightly as they did when first pulled out from my sister's pocket in the eastern yard of our old family mansion, about ten feet, more or less, south from the outer door leading to either the sitting-room or parlor of brother William's house. Mechanics had been using metal upon the *New* Brick meeting-house ; and my precious gems were some bright, "bran-new" sparkling scraps which had been clipped off by the tinman's shears. They were unfading beauties, — "joys forever," — and look just as bright to-day as they did sixty-six years ago. I have brought them here as my contribution to this parish collection of native products. Look at them, — the beauties. If you can't see them, it is only because you don't look through my eyes. They are here : *I* see them just as surely as I do any one of you. And they whisper in my ear that human vision is a faculty of marvellous capabilities and operations ; that it is ever robing in *changing* hues our judgments, faiths, and feelings, and is thus causing us to be ever differing one from another in our estimates of intrinsic values, and also to be ever changing our own estimates of the worth of many things we know or possess. Led by vision, one prizes a scrap of tin much more highly when only four years old than he does when three score and four. So, too, many a belief or notion valued highly in early life seems little more than tinsel at three score and ten. It is a law of human life, that man — spiritual man — shall be ever growing, and ever outgrowing himself ; that growths and outgrowings are essential steps in any healthful progress ; that man must forget many things that are behind, when he wisely presses toward the mark for the prize of the high calling of God upon him.

I limit my offering of personal reminiscences to that one tin plate of thin soup, hoping thereby to whet your appetites for more substantial things I am holding back, — things it would give me keen pleasure to contribute plentifully to your collation now, did they not require more table-room than courtesy allows me to cover. She restricts me to a bare sample.

Far other than the ordinary events of parish history at once crowded in upon my brain when I began to consider what I could say to you to-day ; and I will not hold myself back from hinting

at what seem to me much more important than the solicited
personal reminiscences. The oncoming of this memorial celebration awakened in me a strong desire to delve the darkness
of New England's blackest night, and to report here and now
upon its more latent causes, its intrinsic character, and its ulti-
mate results, — to do what I could to "justify the ways of God
to man." If any of you will arrange for a meeting here within
a few weeks, I will gladly come and spend an hour in my best
possible efforts to show that the scenes of *witchcraft* may have
been the most widely and deeply beneficent, and therefore
intrinsically, the brightest of any in all your parish annals. If
my wish is gratified, your record of this day's doings will contain mention of the fact that one septuagenarian, born and
bred on this witchcraft soil, feels conscious, that the out-
growth from seed planted in him here while yet a lad, con-
joined with the world's general advance in knowledge of
recondite natural forces and laws, and also with observation
and study of marvellous phenomena in modern times, may constitute a torch whose rays can deeply penetrate the dreaded
darkness, which, resting here for nine score years, has bewildered the eyes that looked upon it, making itself appear to
them as a hideous monument of *murderous public phrensy,*
— as an obtrusive remembrancer of what many of you would
gladly consign to the deepest pits of oblivion, — a torch which
may show that the mysterious phenomena of witchcraft here
were the productions of natural forces, laws, instrumentalities,
and processes, — used in part by unseen human intelligences
under *God's* providence, — which in 1692 began to clear, and
have ever since been clearing, ways for mankind's more ready
advancement to freer fields of thought, of sentiment, and of
action, — a torch which may show that the tenacious fidelity
and devotion of hero and martyr to the full requirements of
their own faith and the world's faith, however stern and exact-
ing, commenced the deliverance of broad Christendom from
dire subjection to many wide-spread, hellish, and blood-shedding
witchcraft-dogmas, laws, penalties, and processes of legal trial,
— a torch which may show that the little resolute band of
Devil-fighters here in the wilderness became, though all un-

willingly, yet became most efficient helpers in gaining liberty for the freer action of things nobler than any creed,—for the freer action of *reason and humanity* at the tribunals of justice throughout all Christian lands; may show, that, by their unprecedented and o'erstrenuous obedience to its own rigid behests, they ruptured the vitals of the bloody tyrant whom they and the Christian world were ignorantly serving,—show that the dreaded blackness here is a tombstone marking the resting-place of witchcraft's own mouldered remains. Its inhuman statutes were here developed into such monstrosities, that the world stood aghast at them,—shrunk from them in horror,—and caused that the places that had known them for long centuries have never known them since, and make it our privilege to be standing here to-day on modern witchcraft's verdant grave. One heart in this assembly feels that the soil of this parish—that this witchcraft battle-ground—might fittingly sustain a lofty and enduring monument to that terrific struggle here, which soon partially evolved world-wide mental and spiritual emancipation, and still beckons onward to ever widening freedom.

ADDRESS OF JUDGE MELLEN CHAMBERLAIN OF BOSTON.

Mr. CHAIRMAN,—I cheerfully respond to your call; though I was hardly expecting it at so early an hour, as I am neither native nor citizen of this ancient town. For three winters, when a member of Dartmouth College, I taught school in one of your districts, and during those years formed many pleasant acquaintances, one of which ripened into closer intimacy, and finally resulted in marriage, with a daughter of one of your townsmen. To this circumstance it is owing that I am with you to-day; but not, let me say, with the same feeling that animates the bosom of the native-born, returning after years of absence. Their feelings I fully understand, though I do not share them at this hour and in this place. But there is a quiet little town on the banks of the Merrimac, in Central New Hampshire, every sod of which becomes quickened beneath my revisiting footstep; for there my eyes first beheld the light of day, and "night clad in the beauty of a thousand stars." Every tree, every house, in that old town, and every feature of its landscape, are dear to me as these are to you ; and, whenever I find myself among them, tears unbidden will flow, and the heart is agitated with the old emotion. And even now, when far away from the scenes of my childhood, memory recalls them, and not without deep feeling ; for

> "Our river by its valley-born
> Was never yet forgotten."

If to-day I cannot fully enter into all your joys and sorrows, I am at least an interested listener to all that is said. We are citizens of the same State, or, at all removes, of the same country ; and this instinctive love of locality, which so moves you here to-day, and all of us somewhere, is, when diffused, that love of our common country which we call patriotism. We love the spot that gave us birth ; and this sentiment, strengthening with the unfolding years, finally embraces the whole country within the circle of a common affection. Animated by this sentiment, as a citizen of Massachusetts, and somewhat more, recalling, as I now do, the many sabbaths I have sat in this sacred place, I am glad to be present on this occasion.

The two centuries behind us have witnessed an experiment perhaps without its essential parallel in history. At this hour the result of that experiment confronts us, and we are required to estimate its magnitude.

Our ancestors came to this soil ; and the descendants of some of them still cultivate the same acres which the first emigrants, with painful toil, reclaimed from the primitive wilderness. Those first men were of a hardy, vigorous race, with uncommon aptitude for colonization. They were as intelligent and as moral as any community of men and women of those times, — perhaps of any time. The soil on which they settled required and repaid industrious cultivation. They were a well-to-do people. No inheritance of poverty was theirs. They left the burdens of the old country behind them when they crossed the ocean. Once settled on this soil, "no

hungry generations trod them down." For them there was a
new start in life, and, upon the whole, under most favorable
material circumstances. It is also to be noted that they were
a free people, who had been taught civil and religious liberty
in the same school as Milton and Cromwell. No feudal system interfered with the rights of person, and no complicated
law of tenures obstructed the accumulation or diffusion of
property. In a word, they entered upon these centuries which
we are now reviewing, with an unencumbered soil, civil and
religious liberty, social equality, a free State, a free church,
an open Bible, and the common school.

What more would the most enthusiastic believer in human
advancement require? What condition of success did our
ancestors lack? And now the question of main interest to
us returns: What is the result of this experiment? Success,
beyond question, in every material interest; and, leaving out
of the account the generation of men and women now on the
stage, perhaps because it is wise, and certainly because it is
modest so to do, I think the experiment was a marked success
in training a community of high intellectual and moral culture,
possessing in a special degree that combination of qualities
which we call character. At least, I have been accustomed to
think that Essex County, at the commencement, say, of the
second century, and as the result of its discipline during the
first, entered upon an epoch of almost unexampled brilliancy in
the history of the English race. Observe how the men of
those days projected their influence beyond the limits of their
county, and of the State itself. Recall silently — for I will
not stop to mention them — the long list of names, —

"On fame's eternal bead-roll worthy to be filed,"—

which, in theology, jurisprudence, science, and statesmanship,
have illustrated and adorned your annals. Where upon this
continent, but in Essex, did commerce receive its first impulse, and secure its most substantial results? Who earlier,
or more resolutely, than the men of Essex, met the shock of
the great revolution which severed an empire; or exercised a
greater formative or controlling influence upon the govern-

ment which succeeded? What men, but your fathers and their neighbors of adjacent towns, met England on the deep, and secured our commercial freedom, and for our navy gained imperishable renown? Certainly the second century of your history is grand and almost epical.

But I have not recalled it altogether, nor chiefly, for congratulation; but simply to ask, standing as we now do at the threshold of a new century, what are we to do with all this priceless inheritance of intellectual and moral wealth, and all these precious memories of the past, which are cast into our laps? Shall we transmit them unimpaired? Shall we cause this great estate, which has fallen to our management, to yield its just increase of intellectual power, general culture, good morals, and widely diffused happiness? Is the experiment which yielded such grand results in the second century, to fail in the third,— to fail with us?

Our ancestors had their problem.: we have ours. It was theirs to subdue a wilderness, and erect a State, to organize civil communities, to found free churches and free schools. It is ours to perfect, adorn and transmit unimpaired, these priceless blessings. They did their work well. Ours remains. And we should remember that events unfold more rapidly with us than with them. Causes operate and results mature in briefer periods in these days than in the former. Long before the lapse of two other centuries, the hopes of man in free government will either be sadly frustrated or fully realized on this soil. Failing here, self-government will be likely to fail everywhere; and, succeeding here, men may be encouraged to expect happier days for less favored communities.

I am well aware that there is nothing novel in this line of thought. Our past is full of such questions; and, on such occasions as this, they will and should force themselves upon our attention; and it matters little whose voice gives utterance to feelings which pervade all bosoms. The past is secure; but many thoughtful people, while they find much for encouragement in respect to the future, are not wholly without solicitude. May we of this generation discover the work which belongs to us, and have strength and wisdom to perform it as well, as our ancestors performed their work!

ADDRESS OF REV. ALFRED P. PUTNAM, D.D., OF BROOKLYN, N.Y.

FRIENDS,— It is with feelings of peculiar pleasure and satisfaction that I respond to the kind invitation of the committee to participate in the celebration of the two hundredth anniversary of the establishment of this society. As I have glanced at the pages of your Church Manual, I have been more forcibly than ever reminded how many and how sacred are the ties that connect me here. Among the original members of this church were some of my earliest ancestors in this country. John Putnam, who in 1634 came from England to America, with his three sons, Thomas, Nathaniel, and John, and settled in Salem Village, had died when this society was separated from the First Church in Salem. The three sons, however, survived him, and were among the first to organize the new parish. The descendants of Nathaniel, my progenitor, continued to worship on this spot for successive generations ; and I suppose that I might in some good way claim as my cousins the whole "wilderness" of Putnams here, as Father Taylor would call them. In the list of deacons presented in the Manual referred to, I see the name of Edmund Putnam, who died in 1810, at the age of eighty-six, and who was my great-grandfather. Among those who joined the church in 1832 was my mother, who still remains with us, having passed beyond the limit of fourscore years ; and of those who joined it in 1851, was one who walked with me in my early wedded life, but who has long since gone before. Nor would I forget the name of the first Mrs. Nathan Tapley, who, as the teacher of an infant class, here gave me the earliest instruction in Bible and catechism which I ever received in the church of Christ.

It was about this time, while I was yet a little boy, that an incident occurred which shows how kindly you have been disposed to care for those who go astray. One Sunday after the service was ended, I marched out of the church in advance of

my older sisters, and, confident of my sufficient acquaintance
with the homeward route, trudged on with the crowd that
proceeded towards the turnpike.   As my attendants dropped,
one by one, into their homes along the way, until I was left
quite alone, I dimly remember how I began to look about
me, and to feel that the road, and objects on either side, had a
startlingly unfamiliar aspect.   In short, I was getting to be
considerably frightened, when a good friend who knew me,
and had followed me with gracious intentions, thinking I was
wandering on in the wrong direction, came up to me, and,
having found that it was just as he supposed, took me home.
He struck a bee-line for my father's house, crossing the hills
and fields, leading me when I was able to walk, and bearing
me on his shoulders when I was tired.   I need not say that I
was heartily welcomed by the anxious ones at the old homestead ;
nor need I say how grateful I have always felt to Mr. Moses
Prince, who rendered me this very timely service in my childhood.   I am glad to see him here to-day ; but I somewhat
doubt whether he would be as willing now, as he was then, to
carry me on his back over Lindall's Hill.

How well I remember the old brick meeting-house ; remember how twice a Sunday long processions of carriages, laden
with devout worshippers, rolled along all the roads that here
converge, and poured their living currents of humanity into
the venerable structure ; how, oh ! sweetest, sacredest recollection of life, I used to nestle as a little child at my mother's
side, as she sat in the house of God ; how I was wont to look up
at the minister, and fear that at any moment the *sounding-board*
might drop, and extinguish him utterly ; how, at the other end
of the church, Mr. Henderson, Mr. Berry, the Miss Clarks,
and many others, sang the good old hymns we shall never forget ; how patiently the great congregation stood through what
is oftentimes rather significantly called "the long prayer," at
the end of which they filled the spacious building with a great
clatter, by letting fall the lifted lids of their uncushioned
seats ; how the big boys in the galleries, hidden away in high,
square pews, disturbed the worship of the hour by a still
more unendurable racket ; and how it was necessary at times

to awe these incorrigible offenders, by sending among them the dreaded tithingman.

What able, interesting, eloquent sermons it was the privilege of this society to hear from Dr. Braman in that old brick church, and afterward in this edifice which was erected on its site. Many a text from which he preached when I was a boy, I well remember still, while, what is more, the deep impression made upon my mind by the discourses themselves has never been lost. It has been my privilege to listen to many an instructive and powerful preacher ; but I can hardly name one of them whose pulpit ministrations evinced such rare originality of thought, scholarly research, intimate acquaintance with the heart of man and with the experiences of the spiritual life, as did his. And who, that heard them, can ever forget the famous occasional sermons which Dr. Braman was accustomed to give on Fast and Thanksgiving Days, when intelligent and influential persons came, not only from all parts of Danvers, but from other towns as well, to listen to what he had to say about the various social, political, and reform questions of the day ; or about, it might be, the virtues and sacrifices of the forefathers, and the customs and institutions of dear New England ? Danvers has never had a better preacher than the immediate predecessor of the present worthy incumbent of this pastoral office ; and I shall always regard it as one of the highest privileges of my earlier life, that I was permitted on so many occasions to hear his voice.

Two hundred years, of what eventful and thrilling history, of what consecrated toil and immortal harvests ! Scarcely any other church in the country has so interesting and affecting a record as this. If, in the early time, that record was darkened with accounts of superstitious beliefs and tragic scenes, yet, in subsequent periods, it was illumined with the growing light of truth and peace. Through all the years that have elapsed since this society was established, how many good and faithful souls have worshipped here, and have gone to their reward ? Godly men and saintly women, — not a few, — who were an honor and blessing to the community in which they lived, and who are now with God, here learned the lessons of duty and the way of salvation ; here prayed and sang, rejoiced and sorrowed, loved and served together ; here bequeathed as they departed, to those who should come after them, a Christian example and a precious memory. May their successors be as faithful to the light and opportunities of to-day, and of coming time, as were those who have thus preceded us in the march of life to the light and opportunities which God vouchsafed to them.

Bless God that increasing light is ever pouring down upon us all. and will to the end of time. "The Lord has more truth yet to break forth out of his holy word." It is just as true now as it was when John Robinson of Leyden said it two and a half centuries ago. We have outgrown many an error and superstition which our fathers who first worshipped here regarded as most important truth. Much that we deem to be important truth now may also appear as error or superstition to those who shall, two hundred years hence, stand in our places. Things, moreover, which we to-day hold to be false, may sooner or later be revealed to us, or those who shall follow us, as true. While some of us need to go forward to accept the new, others may need to go back to take up not a little of the old, which they have left behind. We shall all, I believe, meet finally on a common ground, and see eye to eye, reverencing alike the word of God, and loving with equal devotion the Lord Jesus Christ,— members together of the same great fold on earth, and heirs together at last of the same heavenly glory.

ADDRESS OF MR. GRANVILLE B. PUTNAM, MASTER OF THE FRANKLIN SCHOOL OF BOSTON.

MR. PRESIDENT AND FRIENDS, — Like many a New-England boy living away from his birthplace and the home of his infancy, I was accustomed, year by year, to return to the old homestead, to meet with grandfather and grandmother, with uncles, aunts, and cousins, to enjoy that time-honored festival, Thanksgiving. I remember, as I recall those days, that my thoughts, both in anticipation and in retrospect, were of turkey, of chicken-pie, and plum-pudding, not forgetting the blindman's buff in the evening ; but as years passed on, and we missed, one after another, the familiar forms and loved faces of dear ones called from earth, my thoughts were less of the good things of the table, and more of the kind words, the generous deeds, and Christian life, of the departed. So to-day, as we gather, some of us from distant homes, our thoughts are not chiefly of the collation so bountifully provided and so gracefully served by the ladies, but rather of the devoted piety and Christian heroism of godly men and women who labored here in the Master's cause.

While recalling the early history of the church, let us not forget the origin of the sabbath school, whose fiftieth anniversary was celebrated two years since. I call upon you to honor the memory of Joanna Prince and Hannah Hill of Beverly, who, in 1810, gathered together the children of their neighbors, for religious and moral instruction upon the sabbath day ; thus inaugurating a system of sabbath-school instruction in this region. Honor to the memory of their friend Betsey F. Putnam, who, imbued with their spirit, originated in 1818 the "Danvers Sabbath School Village Society." * Nor would we forget the names of those who joined with her in this good work. On that 30th of July, when this society was formed, there were present Edwin Jocelyn, Samuel Preston (who has been spared to preside on this occasion), Betsey Putnam, Hannah Putnam, Harriet Putnam, Nancy Putnam, Clarissa Putnam, Edith Swinerton, Betsey Pope, Eliza Putnam, and Eliza Preston. On the 9th of August the school was opened ; and eternity alone can reveal the good accomplished by these first teachers and their successors for more than a half-century.

I cannot allow this opportunity to pass without mention of

---

* Miss Betsey F. Putnam brought from her friends at Beverly to this place the idea of a sabbath school, and assisted at its formation. She is not to be confounded with Betsey, sister of Hannah Putnam. These two ladies last named, who were also teachers in the public schools, were foremost in efficiency, if not in the very opening of the school, yet in its establishment and maintenance through all its earlier years. — R.

the debt of gratitude I owe to him,* who for thirty-six years was the pastor of this church, and whose name is recorded there. His hand was laid upon my brow in baptism. From his lips I heard, so faithfully presented sabbath after sabbath, those great truths which make wise unto salvation. Week by week, without any adequate compensation, he directed my studies in preparation for college ; and more than all, when, seeking relief from a burden of sin, I had waded for two miles amid the darkness and the storm through the deepening snow to seek his guidance, with a faithfulness and a tenderness I shall never forget, he pointed me to the Crucified One. Who of us cannot testify to the wonderful power of many of the sermons preached by him from this desk? Although the printer's type has preserved but few of them, they will never pass from the tablets of memory.

Mention was made in the address of the morning of young people's meetings held more than a century ago. I would bring to your mind those of a more recent date. In the spring of 1857 a little company of five or six, most of whom had just found the Saviour, met at the house of Dea. Elijah Hutchinson ; and, after a brief season of prayer, we resolved to invite the young people of the parish to meet each week for social worship. The invitation was cordially accepted ; and, accompanied I doubt not by the Holy Spirit, we met for a time from house to house ; but our numbers soon increased to such an extent, that we were obliged to gather in the chapel. I rejoice to know that these meetings have been continued, without interruption, to this day, and that the blessing of God has evidently rested upon them.

Did time permit, I would gladly speak of those Saturday-evening meetings held for years in District No. 4. To the late Stephen Driver, that devoted Christian worker, were we deeply indebted for their origin and continuance ; and I doubt not that he has already united in the music of heaven with some who, through his instrumentality, learned to sing the New Song.

But while we would dwell upon the past, and tell its story,

---

* Rev. Milton P. Braman, D.D.

let us not forget the lesson taught us by this day, and the two hundred years which it commemorates. When the great Napoleon, in his effort to strike a blow at the British power in India, had gathered his troops within sight of those wonders of the desert, he was confronted by a hostile army of Mamelukes, which disputed his progress. To inspire valor in the hearts of his men, he exclaimed, "Soldiers! from yonder pyramids forty centuries look down upon you." The wearied and dispirited ranks were electrified by the thought; and a brilliant victory was gained by the French army. It is true, indeed, that not forty centuries are looking upon us to-day, for we live in an age when ten years are doing the work of a bygone century; but two hundred years are looking upon us, and the thought should inspire us to achieve a glorious triumph for the cause of the great Captain.

In 1820 Daniel Webster, standing by the rock of Plymouth, and speaking of those who a hundred years hence should commemorate the landing of the Pilgrims, said, "We would leave for the consideration of those who shall then occupy our places, some proof that we hold the blessings transmitted from our fathers in just estimation; some proof of our attachment to the cause of good government and of civil and religious liberty." We would catch the spirit of the sentiment uttered by the great orator at Plymouth, and see to it that the record of this day shall witness to those who shall celebrate the three hundredth anniversary of this church, that we are not unmindful of the blessings which we inherit, that we love the faith of the fathers, and that we adore the Puritan's God.

The next speaker was Rev. James Brand, pastor of the Maple-street Church, of whose remarks I have not been able to procure a full report. He spoke with warmth of the affection felt for the First Church by the church of which he was pastor. He alluded to its age, as running back one hundred and four years beyond the signing of the Declaration of Independence, and one hundred and one years beyond the Boston

Tea-party.* He proceeded to speak with force of the refor-
matory power of the Christian gospel, as preached in these
New-England churches, and of its wholesome influence upon
society and upon the institutions of government. He declared
also his faith in the present age, his confidence in its powers
of life and progress, and his firm expectation of future times
at hand, not worse than the past, but better than any that have
gone before.

Address of Rev. Hiram B. Putnam of West Concord, N.H.†

Mr. Chairman, — We are all at school to-day, learning from
the past ; and the very way in which we are conducting these
exercises is an unconscious tribute to the past. The spirit of
the old-time days and the old-time preachers is upon us ; for
we keep the *same theme all day.* This morning we had the
text and argument ; this afternoon we are having the "improvements ; " just the method of Dr. Emmons and others
of his day. Not that we need improve the excellent discourse
of the morning, or improve *upon* it : we are trying to improve
by it. That suggested histories and memories which we are
following out a little more fully. That was a picture of the
past sketched in outline, but of necessity not filled out in all
details. As we bring our individual reminiscences, we are
only letting in a little more light upon parts of the canvas,
where the interest of one and another specially attaches, and

* This reference to the Boston Tea-party leads me, though beyond the exact
limit of this history, to a notice of a most pleasant observance of the one hundredth anniversary of that memorable occurrence, Dec. 16, 1873, at Village
Hall. The hall was filled with tables, separated from each other, and each
under the charge of one of the ladies of the parish, who furnished it in antique
style, and who presided over the group that gathered about it. A choice company was assembled from all the societies and neighborhoods of the town. There
was historic and other speech-making, and much flow of wit with social intercourse ; and the occasion altogether was rare and enjoyable.

Though no longer at the centre of the town, the old parish still claims a certain
right, on these days that look to the past, of calling as children to the ancient
homestead all the families upon its original soil. And the children have not
seemed unwilling to answer the call.

† Installed pastor of the Tabernacle Church, Salem, Dec. 31, 1873.

bringing out in a little more prominence figures about which our memory lingers. We are taking up the threads of our present ecclesiastical history, and tracing them back through these past two centuries to their very beginning. We are trying to weave or reproduce the pattern of the past. The *warp* we had in the historical sketch of the morning; the *woof*, or filling-in, we are furnishing now, as memory and history supply us.

And, sir, we do well to stand with backward gaze to-day, drawing our inspirations from the past, thus consecrating the day. But we do better not to stay in the past. We want to connect the past with the present ; to be instructed from the past, and from its lessons get wisdom for the future. I trust, therefore, it is not from curiosity only, or with the spirit of the antiquary or relic-hunter merely, that we turn back the pages of our history, revive these memories, and bring out these reminiscences to-day. We are taking this survey of what has gone, that we may find the formative, moulding influences of earlier years, which have helped make us what we are to-day. The history of the church in this place, the preaching of the gospel here, during these last two hundred years, have had more to do than we can reckon in producing the thrift and culture, and elevated Christian sentiment, that characterize the homes of this neighborhood to-day. While we acknowledge the mistakes of the past, we ought gratefully to recognize, on this occasion, the helps of the past.

Among the educating, formative influences of our more recent past history, is the ministry of Rev. Dr. Braman. Your committee have suggested that I say a word on this subject. We had hoped almost to the last, that Dr. Braman would be here to-day, by his presence and words to give an added interest to our anniversary. In his absence we can at least make grateful acknowledgment of his very able and faithful service in a long pastorate among this people. It will not be expected of me, in these few moments allowed me, to give a full historic sketch of that pastorate, or to attempt any exhaustive description or analysis of the talents and pulpit power of our former pastor. Even if I could give you full details of the outward features of that ministry, if I had the exact dates and figures, — could tell you just how many sermons he preached to this people, on how many occasions he acted in an official capacity outside the pulpit, how many addresses and lectures he gave here and elsewhere, — all this would be no true or satisfying measure of the real service which he rendered us. And I am sure we could never get these figures from him. He never made a parade of such statistics. He was also very chary of giving his sermons for publication. He shrank from any notoriety from the press ; and in only a very few instances could he be persuaded to allow his manuscript to go into the printer's hands. One of his Thanksgiving sermons, a sermon on the Mexican War, an election sermon, and the discourse delivered at the dedication of this house, were published. But, if we could reckon all the intellectual and moral and spiritual quickening which this people received under the the preaching of Dr. Braman for nearly forty years, — if it were possible to follow out and gather up such results, *moral* results, — we know that we should see that his ministry was abundantly fruitful of good.

Dr. Braman had marvellous power in the pulpit : there was his great strength. His presentations of the great truths of the· gospel system were not only correct and clear, but they were *powerful*. There are many among us who have vivid recollections of particular sermons delivered in this house with thrilling effect. Some of his biographical sermons are well remembered for their discriminating analysis, their acute insight into character, their touches of rare wit, their timely and well-put applications. On a certain sabbath which fell on the Fourth of July, Dr. Braman preached a sermon (from the text, " If the Son therefore shall make you free, ye shall be free indeed ") which made a most profound impression upon all who heard it, and will long be remembered for its theme, its illustrations, and the moving power of oratory with which it was delivered.

Not only on " occasions," but uniformly, were this people helped, educated, stimulated, by the presence and power of such a preacher. Our hearts and lives to-day feel the effects, and we trust bear some results of his inspiring helpful ministry to us. The church was strengthened and blessed under this pastor ; and, when he retired, it was not from a people weary and impatient under his services ; it was not from a people who could see in him signs of waning vigor and diminishing talents : it was against the decided wish and choice of his people that he left his pastorate among us when he did ; it was when his "natural force had not abated," when his powers were only in the early autumn richness of their fruitage, that *he* decided such a step to be the part of wisdom. I am sure our hearts go out in blessing to him at this hour, as we review the past ; while we shall ever hold in grateful remembrance his ministry here, with the impulse to good, and the quickening influence which he was able under divine grace to impart to us.

And now, sir, as we stand here to-day, trying to link the past with the present, we may well have a thought also for the future. Let us hope that the blessings of a faithful, able, devoted ministry may be perpetuated here. It is not a small thing, that for these last two centuries, with their thousands of sabbaths, the word of truth has here been proclaimed, the fire has not gone out upon this altar. May a light always shine out from this church ! May the truth ever be preached here in love, and with power ! May the beneficent results of the preached word always be seen in this place, and the consolations of the gospel of peace abound here to the latest generation !

ADDRESS OF WM. P. UPHAM, ESQ., OF SALEM.

While I shrink from addressing such an assemblage as this, and upon such an occasion, and regret very much the absence of Mr. Goodell,* who is far more competent to answer for the First Church of Salem, still, as I have had such great enjoy-

---

* Mr. Upham was called upon not only as one very familiar with all this local history, but as a representative of the First Church in Salem, from which this church was an offshoot. I have been unable to give the remarks of the president in introducing the speakers, having no record of them.

Mr. Goodell was present in the evening, and took part in the exercises.

ment in attending these commemorative exercises, and in listening to the interesting historical address of this forenoon,
so well arranged, so correct, and interspersed with so much of
wit and pleasing reminiscence to relieve the darker and graver
outlines of history, I do not feel justified in wholly declining
to respond.

There is one thought connected with the character of this
community which a study of its early history and of the first
settlements that were made here suggests, that may be not
without value; namely, the permanency of the ancestral homestead in the same family, generation after generation.   Those
who first occupied and cultivated the region afterwards included within the bounds of Salem Village were men of a
remarkable stamp.   Active, industrious, frugal, and intelligent,
they were well fitted to make fertile and profitable farms out
of what was then but a rough wilderness.   As we look around
us upon these farms, now so conveniently divided into fields,
meadows, and woodland, with good roads leading in every desirable direction, we find it difficult to realize or appreciate the
vast amount of patient labor that must have been required to
first break the soil and make the rough places smooth.   An
enumeration merely of the names of those first settlers, so far
as memory will recall them, will show how many of them were
not only prominent in colonial history, but men whose descendants still live here, and take part in this celebration.

The settlements appear to have spread up the western
branches of the North River, first on what is now Waters
River, then called Cow-house River, or Endicott's River, and
on Crane River and Whipple Brook; then on Frost-fish
River, now called Porter's River, and on Frost-fish Brook,
which empties into it from the north.

On Waters River was the orchard farm of Gov. Endicott,
a part of which is to-day owned by a direct descendant.   At
Felton's Hill, Nathaniel Felton made his home, whose descendants still occupy the same homestead.   South of that was the
farm of Emanuel Downing, leased upon his removal to John
Proctor, whose children afterwards took a deed of it; and the
homestead continues in that family to the present time.   Next

west of Endicott was the Townsend Bishop farm, where Francis and Rebecca Nurse lived, and where to-day direct descendants reside, the children of Mr. Orin Putnam, who receives so courteously the numerous visitors coming, like pilgrims, to look upon the home of that saintly woman, a victim of the terrible tragedy of 1692.

On the spot where we now meet, the first settler was Richard Weston. He and Richard Waterman, who lived near by, removed to Providence, Rhode Island; and were among the leading colonists. They took part in founding there the first Baptist Church in America. Richard Ingersoll and William Haynes bought the Weston grant; and Nathaniel Ingersoll, son of Richard, and Joseph Houlton, son-in-law of William Haynes and ancestor of the Houlton family, gave the land for the second meeting-house and for the ministry pasture. Judge Houlton lived upon part of the same farm; and his descendants live there still.

East of this was Elias Stileman's grant, bought by Richard Hutchinson, who also bought the farm of John Thorndike, including the hill now called Whipple Hill. Richard Hutchinson first ploughed the fields to the south of Whipple Hill, receiving a special grant from the town as a compensation for his services in first opening the soil to cultivation. Here he lived, and descendants have continued to live, to the present time. North-east from Whipple Hill, John Putnam selected his farm. His descendants are now to be found not only there, but in every part of the town and throughout the country. Robert Prince was his neighbor; and part of the Prince farm is now occupied by a direct descendant.

On Frost-fish River were Lawrence Leach and Jacob Barney, whose farms covered Folly Hill, being separated by a bound wall still to be seen running directly across the top of the hill, now the boundary line between Danvers and Beverly. Jacob Barney gave the land for the first schoolhouse in Salem outside of the town proper.* Its location was afterwards

---

* I have no exact knowledge respecting the building of the schoolhouse here referred too, and which appears upon Mr. Upham's map of 1692. But in any case, while standing south of the road, it was not within the limits of

changed for a time to the north side of the road (the old Ipswich Road); but was again removed to near its first site, now
occupied by the East Danvers school.

The Neck, now Danversport, was granted to Samuel Skelton, pastor of the First Church; and next north, including Lindall Hill, was the grant to Samuel Sharp, Ruling Elder; and,
on the other side of Frost-fish Brook, Charles Gott, first deacon of that church, was the first occupant or owner of what is
now the Burley farm.

John Porter bought all these farms, besides others farther
north, and fixed his residence at the head of the creek that
makes up towards the road from Salem to the Plains, a short
distance east of the Unitarian chapel, where an ancient house
was burned down a few years ago. Where Mr. Augustus
Fowler lives, Daniel Rea was the first occupant. We have
just had the pleasure of listening to a descendant of his, who,
in his early years, lived at the old homestead.

And so we might go through the whole village, from farm
to farm, pointing out the grant to Hugh Peters, east of the
Daniel Rea farm, which Henry Brown coming here from Salisbury bought, and where his descendants continued to reside
for many generations (I believe part of the farm still remains
in possession of the family); Thomas Putnam's homestead,
where his descendant, Mr. Wm. R. Putnam, lives; that of
Thomas Flint in West Danvers, which has ever remained in
that family. Robert Goodell's farm and others might be mentioned; but I will not weary your attention with further detail. The list already given is sufficient to show how remarkable this community is in having so many families descended
from men of the first generation here, and occupying the same
homesteads. The importance of this fact in its bearings upon
the character of this people, and the power which the home-
influence thus created and cherished must have in shaping its
future history, is worthy of consideration. Such is the migra-

Salem Village; and, on either side, it was not within the limits of Danvers, save
as by the new boundary of 1857. And nothing here stated by Mr. Upham is
thus in conflict with what has been said in connection with the house built at the
Village Centre by Mr. Green (p. 59). Mr. Barney gave the land in 1692. — R.

tory and ever-changing nature of our social life, that all traditional veneration for the memory of our ancestors might be lost and forgotten, were it not for the existence of such influences. How many there are who now, after years of busy life far away, return again to the old ancestral home, and, quickened by its beloved and sacred associations, renew their allegiance to those great principles of religious and civil liberty in public affairs, and of virtue and piety in private life, which were so dear to their fathers! Let us hope, that, when another century shall have passed, it may find here a posterity still cherishing those principles, and ready, with their lives if necessary, to uphold and defend them.

ADDRESS OF REV. GEO. N. ANTHONY, PASTOR OF THE SOUTH CHURCH IN PEABODY.

MR. PRESIDENT, — I do not forget that I owe this opportunity for participating in your festival, not to my being a son of old Danvers, for such I am not, nor as one bound to this parish by family ties, as some are who have preceded me, but solely to the fact that I am the pastor of a church neighbor to this, and long within the corporate limits of the same municipality. I may not, therefore, trespass at length upon your patience.

This day is devoted to historic reminiscences. The orator of the morning, alluding to the obscure and voluminous records which he has had occasion to consult in the preparation of his memorial address, gracefully remarked, that, with a " great sum of labor," he had bought his knowledge of your parish history. I, sir, have had no such " sum of labor " at my disposal, and may not, therefore, enter the historic field.

While listening to the very able and entertaining address which your pastor gave us, I was reminded of the account of the creation in the Book of Genesis. There were, it seems, dwelling here, in the early days of old Danvers, strong, robust, energetic, and liberty-loving citizens, who contended much with the wilderness, and much with one another. Bickerings and disputes appear to have been a staple production. Moreover, the ancient proverb was illustrated, that "as with the people, so with the priest;" for the ministers seem to have been as contentious as their flock. Like the earth in its earliest condition was the picture; for chaos and confusion reigned. Order was, however, at length evoked. The change was not an incidental, but a permanent improvement; and gentlemen who have spoken to us, and who familiarly knew the leading citizens of a generation now gone, have paid a loving and beautiful tribute to those departed worthies. The records are in harmony with this oral testimony. For a very long period, there has been a happy concord among the people.

Naturally we ask for the secret of this gratifying transformation. Can we be mistaken in believing that the same good Being who brought order out of confusion to the material world, and garnished the earth with beauty, wrought moral order in the character and life of the Danvers population? His religion has, I would gladly believe, gained a more effective hold upon the understandings and the hearts of men. It is instructive to notice, that always and everywhere, Christianity exerts a formative influence. She shapes the opinion and the character of individuals, of homes, and of institutions. There is a deep significance in the fact to which our attention was just now turned by a neighboring pastor (Rev. James Brand), that this parish is by a whole century older than the nation itself. The Christian religion paves the way for civil and social order. One word in the common speech of men pays its unconscious tribute to this very thing. We speak of *society*, and we invariably regard it as the product of a religious life. Where Christianity has not gone, there is no society, in our sense of the term. Only that can be a true *society*, in which each member is a *socius*, a closely united partner, a link in the social chain, a member of a true brotherhood. Wherefore, the history of old Danvers attests incidentally the value of the religion which has here wrought out these social results. Your history is of itself a *homage* to the system of truth to which you have clung.

There came, we know, a measure of distrust of this system, and a breaking-away from it. If we ask why, one answer, doubtless, is, that certain terms and phrases embodied in the religious vernacular of New England were unhappily chosen ; and another answer may be, that the protest and re-action came, when as yet the memory of contentious and uncomfortable men prominent in religious affairs had not passed away, — a memory not suited to commend any religion with which it may be joined.

To-day we look back gratefully upon the trial of two full centuries of New England Christianity in this place. And, although this occasion is mainly devoted to the past, it is admissible to turn our thoughts also to the present and to the opening future. While we do cheerfully believe that the God who has guided these communities thus far will preserve and bless them still, and while we confide in those doctrines which he has so signally honored already, we are not to forget that new conditions may devolve on us new responsibilities. It must be confessed that there are some aspects of the present and prospective condition of our population, as a whole, adapted to create alarm. Let the lighter divergences of religious opinion be adjusted as they may, we are summoned to meet the question, " What shall be done for the many thousands now in our land who acknowledge neither sabbath, nor Bible, nor even God himself ? " We are annually importing infidelity from abroad, and assimilating with it the irreligion which is native-born. We are driven by the present condition of affairs to ask whether any thing better for substance can be found than that system of religious faith and worship, which, for two centuries, has wrought so beneficently here. May we not to-day study history with advantage, and looking at what we need, and what has been accomplished, say devoutly, *Deus monstrat viam ?*

In closing, I know not how to reciprocate the courtesy which has included the South Church in Peabody among your guests, except by reminding you, that she, too, has a history, and is no modern growth. She looks forward to her bi-centennial ; and when it shall come, — it will soon be here : only forty-one years intervene, — she will expect the church in old Danvers to be with her. These churches and parishes are intimately joined.

Ties of consanguinity and of marriage unite the families. We have members received from you, and you have members received from us. Please not to forget, therefore, the South Church, Peabody, invites you of the First Church, Danvers, to be at her bi-centennial in the year 1913.

ADDRESS OF REV. A. H. CURRIER OF LYNN.

MR. CHAIRMAN, — I esteem it to be an extraordinary favor that I am invited to speak here to-day. Certainly I cannot ascribe the privilege to the fact of birth, or matrimonial alliance, or to any of the other reasons which have guided you in the selection of the other speakers. Perhaps it is due to a happy circumstance in the beginning of my work of the Christian ministry.

It was here, in this honored pulpit, within the walls of this church, that I first tried my unpractised voice in preaching the gospel. In the ears of this people my first sermons were spoken. It has seemed to me ever since, in view of the marked kindness which I have experienced from many of the people here, that the fathers and mothers of this church then took me into their hearts, and adopted me as a son. In gratitude for that kind and affectionate interest, I have been made to feel, in return, an unusual interest in your history and locality.

I have endeavored, so to speak, to fit myself for the place of foster-son, to which your partial favor had received me. As a result, I have been an eager and diligent student of your annals. There is no local history with which I have made myself so well acquainted. Under the guidance of Mr. Upham, as proffered to me in his valuable History of Salem Village, I have extensively traversed, in thought, the region embraced in the ancient limits of your town. With the plan of that region furnished by him in my mind, I have often gone from Hathorne Hill to the Orchard Farm, and from Cherry Hill to the Cow River. By the favor of his introduction, also, I have conversed and become acquainted with the ancient worthies of the village, — with good Nathanael Ingersoll, whose hospitable dwelling stood on ground near to where we are ; with Thomas Putnam, the faithful clerk of the church ; with honest, manly John Procter, whose discernment penetrated and justly weighed the nature of the fearful delusion which sprang up in this neighborhood, and at length made him one of its victims.

When he heard of the feigned revelations of the afflicted children, he said they ought to be sent to the whipping-post rather than to have their accusations of the innocent and infirm heeded. Would that such sound advice had been received and acted upon !

It would most effectually have cured those informers of their mischievous malady, and saved your church and village from the stain which rests upon their early history.

Permit me to dwell a moment upon that sad episode in your history. It may be thought, by those unacquainted with the facts, that the preacher this morning, in referring to Samuel Parris, the chief actor in that melancholy business, was too severe in his condemnation and treatment of one who exercised the sacred office of a Christian minister.

But in my judgment, and if my knowledge of the case is not entirely erroneous, Samuel Parris received a lenient treatment at the preacher's hands.

When I came into the church this morning, and saw on the front of the gallery encircling the house the names of the different ministers who have served this church and people from the beginning until now, framed in evergreen, and ranged in the order of succession, I felt a secret disapproval at beholding among them, and holding a place of equal honor, apparently, with the rest, the name of this man Parris. Justice seemed to require some indication of the guilty part he played in that public tragedy, which cast a cloud of darkness and horror over this region in those early days. I thought of something which I saw in the old city of Venice last year.

In the ancient hall of the Grand Council in the doge's palace, the portraits of the long line of doges who ruled the old Venetian state are ranged around the top of the room, like a frieze. At one place in the historic line a single vacancy

14

appears. Instead of a portrait, one sees the semblance of a black veil, and above it the inscription, " The place of Marino Faliero, who was decapitated for his crimes."

When I saw the name of Samuel Parris inscribed on the front of the gallery, and to all appearance equally honored with the rest in the worthy line, I thought you had tenderly treated him ; that you might have been justified if you had refused him an equal place with the rest, and even if, like the treatment given to her traitorous doge by the Venetian Republic, you had put a black veil, instead of his name, in the enclosure of evergreen, and written over it, " The place of Samuel Parris, gibbeted in infamy, on account of his misdeeds and unchristian conduct."

And now, sir, will you suffer me to say one word as to the lesson taught us by that sad chapter in your history ? The great lesson, as I read it, which that tragical business teaches us is this : the law of charity is to be considered as always in force. It stands paramount above all others, and is never to be disregarded or set aside upon any pretext. If there is any thing in the Bible which seems to contradict and oppose it, if there is any precept or teaching contained there which seems to enjoin a conduct at variance with its promptings, consider that you have made some mistake in interpretation, that you have not yet arrived at the true meaning, that you must not accept any thing as true, which may command you to violate the law of love.

That law is supreme, and cannot rightly be violated. If this truth had been observed by your forefathers and the civil magistrates of their day, there would have been no Salem witchcraft tragedy to deplore.

The same truth acted upon would have prevented the cruel persecutions for heresy which have disgraced the name of Christianity ; and in the future will be a sure safeguard against similar mistakes.

ADDRESS OF DR. JEREMIAH SPOFFORD OF GROVELAND.

MR. CHAIRMAN, — I have very little claim to occupy even the brief space allotted to each speaker during the short hour that is now fast passing away. I have neither resided here, nor descended from any one who ever did ; but, did time and memory serve, I could find many facts and reminiscences of intense interest, at least to the speaker, in connection with this place. My wife and family descended from a Danvers ancestry, and are probably related to every Putnam and Flint in the town, and all the Danvers families with whom the Putnams and Flints intermarried, previous to 1764, when Eleazar Spofford married Mary, daughter of Capt. Elisha Flint and Mary Putnam, and ultimately administered upon his estate, and transmitted to me, his son-in-law and executor, many deeds and partitions of old Danvers lands, one parcel of which, I recollect, is conveyed to the family by Giles Cory. We have now in our family a gold clasp inscribed with their names, and presented by Elisha Flint to Mary Putnam previous to their marriage, which could not well have been later than 1744 ; and a gold ring with the same inscription is still preserved in another branch of the family. I recently visited with much interest the old mansion, with massive timbers and huge chimney, where the recipient of these love-tokens was received, a blooming bride, a hundred and thirty years ago, and was happy to find still well kept and in good hands.

But I have many other interesting reminiscences. In 1795 Thomas Peabody removed from Rocks Village, in Haverhill, to Danvers, with his wife (who was a favorite niece of my mother), and two interesting children, David and Achsah, my early playmates. A constant intercourse was maintained between our families ; and in February, 1796, I first visited this locality with my parents. We moved in primitive style, with horse and sleigh, along the Topsfield road. I remember the white spire of Mr. Wadsworth's church in the distance, soon after burned, and succeeded by the brick church. We arrived at Danvers Plains, and called at " Putnam's Corner." I remember the genial landlord, whom they called Col. Putnam. We passed round by Dr. Putnam's brick house, by West's farm, Derby's garden, and along among the potteries, and the old flax-colored church, whose frequent enlargements had left it, with its numerous windows, and two pulpit-windows standing out of the ranks, with much the appearance of an unpainted wooden factory. Still on, round by the old "Bell Tavern," —for there was no street then through by the tanneries,— until we arrived at Mr. Peabody's. His father-in-law, Jeremiah Dodge, had by this time removed to Danvers, and purchased the Needham place on the Lynnfield road ; and by the attraction of hospitable friends, and the repulsion of a powerful rainstorm which spoiled the sleighing, we were retained three days.

By this time a third child was added to the Peabody family, not near as attractive in his childish days as his elder brother and sister ; for, in his earliest years, George had much of that decision of character which was a distinguishing characteristic of his after-life. I was therefore conversant with the life and fortunes of your distinguished benefactor, from infancy till I found myself in the long procession which wended its way from North to South Danvers, and at the table and on the platform an invited guest at the dedication of the Peabody Institute.

I came from Georgetown with Mr. Peabody on his last departure for Europe, and parted with him here as he left the cars for Salem. And, again, I was at his funeral ; and I viewed from one of the slow-moving coaches which followed his remains to his last resting-place, the unnumbered throng, which, regardless of the thick-falling snow, filled the street from the church to the cemetery.

I have been acquainted with one of your most talented pastors from infancy to age. His father was my pastor during all my youth, and tutor for a time ; and his estimable wife is of the blood of the Spoffords.

I will name but a single other reminiscence. In June, 1813, I closed my three-years' medical studies by an examination at Worcester ; and quite happy, with my diploma in my pocket, I made my way to Boston, to see its Common covered with soldiers and arms, and the British ships, which had a few days before sent the old "Chesapeake" off to Halifax, lazily blockading the town. I came to Salem in the stage, over the turnpike and the water-logged floating bridge ; moved slowly on foot to North Danvers; and spent the night at your then young Dr. Osgood's,* with my good friend and relative, Israel Adams, then a clerk in Mr. Warren's store, who settled among you, married a descendant of Judge Holten, and owned, resided in, and valued his ancient mansion near this spot. A cordial intimacy with this esteemed relative and friend, and your excellent citizen, from youth to age, may account for the interest I still feel in what is still Danvers.

Hon. ALLEN W. DODGE of Hamilton, treasurer of Essex County, was next called upon; and he responded with the expression of his interest in the occasion, and with graphic comments, of which I have no full report, upon matters belonging to the times of Peter Clark and Dr. Wadsworth. He commended especially that style of manhood, of which he took "the monosyllabic Clark" to be a representative, that is able to say "Yes" and "No," and to stand by what is said.

Deacon SAMUEL P. FOWLER of the Maple-street Church referred to the general tone of disparagement in which Rev. Samuel Parris is always referred to, and spoke in terms of apology for the course of that minister, arguing to show that the idea of witchcraft in connection with sickness in his family was first suggested to him by his family physician. His children were sick; and the doctor said they were bewitched. He sent to Boston and got Perkins's "Art of Damnable Witchcraft," and found their symptoms were therein delineated. He called a meeting of the ministers; and they pronounced them bewitched; he believed they were going to start the Devil's

* Dr. George Osgood was a prominent man in Danvers society forty years ago, during the period of his middle life. He was active in parish affairs in the later years of Dr. Wadsworth's ministry, and at the coming of Dr. Braman. He was inclined toward Unitarian views, and was earnest in the wish that his minister should exchange pulpits with preachers holding those opinions; on which topic the persons interested had some sprightly conversations. The doctor had a fondness for botanical studies. And he is specially well remembered by all who were boys and girls in his later life, for the somewhat remarkable manner in which he carried his cane as he walked. His residence for the most of his life was at the Plain. He was a practising physician fifty-five years; and he died May 26, 1865, aged seventy-nine years. — R.

kingdom here. The courts appointed him to take the depositions ; and that was the reason he came before the courts as the principal witness. He supposed the parsonage was given him with two acres of land : the society denied it, though it was on the records. All the councils gave him a good moral character ; and he was not to blame because he did not know more than Lord Chief Justice Hale and others since then.*

Rev. GEORGE J. SANGER, pastor of the Universalist Church, and representative in the State Legislature, followed with a brief and concluding address.† He spoke of the respect he had for this church, and the denomination to which it belongs. He referred to the efficient help furnished by the Orthodox churches of New England in the great struggle against slavery ; and expressed in strong terms his sympathy with them in the foreign missionary work they are carrying on. For the old Puritan stock of New England, he said that it had been much spoken against, even as fruit-bearing trees are most pelted with stones, but that the fruits, at least, had been worth the gathering ; and by these it could afford to be judged.

Letters from various persons invited to attend the celebration, and not able to be present, were read during the afternoon session by Mr. Edward Hutchinson, secretary of the general committee.

LETTER OF HON. CHARLES W. UPHAM.

SALEM, Aug. 28, 1872.

, EDWARD HUTCHINSON, ESQ.

DEAR SIR, — I cordially thank you for the honor of an invitation to attend the *two hundredth* anniversary of the First

---

* From the report in the Essex County Mercury, indorsed by Deacon Fowler.

† Mr. Sanger was called upon, ingeniously as he judged, in behalf of *the school committee*, of which he was a member ; which committee in former times had been chosen, after some sort, in these parish meetings. I regret that I have no full account of his remarks.

Church and Society in Danvers, and regret exceedingly that it will not be in my power to be present on the occasion; but few can have higher attractions to me. The congregation, soon after its organization having a church established, at old Salem Village, has a strange interest, and occupies a conspicuous place in the world's history, from the fact, that a fearful superstition that had brooded for long centuries over Christendom there came to a head, and received its death-blow.

Outside of that, the history of the Salem Village church, or First Congregational Church and Society of Danvers, is truly honorable. In the character of its pastors, particularly subsequent to 1692, and of its people, it is most worthy of commemoration. It has been an example and a model of a Christian society pursuing a course of peaceful and unsurpassed usefulness, fulfilling the best purposes for which the people of the New-England communities have been, from the first, gathered as worshippers into religious associations for edification and instruction. May its harmony, prosperity, and usefulness be perpetual!

Begging, through you, to thank the committee for their kind invitation, I am,

Very truly yours,

CHARLES W. UPHAM.

LETTER OF REV. LEONARD WITHINGTON, D.D.

NEWBURY, Aug. 29, 1872.

DEAR SIR, — Your polite note and invitation to the two hundredth anniversary of your church has been received; and it awakens sad regret that my age and health forbid the idea that I can attend. My heart, however, is young, and flies to the spot, and will give all its sympathies to your celebration; for I love the Pilgrim Fathers with a specific love, for I am descended from them. I send you this sentiment: "May we build on their foundation; carry the edifice indeed higher, but never forget or forsake the corner-stone! Whither they went we will go, and where they lodged we will lodge; their people

shall be our people, and their God our God ; where they died
we will die, and there will we be buried.   The Lord so do to us,
and more also, if aught but death part them and us."

Yours truly,

LEONARD WITHINGTON.

Letters, of which portions were read, were also receivd from
HIRAM PUTNAM, Esq., of Syracuse, N.Y., a native of Danvers ;
Rev. MOSES K. CROSS of Waterloo, Io., also a native of the
town ; Rev. JAMES FLETCHER of Groton, formerly of Danvers ;
Rev. WILLIAM S. COGGIN of Boxford ; Dr. C. G. PUTNAM of
Boston ; Prof. JOHN S. SEWALL of Brunswick, Me., formerly
minister at Wenham ; Rev. E. P. TENNEY, now of Ashland ;
and others.

The services of the afternoon closed with singing, and with
the benediction by the pastor.

And here the formal exercises proposed for the celebration
ended.   But the people were slow to depart.   A social gathering in the evening had been before suggested.   The weather
abroad had now become fine ; for the day itself, in its progress
from the stormy morning, was answering to the history of the
parish and the church ; and it was known that ample provision
for supper was still to be found in the rooms below.   Many,
therefore, remained ; and by early evening the Village Hall
was filled with people, among whom were many friends and
former residents from abroad.

The occasion was largely given up to social enjoyment.   The
making of speeches, and reading of letters, however, still continued to be in order.

Remarks were made by Abner C. Goodell, jun., Esq., of
Salem, throwing light upon the ancient. times.   Mr. Goodell is
of the VILLAGE stock, and is thoroughly conversant with our
local history ; but of his remarks I have been furnished with
no report.   He gave a sketch of the condition of church-
music, if it might bear that name, in former times, with

an account of the versions of the Psalms, and the hymn-books formerly in use ; illustrating his theme by copious citations, given from memory.

Mr. DAVID STILES of Middleton gave an account of the church and parish in that place since the separation from us. With the addition, that has since been made, of some details, he spoke substantially as follows : —

MR. PRESIDENT, LADIES AND GENTLEMEN, — I am highly gratified in meeting with you to-day. In the first place, I have some claim to speak, as my wife was a resident, and therefore myself half-resident ; and, second, a part of my early days was spent among this people, and under the ministrations of the venerable Dr. Braman ; and, third, I am to speak in behalf of the oldest child of this church.

I will relate a little story that has never been in print, showing our intimate connection nearly two hundred years ago. At the time of the witchcraft excitement, in 1692, a sister of Joseph Putnam (who lived where now is the residence of Dea. William R. Putnam), and aunt of the famous Gen. Israel Putnam, had a wish, like many others at that time, to see the proceedings of the court, then held in the first meeting-house, a little east of where we are now assembled. But, as she entered the house, she was accused of witchcraft. The officers of the law were advised by Mr. Parris not to arrest her till the trial then going on was closed. Meanwhile the poor girl fled to the house of Bray Wilkins, living under the brow of Will's Hill. She took her weary and anxious way through the swamps, among the thorns of the wilderness, fording Ipswich River, leaving behind one or both shoes lost in the mud ; and, with her clothing nearly torn from her body, she entered the house of this well-known good man. But the officers were already upon her track, and were soon seen on the plain land below. Again she ran with bleeding feet to the dismal locality at the head of Middleton Pond ; and there among the thorns and briers, wild beasts and reptiles, she secreted herself till the search was given up.

Bray Wilkins had lived on this spot since 1660, having bought Richard Bellingham's claim the year before.   He was well known at Salem Village for forty-two years, as a pious and good citizen, and a firm supporter of the church and parish, till his death in 1702.

He was the son of Lord John Wilkins of Wales ; * and the genealogy of the family, which I have seen, goes back to 1090, or seven hundred and eighty-two years.   The honorable titles attached to some of their names indicate that this family took a high rank among their countrymen.

Tradition says, that Wilkins, Bellingham, and others came over with Gov. Endicott in 1628 ; and it is thought that the intervening years, up to 1660, were spent by Wilkins in Lynn. He was, however, the first English settler in *this part* of Salem Village ; and his tract of land was added to that of the Village, through his influence ; which accounts for the long and peculiar shape given to the Village boundaries.

William Nichols bought a claim of land of Bartholomew, and settled on the same in 1652 ; and William Hobbs, in 1660. These lands are in the east part of the town, near the residence of William Peabody ; and for some time they were claimed by " New Meadows," now Topsfield.

In 1663 Thomas Fuller of Woburn bought a claim of Major-Gen. Dennison, which lay upon the east side of that of Wilkins, beginning at Pierce's Brook, and running north. This brook passes in front of the house of Abijah Fuller ; and upon this spot Thomas erected his first dwelling.   He was a blacksmith by trade, and thus made himself useful both to the Village and Hill people.   His voice was listened to with respect in parish meetings at Salem Village.   His grandson, Jonathan, made the presentation of the charter for our town, procured from the General Court.   This took place at the

* Whoever his father may have been, Bray was a sensible man ; and his own sufficiently honorable title was " Bray Wilkins, husbandman." — R.

house of Dr. Daniel Felch, in 1728. A remnant of the Felch
cellar is now seen opposite the house of Mr. Addison Tyler:
this was the dividing line between Salem and Rowley. Mr.
Fuller was called Lieut. Thomas in our early history; being
probably an officer in the Indian wars. It seems that he and
his friend Wilkins, and their families, were not much affected
by the witchcraft delusion.* A grandson of Wilkins, however, John Willard, was hung for witchcraft, on Gallows Hill,
for choking Daniel Wilkins to death. (Probably this Wilkins
died of some throat-disease.) The foundation of this Willard's
house is now seen near the residence of Samuel H. Wilkins.

But I suppose you wish to hear how God has prospered this
child of yours, — the church in Middleton. Unlike the mother-
church, our first ministers were godly men. It was during
the ministry of your second *good* pastor, Mr. Clark, that the
church was formed; and no doubt he was consulted in making
the selection of our first pastor. The act of the incorporation
of the town enjoined upon the people " the settling of a minister, and the hiring of a Schoolmaster, to teach ye young to read
and write." The church was formed Oct. 22, 1729, with fifty-

---

* My friend Mr. Stiles has, no doubt, a desire, natural, and, within due
bounds, praiseworthy, to make it appear that these early townsmen of his were
less deluded than the other inhabitants of the Village. But I cannot quite suffer this to pass. These were families of character; and of intelligence, for those
times. But the complaint against this John Willard was made by Thomas
Fuller, jun., and Benjamin Wilkins, sen., both members of these families; and was
concurred in by Bray Wilkins himself, Willard's grandfather, and, apparently,
by nearly all of the family connection. And the offence was charged to have
been committed to the injury of Bray Wilkins, then an old man, and of Daniel
Wilkins, a great-grandson of Bray Wilkins, as I suppose.

"Lieut. Fuller," also being present at an examination of persons charged
with witchcraft, declared that the witches had been trying to persuade a certain
child to "cut her head off with a knife" (*History of Witchcraft*, vol. ii. p. 25).

On the whole, Mr. Stiles should be satisfied with claiming, what was certainly true, that these Will's Hill people were as good as the rest of the villagers.

It may, however, be added, that Thomas Wilkins, son of Bray Wilkins,
entered early into the opposition to Mr. Parris; along with Samuel Nourse,
John Tarbell, and Peter Cloyse, which may indicate that he began to get light
sooner than some others. — R.

two members : twenty more were added the next year. From this, we conclude that the population was then about four hundred. Rev. Andrew Peters, the first pastor, was settled Nov. 13,* 1729, and remained twenty-seven years. He was a devoted minister ; and the church prospered under his ministry. He died Oct. 6, 1756, aged fifty-five years. His remains rest among the people of his charge. Mr..Peters was a graduate of Harvard College, and son of Samuel Peters of Andover.

It is related that Mr. Peters's negro, while driving his master's cows to pasture, had several times been molested by a troublesome neighbor ; whereupon Mr. Peters one morning concluded to go himself. As he proceeded on his way, he met the hectorer of his negro, with whom he expostulated, but without satisfaction ; then, without any hesitation, he took off his coat, saying, as he laid it upon a stump, " Lie there, divinity, while I whip a rascal," and gave him a sound thrashing. This story, whether true of any other minister or not, is true of Mr. Peters ; and the place where the stump was is near the house of Capt. Simon F. Esty, as stated by Deacon Symonds, who pointed it out within the remembrance of some now living.

In 1759, Jan. 10, Rev. Elias Smith was settled. He, also, was a graduate of Harvard, and a successful minister. He died Oct. 17, 1791, aged sixty-one years. His was a ministry of nearly thirty-three years. His remains rest with us. Mr. Smith once had a call from a church in Marblehead, with a larger salary. His reply was, that he " would not leave his little flock in Middleton for all Marblehead ;" being unlike, in this, to some pastors at the present day, who are induced to leave their people for a small additional sum of money. Mr. Smith was one of the trustees of Phillips Academy, and so remained

---

* Here is still another date. (See pp. 72, 73.) This is from The Church Manual. I have been to look the matter up. The records of the church have no mention of the ordination. By the town records it appears that it was voted to employ Mr. Peters, March 17 ; and that it was proposed, Sept. 16, that he should be ordained on the second Wednesday of November. But that day fell on the 12th of the month. There is no mention of a postponement which, I think, occurred. The ordination was probably, in fact, upon the 26th ; and for the date, as given in the Manual, there seems to be no authority at all. — R.

till his death. He was qualified to fill almost any station in life. He was the grandfather of George Peabody, and of the late Col. Francis Peabody of Salem.

Rev. Solomon Adams was settled Oct. 23, 1793, and remained twenty years. He died Sept. 4, 1813, aged fifty-two years. He was the last of our ministers to be buried among us.

Rev. Ebenezer Hubbard was settled Nov. 27, 1816, and remained twelve years; and was dismissed April 30, 1828. It is said that he died a few years ago in Tennessee, in destitute circumstances.

In 1831 a call was given to Rev. Forrest Jefferds; but the parish, desiring unevangelical preaching, refused to concur with the church. Accordingly the church withdrew, leaving· behind the church-funds and communion furniture, their meeting-house, where they had worshipped one hundred years, with a new stove and funnel (the first ever within its walls), and a new sabbath-school library and case. These things were purchased mostly by these now outcasts. This was a sad day for the church in Middleton; with no place of worship, no pastor, without funds, "cast down, but not destroyed." I well remember the day. Strong men wept. They cried unto God; and he heard them, and delivered them out of all their troubles. The good man Mr. Jefferds cast in his lot with them, and was settled May 2, 1832. A new meeting-house was soon built, costing about two thousand dollars, of which sum only seven hundred could be raised by the people. The remainder was given by Salem Village people, and others whose sympathies were enlisted by our forlorn condition.

Mr. Jefferds's salary was five hundred dollars: one-half of this sum was given by the Home Missionary Society for some years. Great praise is due Mr. Jefferds for his faithfulness in the hour of peril. Under the two last pastorates, the parish had gone over to Unitarianism; while the church had seldom listened to a gospel sermon. A new foundation must be laid: but, fortunately for us, the most of the church were regenerated men and women; and with the blessing of God upon their labors, with those of their minister, a better day was soon at hand.

Mr. Jefferds was dismissed May 15, 1844.

The succession continued in the following order: Rev. Thurston Searle, settled May 8, 1845, dismissed Dec. 23, 1846; Rev. J. Augustine Hood, ordained Jan. 2, 1850, dismissed May 17, 1854; Rev. A. H. Johnson, ordained Jan. 1, 1857, dismissed April 5, 1865; Rev. James M. Hubbard, installed April 5, 1865, resigned Dec. 28, 1868; Rev. Lucien H. Frary, ordained Oct. 7, 1869.*

Within a few years we have built a new church and parsonage, costing over ten thousand dollars. Fifteen hundred dollars is now assessed on the pews to pay current expenses. Rev. Mr. Frary, our beloved pastor, has full audiences on the sabbath; and the sabbath school is well attended. The church now numbers about one hundred and fifty.

Thus hath God prospered us; to him be the glory.

From the first, the people of Will's Hill have lived on good terms with those of Salem Village. We heartily thank you for your sympathy and help in the hour of our need. We are confident you have not forgotten your daughter-church; and we trust that that bond which binds us together will never be sundered. When the hand on the dial of time has made another revolution, and points to 1972, we shall all be laid in our final resting-place, till the sound of the last trumpet; but we believe that our children's children, unto the third and fourth generation, will meet on or near this consecrated spot, to recount God's mercies. They may narrate thus again the names of Christian pastors, and of church-officers that are yet to come; and there will be others, also, whose names will long

* There is here appended a list of deacons in the Middleton church, with the time of their election to the office:—

John Berry	1729	Joseph Symonds	1820
Samuel Symonds	1729	Joseph Peabody	1821
Edward Putnam, jun.	1738	David S. Wilkins	1829
Samuel Nichols	1749	David Stiles	1831
Francis Peabody, jun.	1756	Allen Berry	1840
John Flint	1778	William A. Phelps	1857
Samuel Symonds	1780	James N. Merriam	1868
Benjamin Peabody	1794	Edward W. Wilkins	1874
John Nichols	1794		

have been forgotten, but whose labors for the cause of Christ will never die, and whose prayers will be answered in the salvation of mankind, upon every land under the sun.

The following letter, from Judge TAPLEY of Saco, Me., was received too late for use on the day of the celebration, but is here printed, as belonging in intent with these proceedings : —

GENTLEMEN OF THE COMMITTEE, — I received with pleasure your kind invitation to be present upon the "memorial occasion," so fitly chosen and arranged by those who love their native land. I fully determined to avail myself of the opportunity offered to meet many dear friends yet remaining in the home of my childhood ; but I find myself compelled by a press of public and official duties to forego the great pleasure anticipated.

The reflections suggested by the occasion bring to my mind with great force the words of Woodworth, when he says, —

> " How dear to this heart are the scenes of my childhood,
> When fond recollection presents them to view ! "

We, too, can see

> " The orchard, the meadow, . . .
> The wide-spreading pond, and the mill which stood by it."

And we remember

> " The bridge, and the rock where the cataract fell,
> And e'en the rude bucket which hung in the well."

But how changed are even these now ! Being material, they could not escape the ravages of time, but in their change mark its flight. Change is God's time-keeper : by it we note the flight of years. Infancy, youth, manhood, and old age are but marks and points upon the dial-plate of time : were they everlasting, we could not note time. Life is limited, and time illimitable. Upon the infinity of one is marked the finiteness of the other. To-day we contemplate two hundred years

passed and gone, two centuries born and dead.   This space of
time to us seems great ; and how vast and varied have its
changes been !   The postilion has given way to the steam-car :
in communication of thought, space and time have been almost
annihilated by the telegraph.   The genius of invention has
been crowned with such wonderful success, that there seems
but little more to be done in material advance.   This we call
progression : it is progression ; but it is temporal, except so far
as man is improved, and brought nearer to the estate of Him
whose image he bears.   This progression, and these advances,
we contemplate with pride and satisfaction ; but, grand and
magnificent as they are, they sink into insignificance when
compared with those whose influence must be felt throughout
eternity.   Those which elevate man in his action and compre-
hension are not simply grand, but sublime : their results are
not seen alone in matter, but are also manifest in mind.   From
this standpoint we find much has been accomplished in the
past two centuries.   A barren wilderness here has been
peopled, and civil and religious freedom established and maintained against the power of the Old World.   Although two
political revolutions have been witnessed in the progress, and
the scourge of war has visited the people in their march, it is
not the result of arms.   They were not the motive-power, or
even the means whereby the ends were produced : they were
simply resistances offered to the progress of right, and rebel-
lions against just and immutable laws, which must be met in
kind, and as surely to be overcome as God's laws are to pre-
vail over man's.   The selfish bigotry of the past has yielded
much to a more charitable and enlightened liberality of both
thought and action.   More and more every day is man inclined
to view his fellow-man as a brother, and to praise and appreciate his well-meant efforts by whatsoever creed worked out.
In their religions, men love more, and hate less.   Education
and intelligence have forced out superstition and intolerance.
The means of education have kept well apace with all the
advances made ; and the light of intelligence is now as freely
offered as the light of the sun, and the free school is now
almost a birthright of American children.

These things illumine the past ; and, while they move us in grateful remembrance, they create a high respect and regard for those who have gone before, and do much to stimulate us to action.

In contemplating the past, we naturally turn our eyes to the future, and wonder and surmise what it will be. While it is true that "the lamp of the past is the light of the future," we are not left to reason entirely from experiences ; for we know certain laws must produce, in time, certain results. May we not reasonably expect a continued progression till we reach that perfection which shall constitute in itself a heaven of God's created things ? In the progress of the events that shall thus be crowned, we anticipate our country and nation will be both a leader and teacher ; and that its wise and benefi- cent institutions, and its just appreciations and recognitions of the rights and duties of man, may and will be a continued sample for others ; and that, if there be one place above another in the great and final gathering, we, as a nation and a people, shall be found in the most favored place as the example which hastened the glorious day.

Respectfully yours,

RUFUS P. TAPLEY.

There was also received, at a subsequent date, the following communication from Rev. MOSES K. CROSS, which, although previously printed in "The Iowa Instructor and School Jour- nal," is appropriately furnished by him for a place among these local reminiscences : —

THE OLD BRICK MEETING-HOUSE.

The Old Brick Meeting-House stood on a gravelly knoll, at an obtuse angle in the highway, in the town of Danvers, Essex County, Massachusetts, and could be seen at a great distance, in every direction. On the same spot had stood two similar structures before ; and a fourth one now occupies its place. It was near the scene of the notorious Salem witchcraft ; and the blighting influence of that sad exhibition of human weakness seemed to rest on the neighborhood for many years.

The Old Brick was "erected," as all passers-by were duly notified, in 1806. It was neither an elegant nor a substantial structure ;* for the tower had settled and separated from the house, leaving a huge and horrible crack between them. It was a disputed point, whether the tower had separated from the house, or the house from the tower ; but there could be no doubt about the fact of a very grave schism in the sanctuary.

Rev. Dr. W. was the first minister in the Old Brick Church. He was a very dignified, venerable man, and always wore bands. His voice was weak ; and he could be heard only with the closest attention.

The pulpit stood on six fluted columns, and was very high. The entrance was by a door, which was always shut, except when the minister went in and came out. We used to watch and measure the time after he closed the door, before his head appeared above ; and, as near as can now be remembered, it was not far from half a minute. Over his head hung that mysterious hexagonal sounding-board, suspended by an ornamental rod some thirty feet in length. When he stood up, it was about eighteen inches from his head.

Opposite the entrance to the pulpit was another door, which was always kept shut and locked, so far as we were permitted to see. It was a very curious question to us boys, what was kept in there. It must be something sacred, of course, we concluded ; but whether it were Aaron's rod and the pot of manna, or some more modern institution, we were not permitted to see. We now believe that the communion service and baptismal font were kept there ; and what else, we cannot say.

The galleries were occupied chiefly by the choir, the mice, and the boys, especially the last. It was a great feat when

---

* There was a different opinion, on the first point, when the house was built, and before the crack appeared. (See pp. 99–102 ; and also, for the matter of permanence, p. 139).

Moreover, as there was more moisture in the soil, and a poorer foundation, under the eastern end of the building, we ought firmly to believe that the settling was in that direction, and that the *house separated from the tower.* — R.

a boy got old enough to sit up gallery. He was the next step to a man, surely. Opposite the pulpit, and behind the orchestra, were the negro-seats, which were never occupied by white folks, and seldom by colored. The high box-pews, in a high gallery, afforded a fine place for the boys to trade jack-knives, and perform other irreverent ceremonies, during sermon-time. I remember swapping watches in one of them, and getting a first-rate bargain, one Thanksgiving Day, not on Sunday. I remember, also, the exceeding mortification I felt once, on Sunday, at having the sexton come into the pew, and roughly separate us boys, taking his seat between us during the rest of the sermon.

The belfry was a never-ceasing marvel and astonishment to us. It was reached by successive flights of winding-stairs, through the dark, unfinished tower. The bell, which could be heard many miles, was one of Holbrook and Son's of Medway, Mass., and had this solemn motto on it, which always preached a little sermon to us when we went up there, and when it tolled for a funeral, —

> " I to the church the living call,
> And to the grave do summon all." *

The large ball and weathercock above the bell were the most wonderful things of all that pertained to the Old Brick Meeting-House. How they ever got there, who could have the courage to go up and put them in their place, when it was all that we dared do to look over the railing, were questions that were never fully solved to our childish understanding.

But, in process of time, the old sanctuary must come down. The lofty brick tower was carefully undermined ; and at a signal from the bell, on a certain day, it was to fall over, full-length, in the sight of all the wondering and expectant people of the parish. Instead, however, of conforming to the programme which had been adopted, it ignobly crumbled, and crashed down in one general mass of confusion and dust.

---

* The same bell is now in use. Spanish doubloons were put into it, it is said, when it was cast ; and a committee went to the foundery to see it done. — R.

Thus ended the Old Brick Meeting-House, and with it many a dream of boyish imagination.

An interesting letter was read, during the evening, by Augustus Mudge, from Mrs. MARY P. BRAMAN, the wife of the former pastor; and, in connection with the reading, Mr. Mudge made appropriate and just remarks upon the great efficiency of Mrs. Braman in the sabbath school and the ladies' circle, and upon the extent and value of her influence throughout the parish.

And thus the hours of our assembling, though so far prolonged, drew to a close.

Much, and perhaps the larger part, of that which engages our thoughts, and affects our feelings, upon such an occasion, it is not possible to record. There is a sacredness in the past to which we cannot be insensible, and which these memorial days bring freshly upon us. And the past, at such times, is scarcely separated from the future, and from all the life of man. We felt the power of these impressions, and we should not wish them to be taken from our recollection. Except for the storm of the morning, — which also made brighter, by contrast, the hours that followed, — it was thought that there was little connected with the day or its services that might not be remembered with pleasure. We are glad, therefore, for the observance we have kept, the rec rd of which is here about to end. It has made us better acquainted with the history of our neighborhood and town, from near the time of its first settlement. It has increased our interest in these Christian institutions, whose history we have reviewed ; and it has made us to feel more of concern for whatever may have to do with the well-being of this community in the times that are to come. But, besides this, it has quickened our feelings with respect to all that belongs to mankind. We have paused, and looked upon human life ; we have enlarged our sympathies ; and we have more of kindness and of hope. And thus from this eminence upon which we have stood for a little, by the way, we have given to our brethren, to the generations of our fathers and our children, our affectionate greetings and our farewell.

APPENDIX.

---

no question had ever been raised upon it. After the stereotyped plates for the history had been finished, and when a change of large extent could not well be made upon them, I chanced to notice, in looking over the published records of the Massachusetts Bay Colony, that the date of Oct. 11 was set in the margin against this act of incorporation. It immediately occurred to me that the date of Oct. 8 was only given as covering all the acts of the General Court assembling on that day. And this is the truth. The assembling, indeed, of the legislature in those days gave some better indication of the time when business might be transacted than it would at present.

But further, upon going to the State House, and examining the original records, — both the book from which the printed record was copied and the books containing files of the original papers, — I became convinced that the date Oct. 11 was no more correct than the other. Upon calling to this matter the attention of an expert, long employed in the secretary's office, he remarked, that though no one had ever spoken of it before, yet he had been aware *that these marginal dates, as given in the volumes of the printed records, are not to be altogether depended upon.* They are certainly doubtful, probably wrong, in other cases besides this, and in the same immediate connection.

It appears from the original papers, that, on the 15th of October,

POSTSCRIPT.— Not till these sheets were in the hands of the binder, did I notice, in the preface of the *third volume* of the Mass. Colony Records, that the Editor has himself called attention to the possible inaccuracy of the marginal dates.

A more careful reading at an earlier day, would have changed the form of the reference made to this matter.

APPENDIX.

THIS date, Oct. 8, for the act of incorporation, is wrongly given, and the celebration itself of the day was of course also misplaced. It was taken from a copy on the parish records of a paper, attested by Edward Rawson, Secretary of the Colony, and dated "at a General Court held at Boston, 8th of October,. 1672." The document may be seen upon page 15. The titlepage of the record-book also refers the order of the court to Oct. 8. And no question had ever been raised upon it. After the stereotyped plates for the history had been finished, and when a change of large extent could not well be made upon them, I chanced to notice, in looking over the published records of the Massachusetts Bay Colony, that the date of Oct. 11 was set in the margin against this act of incorporation. It immediately occurred to me that the date of Oct. 8 was only given as covering all the acts of the General Court assembling on that day. And this is the truth. The assembling, indeed, of the legislature in those days gave some better indication of the time when business might be transacted than it would at present.

But further, upon going to the State House, and examining the original records, — both the book from which the printed record was copied and the books containing files of the original papers, — I became convinced that the date Oct. 11 was no more correct than the other. Upon calling to this matter the attention of an expert, long employed in the secretary's office, he remarked, that though no one had ever spoken of it before, yet he had been aware *that these marginal dates, as given in the volumes of the printed records, are not to be altogether depended upon.* They are certainly doubtful, probably wrong, in other cases besides this, and in the same immediate connection.

It appears from the original papers, that, on the 15th of October, a bill was passed by the "magistrates"* for the incorporation of Salem Village, and which would have conferred upon it powers in little or nothing short of those of a distinct town.

To this the deputies "consented not." But on the next day the deputies agreed to the act as it now stands, and the magistrates upon the same day concurred. The paper is signed by the clerk of the deputies, and the secretary of the colony, Edward Rawson, — who was also secretary of the magistrates' branch of the court, — apparently with but one date. And, in any case, the date of the final and only conclusive action was OCT. 16 (O. S.).

And this is the day which should have been commemorated ; or rather more exactly, adding ten days for the change in the calendar, the precise time of the year would occur upon Oct. 26.†

I think, however, that we will not now disturb what was done nearly two years ago, on the 8th of October. We are at most but a few days younger than we thought.

I have set this matter forth so at length as being one of some interest to those who are curious or careful in such concerns, apart from its connection with us in this Village Parish. It may be of importance, too, in some cases, to know that these marginal dates in our printed and widely circulated colonial records are not to be implicitly relied on. While thus speaking, I do not mean to imply that great care was not taken by Dr. Shurtleff, the editor, in the printing of those records. The books from which the copy was made are in parts obscure, having marginal dates the intent of which it is difficult to make out. It is not easy, and as I think not possible, in many cases, to fix the time of the passage of an act with certainty, except by comparison with the books in which are preserved the original papers themselves ; and this it could hardly have been expected that the editor should do.

---

* The General Court was composed of two bodies : the governor and his assistants, or "magistrates" as they were termed together, in one, a body answering in part to the Senate, and in part to the Governor and his Council, as we now have them ; and the "deputies," or representatives of the people from the several towns, in the other.

† This matter is often misunderstood, as if the change of the calendar did not affect our fixing upon the same point of the natural and actual year. But it does. What I mean is, that to find the *same real period of the year*, the days must be added. The two hundred yearly revolutions of the earth were not completed in this case until Oct. 26, and a few hours later in the day withal, at that reckoning. If the reason is not plain, I hope at least the *assertion* is.

The incorporation of the parish being thus again referred to, it may be added that a movement for separation from Salem was begun as early at least as 1666. It was a matter of sharp contest. And moreover, after the passage of the act of 1672, the people of Salem still made opposition, a few of the inhabitants of the Village apparently joining with them ; and the business was brought again before the General Court in 1673. The deputies would have been willing to reconsider the case ; but the magistrates declared that it had been "fully heard and settled already."

It may be noticed that the name itself, SALEM VILLAGE, is not given in the order of the Court, though it did occur in the form of the order rejected by the deputies. In official documents the more frequent title at first was " Salem Farms." The other, how ever, soon came into popular and universal use.

I will observe also, with respect to the early dates in our history, that the time of the formation of the church, and the ordination of Mr. Parris, has been given with variations. But it is open to no doubt whatever, that both these events took place, as stated in the history, Nov. 19, 1689 (O. S.).

The date is given erroneously in Mr. Felt's " Annals of Salem," but is corrected in the appendix ; which correction, not being referred to in the body of the work, has probably escaped notice by some. The church record is clear as to the date of the organization, or " embodiment ;" and the preface to Mr. Parris's ordination sermon makes it certain that his ordination took place on the same day.*

* There is in the possession of the Connecticut Historical Society, at Hartford, a manuscript volume of sermons by Mr. Parris. They are mostly discourses preached at the Communion. They are in his clear and elegant handwriting, and were bound also by himself. The volume is kept, I may add, with great care ; being safely locked beyond the reach of the assistant librarians, and only accessible to Mr. Hammond Trumbull himself. His own courtesy in the matter is ample. But I do not know whether he is under any apprehension that the book may be in danger of flying upon a broomstick to this spot of its origin where it might suppose itself likely to be more at rest.

The 19th fell on Tuesday, not Monday, as Mr. Upham has inadvertently given it. (Compare Mr. Parris's entry in the church record immediately follow- ing : " 24, November, 1689, Sab. day.")

I cannot omit here to make an acknowledgment, which should have been more conspicuously placed at the opening of the volume, of the courtesy and helpfulness uniformly shown to me by the officials at the State House, in charge of the books and papers to which I have had occasion often to refer.*

B. — Page 45.

It has been mentioned, that, while Mr. Parris gave up his ministerial work in this parish upon the last sabbath of June, 1696, he continued to have some nominal and legal hold upon the pastoral office to a later date. The last entry he left upon the church records, and the only one he made after the close of his public ministry, is of date "October 11. 1696. Lord's day." It is as follows : —

The dismission of our Brethren and Sisters Wᵐ· Way and Persis his wife, and Aaron Way and Mary his wife, together with their children to ye church of Christ lately gathered at Dorchester in New England and now planted in South Carolina, whereof the Reverend Mr. Joseph Lord is Pastor, was consented to by a full and unanimous vote at ye motion and desire of ye Brethren and Sisters : and accordingly letters Dismissive were written, 17th instant.

Mr. Parris being at hand, his clerkly gifts were called into use, we may suppose, upon this occasion.

A matter of considerable historic interest is here touched upon. The Dorchester church referred to was a missionary organization in reality, formed in answer to an appeal from certain Christian settlers in the southern part of Carolina (a colony then in its infancy) for help in the maintenance of religious institutions.

The main portion of the expedition had sailed in December, 1695, and had made an establishment on the Ashley River, which they named Dorchester. To this point, the two families dismissed from

---

* I am moved also to speak of the unfailing patience that has been exhibited in the preparation of this volume for the press by the gentlemen of the firm of C. J. Peters & Son, stereotypers, of Boston. Moral qualities are held to be transmissible by natural descent ; and I am persuaded that some progenitor of theirs, though even in distant times, must have laid up that store of enduring and unruffled temper, at this very work of compiling himself the history of some old parish.

It is my wish that the continuation of this publication, through coming centuries, should be with the assistance of the members of this same firm and family stock.

our church doubtless went. A Congregational form of church government was there set up ; and the colony prospered. But, the location proving unhealthy, the larger part removed, in 1752, to Georgia, to a location which they called Midway, lying between the Altamaha and Ogeechee Rivers. They numbered here eight hundred and sixteen persons, of New-England origin and New-England principles, and differing widely from the surrounding population. They gave a flavoring of their own character to the parish or county of St. John's, in which they lived. With the coming-on of the Revolutionary period, this parish chose the first, and, for some time, the only delegate from Georgia to the Continental Congress of 1775. For its zeal in the cause of Independence, the name was changed to "Liberty County ; " which name is still kept.

The county is said to have preserved to the present time a distinction for intelligence and public spirit. Though Southern in feeling, it went reluctantly, and with strong efforts at resistance, into the movement for secession and rebellion. And the original church itself at Midway is believed to have maintained its Congregationalism to the present time.

It would be pleasant if there might be resumed some fraternal intercourse between this church and the churches from which its founders and early members went forth.

For further particulars see an article entitled, " THE FIRST HOME MISSIONARIES OF NEW ENGLAND," in "The Congregational Quarterly," for April, 1868, by Rev. James H. Means of Dorchester.

C. — PAGE 142.

THE SHOE-TRADE OF DANVERS.

BY MR. EDWIN MUDGE.*

SHOE-MANUFACTURING has long been prominent in the business of the town. For the past sixty years the number of manufacturers has averaged twenty or more ; and the average yearly value of boots and shoes produced, from one half a million dollars, to a million, and in some years exceeding the latter amount. The Danvers brogan, the unbound kip, the women's calf, the women's, misses', and children's grained and goat shoes, have had an excellent reputation in the different markets of the country. As we were among the

* Senior member of the firm of E. and A. Mudge & Co.

earliest to commence the wholesale trade, which has been continued to the present time, a somewhat extended account of the shoe-business here may be of interest to those who shall come after us, as it will show to some extent its rise and progress in this country.

We have not confined ourselves to the shoe-business so exclusively as some other towns. It used to be said of Lynn, that all the inhabitants worked upon shoes except the minister, — and that he made his own. It was not so with Danvers. It is told of the Rev. Dr. Wadsworth, that one day, as he was going to get a pair of shoes made, he was seen coming, and the shop was all swept before he came in. He looked around, and remarked that it did not look as though there was much work done there! When he came for his shoes the floor was well covered with leather-chips. He then observed that "it looked as though they did something." The good doctor was wise and prudent in regard to the treasures of this world, as well as those of the next; and he liked to see his people industrious and thrifty.

Until the present century there was nothing done except what was called custom-work. A person bought a side of sole-leather, a side of upper-leather, a calf or a morocco skin, and had the shoemaker come to his house, and make a pair of shoes for such of the family as might be in need. Or the shoemaker would provide himself with the different kinds of leather; and those in want of a pair of shoes would call upon him, have the measure taken, and the shoes made as directed. Early in the present century the wholesale trade was commenced here. At first men's sewed slippers were made, and packed in barrels, and sent by sea-captains to Baltimore and other places to be sold, if they would bring a fair price and ready pay: if not, they were brought back. During the war of 1812 they were sent by horse-teams.

At this time the soles of shoes were all sewed on. The making of pegged shoes had not been thought of. One of our manufacturers tried the pegging on of soles, and it soon became common. In a few years our manufacturers became largely engaged in making thick brogans for the Southern slaves. Instead of sending them to market, and getting ready pay, the buyers or commission-dealers would come to Danvers for the goods. They had to be sold for eight-months' notes; the Southern planters being always short of money, as they spent so much not only in buying their plantations, but in buying their slaves.

They wanted to get trusted through the year, until they raised and sold their crops ; and, if their crops failed, their debts were put over until another year. Sometimes the streams would be so low that their crops could not be floated down to the sea : this, and various other causes, would produce delay in their payments ; so that our Danvers manufacturers needed all the "time" they could get on their stock and work. This led them to pay their workmen in orders on the stores, where they could obtain their groceries and dry goods. These orders were not as good as the money ; but still the work with this kind of pay was a great advantage to the people, as all of a family who were old enough to work could assist in some way, either upon the closing, binding, or making. This could be done when work was not needed upon the land, in winter as well as summer, in the evening as well as daytime. These orders were more convenient for the storekeeper than trusting a large number of workmen for small amounts ; for he would receive a note for them, which he could usually obtain the money on by getting it discounted at some bank. The demand for bank facilities created by the shoe-business led to the establishing of the Village Bank, in 1836, now the First National Bank of Danvers. Sometimes the manufacturer would connect storekeeping with his shoe-business, so as to pay his workmen with his own goods: but this was never very satisfactory to the workman, as he was obliged to take such goods as the manufacturer happened to have ; while, when he took an order, he could usually have it upon any store in town or in the vicinity. The shoe-business wrought a great and happy change in many families in town. Until that was introduced, the sons and daughters of those who had not a farm large enough to employ them at home had to go out to live, causing sadness to parents and children ; but they could all remain at home, and work upon shoes.

When the large farmers could not find a supply of help from their neighbors, they found it in New Hampshire. Many will remember the stalwart young men and women who came from that State some fifty years since to assist the farmers and their wives. In this way, in part, as well as towards the West, commenced the drain, from the "hill towns" of New England, of their young people.

It was the custom of those who manufactured thick shoes to store them in the attic until the selling season, when they would be prepared, and put in cases for the market : those of the same kind were put together, although made by different persons.

When brought in by the workman, the manufacturer would examine and count them, throwing them upon the pile to which they belonged.

It was said of some of the shoemakers, that when any of the shoes were damaged by cutting, or otherwise, that they would try to assist in counting, throwing the bad shoes over the top of the pile, so that they would not be seen ; but, if they succeeded at this time, they were liable to be caught when the shoes were packed for market, as the trained eye of the manufacturer could distinguish the shoes made by the different workmen. The shoes to him were like the book whose author was asked why he did not sign his name to it : he answered, that his name was written upon every page.

The shoe-manufacturers of this town were quite prosperous until the great financial crisis of 1837, when they suffered great loss by bad debts and general shrinkage of prices. The shoe-business had become well distributed about town ; a considerable amount being done at the Plain, the Port, Putnamville, and in the school-districts Nos. 4 and 6. About this time several young men in School District No. 5 commenced manufacturing shoes : they made kinds somewhat different from those manufactured in other parts of the town, and sold them in a different manner. The kinds were women's, misses', and children's grain, goat, and kid, pegged shoes. They would take them to Boston with horse and wagon, and there exchange them for part money, and the balance in leather. This furnished them with money to pay their workmen with, instead of orders. The profits, if any, were very small. The manufacturers in other parts of the town would rather look down upon these young men ; but in a season when many of the Southern notes came back protested for non-payment, they began to think that those "Meeting-House fellows," as they were sometimes called, were better off than themselves.

They were called "Meeting-House fellows" because they lived in the vicinity of the Brick Church, at that time the principal one in that part of the town now retaining the name of Danvers.

For twenty years, from the crisis of 1837 to the great crisis of 1857, the shoe-manufacturers of this town enjoyed a good degree of prosperity. The principal change in the mode of manufacturing in this time was in the use of some machines. The manufacturers of Danvers have not been behind those in other towns in the invention and the owning of patent rights of machines, and in intro-

ducing them into their manufactories.   At the commencement of
the twenty years referred to, about the only machine in use was a
roller of some two feet in length, which the manufacturer used to
roll the softer pieces of his sole-leather, and a shorter one which
the shoemaker used to roll the soles instead of hammering them
upon the lapstone, as he had formerly done.   Soon one of our
manufacturers invented a splitting-machine, by attaching a knife
to a rolling-machine, just back of the rollers.   This was very convenient for splitting the thick pieces of sole-leather.   From this
time during these twenty years, there were many machines invented,
and brought into use, with more or less success.   The most important ones that came into general use were the machines for cutting
the soles, and those for closing and stitching the uppers of shoes.

Pegging-machines were used to some extent.   One of our shoe-
manufacturers, Mr. Samuel Preston, invented and obtained the
first patent ever issued for a machine to peg shoes.   The paper is
dated March 8, 1833, and is signed by Andrew Jackson, President
of the United States.   Mr. Preston still has the shoe from which
he obtained this patent.

The four years from July, 1857, to July, 1861, were very disastrous
to the shoe-manufacturers of this town.   Few, if any, made money
during this time, and a large proportion lost all they had by bad
debts ; and it was the same generally with the shoe-manufacturers
throughout New England.   Those having a Southern trade suffered
least in the crisis of 1857 ; but in 1861, when the slaveholders'
rebellion commenced, and the South repudiated her Northern
debts, if one's trade was mostly at the South, there was no way for
him to escape the loss of all he was worth, unless his capital was
unusually large for the amount of his business.   This is probably
the only time in the history of the trade when it was not comparatively safe for one to extend his business, so that his indebtedness
would be three times the amount of his capital : that is, if he was
worth $25,000, he could owe $75,000, having property amounting to
$100,000 to pay it with ; he could then suffer a shrinkage of twenty-
five per cent upon all trusted out, and upon all property on hand,
and meet his payments in full.

It was a rule of the late Amos Lawrence to keep his business so
that he could suffer a shrinkage of forty per cent, and meet his
payments ; but he was in the dry-goods trade, where the fluctua-
tions are greater than in the shoe-trade.

The shoe-manufacturers of this town were very prosperous during the war, and since that time the business has yielded a fair profit.

Within the last few years there has been with many a complete change in their mode of manufacturing, almost as much as in making of cloth when the factory was substituted for the house spinning-wheel and loom. Instead of having the workman take the stock to his home, and there make the shoes as formerly, all parts are now done at the factory, with many different machines run by steam or water power.

Perhaps the present mode of manufacturing can as well be shown, and also the size and shape of a factory considered convenient for a given amount of work, by describing one of our Danvers factories, as in any other way.

The capacity is for 1,500 pairs daily of women's and misses' pegged or sewed shoes ; and the average value of the goods about two thousand dollars a day, or six hundred thousand dollars a year. The building is 125 feet by 33 feet, with a boiler-room on the rear end 33 feet by 20. The building is three stories high, besides basement and attic, which are good rooms ; making five floors, all well lighted. It is without plastering. The rooms are ceiled on the sides with hard pine, and varnished ; overhead they are finished and painted. A boiler of 50-horse power and an engine of 25-horse power are used for heating the whole building, for running the machinery and elevator, and pumping water to a tank in the attic for the supply of all parts of the building. In cutting and preparing the sole-leather, machines are used for stripping, rolling, splitting, sole-cutting, dieing-out, rounding-up, moulding, channelling, shanking, thinning edges of soles, and skiving stiffenings. For fitting the uppers, there are also various machines for closing, stitching, and binding, and for stamping, scalloping, punching, eyeletting, staying, rubbing-down, rolling, and bobbin-winding. In the making-room, machines are used for lasting, sewing, pegging, beating-out, edge-setting, heeling, heel-grinding and burnishing. In the room for finishing the bottoms are machines for sanding and brushing.

It is estimated that the cost of making shoes with machinery is only about three-fifths as much as by hand-work. The labor is only about fifty per cent as much ; and the use of the building and machinery, and the cost of running, about ten per cent ; making sixty per cent, or three-fifths.

When making fifteen hundred pairs daily, about one hundred and fifty workmen are employed. The number of males and females is nearly equal, with some young boys and girls. The pay of those old enough to do a full day's work ranges from two to four dollars a day for males, and from one to three for females. Males and females receive the same pay for the same work. Most of those employed work by the piece; that is, they are paid a certain amount per set for the part of the work they perform.

The manner of selling boots and shoes has changed, as well as the mode of manufacturing them. Many of the manufacturers have stores in Boston, where they sell their goods; having several factories located in different towns, and making a different line of goods at each factory. The buyers from a distance go out of Boston only to a few of the towns where a large number of manufacturers are located. There are advantages in being able to sell goods at the factory; but, on the other hand, much is lost in manufacturing by using dark, inconvenient rooms, occupied because they are situated in a favorable place for the buyers to call. It is thought by many that the time will soon come when all the sales-rooms will be separated from the factories in the shoe-business, as is now the case in the cotton and woollen business.

The manner of paying the workmen with orders upon the dry goods and grocery stores passed away some twenty years since. They are now paid in money, once a week or once a month. At the commencement of the war the shoe-manufacturers changed the terms of selling their goods from eight months' time to cash, or thirty days' time, which continued some years; but the buyers soon began to ask for more time, and now most of them who are in good standing buy on six months, some with the privilege of pay-ing in thirty days, at a discount of five per cent, if they prefer to do so, instead of giving a note.

Within a few years the shoe-manufacturers and other business men have adopted a change in regard to notes. They have printed upon their bills or statements, " All notes payable to your own order : " so that the receiver can sell them without putting his own name upon them, or being held for their payment, provided he can find any one to buy them. Upon single-name notes, as they are called, the rate is higher than upon indorsed notes, if the indorser is in good credit ; but it is very convenient for the business man to be able to sell a part of his notes, if he holds more in amount from one party than he likes ; as it gives him an opportunity to sell the same party more goods, and hold only the desired amount of notes.

The rate at which a person's note sells is usually the best test that can be had in regard to his standing, if he has been long in the business, or has done enough to be known in the market. By disposing of a part of his notes in this way, the seller can learn the value of the rest.

Note-brokers do a large business at selling notes on a commission of $\frac{1}{4}$ of 1 per cent.

Unless one's note averages to sell below ten per cent, it is very difficult for him to succeed in business, as he is not able to buy his stock low enough to sell at a profit. It is probably better for him to reduce his business, or try and obtain more capital by taking a general or special partner, as many do who have more ability and energy than money.

The capacity of the shoe-manufactories of this country at the present time is said to be much larger than is needed to make the amount of goods used. Some suppose enough could be made in six months to meet the demand for one year. This leads to sharp competition: as all wish to run their factories as much of the time as possible. It also makes the business very irregular. The buyers want most of their goods sent in January, February, and March, for summer wear, and July, August, and September, for the winter. Boots and shoes are made largely as they are ordered ; and the buyers are not willing to give their orders but a short time before the goods are wanted. This leads the manufacturers to do all they can through the two selling seasons of the year, of about three months each ; which are followed by about the same length of time when many of the workmen are out of employment. This is hard for the workmen ; and the manufacturer suffers loss and inconvenience by having his factory stand idle, and his workmen scattered twice a year. This loss has to be made up — together with the profit, if there be any — in the six months while the factory is in operation. One cause that has helped produce the large number of shoe-factories is, that a few years since efforts were made to introduce shoe-manufacturing into many places where it did not exist, in the hope of building up the towns. Individuals offered buildings free of rent, and proposed to loan money on favorable terms. Towns offered to exempt from taxes ; and stock-companies were formed to carry on the business. These efforts were not very successful ; but they undoubtedly did something towards causing the over-supply of shoe-manufactories which we have in New England at the present time.

D. — Page 160.

Previous to 1849, the books of the town appear to contain the account only of taxes assessed upon the inhabitants, without any statement of the total valuation, although it is very likely that there may be some such statements which I have not happened to see. There are among the papers of Judge Holten, in the possession of Mrs. Philemon Putnam, certain schedules showing the amount of property of various descriptions in the town, one of which, for the year 1771, I will transcribe. It is entitled, "A Copy of the Valuation of the Town of Danvers;" it being, of course, the original and undivided town.

Polls Rateable	427
Polls not Rateable	66
Dwelling-Houses, Shops under the same Roof, or adjoining to them	278
Tan-Houses, Slaughter Houses, Shops seperate from Dwelling Houses Pot and Pearl Ash-works	57½
Still-Houses	—
Ware-Houses	5
Superficial Feet of Wharf	8566
Grist-Mills, Fulling mills and Saw Mills	13
Iron works and Furnaces, and all other Buildings and Edifices	3
The Annual Worth of the whole Real Estate without any Deduction, for more than ordinary Annual Repairs	£3163 17s. 8d.
Servants for Life between 14 and 45 years of age	33
Tons of Vessells	340
An Account of each Persons stock in Trade	£2711 6s. 8d.
Factorage or value of Commissions or Marchandize	—
Money at Interest	£5209 6s. 0d.
Horses	287
Oxen	297
Cows	888
Goats and Sheep	1414
Swine	317
Acres of Pastorage	6798½
The Number of Cows s⁴ Pastorage will keep	1411¼
Acres of Tillage Land	897¼
Bushels of grain	16035
Barrels of Syder	2401
Acres of Salt Marsh	89¼
Tons of Salt Hay	98¾
Acres of English Mowing	2421½
Tons of English Hay	1271½
Acres of Fresh Meadows	1265
Tons of Fresh Meadow Hay	984

A general valuation was ordered throughout the province for this same year; and the returns, so far as they are to be found, give the names of individuals. But there is only a fragment of the return from Danvers to be discovered; though it is possible that a more thorough search might disclose the rest.

There is, however, a memorandum at the State House, containing an account of the property of Danvers for 1781, somewhat similar to the one printed above, which I also give herewith.

The sums in the second column are the totals of what is called "income" under each head. This income appears to have been the thing aimed at throughout.

STATEMENT OF PROPERTY IN DANVERS IN 1781.

			"Income." £ s.
283 Houses,	"Income" on, 65 shillings	. . .	919 15
242 Barns	" " 18 "	. . .	224 0
59 Stores &c.	" " 24 "	. . .	70 16
6 Distilleries, Mills &c.	" " 80 "	. . .	24 0
1986 Acres and parts of an acre English Mowing, 13s.		. . .	1291 18
1101 Barrels of cider	2s. 6d.	. . .	137 12
810 Acres of Tillage Land	10s.	. . .	405 0
1353 Acres of Salt and fresh meadows	7s.	. . .	473 11
5878 Acres of Pasturing	3s.	. . .	881 14
1183 Acres of wood and unimproved land	80s.*	. . .	78 18
4833£ Money on Interest	.	. . .	289 19
678£ Amount of Goods and Wares and Merchandise .		. . .	40 13
206 Horses Value £6 . £1236 0			
274 Oxen " 7 . 1918 0			
880 Cows " 4 . 3520 0		. . .	439 12
1039 Sheep and Goats " 6s. . 311 14			
182 Swine " 12s. . 109 4			
232£ Coaches, Chaises &c. . . . 232 0			
25 Ounces Gold, coined or uncoined }			
2552 Ounces Silver " " " }	. . . . .		58 12
80£ Wharves &c. at 3 per cent.	. . . . . .		2 8
380 Tons Vessels &c. 3s. income	. . . . . .		57 0

£5395 8

There are apparent discrepancies between these two statements, which I cannot undertake to adjust. Certain figures, also, in either list, but especially in the second, are difficult to be accounted

---

* The figures at this point seem to be plainly as here given; but I can render no satisfactory account of them.

for. In 1781 there are reported fifty-nine "stores," whatever that may stand for; while the whole value of "goods, wares, and merchandise," amounted to but a small sum, and the "income" on these articles was ludicrously small. The account must, it would seem, be open to some misapprehension at this point; since, from what we now know of this class of men, we may not believe that fifty-nine storekeepers would live upon a business no more productive, to say nothing of the six owners of "distilleries and mills."

The number of swine appears, also, to be relatively small; and it hardly bears out Mr. Proctor's assertion, that the Revolutionary heroes of this town were fed mostly upon "salt pork and bean-porridge;" unless, indeed, we understand, that in 1781, the war being nearly ended, those heroes had eaten a considerable proportion of the swine, beyond the annual production. But, in fact, live stock of all descriptions, excepting cows, had fallen off heavily within those eventful years. The comparison of the two accounts will furnish, also, other indications of the severity of the times.

Of "coaches and chaises," there could have been but few; and the catalogue of pleasure carriages for that period does not go much further. It is doubtful if there was at that time a wagon, or light four-wheeled carriage of any description, in the town, or, indeed, anywhere in the neighborhood.

The increase of wealth of all descriptions within the last one hundred, or even the last fifty years, has been very great, — far beyond what most persons now living are aware of. The change is to be seen in the improved quality and greatly enlarged variety of food in most households; in the possession of clothing much more abundant in amount, and better suited to the extremes of the climate; in the larger size and better aspect of dwelling-houses, in their greater comfort for light and warmth, and in their more convenient, ample, and elegant furnishing; in the multiplication of books and of objects of art, of which the former were rare, and the latter almost unknown, in earlier times; in the great improvement in tools of all descriptions, and of carriages, not to speak of railroads, and in the increased ability and opportunity for travelling; and in some lightening, in general, of severe and continued toil for subsistence. Proofs on all these points are ample. All classes of our population have felt the change, — the poorer not least. Within the memory of persons not old, men worked in brick-yards in winter for fifty cents a day, and got such jobs as a personal favor. This is but a specimen. The cost of the necessaries of life, though less than now, was not low in proportion.

The occupation of New England was a thing of hardship, wrought out with toil. It was very unlike, in all its conditions, to the settlement of new lands now going on at the West. Beyond the means of bare subsistence, earned only by the greatest diligence, our fathers, in all the early generations, had but little.

Altogether, while the enervating and corrupting tendencies of wealth are to be guarded against, there is abundant occasion for gratitude to God for the enlargement of the blessings of the present life bestowed upon us in these later times.

E. — PAGE 117.

SINCE preparing the account given above of the formation of the sabbath school, there has come into my hands a fuller and authentic record, from which I am able to make some additions and corrections.

The organization as first formed, at the meeting held at Dr. Wadsworth's house, July 30, 1818, was an organization of *teachers* only, and not of the whole school, as in later years. The first members were Samuel Preston, Edwin Josselyn, Betsey Putnam, Hannah Putnam, Harriet Putnam, Nancy Putnam, Clarissa Putnam, Edith Swinerton, Betsey Pope, Eliza Putnam, and Eliza Preston. They voted to form themselves into a society "by the denomination of the Danvers Sabbath-school Village Society." Samuel Putnam and Philip Dale, jun., were admitted as members, by vote, at the first meeting. These persons were the first teachers ; and their names should have been given as such upon p. 117, since the list at that point embraces only scholars. Asenath Preston, Polly Preston, Mary Pope, and Porter Kettelle were chosen members in the August following ; and in September, Gilbert Tapley, Polly Browne, Betsey Dale, Sally Flint, and Emma Putnam were appointed "assistant teachers ; " and these, with several others, were elected members in the next spring.

At the first meeting Samuel Preston was chosen "director," and Betsey Putnam "directress." They had for "assistants" Samuel Putnam and Clarissa Putnam ; and Edwin Josselyn was treasurer. For several years meetings were held annually, in the spring, for choice of officers. The school was not held through the winter months.

Miss Betsey F. Putnam, who had suggested the project, was prevented by her deafness from taking an active part in it ; and, among the ladies, a great share of labor was borne by the sisters Hannah and Betsey Putnam.

It was provided in the constitution, that the sessions of the school should not exceed an hour and a half in length, "lest the children, being wearied by long confinement, religious exercises should become tedious, which would defeat the design of the institution." The exercises appear, in fact, to have occupied only about half an hour. They consisted largely, at first, of recitations of texts of Scripture ; and, of these texts, some of the children learned a large number. A catechism was also used for the younger classes. There was an elaborate system of record, and of rewards for punctual attendance, and for committing the Scripture to memory. The prizes consisted of "a printed hymn," or "a tract, with an appropriate cover."

There was also a provision, which would be singular in our time, for "punishments and forfeitures." It was to the effect, that scholars "absenting themselves from school without sufficient reason, after having been called on three times, should be liable to exclusion ; " and that any scholar "found guilty of lying, swearing, fighting, stealing, or any indecent or immodest conduct, and who, after repeated admonitions, will not desist from such conduct, shall be dismissed, and forfeit the rewards to which he was entitled at the time of his exclusion."

It is worthy of notice, that not more than one or two of these teachers were professing Christians at the opening of the school ; though a large proportion of them became such in later years. We may learn thus, that, though none should delay entering with the whole heart upon a Christian life, yet, where this has not been done, it may be a suitable and hopeful thing to engage in the study of the word of God, and in the effort to impress its truths upon the minds of others.

F. — PAGE 51.

I adhere to the conclusion at first announced, that there should be no attempt in this book to set forth the particulars of the witchcraft history. But I have been since led to think that there should be furnished some brief sketch, not of the historical and personal details, but of the general principles and methods which characterized those strange proceedings. So much may perhaps be necessary to make intelligible the references contained in this history, and to render thus complete what may properly be regarded as the record of the parish itself. This narrative may fall, also, now or in future times, into the hands of those who will not possess the larger work in which the whole topic is so amply treated.

The theory of witchcraft, as held in New England and throughout Europe, at the period under review, was substantially this: That the Devil, in his desire to torment men, could not visit them readily with bodily sufferings, except through the agency of some human being, employed as a confederate. This confederate was a witch (the term "wizard" was little used). With this ally the Devil made a formal bargain ; and he had it in writing. He required the . name to be signed in a book. Very unfairly, he kept the record himself, and does not appear to have furnished his partner with any copy. He set a mark upon the bodies of his followers, not readily discernible except to himself, though much sought for, and often supposed to be found, in the witchcraft trials. He had his infernal imitations of the Christian sacraments, and caused his confederates to be baptized ; and met with them to drink, in pledge, the blood of men. One such notable observance was declared to have been held upon the parsonage lands in this place ; but the spot has never, that I know of, been determined. The terms of the contract, so far as they came to light, seem to have been unfair throughout ; which, perhaps, was to have been expected of the Devil. The witch made herself over to the Evil One, to do his work, and to be his. She got little, apparently, in return, except that she was furnished with his work to do, and with certain preternatural facilities for its accomplishment. The witch had, it might be, a yellow, or other bird to take care of ; but not for music, and scarcely for company. She had also, perhaps, a spider or two, especially if her rooms were rudely finished, and dusty, to do her bidding as "imps;" but these were useless for common housework. She was allowed also, at times, to ride rapidly through the air upon a pole or broomstick ; but only upon business-trips apparently, and seldom or never for pleasure.

For mischief, the equipments were ample. The witch could torment by the look of her eye only, and with every imaginable pain, whomsoever she chose, or whosoever might be chosen by her master. This was akin to the old and world-wide vexation of "the evil eye." For an absent person, the witch might make a "puppet," or image, with a shawl or a rag ; the form and material were not essential; and the person himself might be tormented at leisure, by the sticking of pins into this his representative image, or by any other violence put upon it. If personal visitation were required, the witch could ride lightly to the victim, as we have seen, in bodily form; or she could go in her "apparition," or spectral shape, without help from the buoyancy of a broomstick, and do the work with equal effectiveness.

When a person was suffering in an unusual manner from some strange disease, it was common to conclude that "an evil hand" was upon him; that is, that he was bewitched, or tormented by some one in league with the Devil. The physicians themselves were not slow to suggest this explanation, which was a continuation, or reproduction of a belief that has prevailed in all ages among savage tribes.

About this nucleus of witchcraft doctrine, there was gathered a vast and indefinite haze of traditional follies and fears. The practices or pretences of fortune-telling and enchantment, of jugglery and magic and conjuring and necromancy, were all concurring, with some power, at least, to bewilder the popular mind. Ghost-stories were in common circulation; and ghosts themselves, always visible, as they are feared and talked of, were abundant.

These dark beliefs were not held in equal fulness by all classes of people; but there were few, if any, that were wholly free from their influence. They did not exhibit themselves in prominence and force at all times; but they were always in existence, slumbering, and ready upon occasion to be awaked. The power of such delusions is subject to certain laws of periodicity. They rage for a space, and then are in comparative rest; and after a time they break forth again, and in forms varied, it may be, from those they had borne before. Peculiar local and temporary conditions may also have much to do with their force and direction. The public mind is ever liable, withal, in some degree, to be struck with some sudden paroxysm or panic of fear or passion, by which the powers of reason may be, for a while, overborne and silenced.

In intelligence, this place was not behind the rest of the Colony; nor the Colony, still less, behind the country: yet it was relatively the dark period of our history. The first settlers were of exceptional intelligence. But they were poor, and could not at once provide schools equal to the work that needed to be done; and the children of the next generations were beneath the standard both of the earlier and later times.

There had been a few cases of trial and execution for witchcraft
in the Colony previous to 1692. The matter had also been in
divers ways stirred up just before that time, and when, as yet,
nothing unusual had occurred in this place. Sundry houses had
been visited with inexplicable noises, and movements of things not
seeming to be touched with hands, as has happened in later times.
And this may bring to notice, what has been often observed, the
resemblance, in some points, between these witchcraft doings, and
the phenomena of modern "spiritualism." Certain children also,
and usually about these same houses, became bewitched, or came
to be witches, whichever it might have been; and astonished
their elders by performances which it was thought the Devil only
could have suggested. Full accounts of these proceedings were
prepared, unwisely, with stress laid upon their wonderful nature,
and with little note made of the deception that should have been
manifest in some of them, and of the unwholesome and altogether
useless quality that marked them all. Such narratives were probably in the library of the minister of this parish; and they got into
the hands of the children. The minister had also in his household certain servants, or slaves, of Indian or of mixed extraction,
whom he had brought with him from the West Indies, and whom
he might better have left behind. Their heads were full of every
barbarian folly; and they were most unfit to be the companions
of children. Presently there came to be formed at the parsonage
a little circle, meeting in the evening it is likely, consisting of the
children of the family, with these servants, and some girls of the
neighborhood, to read these books, with Indian annotations, and to
put in practice as they might, of what they read, and to stock their
minds with stories of murder and darkness, and devils, and the
dead that could not rest in their graves. Nearly all of them were
under twenty years of age; some were not twelve. How far their
parents knew what they were about, we may not be sure. But they
ought to have known. Here was the breeding-place of the whole
plague. Had the minister sent away these slaves with their freedom and his final blessing, and had these parents kept their children at home, where all children belong, and had them busied
with work or studies or plays, and rested with sleep, the Salem
witchcraft would never have been heard of. As it was, with their
winter-evening suppers of wonders and witches and ghosts, it is
not a wonder that they were shortly themselves bewitched. They
began to act and to suffer strangely. They could not be stopped,

or they would not stop. The astonished and appreciating notice that was taken of them made them worse. What exactly they meant to do at first, or, indeed, at any time, and with what motive they did it, no one now can certainly tell. It is not certain that they ever knew themselves. This only is clear: they had gotten into an utterly morbid state of both mind and body. And this is really what is most important to be known. It is of more account to understand, concerning such a condition, that it is one of disease to be guarded against, or cured, than it is to be able to determine the exact quality of all its unnatural and unreasonable manifestations. The truth is of wide application in our own times. The trouble with these girls arose with the long listening to stories which were bewildering, exciting, terrifying, and fascinating. These stories wrought upon their imagination, and their imagination upon their nerves. In a little time they were scarcely able, we may believe, to distinguish between what they imagined, and what they saw, heard, or felt. They grew to be excited, bewildered, bewitched. They were unnerved, unbalanced, unstrung, and in all ways unlike healthy and sensible girls.

Beyond this, it may be of little use to undertake the analysis of these experiences. They were unhealthy and undesirable, and deserving chiefly to be avoided ; and they were of a sort possible also, ordinarily or always, to be escaped from. We need not inquire, therefore, whether they did actually see or hear what others did not ; or have any knowledge, according to their pretension, of what was hidden from those about them. If they did, as I think they did not, it was of nothing profitable to themselves or to any one else. So as to their motives and moral standing in the public proceedings soon begun. There are the clearest evidences of what, in persons of sound body and mind, would be carefully meditated falsehood and shocking malignity. I believe they came to be both false and malicious. But what mixture of other and modifying qualities with these there may have been, in their disordered state, no one can tell.

But they were bewitched. So the minister thought; so the family doctor said ; and so the whole community agreed, with scarcely one to differ or doubt.

The next step was to find out by whom the thing was done ; that is, who the witches were. The people were aroused and excited, and were in earnest to know. The performances of "the afflicted children," of whom there were, at the first, eight or ten, had been spread abroad. Multitudes had witnessed their uncouth actions, and the horrible appearances of their sufferings ; for the fashion after which the girls suffered was not common. With due urgency, and after some real or feigned reluctance, the children began to name the individuals through whose agency, as they averred, the Devil was so besetting them. There was method in their selections. Some were persons of ill savor in the neighborhood, whether with or without good cause ; some, and a larger number, were those against whom personal or family enmities had been stirred up during the quarrels that had prevailed in the village, and who seem to have been accused to gratify some spite, or because the children had heard their friends mention their names with bitterness of feeling ; others, still more numerously as the trials went on, were singled out because they or their friends had spoken slightingly of the proceedings, or of some one connected with them.

The first warrants for arrest were issued on the last day of February, 1692. The preliminary examinations were held at first in the village meeting-house, — afterwards more frequently at Salem. The hearings began before the local officers ; that is, the magistrates or "assistants," resident at Salem. But soon after, these opening examinations were taken in hand by the "council" itself, the most dignified and authoritative body in the Colony. There was no special local responsibility, therefore, for what was further done. After commitment, the trials proper, which were before a jury, were conducted by a special court, composed of six judges, appointed for the purpose.

One story will serve for all. The court, the alleged culprits, the afflicted children, and a great crowd of people, were assembled. The judges, who showed their impartiality by assuming at first the guilt alike of all the accused, began by asking the prisoner why he did so foully, and with what particular devil he had agreed to torment those children. The prisoner denied that he had done them harm. The children said he had ; and he denied it again. Then they were tormented. Then they were struck, pinched, pricked, choked, thrown down, and in all other ways beset that they could themselves think of. The judge then bade the prisoner, see what he was doing. When he looked upon them, their sufferings increased. As he turned his head, their necks were twisted that way ; for they were not so afflicted as to be blind. Looking the other way, their heads went on that side with a wrench, and would not go back. Then the children cried out that his apparition was on the great beam, with a yellow bird in its hand. Then one of the afflicted cried that the appearance was coming to torment another of the afflicted, whom she called by name, and that one was tormented ; and she cried that it was going to another, and that other was tormented ; for they were not so afflicted as to be deaf. Then they yelled, and had fits ; and the fits were such as would never be come out of except at the touch of the prisoner's hand, that the " fluid " might run back into the witch again ; and with that they had rest, for so it was written in the witchcraft-books ; and these were not such fits that they might not feel when they were touched. If the calm demeanor of the person under trial affected the court, or if the knowledge of previous irreproachable character were likely to make a condemnation doubtful, then the sufferings of the children waxed great beyond measure. They earned then the name they bore. They wrung their hands and their necks, and twisted and twitched, and were bitten and strangled and sat upon ; they leaped and were lame ; they howled and writhed, and tumbled, and rolled over, and foamed at the mouth, and bled ; they rolled their eyes horribly in their sockets, and held them cold and stony and set, and put upon their faces the pallor and ghastliness of dissolution ; and they would lie, if need were, for hours, and well nigh for days, to all sight of those that beheld them, at the very door of death. So the witch was convicted and hung, and again the afflicted had relief; for they were not so dead as to be dead when the witch was hung.

In like manner, justice was done to the next witch, and the next, until nineteen were hung ; and one, an aged man, was pressed to death, according to the old English law, for refusing to make answer before this variety of court.

The prospect for a defence, in fact, was not cheerful for any. The evidence most thought of was the testimony of these children ; and they told of things that lay out of the line of all other persons' knowledge. They said they saw the accused going to torment them and others, in a form invisible to common sight. If this kind of evidence was allowed, it was not, in the nature of the case, possible to make any defence. The most decisive proof of being somewhere else while torments were alleged to have been inflicted was of no account. This proof was given continually ; since the accused were declared, by these children, to be engaged in that very work of mischief, while they stood in bodily form before the judges' own eyes. If, therefore, the children would tell such stories, there was nothing for whomsoever they might accuse, but to be hanged.

Unless, indeed, they would confess. None lost their lives of those that acknowledged their guilt. The way, therefore, to escape being hanged by these remarkable judges, was to furnish them with this only possible proof that one ought to be hung.

For the trustworthiness of the accusers, their extraordinary sufferings were thought to be ample guaranty ; and it was not considered, that, admitting their sincerity, they might be themselves deceived ; and that there was a double exposure to such misleading, in the illusory nature of the things to which they testified, and in their own manifestly distempered state.

The excitement raged until autumn. Of the executions, one was in June, five were in July, five in August, and nine in September. Not all, nor the larger part of these persons, were residents within this village parish : they were taken from throughout the whole town, and from nearly every town adjoining. The most of those that suffered death exhibited throughout their trial and imprisonment, and to the last, a genuinely Christian combination of meekness and courage. Their conduct reflected honor upon that humanity, whose nobler traits, in that time of darkness, were visible upon themselves almost alone.

More than twice as many, to save their lives, made false confession.

The fury was checked, partly by the natural effect of time, with slowly awakening reason ; and partly by the course of the accusers, in bringing charges against persons of such standing and character, that it was felt to be impossible that they could be guilty. Trials, however, continued to be held, and even with a few convictions, though without further executions, through the winter, until May of 1693 ; when the jails were opened by the governor's proclamation. The whole number of imprisonments, of several months' duration, cannot have been less than three or four hundred. Imprisonment in those days was fearful. It brought also poverty after it, for at the end no one went free till he had paid himself the whole cost of his own wrongful imprisonment.

Belief in witchcraft was not altogether given up when the innocence of these particular victims was conceded ; and public acknowledgment and reparation came but slowly. Too many persons, and of too great note, had been involved in the wrong. Partial acts of justice and relief were passed by the legislature, at different times within the half-century following ; but there are some of the sentences still left, though by inadvertence, without the poor, but only possible remedy of reversal.

In justice to the men concerned, it should be considered that, the persons afflicted being young, it was natural both that their condition should awaken the deepest sympathy, and that their own statement of its cause should be believed. The confession, also, of the crime itself by so many persons, though now known to be false, and though the pressure under which it was made should then have been more thought of, was still calculated strongly to confirm the delusion.

We may wonder, in reviewing this account, that the children, the accusers, were not themselves thought of as the witches, if there were to be any. They were the only ones that *claimed* to exercise any preternatural powers or faculties, or to have any particular acquaintance with the Devil or his works. The persons accused and executed had never made any such pretence, but had made denial. They were distinguished by this from the whole brood of ancient witches, and of sorcerers and their kind, ancient and modern, — with all of whom pretension has been the essential thing. It was the astonishing severity of the sufferings these persons appeared to undergo which warded off suspicion from them, and which confused the minds of the beholders, as to the real bearing of the whole demonstration.

I have spoken already of the connection between this witchcraft, and the teachings of the Bible. I will only add that nothing affirmed as real in the Scriptures bears any resemblance to what was here enacted, unless it be the demoniacal possessions of the New Testament. And to the proposition that it might be possible, even now, for a spirit of evil to gain some mastery over a mind and body grievously disordered, and willingly, or even temptingly, exposed in the beginning and continuance of its maladies to such an unnatural control, I might have little care to oppose any very earnest denial. But let us have, then, the biblical remedies, along with medicine, and as themselves indeed medicinal. We may wish that into that ancient place of worship, while the uproar called a trial was going on, with those young women tearing and screaming and swooning, and the court and all the multitude besides half out of their wits with fright and horror, there might have entered one with somewhat of the composure and presence of the Son of man, advancing with calmness and authority into the shrinking crowd, quelling the unseemly tumult, casting his look of search and indignation along that line of ministers and magistrates, rebuking the devils of every name and number, and bidding them be shortly gone ; and taking to himself with reproof, and with sheltering confidence and decision, those distracted children, who might well have been healed at his coming. Such an interposition by one of answerable bearing and dignity, and with a courage befitting a disciple of the Master, even though without the superhuman endowments the Master bore, might possibly have sufficed to turn the tide of folly ; and would, in any event, have been a procedure of which none other of his followers would ever have had occasion to be ashamed.

As to original blame, the ministers deserve most. It was their business to have known, taught, and practised better. But afterward they did do better, in holding back, coming to their senses, and making reparation, than most others.*

For all that was done, we freely admit the errors of our fathers. We hope the representatives of other sinners of those days will do as much. But in comparisons, if so pressed, we yield nothing. We are not slow to fight. The war, be sure, will be one of onset, not mostly of defence. There have been crimes as great in other parts of our country, and later. The Papal Inquisition, or any of the great allied tyrannies, would have swallowed the witchcraft victims, and would never have known that any thing had been in its mouth. Grappling with these despotisms, the Puritans got what undue severity they had. They are railed at now by men whom their stern vigor only made free to rail, or to think. The faults of the Puritans are made great, withal, by the issues of the work they wrought, and by the gaze of succeeding generations drawn upon it. It is of their fame that their sins are known. And this witchcraft darkness is a cloud, conspicuous chiefly by the widening radiance itself of the morning on whose brow it hung.

We shall stand by our fathers   But we are willing rather to join with all our fellow-men in putting away the wrongs of the past, and in reaching toward the better things that are to come.

---

* History of Witchcraft, vol. ii. pp. 350, 363, 364, 455, 459, 477, 478, 482, 483, &c. This village church is also entitled to the credit of a comparatively early and an ample acknowledgment of the wrong that had been done.

INDEX OF SUBJECTS AND NAMES OF PLACES.

INDEX OF NAMES OF PERSONS.

The spelling of many of these names has varied with different periods of time, and with different families. It has not been attempted to bring it to entire uniformity. Changes of name by marriage may not in every case have been correctly indicated.

It is likely that there may be mistakes in the distribution of references among persons bearing the same name, either contemporaneously or in successive generations. This is a matter not to be accomplished with absolute accuracy without more of research than the importance of the case would justify. There may possibly, also, be errors of inadvertence in this respect. The natural liberty of the reader to revise the work according to such better knowledge as he may think he has will not be interfered with by the author of this sketch.

* If the name of any person living, or that has ever lived, in this parish that should have been mentioned in this book, has been omitted, there need not be the least unpleasant feeling on that account ; since, if the individual interested will furnish a statement of the facts, I may readily cause it to be laid up until the time of the next corresponding publication, when the matter can easily be set right.